Brothers
of the
Capucine

ROB MCLAREN

Brothers of the Capucine

This paperback edition published in 2021.
Lulu Publishing — www.lulu.com

A CiP record for this book is available from the National Library
of Australia and the State Library of Queensland.

Text and illustration copyright © 2018 Rob McLaren
Graphic Design, typesetting and map illustrations by Matthew Lin
www.matthewlin.com.au   .

Paperback ISBN 978-0-6484-716-9-1
E-book ISBN 978-0-6484-716-1-5
Hardcover ISBN 978-0-6484-716-2-2

Typeset in Bembo Semibold 12 pt

To Dylan

My brother who ensured I made it home
- every time

Brothers of the Capucine
Acknowledgements

I wish to sincerely acknowledge and thank the following people for their contribution to the work:

Sophie Walker - My beautiful, talented and patient wife.

Peter Cross – for his unwavering friendship and support, access to his excellent collection of Napoleonic books and artefacts, and his vast collection of exquisitely painted Napoleonic figures, the largest collection of 28mm Napoleonic wargaming figures in the Southern Hemisphere, which have been kindly provided to create selected images.

Joe Tapping – for his sincere encouragement, his extensive research into the Nelsonian navy and his market experience in online publishing.

José de Andrade – for his friendship, access to his Napoleonic library and extensive collection of Napoleonic figures.

Katie Whiffen and Andrew Koranski – two dear friends whose own writing inspired me.

This story culminates within the siege of Toulon in December 1793. For the depth of detail woven into the story, I am very grateful for one particular reference, the in-depth research of Robert Forczyk, PhD, laid out in his excellent work *Toulon, 1793, Napoleon's first great victory*.

Cass Moriarty, Lauren Daniels, Gail Cartwright, Belinda Pollard and Geneve Flynn - for their superlative editorial support.

Brothers of the Capucine
Maps

Brothers of the Capucine

Appendices

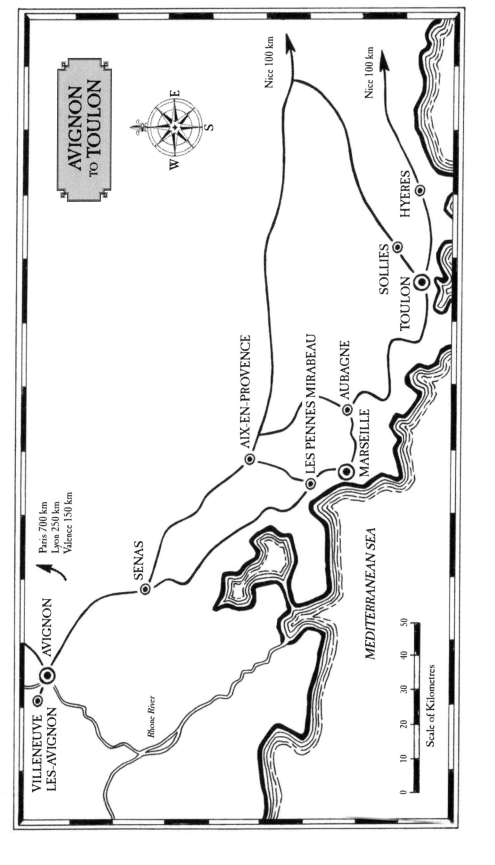

Prologue
December 1793, Toulon, France

Blood oozed from Captain André Jobert's scalp, dribbled down his neck and pooled inside his collar. The splatter of grey rain against his hunched shoulders encouraged clotting blobs to wriggle icy trails between his shirt and his back. The congealing tendrils pulsed dread down his spine to puddle heavily in his guts.

I have risked my arse too many times this year, he thought, *but this stunt is just idiotic beyond reason.*

Jobert's gaze drifted across the wounded having their injuries dressed, squirming against the wrapping of bandages and the pelt of icy rain.

My arse … and theirs. I have committed eighteen recruits to achieving what? No-one will know if we fail. This time there will be no shame in —

A soldier crouched beside Jobert. 'I need to bind your head wound, sir, and put your arm in a sling.'

Jobert hung his head toward his sodden wool jacket, a coat of the Spanish infantry. Blood seeped from the left elbow of the grubby, white jacket into the linen of the sling. *Why did I ever say 'yes'?*

A squelch in the mud beside him caused Jobert to jerk. The cold water reached deeper inside his shirt. Sergeant Major Koschak grunted as he squatted stiffly beside Jobert. The crimson bandages binding Koschak's forearm and thigh were leached by rivulets of rain.

Koschak's green eyes, red rimmed in a pallid face, searched Jobert's face. *He too doubts we will make it.*

'General Masséna has begun his attack on Fort D'Artigues,' said Koschak. 'The wounded are ready to march. We await your command, sir.'

Chapter One
March 1793, Avignon, France

It was time to go.

Yet he hefted the sabre in his hand and regarded it closely. Something he did not often do.

André Jobert paid attention to its cutting edge when standing by the armourer's spinning grindstone. He fussed over the speckled rust caused by brushing against the sweaty flanks of his horses, as he twirled his rag-wrapped, polish-soaked fingertip in tight circles. He inspected the tightness of the fit of the blade's tang into the hilt, both by eye and feel, when examining the brass-wire woven around the leather grip.

To wonder at the simple flesh-cutting tool itself was a rare indulgence.

When he drew it from its scabbard, Jobert felt its weight through his wrist. To fence in the mornings, his mind filled with the relationship of his opponent's sabre tip and weight shift in relation to his own wrist. In the charge, with knees gripping the bounding saddle, Jobert's eyes flicked between the path over which his horse raced towards his target. He never thought of the blade extending from his locked right arm. Just the delivery of the floating steel tip to his foe.

But today is different. Jobert's mouth creased in uncertainty. *Another beginning.*

Today Jobert was to enter a new home. He was to join a different family where his total worth was measured in his knowledge of this tool.

Not my total worth. There are four essential elements of a cavalry-man. My skill with a sabre is just one.

Jobert returned the steel sabre to its brass scabbard in a long-practiced, fluid movement. He drained his wine cup. With spurred heels clumping across the tavern's ancient floorboards, he strode along corridors with low beams and greasy walls. Begrimed servants pressed into doorframes and corners as he passed.

Stepping down from a stone threshold he entered the tavern yard. The warm internal reek of stale urine, smoke and garlic, with its upstairs' footfalls and murmurs changed to the sharp cold of churned horse dung, mouldy hay and the shouted curses of stable boys.

Bleu, always impatient, stopped his pawing hoof and greeted his rider with a thrust of his great nose into Jobert's midriff.

'No, lad.' Jobert raised a warning finger at which the bay gelding stepped back. 'Today I must not be covered in your hair and snot, thank you.' Jobert gave a gentle rub with the back of two fingers, showing his affection without soiling his dress gloves.

The groom had Bleu ready to mount. Jobert shortened the reins, twisted the stirrup leather and placed his polished toecap in the stirrup iron. Then with a muscular hop, Jobert rose up towards the grey clouds and seated himself on his sheep skin saddle cover as lightly as he would put a hat on his own head.

Horsemanship. The second essential element of a cavalryman.

Jobert's knowledge in this regard would be scrutinised over the coming days, by superiors, peers and subordinates alike. As his groom wiped both of Jobert's boots clean of hay chaff and wet sand, Jobert reflected on his ability to communicate the rapid dance of mounted combat to his horse, through weight shift and muscular tension.

His valet held up his helmet, a moulded leather casque. Before placing on the peaked helmet with its thick horsehair crest, Jobert regarded the long, feathered plume. The feathers of the lower two-thirds were dark green, the same colour as his braided dolman jacket and his snug-fitting Hungarian breeches; the colour identified him as a *chasseur.* A hunter.

A hunter of men.

The remaining top third of the plume, the tip, was yellow. The facing colour of his last regiment. A military family he had called home for his entire life. *My home no more.*

Within the hour he would join a new regiment. By sunset this day a new plume would adorn his helmet. Jobert placed the helmet on his head and adjusted the fit with a wriggle of the leather peak.

Jobert turned Bleu towards the tavern gate. With a squeeze through the saddle, Jobert and Bleu departed at a smart walk into the raucous Avignon lanes beyond.

'Excuse me, gentlemen. Captain André Jobert.'

As doors closed behind him, Jobert's eyes adjusted to the morning light now streaming through the tall windows, the dust motes rising on the air currents as the room warmed. The room smelt of fire smoke, furniture polish and parchment. His gaze swept the room, identifying two men: the regimental colonel and a lieutenant colonel.

'Jobert, very good to see you again,' said the lieutenant colonel. 'May I introduce Colonel Morin?'

Jobert's recognised the lieutenant colonel, but he remained focused on the commanding officer. 'Good morning, sir.' Jobert saluted.

'Welcome to the 24th *Chasseurs à Cheval*, Captain Jobert,' said Morin.

Morin's eyebrows bristled. Jobert felt the colonel's scrutiny glide across his face, hair and uniform. Morin made a flourish towards the other man.

'I was informed in the last day that you are both known to each other. Lieutenant Colonel Raive speaks highly of your service together under General Dumouriez in Belgium last November. Were you aware that Lieutenant Colonel Raive was the regimental second-in-command?'

'No, sir, I was unaware of Lieutenant Colonel Raive's posting to the 24th Chasseurs.' Jobert took in the extra lace on Raive's coat sleeves, as well as the new facings of the 24th Chasseurs on his coat and trousers, noting to have all his old regimental uniforms changed over to the new facings. 'Very good to see you also, sir. Congratulations on your promotion.'

'Sir, I must away,' said Raive. 'Again, good to have you with us, Jobert, but correspondence awaits. I will have your company second-in-command summoned. He will have with him your new regimental plumes.'

Morin indicated a chair, as an orderly with a fresh pot entered the room. Jobert adjusted his scabbard and *sabretache* to sit.

'With the recent execution of His Majesty ...' Morin sought a reaction. Jobert's face remained stern. '... and with the recent declaration of war by the British and the Dutch, the constant climate of both civil war and foreign invasion has heightened to an alarming degree. Another twelve regiments of chasseurs are to be raised. I am ordered by the War Committee to raise a regiment of six squadrons.'

Six squadrons! Jobert's face tightened. *The old regiments with a war establishment of four squadrons barely manned three.*

'In total, over one thousand two hundred men and horse,' said Morin. 'My staff and I arrived ten days ago. To raise the 24th Chasseurs, the regiment will be based on the five hundred sabres of the recently disbanded *Chasseurs Volontaires* Regiment. In the spirit of patriotism and with the War Committee's recent *levee en masse* for three hundred thousand men, the districts will have our seven hundred recruits here within days.

'Somewhere out of the chaos issuing from Paris, I am informed trains of equipment and supplies will arrive within weeks. With the enthusiasm and flood of promissory notes, it appears every village in the land is sewing breeches, weaving blankets, hunting hares for hat felt and melting church bells for cannon.' A bitter cloud crossed Morin's face. 'Except of course, for those towns in open revolt.'

Morin scoffed his tea. 'Lieutenant Colonel Raive and my staff are busy as a result. With His Majesty's execution, manning the regiment, equipping the regiment and training the regiment cannot occur quickly enough.'

Morin flicked thick fingers at a stack of documents on his desk.

'As well as your own letter of introduction, Jobert, I have a most agreeable letter of recommendation from your previous commanding officer. You served on campaign against the Austrians and Prussians as a company commander. With your previous regimental commander and Lieutenant Colonel Raive as your referees, I am entrusting command of 2nd Company to you.'

A tightness gripped Jobert's chest. *Command of a senior company. Man, equip and train.* 'I am at your service, sir.'

Morin's baleful glare locked on Jobert. 'I am absolutely committed to raising a regiment ready for war in the coming weeks, Jobert. I only accept utterly focused men to make this happen. I will not accept verbal assurances from my officers.' Morin stabbed a finger into the desk. 'I only accept resolute action.'

Jobert rose and saluted.

Morin dismissed him with a curt nod. 'Again, welcome to the 24th Chasseurs, Jobert.'

'Excuse me, sir.' A short, stocky man saluted, his intense brown eyes drilling into Jobert. 'Welcome to the regiment. I am Lieutenant Geourdai, your company's second-in-command. May I introduce our company sergeant major, Sergeant Major Koschak.'

As blond as Lieutenant Geourdai, Koschak had a muscular neck, deep chest and powerful arms, which flexed within his jacket as he saluted. 'Welcome to the 24th Chasseurs, sir.'

Jobert noted that both Geourdai's and Koschak's uniforms were in the correct regimental facings. 'Colonel Morin informs me there is much to do. I am keen to start immediately. Where can we talk?'

'Before we go, sir,' said Geourdai, 'the regimental second-in-command gave me a regimental plume and a company pompom for your headdress.'

Jobert took the thirty-centimetre plume of bound feathers, the lower three-quarters dyed chasseur green and the top quarter dark orange, the facing colour of the 24th Chasseurs à Cheval. At the base of the plume, just above a small brass spike which fitted into the chosen headdress, was a woven-wool sky-blue pompom, an indicator that the wearer was of the 2nd Company.

'For a regiment that did not exist ten days ago, I am told, I note you are all in the new uniform. What is the dress of the day?'

'The Colonel is adamant the regiment maintains a common dress,' said Geourdai, 'to bind members of previous regiments with the daily influx of recruits and in the face of uniform supply shortages. To that end, linen pants over boots worn with your number-two tailcoat. Officers are to wear bicornes with plume, so the recruits know who to salute. Non-commissioned officers are to wear helmets with plume, again to orient the recruits. All troopers, either old hands or new recruits, are to wear *bonnets-de-police*. Until more uniform stocks arrive in the unit, that is dress of the day.'

Jobert placed the plume into his sabretache, the stiff, embroidered pouch which swung off his sword belt, beside his scabbard. 'Very well, Lieutenant, then you and I need to speak of my accommodation and how I might get my current uniforms changed over to these new dark orange facings.'

'Capucine, sir,' said Geourdai.

'I beg your pardon?'

'We are informed, sir, the dark orange colour is called capucine. You sought a place to speak, sir. May I suggest the stables? As there are no horses in now, we will be free of interruption. From there, you might consider your accommodation. Our two troop commanders and I have taken rooms in a nearby tavern, just a short walk from the barracks entrance. We could visit that establishment, if you are agreeable.'

'A fine plan, Lieutenant. Shall we proceed?'

As the three made their way from the headquarters' steps to the stables, Jobert accepted the salutes of the non-commissioned officers observing the drilling of a new company. Geourdai and Koschak marched in step with him, spur rowels and metal-capped heels making a harsh military beat.

Within the chill air of the empty stables, rows of stacked wooden crates and hessian-wrapped bales shielded the noise of bellowed orders and crunching gravel emanating from the drill lessons.

Jobert turned abruptly. Geourdai and Koschak faced him.

'Let me introduce myself,' said Jobert. 'I was a sergeant when my regiment mutinied. I was elected company commander. When the Austrians and Prussians invaded last year, my regiment served under General Dumouriez at Valmy and Jemappes. That is me. Who are you?'

Geourdai shuffled his feet, then raised his face, his jowl clenching as he spoke. 'Sir, I am from the 7th Chasseurs. When the old officers departed, I was elected from sergeant to second lieutenant troop commander. My troop saw action with the Army of the Rhine last year. I joined the 24th Chasseurs a week ago on promotion.'

'And you, Sergeant Major?' asked Jobert.

Koschak squinted at Jobert and raised his chin. 'I too was present on the field at Jemappes last November. Lieutenant Colonel Raive was my squadron commander there and we arrived also on promotion, ten days ago. Furthermore, sir, ...' Koschak scowled as he shifted his stance. 'I have the clear memory, sir, of charging the Austrian trains beyond Jemappes. I remember looking over my right shoulder and observing the Austrian hussars about to hit us in the right flank and those hussars looking over their left shoulders as you, sir and your company of 5th Chasseurs butchered your way through their left flank. For that, sir, I am much obliged.'

Jobert shifted his gaze from Koschak's stony face to the marching men and the shouting non-commissioned officers outside. 'Here we are, then. Old sergeants with campaign experience with the job of taking recruits to war within weeks.'

Inhaling the strong smell of musty fodder hanging from the old spider webs on grimy walls, Jobert indicated they sit on the closed crates and bales, stored just inside the stables' doors. 'The Colonel is intent on manning, equipping and training the regiment as quickly as possible. The quality of our company leaders is key to our survival as a company. Focusing on our own 2nd Company, would you update me on manning?'

Geourdai cleared his throat, exchanging glances with Koschak before proceeding. 'Company headquarters is not yet complete. There is the three of us, but we have not been allocated a trumpeter, a farrier or a quartermaster corporal.

'At troop command level, sir, we have two second lieutenants. One is away with the regimental remount group. The other, Second Lieutenant Voreille, arrived yesterday from the *École Militaire* in Paris. His class graduated early to fill the new regiments.'

'Platoon sergeants?' asked Jobert.

'We have four sergeants, sir. One is away collecting our recruits. Another is with the remount group. Two sergeants remain in barracks, both working in the armoury.'

'Where do we stand, Sergeant Major, with our corporals and chasseurs?'

Koschak grimaced at Geourdai. Geourdai's face soured.

'We have all eight section commanders for our company,' said Koschak. 'Every one of them was a trooper with the Chasseurs Volontaires. They have neither prior regimental experience nor have seen active service. I foresee a range of difficulties arising from corporals who have eighteen months experience in a gentleman's riding club.'

'The whole French Army appears to be on promotion, Sergeant Major, with little or no experience for the roles they hold. The three of us are no exception. But we have survived our first battle and we are all that France and 2nd Company has.'

'Yes, sir. Of the company's eight sections, we have manned our sections with three ex-Chasseur Volontaires and the other eight men will be recruits.'

'We are three-quarters recruits? We will be at war with Austria once the Alpine passes thaw in the next four weeks. Where are these recruits? Who do we see on the square?'

'Lieutenant Colonel Raive is bringing in a company of sixty recruits from the districts every day,' said Koschak. 'Those are the 1st and the 7th Companies' recruits. We expect our recruits tomorrow.'

'What can you tell me about weapons?' asked Jobert.

Koschak's jaw clenched. Geourdai wriggled on his crate. 'The regiment has not yet received its issue of sabres, sir.'

'What?'

Head hung, Geourdai looked at Jobert from under his brows. 'Indeed, sir. Corporals and chasseurs on guard are issued the sabres we do have. There is a limited supply of wooden swords for drill, sir.'

Jobert rubbed his jowls. 'This is not good, gentlemen. Firearms?'

'The armoury has just received two thousand examples of every calibre of musket, rifle, musketoon, carbine and pistol imaginable, from every war France and her enemies have fought for the last hundred years. Regimental work parties are still sorting through a veritable nightmare. The regimental second-in-command is not impressed.'

'Cartridges?'

'No ammunition has arrived yet, sir. But we can appraise you of uniforms and equipment, if you wish, sir?'

An invisible vice crushed his chest. *No sabres!* Jobert's gaze drifted towards the parade ground activity. 'Without sabres, does it matter how we are clothed?'

Chapter Two

'Gentlemen, salute.'

With heels together, the six ranks of nine to ten officers, each two ranks facing each other, each officer stripped to waistcoat and shirt, on the command of the regimental fencing master, saluted the man opposite with his wooden sabre.

Jobert stared his opponent in the eye, brought his sword hand up to his chin, the sword hilt at lip level, the action based on ancient custom of Christian knights kissing the crucifix. Then the sabre hand was brought smoothly back to just past the hip, the sabre held low, the blade tip at ankle level from the ground. This elegant sweep of blade originated from the Crusades, where Muslim warriors would draw back their lance tips as a form of recognition. Halting momentarily in this lowered position, the sabre hilt swept back up to Jobert's lips before returning to the carry position, where the upper arm hung naturally against the ribs, the forearm perpendicular to the ground, the blade balanced directly over the wrist.

'Gentlemen, on guard.'

The sun had not yet penetrated over the barrack rooftops. With dust from the movement of horses as stables were mucked out and smoke from the kitchen fires hanging across the chilly morning square, the officers prepared themselves for action.

Jobert's left foot slid rearward taking the body weight for any forward launch. His torso twisted so his heart was furthest from his opponent's sabre tip. His right hand holding the sabre, lowered to mid-thigh level, allowed his sabre tip to align at his opponent's upper abdomen, centrally ready for offensive or defensive movement, higher or lower, left or right.

The regimental fencing master strolled between the ranks with his fencing foil reclining on his right shoulder.

'Gentlemen, listen carefully. Odd-numbered squadrons, salute.'

Three ranks saluted again.

'You gentlemen will make four attacking strokes on your opponent and then prepare to parry. Once you have completed the five actions, step one opponent to your left and repeat without hesitation until you return to your original partner.

'Gentlemen, on guard.'

The three ranks of officers returned to a position of balance.

'Now, gentlemen, even-numbered squadrons, salute.'

The other three ranks, including Jobert and Geourdai, saluted.

'You gentlemen will make four parries against the attacking strokes and then counter-attack with a cut of your own once your opponent completes his fourth stroke. Be prepared to hold your ground as a new opponent engages you from your left with the repeated pattern.

'Gentlemen, on guard. Gentlemen, attack!'

The near instantaneous crack of sixty wooden blades colliding was heard throughout the barracks. Soldiers and non-commissioned officers raced to the dormitory windows and stable doors and observed the spirited melee in the centre of the square.

Within the delivery of the first four cuts, a simultaneous roar of sergeant's invective for men to return to their duties caught many sabreurs by surprise. More than a few wooden sabres found their mark on the thighs, ribs and arms of the distracted young gentlemen.

Each rank was given the opportunity of each exercise and many others beside. The fencing master would whip with his foil the target areas on the bodies of those to whom he directed his suggestions. Some of the younger fellows were forced to vomit between the rain of blows, swearing to themselves and at themselves, for their over-indulgence in spirits from the night before.

Jobert watched the scene of riotous gaiety as the recruits entered the barracks square.

Laughing young men with tricolour cockades and ribbons in their hats and caps, some with tricolour sashes, some with sloshing beer steins, strolled the length of the regimental parade ground as if entering a town fair during a harvest holiday. Two young fellows, one with fiddle and one with fife, played for a merry, dusty dance cavorting in the centre of the ramble. Around them, recruits who arrived yesterday, stopped drilling and cheered the happy crowd. Non-commissioned officers bellowed to retain control of their drill lessons.

Sergeant Major Koschak sat on his war horse like a bemused pillar, watching the shambolic merriment enter through the stone entrance to the barracks. Beside him, mounted on a grey horse, sat a headquarters' sergeant carrying the tricolour regimental standard.

Koschak spied a mounted sergeant, 2nd Company's own Sergeant Bredieux, a wiry man with a fat-bowled pipe curving from the side of his mouth, pass through the stone entrance and wave to him, indicating he was the last man in the column.

'Who wants lunch?' called Koschak. 'Gather around the tricolour, lads.'

With a cheer, the revelry gathered in a circle around Koschak and the standard bearer.

'*Vive la République!*' Koschak bellowed. 'Welcome to the 24th Chasseurs à Cheval.'

The square boomed with response from the recruits, as well as those drilling nearby. The two horses in the centre of the crowd skittered at the roar, causing those closest to press back. The standard bearer held the regimental standard aloft and wafted its silken folds.

Koschak leant on his saddle bow, looking into the faces about him. 'Who wants lunch?' That question resulted in a deafening cry.

'You.' Koschak pointed at one of the young musicians. 'Yes you with the fife. What is the loudest, shrillest note you can play?'

The young musician blew a loud squeal at which everyone recoiled and groaned.

'Excellent. Listen, friends, that is our signal for silence. Lad, if I point at you, you split our ear drums. Understand?' The boy grinned and nodded.

'Lads, my name is Sergeant Major Koschak. You will address me as "Sergeant Major". Now, listen carefully. We want to get you to lunch, but there are a few tasks to be done to make that happen. I need your help. Keep quiet, listen carefully, do as I ask quickly and a hearty soup, fresh bread and wine will be yours before long. I am going to request that you all line up, in your village groups, friends and family together, with your recruit paperwork in your hands. All right, off we go.'

Jobert watched Sergeant Bredieux and the corporals who accompanied the men for the last twenty-four hours, with good humour, press the chattering crowd into a single rank facing the Sergeant Major.

Koschak pointed to his piper and winked. The piper produced a piercing blast. 'Men, you are all members of the 2nd Company. Yes, the 2nd Company. In this formation, I look at you now and I know the Austrians are trembling in their boots.'

A spirited 'Hurrah!' erupted from all. Koschak pointed to his piper. With the signal, all stood silent.

'When I give you the command, you are all going to turn to the right towards those tables, move forward and receive your new uniforms. Wait for it, wait for it, wait for my command, 2nd Company. Now ... 2nd Company, will move to the right in file. Right turn!'

As the company's first drill movement, the resultant chaotic shuffle caused deep breaths, rolled eyes and wry grins from all uniformed personnel watching.

Koschak and the standard bearer dismounted and strode down the file of recruits to a series of trestle tables, besides which waited unlimbered wagons laden with bundles of equipment. Upon the tables were laid out all the items that the new soldiers were to receive.

Reclining on a camp chair, Jobert watched as the corporals managing the head of the file checked the recruits' documents. One by one, a recruit moved forward to one of the two trestle tables where Sergeant Pultiere, a bull with a heavy moustache covering acne-pocked skin, was waiting.

'Welcome, lad,' said Sergeant Pultiere, 'to the 2nd Company of the 24th Chasseurs à Cheval. The corporal will read out an item on the table and you will put that item into either your satchel, your paillasse, or your saddle portmanteau.'

As the recruit packed away his equipment on one table, the other table was laid out by an attendant old hand from the nearby wagons ready for the next man.

'Well done, young fellow, well done. Now, go to the next table and hand over your paperwork.'

'What is this, sir?' a recruit might ask.

'Do not call me "Sir", I work for a living. That, my lad, is your paillasse. It is a mattress cover you fill with straw, so you may sleep each evening like a babe at your mother's breast and awaken each morning ready for a new adventure. Now keep moving, well done.'

A further twenty paces away from Pultiere's equipment table, Second Lieutenant Voreille and another sergeant were seated at a table, beside which the standard hung in the morning air. As each recruit approached the table, Voreille receipted the man's documents from the central recruiting office and entered each man's name on a growing roll.

Sergeant Huin then took the equipment issue paperwork and passed the recruit a slip of paper upon which was written his name, company, troop, platoon and section. Despite having the build of a skinny, petulant teenager, Huin evaluated the recruit with grey, unblinking eyes.

'Keep this piece of paper on you at all times. Produce it whenever you are asked. You need this piece of paper to eat and be paid. Lose it and you will be punished. Now wait here until summoned by the Sergeant Major. Do you understand?'

Each man's face showed a sobering foretaste of the days to come.

'Next man,' called Koschak. 'Yes, you lad, over you come. Bring your kit with you, lad. The Republic has gone to great expense and provided you the best equipment in Europe and you lose it the first time you put it down.'

Beyond the tables, Koschak was laying out a seated formation, building up the company one section of twelve men at a time.

Ever so slowly, one section became two sections, or a platoon. Then a further two sections became a second platoon, or troop.

As the initial long file diminished, each recruit receiving equipment and handing over documents, the second troop slowly filled out to become the full 2nd Company.

Because of their original groupings of friends, the recruits came across from Huin's table and sat with known village friends or family members. The section corporal and the troopers welcomed each fellow to his seating position in the mid-morning sun and kept the new recruits from wandering off or spreading out their new equipment in the dirt.

Jobert kept a keen eye on each parcel of equipment, watching if sufficient stock was on hand for each man. Each recruit received an initial issue of one linen satchel, with mug, bowl, towel, knife, fork, spoon, soap, candle and uniforms. Two shirts, two underdrawers, two stockings, one set of linen parade breeches, one set of hemp stable breeches, one pair boots, one pair stable clogs, one summer waistcoat, one stable jacket, one undress tailcoat, one cape, one bonnet-de-police, one paillasse, one blanket and one saddle portmanteau to carry it all in.

That equipment would allow the recruits to sleep their first night in barracks. Sword belts, cross belts and cartridge pouches would be issued the next morning and whitened with pipe clay that day. The following items would be issued as stores arrived; a second pair of boots, winter waistcoats, full-dress tailcoats, dolman jackets, sashes, full-dress Hungarian breeches, over-breeches and helmets.

Sergeant Bredieux accompanied the last man to be processed. Jobert watched the sinewy man, hair swept back into a queue, with thick hussar plaits against each temple, a drooping moustache framing his weathered pipe. Jobert marked Sergeant Bredieux down as rogue until proven otherwise.

Koschak signalled to his piper. The shrill squeal created silence. 'Men of the 2nd Company, well done on achieving that task so well. Each of you now sits in your sections. Ensure, right now, you know the face of one of your friends in your section, one old hand and your section commander.'

The invitation to look about them caused another sharp note from the fife.

'Men of 2nd Company, your sections are grouped into platoons. Myself and these three men,' Koschak indicated Pultiere, Huin and Bredieux, 'will guide you as platoon sergeants over the coming days. You note your section corporals, platoon sergeants and I wear helmets. If you are addressed by any person in a helmet over the next few weeks, you are to listen respectfully and act immediately. As eagle-eyed chasseurs, you will have noticed the sky-blue pompom on each of our plumes. That sky-blue pompom indicates a man of the 2nd Company, your company and therefore a man who is concerned with your welfare.'

Koschak looked across to Jobert and gave a slight nod.

'Now, I want to introduce some very important people within our company, also with sky-blue pompoms on their plumes. The commissioned officers of the 2nd Company. The men who will lead us to victory in battle against the Austrians.'

Jobert, Geourdai and Voreille stepped forward.

'You will note these gentlemen wear bicornes. When any person wearing a bicorne enters a room, you must cease what you are doing, remain silent and listen respectfully.'

All eyes watched the three officers with a mix of suspicion, confusion and awe.

Jobert stepped forward into a central position, surveyed the company in three ranks with a frontage of over thirty men.

'I am Captain Jobert. I am your company commander. I began my service to France, as you are today, as a trooper thirteen years ago. Welcome to the 2nd Company of the 24th Chasseur à Cheval Regiment.

'The War Committee of the National Convention has tasked the Sergeant Major and I to prepare us all for victory on the battlefield. The Sergeant Major and I take such responsibility very seriously. I echo the Sergeant Major's comment. As I look at you all, on our first day together, I despair for the Republic's enemies. Sergeant Major, carry on.'

The dining room was set for lunch. Tureens of soup, bowls of apples, platters of bread and carafes of wine sat on buffets to the side of the room under the tall windows.

'Gentlemen!' boomed a captain standing by the door. 'Colonel Morin.' The officers braced to attention.

Morin surveyed the room. 'Please sit. Allow me to make a few remarks before we dine.'

Once seated, Jobert watched Morin pace to a central position, in the room. Stepping forward to the table, he poured himself a glass of *vin de noix*.

'Gentlemen, as you know, last month Britain and the Netherlands joined Austria, Prussia and Sardinia as our declared enemies. I am informed that, first, the National Convention has now declared war on Spain.'

The creaking of chairs was pronounced as fifteen silent officers adjusted their weight to accommodate the news.

'Second, France's gains in Belgium, in the last few months,

have just been lost with our defeat at Aix-la-Chapelle to the Austrians last week, with the loss of three and a half thousand casualties and one and a half thousand captured.'

The audience collectively breathed out in astonishment and slumped deeper into their chairs.

'Gentlemen, today France is in anarchy. Throughout the last four years the energies and emotions of our fellow countrymen remain unsettled, as we all seek a common understanding of liberty, equality and fraternity. Four years of fear and greed dominate the lives of ourselves, our families, our communities and our soldiers. Should we, as brothers, disagree, the waste of civil war threatens every home, every day.

'Ancient families who rule the people of neighbouring nations are terrified of the simple idea that the people of France can determine their own path. It terrifies these noble houses that their own people may erupt with the same energies and emotion and choose to determine their own path.'

Morin sipped his *eau de vie*.

'Acknowledging there are many who disagree within our nation, and without, the National Convention remains the current legitimate government of France. The National Convention raises taxes from the people of France to create this regiment. The National Convention causes this regiment to exist on behalf of the people of France, to protect the people of France.

'On this very day, hundreds of regiments are forming and preparing for war. Civil war and foreign war.

'On this very day, hundreds of thousands of energised young Frenchmen are farewelled with cheers and tears to join such regiments and protect the terrifying values France now embodies.

'On this very day, millions of men and women labour ceaselessly across the length and breadth of this land and supply not only their menfolk but all the accoutrements of war.

'Here we all are. All sons of France. My regimental brothers. On this very day, raising a regiment of one thousand two hundred men and horse. On this very day, preparing for war tomorrow.'

Morin walked to the table, poured himself another glass and took a long sip.

'Why, might we ask, has France ordered another levee en masse of three hundred thousand men? Why has the Army doubled the number of chasseurs à cheval regiments, increasing regimental establishments from four to six squadrons, in essence, tripling the Army's number of chasseur squadrons?

'A number of possibilities emerge. To create nation-wide manufacture through nation-wide expenditure. To harness the energies of the young men of France. To demonstrate to all French people if you wish to maintain liberty, equality and fraternity, then you must participate to ensure such values are sustained.

'Another military possibility exists. That in light of our experiences from the last war against Europe thirty years ago and in recent campaigns, that France can only succeed by overwhelming her enemies with so many bodies that her enemy's arms and ammunition are exhausted by our weight of numbers. In the end, whichever few French soldiers survive become the core of a most fearsome legion.'

Morin drained and then refilled his glass.

'Although tasked with raising six squadrons, I will not be satisfied with a regiment of quantity. I strive to my utmost to create a regiment of the most disciplined and hardest quality. To that end, I demand your best. France demands your best. Your soldiers demand your best. I daresay it, your horses demand your best. If you cannot or will not give your best, you will be sent quickly from this place.'

Morin paused to drink again.

'In the twelve months following the fall of the Bastille, one-third of the officers remained in the regiments. On the raising of the volunteer legions, halfway through 1791, only one-sixth of the experienced officers continued to remain in the regiments. The majority of these officers promoted far beyond their experience. A new generation of officers arose to fill the void, originally sergeant majors and sergeants.'

Jobert reflected on his own rise from sergeant to captain.

'As sergeant majors were promoted to officers, our sergeants became the fresh new sergeant majors. Our corporals became the fresh new sergeants. Our best chasseurs became the fresh new corporals. New blood, new ideas, new energies. But now, with the Army tripling its number of squadrons, another void of experience is created. Now our sergeants are yesterday's troopers, our corporals are yesterday's volunteers in the hastily created legions.

'In the next ten days, over seven hundred raw recruits will be placed in the hands of such non-commissioned officers. Civil war, foreign invasion and now, as the recent defeat at Aix-la-Chapelle reminds us, we are threatened with severe regimental inexperience. Not only am I calling on you to do your best in the role of captains, you must also do your best in the role of corporal.'

Morin considered his glass.

'Man a regiment, equip a regiment, train a regiment. Let us speak of training a regiment. Any idiot can be trained to charge. He need only sit on the back of a galloping horse, wave his sword in the air and scream his silly head off. The lesser training challenge is to identify those who will, at the end of executing a charge, remain in the saddle without bleeding and think clearly. The greater challenge is getting one thousand two hundred men and horses, who are forced to eat and sleep in their own filth, without succumbing to disease and desertion, and arrive at that point of charge.

'On my honour, I swear to you now, I will give my best to overcome these challenges. If you are willing to give your best to the regiment and to France, I welcome you by my side and by the side of my chasseurs.'

Morin surveyed his audience, holding each man in his fierce gaze. 'Second-in-command!'

'Sir!'

'Your parade.'

'Gentlemen!'

The officers stood. The Colonel departed.

Chapter Three

A thick mist hung over the Rhône valley. On this freezing March morning, sixteen chasseurs, riding one horse and leading four others, were having their skills as horsemen extended. Households lining the Lyon road into Avignon rose early and enjoyed the morning display of horses entering the barracks, taking great delight in the jostled discomfort of the troopers.

For the eighty horses, despite walking for two hours, the sights, sounds and smells of the outer suburbs of the city were providing extra stimulus. Their incessant non-verbal conversation went back and forth to the irritation of the weary horsemen. With ears flickering, eyes rolling, snorting and throwing of heads every horse tried to understand the new environment.

Some horses leant on their lead ropes at the slowest walk; some horses unable to walk due to excitement, jig-jogged. Junior horses, awaiting any opportunity where the seniors would be unable to respond, bit at the faces and necks of senior horses. Senior horses responded by baring teeth, nipping at chests and barging with shoulders. Woe betide any rider's horse who was considered junior to the horses led beside it. The led horses would bite at the rider's horse then lean back on their lead ropes.

The rumps of the five horses in front invited more opportunities to bite by those who followed. When the clear warning of flashing black tails was ignored, the section in front slowed and sought any chance to kick out at those behind who might lunge forward and nip.

The air was as thick with the troopers' colourful language as it was with fog.

Jobert and Geourdai sat by the side of the street and watched the procession approach. Jobert's mount, Vert, experienced in the company of unfamiliar horses, stood patiently and flicked an ear back towards Jobert should Jobert shift a hand or adjust his seat. Geourdai's less experienced horse played with Vert by slowly reaching across and nipping Vert's muzzle. To the annoyance of Vert, who threw his head out of reach, and Geourdai, who slapped his horse's neck with the reins.

Jobert looked up the street towards the barrack's entrance some four hundred metres away. Eight sections of the company lined that distance, two dismounted men on either side of the street. As a rider came between a pair of dismounted men, the rider halted his team of horses and the dismounted troopers sprang forward and took the lead rope of a single horse each. The mounted platoon sergeants then shepherded their two sections with twenty-four new horses onwards up the street towards the barracks stables.

'Good morning, sir. Second Lieutenant Neilage. My report on the remounts, sir.'

Jobert glanced at the young officer in the uniform of the recently disbanded Chasseurs Volontaires. Neilage was of slim build, his reddish blond hair swept back into a queue, with a bristling moustache under a rather pointy nose.

Neilage extended a sheaf of papers toward Jobert. Jobert continued his detailed observation of the bay remounts filing past.

Geourdai clicked his fingers and extended his hand for the documents. 'Lieutenant Neilage, your section has completed its task. Sergeant Major Koschak will now take responsibility for your men and your horses. You may now retire to the tavern. You and I will lunch there together at noon.'

'Yes, sir, I am obliged. Would you excuse me, sir?' Neilage saluted, his eyes betraying his disappointment at not being welcomed more warmly.

Jobert turned his head from the procession to watch Neilage join the remaining flow of horses along the street. 'What had you said about him? Joined the volunteers without any prior experience, elected sergeant major in less than eighteen months and the Colonel promoted him to troop commander.'

'Sir.'

'I am interested in where our commanders call home. There are a range of divisions which may impact on our ability to form the company. You, Koschak and I, as old, royal army, versus volunteers like Neilage and the sergeants. Yet all the sergeants were all old army prior to the volunteers. Are they at odds with their local corporals? You and I need to know where our people's allegiances lie.'

'Absolutely, sir.' Geourdai flicked his eyebrows at Koschak approaching behind Jobert.

'Sergeant Major,' Jobert said, twisting in the saddle, 'I note the horses have only their front feet shod. The company farrier ought to be holding the remaining shoes. Do not have them tacked on. Keep them in store. Also, no manes are to be hogged, nor tails shorn on any 2nd Company horses without my explicit orders.'

'Sir.'

'Once settled in barracks, I will have all the horses' manes hogged. Geourdai, find us a mattress maker who will give us a good price for company funds. I want to purchase water gourds for the men. Remember, manes only. I want the tails left long, not bobbed, as summer's insect season approaches.'

'Take two,' Jobert insisted.

Lieutenant Geourdai and Second Lieutenants Voreille and Neilage took two *marc de provence* each from the soldier with a tray of aperitifs at the dining room door.

'2nd Company.' Jobert consumed the glass in a gulp.

'2nd Company,' toasted the others in return, placing their empty glasses back on the tray.

'Thank you, Chasseur,' said Jobert to the soldier holding the tray. 'Which company?'

'Ah, 4th Company, sir.'

'You are doing a good job, lad. Well done.'

The four 2nd Company officers strolled deeper into the room with their other glass.

The dining room brimmed with officers. At four officers to a company and twelve companies in the new regiment, Jobert calculated there will be approximately fifty to sixty officers, including regimental headquarters, at dinner this evening.

With the officers not yet having their uniforms amended, a variety of French cavalry uniforms were on display. Pre-dominantly chasseur à cheval uniforms, especially those of the recently disbanded Chasseur Volontaires. There were green dragoon and blue heavy cavalry uniforms and at least a dozen multi-coloured hussar uniforms within the crowd.

The Colonel was announced into the room. Silenced descended.

'Gentlemen, thank you,' said Morin. 'What a pleasure to have us all here together at last. May I ask you to charge your glasses?'

Glasses, with varying levels of eau de vie, were snatched up from tables and trays.

'Gentlemen, the 24th Chasseurs à Cheval.'

'The 24th Chasseurs!' boomed back the chorus. The room returned to noisy conversation.

As Jobert turned back to Geourdai, Voreille and Neilage, a raised finger caught his attention. A pair of dark eyes drilled into Jobert before the man's athletic frame, enhanced by a well-tailored uniform with correct 24th Chasseur facings, strode across the room towards the 2nd Company officers.

'Gentlemen, Captain Fergnes, 1st Company, 1st Squadron and regimental fencing master.'

Jobert regarded Fergnes' dark curls cut in the latest style, a well-curled moustache and emotionless eyes. Jobert recognised Fergnes' fashion and speech as an officer of common, or bourgeois, extraction. Neither nobility nor up from the ranks.

'Captain Jobert, 2nd Company, 2nd Squadron.'

'Sir, that the army is unable to issue our regiment sabres is scandalous. I am alarmed that I have received a company of soldiers of which one-quarter admit to having knowledge of horses. Upon inspection, I have grave doubt as to the ability of at least half. I predict a disaster. Acknowledging you have only just arrived, may I prevail on you, sir, for your initial thoughts on the matter?'

'I am considering training my company under canvas. My desire is to accustom them to field conditions and the duties of setting, guarding and breaking camp. In line with Colonel Morin's dire warning of impending combat, I hope to avoid the beguiling comfort of barracks.'

A smile lifted Fergnes' curled moustache. 'Splendid. I shall join you. Where might one site our companies? I do not know the country hereabouts.'

'I do,' said an urbane voice. The party turned toward a tall, blond man, his face affable as he bowed. 'Captain de Chabenac, 8th Company, 2nd Squadron. I am at your service, gentlemen.'

Nobility! The group froze their expressions. De Chabenac sought a reaction.

'Forgive my intrusion, gentlemen, but your topic is at the forefront of everyone's mind, apart from, of course, Madame de Rossi's impending ball. To overhear potential solutions to an approaching calamity demonstrates I have placed good manners aside. Then to be given the opportunity to step forward and offer the smallest contribution to your project, I simply could not resist, although it may blacken my name amongst my esteemed regimental brothers. Gentlemen, I beg your forgiveness.'

Jobert maintained a stern mask as he sipped his marc. 'I will forgive any man who knows what capucine is. You heard our scheme, sir. Do you have information which might strengthen our hand?'

'My family is from this area, although my family's influence has passed. My father, until recently the Comte de Chabenac, still enjoys the company of the major landowners around the city. I have hunted the surrounding countryside since a boy. I can think of many sites which would accommodate the numbers you have in mind. My family owes a debt of honour to Colonel Morin, so in facilitating the potential location of your scheme, sir, I am at your service.'

As the room was informed to take their places for dinner, Geourdai shuffled in beside Jobert.

'Have you heard of the coming ball to which the officers of the regiment are invited? Madame de Rossi's ball?'

'Forgive me, sir, having only recently arrived I have much

information to consider. That particular piece of news I have not yet received.'

'Then forgive me, sir, but yes, a ball will be hosted in about ten days. But to the heart of the matter, sir, as an ex-sergeant, can you dance?'

Jobert guffawed with surprise at Geourdai's alarm. 'No, sir, I cannot dance. Well, certainly not the steps required at a society ball. I take it, neither can you?'

'I do believe I will be choosing to charge the Austrian Army single-handedly on that particular evening.'

'If we can put our men under canvas to instruct them in the arts of the battlefield, surely as brothers of the capucine, we can do our best to secretly instruct ex-sergeants to dance.'

Taking his place at the long dinner table, Jobert leant towards Voreille. 'Are you aware that a society lady, Madame de Rossi, is hosting a ball to which the regiment's officers are invited?'

Voreille' eyes widened. 'Yes, sir. The regimental aides are most excited.'

'As a School man, can you dance?'

'No, sir. Perhaps there was dance instruction before, but certainly not now. No.'

'I inquire not to determine the nature of the syllabus of the esteemed École Militaire, sir, but to determine if you, sir, a gentleman of good breeding, education and connection, can dance.'

'I am capable of a few routines, sir. But I do not profess to be proficient.'

'Voreille, in the eyes of an ex-sergeant, any man capable of dancing a few routines in Paris is a bona-fide dance master in Avignon. Second Lieutenant Voreille, as the messing officer of the Tavern of the ... the ... the Sky-blue Pompom, you are to secure the services of a local dancing instructor. Is your mission clear?'

'I am at your service, sir.'

'Then I am obliged, sir.'

The ringing of a small bell quietened the room.

'Gentlemen, Colonel Morin.'

The long tables thundered as they were patted in applause. A chorus of 'Hear! Hear!' was subdued by the Colonel with a wave.

'Brothers of the 24th Chasseurs, an exhausting ten days for us all. Whether by the extraordinary administration required of many of you, or by those who have journeyed from afar to join us. Such effort will be rewarded. Such exhaustion will pale in comparison to what lies ahead. Nevertheless, let us relax in each other's good company for one brief evening.'

A further chorus of table patting ensued, the candelabra on the table shaking and the dim light in the room wavering as a result of the movement.

'Second-in-command, take note to halve the wine allocation at our next dinner.'

Raive's 'Sir!' was drowned as the chorus hissed and stomped on the floor.

'Enough from me. Now for the soup. I am aware of the wave of rabbit soup flooding the city, as milliners seek felt for our bicornes. I have sent out a proclamation seeking the top twenty lads who bring in the most rabbits. I will enlist them immediately. But no rabbit soup tonight!'

The chorus roared its good cheer.

'Tonight, I am assured, it is hare soup.'

Jobert scrutinised the three ranks of chasseurs, standing beside their led, but saddled, horses, on the quiet lane. The dew on the gravel surface had kept the dust to a minimum during their one hour dismounted march. As the morning fog lifted, the sunshine was delightful across the pungent meadow they faced.

'I wish to make clear my directive on padding under the saddle. We are not issued with saddle pads to make the wooden saddle trees fit better. Nor do we seek extra weight in acquiring saddle blankets. To that end, I require every man in the company to fold his bedroll as a saddle blanket.'

The sergeants stiffened. Their eyes slid towards Koschak. Koschak's mouth tightened, eyes never shifting from Jobert. Geourdai lifted his head to gauge Jobert.

Jobert held each man's gaze. 'There are two initial concerns with this approach. First, the men's blankets become wet with horse sweat, let alone smell of horse. The solution is to fold the blanket within the paillasse. The resultant second concern becomes that the men then need to empty paillasses of straw each morning and re-fill each evening.'

Jobert leant towards them, two fingers of his right hand stabbing his left palm. 'Allow me to make this easy for the company to understand. The Republic paid for the horses and pays the chasseurs to be ready to make war on the Republic's enemies. Within days we will be living under canvas and within weeks we will be on campaign. More than likely not sleeping in billets but sleeping on the ground without access to straw. As the senior representative of the Republic within 2nd Company, those horses' backs are my responsibility. I will not discuss the mild inconvenience of re-stuffing a paillasse in barracks when the battle-readiness of our horses is at stake. Is my requirement clear?'

'Yes, sir,' the chorus responded, with Koschak the loudest.

'Sergeants, carry on.'

The sergeants' bellows became a flurry of action. Men broke ranks, formed in sections and unsaddled, some holding each other's horses, some stacking saddles in section order, a few racing to receive the reins of the officers' horses.

Rummaging in their sabretaches for their notebooks, Neilage and Voreille moved stiffly to join Jobert, Geourdai and Koschak. From this morning's fencing, Neilage's swelling would become a black eye by lunch and Voreille still bled from his split lip.

'Neilage will record our findings on horses,' said Jobert. 'Voreille will record on soldiers. First, horse assessment. We three,' indicating himself, Geourdai and Koschak, 'will triage the horses. Reporting to Neilage, a score of one means the horse is very capable and you would be happy to take him on campaign. A score of two means the horse is a little hard, not impressive, sufficient. A score of three means this horse is not good enough and needs work. Remember, we are assessing horses today, not schooling them. I am interested in the horse's desire to listen, to bend willingly, transition to trot, both canter leads and back-up. If the horse is up to it, move sideways and pivot over the hocks.

'Neilage, ensure you have the section corporals telling you the hoof brands, stamped onto bridles, before the horse is given to the assessors. Voreille, ensure the sergeants are swapping our saddles onto each new horse, we will check girths as we receive them. Also, wash your face as you have blood on your cheek and reverse your stock as it too is bloodstained.'

For each assessor scoring each horse took only five minutes in the saddle. From mounting, riding and returning the first horse, reporting to Neilage while saddles were swapped, then mounting the next horse took ten minutes. At thirty-odd horses per assessor, it took five hours of dusty effort to complete the initial horse assessment.

Under the warm noon sun, the men lunched on bread and cheese, sitting in the long, roadside grass, upon which their horses grazed and lazily flicked tails at flies. While men and horses rested, the command group collated their findings and determined that approximately twenty percent of the horses were very good, forty percent were satisfactory and forty percent needed extra training.

'With your permission, sir,' asked Koschak. 'Sergeants, has anyone else started to notice eyes rolling, sly comments and quiet groans from the corporals? And if so, what is the issue?'

Pultiere cleared his throat to break the awkward silence. 'I found the newly promoted corporals very unsure of themselves in the company of their old section-mates, before they departed as members of the recruit and remount group. But they certainly have returned with a swagger.'

'Perhaps the freedom away from the regiment filled them with an inflated level of importance,' said Bredieux, grinding his teeth on his pipe stem. 'Returning to barracks life and wiping the arses of recruits might be taking the shine off their new rank.'

'Would you say there is any old royal army versus volunteer legion frictions?' Geourdai asked. The sergeants looked slyly at each other.

'Perhaps, sir,' said Huin. 'I feel that sentiment may well be there due to the workload required to stand up a company of recruits. The corporals have never experienced that pressure before.'

'Thank you, men,' said Koschak. 'That gives me a decent insight in how to support our fellows. I might have a quiet word in the corporals' little pink ears in the next few days.'

'Next, rider assessment,' said Jobert, his mouth full of bread and cheese. 'The twenty-odd very good horses will be divided between the four platoons. The rider will come out on his own saddle. The exercise is simple. Trot to the turn-around point and canter back on a right lead. Canter back out on a left lead and trot back.

'A score of one means the man rides smoothly and is well balanced. A score of two means he has satisfactorily completed the exercise. A score of three means the soldier is rough and ungainly. Voreille, maintain the scores against the company roll. Neilage will assist to keep the process flowing. With men waiting saddled and mounted, we should have no reason for any delay. Keep them coming like sheep down a race.'

The next three hours flew by with men saddling and unsaddling, nervously taking their turn at the mounted exercise in front of their assessors or attending to horses not in work. Sergeants and second lieutenants barked to maintain the flow of riders and connect the called assessment with the rider to which it pertained.

By late-afternoon, the results showed twenty-five percent of the men were very capable horseman, fifty percent of the company could control a cantering horse and the remaining twenty-five would need to show a distinct improvement in their riding skills, if they were to remain in the company.

Jobert coughed from drinking too deeply from a water flask. 'Geourdai, you have one hour to allocate each man a horse based on Neilage's and Voreille's lists. All the good grade-one riders and all corporals to receive the poorer grade-three horses; that will be my training group. All the poor grade-three riders will receive a good grade-one horse and they will be Sergeant Major's training group. Then the medium grade-two horses will be allocated to the medium grade-two men.

'Once this combined list is created, we will form up on parade, exchange horses, saddle and ride home. We still have a troop guard to mount tonight, yes?'

Chapter Four

Seated in squadron order down both sides of the dining table, Jobert waited for Raive's regimental administrative notices, drawing a notebook and pencil from an inside pocket of his tailcoat.

Lieutenant Colonel Raive's eyes twinkled with his customary merriment as he entered the chilly dining room with a steaming cup of coffee. 'Good morning, gentlemen. How are we all?'

The captains and their seconds-in-command groaned their response, arching their stiff backs and shoulders from the strain of the morning's fencing.

'Down to business. Man the regiment, equip the regiment, train the regiment. In the past two weeks, interaction with the War Committee, city administrators and local suppliers, for the collection of men, horses and equipment, has been the focus of the headquarters. As that flow has begun, Colonel Morin has planned a locally situated regimental field camp.'

The audience sat upright in their chairs, muttering to each other.

'This is possible with the arrival of the regiment's tentage stores yesterday. I might say the regiment is most grateful to the family of Captain de Chabenac in facilitating the project by identifying and securing potential campsites.'

The table chorus patted the table with a resounding, 'Hear, hear.' De Chabenac responded to all by looking up and down the table, nodding with his gracious smile.

'The Colonel's intent is to open the six-hundred-man camp in about four days' time. This week, the Colonel will lead a training ride to the campsite where the requirements of a site will be discussed. From there a plan will be devised and orders given as to the programme of occupation and rotation. Are there any questions of a general nature?'

'Yes, sir,' said Jobert. *We are running out of time before* ... 'When will sabres be issued?'

Raive's merriment evaporated. 'I do not know, Captain Jobert. I assure you all, this parlous situation is uppermost in Colonel Morin's mind.'

Notebooks were scanned in the uncomfortable silence.

Raive evaluated the sullen young officers over the rim of his coffee cup. 'An item of good cheer, the de Rossi ball. Wear whichever full-dress uniform you currently have. Head dress for all, without exception, will be bicorne with the 24th Chasseur's plumes. Officers will assemble here in the square at six o'clock that evening. The ball will commence at seven o'clock, supper at ten o'clock and the dance programme to conclude at two o'clock. Any questions?'

'Excuse me, sir,' said from someone further down the table, 'will there be fencing the morning after?'

'What an excellent idea. Why not?'

Groans and creaking chairs from slumping issued from around the table.

'Any further questions? No? Good. Am I correct, Captain

Jobert, you wish to make a quick remark upon the subject?'

'Yes, sir,' said Jobert, 'I would indeed, if this is an appropriate moment?'

Raive indicated with a sweep of his hand that the floor was his. Jobert noted Captain Fergnes' emotionless dark eyes narrow, resting his chin upon his hand with his elbow on the table.

'Thank you, sir, for this opportunity,' said Jobert. 'Gentlemen, I shall not detain you long, as your duties await. Our Colonel and senior regimental gentlemen maintain our focus on the perils of military operations that lie in the days ahead. For many of us, our experience in such intensive manoeuvres is scant. We would also be aware of the threat to our success in the shape of foreign and domestic agents and spies. To that end, I am forced to make my following remarks with discretion and in code.'

Some at the table glanced toward Raive for enlightenment. Some noticed Geourdai leaning back, his lop-sided grin in place. To those prescient, something was afoot.

Jobert looked over both shoulders to the closed doors of the room, then leant forward to whisper. 'I refer to the loss of honour that will ensue should we fail in an impending regimental operation, to which I can refer in present company as ... Madame de Rossi's ball and the risk and subsequent misery that lies within "dancing". I am not saying that any man present is inexperienced in ... "dancing", but you may be aware of other brother officers, who may need instruction in the brutal art of "dancing".'

Geourdai led a growing chorus, who, seeking the cue, chimed in with "dancing" themselves.

'Are you saying, sir,' asked Raive, 'that you are aware of whispers desiring instruction in ... "dancing"?' The chorus picked up the cue, as Raive waved in their participation.

'My own agents, sir,' said Jobert, 'have made me aware of regimental limitations in ... "dancing".'

Raive's moustache twitched. 'I have bitter experience from this form of military operation, sir. I am aware that any instruction of "dancing" would require a master of such dark arts in attendance. Are your agents aware of a master of "dancing" in our midst?'

Various 'oohs' and 'ahs' emitted from those present.

'I am informed, sir, that such fellows can be found for a price.'

'Again, from harsh experience, sir, I am aware that ...'

'Dancing,' anticipated those seated.

'Or similar military operations require a large, open area, a veritable Champ de Mars, on which to practice the dreadful drill. Are your agents aware of such a location?'

Jobert checked if all was clear. 'Of this location I do not know, sir, but I am aware of its codename. I believe this terrible location is referred to as ... the Tavern of the Sky-blue Pompom.'

A drawn-out 'ooh' was shared from the chorus at this information.

Raive rapped the table. 'This is a most serious situation, gentlemen. A situation I know to be doomed to failure unless ... unless there is a captive enemy force on which to practice such wicked evolutions. Is there, sir, captive enemy at this prepared terrain to which you refer, that other officers might complete manoeuvres in "dancing"?'

Many leant forward keen to commit if the right answer was provided.

'At this dreadful place, yes, sir, there are those of whom you suggest.'

Not just 'ooh', but knowing grins were shared around the table.

Raive put a finger to his lips. 'Then may I suggest, gentlemen, since no man here would admit himself deficient in the wicked art of "dancing", that there is no more to discuss. And with that, I dismiss you all to your duties.'

The officers stood. Raive departed and the entire group followed. As he fell into step with Jobert, Geourdai asked, 'What enemy force?'

'There is a suite of obliging ladies across the lane.'

'Oh, them. Young Voreille will be busy with his negotiations.'

By the light of the fire, Jobert's groom, Duque, polished boots. Orlande, Jobert's valet, ladled out bowls of a fragrant chicken and bean soup onto the scrubbed kitchen table, where sat bottles of wine, fresh baguettes and cloves of roast garlic.

Wincing, Voreille took a letter from the inside of his jacket and passed it to Jobert. 'Between the wooden sabre and the quill this morning I can barely raise my right arm. I prided myself on my fencing at the School, but those fellows from 1ˢᵗ Squadron we opposed this morning were brutal.'

Jobert and Geourdai could see Voreille was hurting.

'If you think 1ˢᵗ Squadron is uncompromising,' said Geourdai, 'wait and see what Fergnes has in store.'

'But we did not stop to refine our actions, sir. It was blow after blow for an hour. Why are we required to parade in gloves tomorrow, sir?'

'Because the sabre is harder to grip with gloves. If you think your forearm aches now, wait until this time tomorrow. I promise you it will get worse.'

'In battle, combat will be over in minutes,' said Jobert,

pointing his envelope at Voreille. 'You will barely trade more than three cuts with each face you see in a melee, but that is not the point of the morning's fencing. You, as an officer, need to know, deep in your bones, that you are good for a fight. This sense of hard-earned confidence must emanate from each movement, look and word prior to an action. The men will look to you for this confidence. Their white-knuckled grips on sabres and reins, vomit in the back of their throats, hearts pounding out of their chests and every eye on you. And there you are, knowing your enemy can not match the hours of suffering produced by Captain Fergnes.'

Jobert nodded his thanks to Orlande as he had his first spoon of the soup. 'Voreille, have you finished writing letters home for the chasseurs in your troop?'

'No, sir, I have a few more tomorrow night —'

'Is not our first dance class here tomorrow night?'

Voreille's freckles flushed. 'Yes, sir.'

Jobert continued enjoying his soup. 'And have we secured a dance floor in the tavern?'

'Yes, sir. For only one franc per dancer.'

'As much as that? Have we secured a dance instructor?'

Voreille looked into his soup bowl. 'Not yet, sir.'

'Why not?'

'I have no excuse, sir.'

Jobert scowled at the response. 'What you want to say is you have not had any time. If you wish to be a troop commander of chasseurs, Voreille, you ought to make better use of the resources around you. What is your solution, Geourdai?'

Placing down his soup spoon and taking up his wine, Geourdai screwed up his face. 'Knowing Orlande and Duque are able to undertake certain tasks for us, sir, at one franc per day, I would have paid Orlande to find our instructor.'

Orlande exchanged a wink with Duque.

'And did Orlande find an instructor?' asked Jobert.

'Yes, sir,' said Orlande, concentrating on ladling stewed brandied plums into bowls, 'At five francs a lesson, he brings his own fiddler. I got the tavern keeper down to three francs for the hour.'

'Voreille, you owe Orlande one franc. What of the ladies to assist our dancing?

Voreille slumped back in his chair.

'Duque?' asked Jobert

'Yes, sir. Eight ladies will be in attendance.' Duque's weary moustache twitched as he changed his grip inside the boot. 'At two francs each.'

Jobert looked at the bewildered Voreille over the rim of his wine. 'Now you owe Duque one franc. What will it cost? Sixteen plus five plus three equals twenty-four francs. Will we have at least twenty dancers at three francs each?'

Geourdai's head gave an affirmatory twist.

'Then, gentlemen,' said Jobert, 'we shall make a small profit for company funds.'

Paris
7th March 1793

My dearest André,

Jobert breathed in the hint of lilac that lifted from the unfolded pages.

I have just received the latest news from the farm.

Grandfather writes to Aunt that he is so proud of you both. He was so thankful you visited the farm as you travelled south to your new regiment. I know your father and mother are looking down lovingly on their very clever sons.

Jobert winced. *He had all those years. I have barely weeks. And without sabres.*

I also know my father would be very proud of your new promotions and positions, but you know how he is. Although he would say nothing, he would crush you and Didier with a bear hug, plant a bristly kiss that would remove skin and send you both off immediately to work colts. Needless to say, Aunt and I are so very pleased for you both and we send all our love and best wishes.

Our great aunt remains very well; she is energised by the activity here. I find it quite frightening just as it was last August with the invasion and then Valmy. With the defeat at Aix-la-Chapelle and now at war with Spain as well as Austria, Prussia, Sardinia, Britain and the Netherlands, our friends within the War Committee are in chaos. The Jacobin faction are beside themselves with rage and their support here grows daily. Not satisfied with the King's head, the number of executions grows daily, which is quite sickening.

Sadly, our family does well as a result.

The War Committee continues to raise more of the new horse batteries, so Grandfather's horses and harness are in much demand by the officers, despite the market flooded with horses because of the levee en masse. Ironically, cheap horses and father's reliability in filling contracts means we are selected for more and more supply contracts.

The levee en masse is also emptying surrounding towns of women, children and the elderly. Our workhouses here are overwhelmed. I intend to open another as we cannot accommodate the women we have. Demand for our sewing grows, especially in the manufacture of headdress alone, so there is more than enough work to sustain us.

Apart from the chaos in the streets, I am busy, well and happy. I know you will laugh when I tell you suitors abound, but I am too engaged with our projects for all that.

Didier's regiment is desperate for horseshoes, so I am having our friends to dinner soon. Is there anything in particular that you need?

Jobert stiffened.

'Is everything well at home, sir?' asked Orlande from beside the hearth.

'All is quite well, my friend. Just a whisper of opportunity.'

With a nod from Jobert, Geourdai banged a tavern chair several times on the ancient floorboards. Lit by candles set into the smoky, low beams the throng of cheerful young faces turned towards them.

Geourdai stood on the chair and held up his hands for quiet. 'Gentlemen, welcome to the Tavern of the Sky-blue Pompom.'

'If you are going to rename my tavern,' boomed the tavern keeper, as he pushed tables and benches aside to make room for the dance class, 'that will be another five francs.'

'Yes, yes,' said Geourdai. 'I recommend you unsling your scabbards and give them to Corporal Duque, there, for safe keeping.' Duque indicated his position by raising his beer tankard.

'I have appointed six squadron representatives,' continued Geourdai, 'who have the choice of receiving three francs from each member of their squadron tonight or paying ten francs themselves.'

'Hurrah!' erupted the majority. Six second lieutenants pointed fingers at their squadron colleagues, acknowledging the debt due.

'Gentlemen, this would not be possible without our orchestra.' Wobbling on his chair Geourdai indicated the dance master's violinist, the two musical brothers from 2nd Company with their own fiddle and fife and Corporal Duque with a mouth harp and tambourine. The musicians bowed low as the crowd gave a hearty round of applause.

'Yes, well done.' Geourdai waved to regain the crowd's composure. 'Our next thanks are to Anissa and her friends who will support our class this evening.'

Eight women aged between fifteen and forty-five curtsied low to the officers, their simple above ankle-length dresses adorned with tricolour sashes, either wound tightly around their waists or over their shoulders. Many with low cut bodices, all with merry eyes, cheeky smiles and their hair tied up with ribbons, with loose curls on foreheads and necks according to the latest Parisian style. The officers applauded and bowed in response.

'Now I beg you to give your full attention to our dance master, Monsieur Inoubli.'

Inoubli, a slim, clean shaven man in his early thirties, in matching purple satin jacket and breeches, with a vibrant orange waistcoat, white stockings, purple shoes with orange bows and his hair slicked back into a queue held with a purple ribbon, bowed low to the officers with a theatrical flourish. Nodding to the officer's applause, Inoubli stepped into the centre of the group and with rolling hand gestures to Geourdai, the musicians and the ladies in turn, extended the applause.

With another bow and a raised hand, Inoubli returned the room to silence. 'Good evening, ladies and gentlemen, my name is Inoubli. It is my pleasure to be here this evening to assist you in any small way that I can. I can assure you Madame de Rossi has confided in me her selection of dances for the ball to ensure maximum participation from her guests by minimising the number of dance styles. To that end, I have placed myself at the disposal of the regiment for four evenings. I propose to introduce a particular dance during the first three evenings and review our progress, on the fourth evening, prior to the ball. If that is to your satisfaction, then we might commence the evening with the *gavotte*, a harvest festival and wedding favourite. If all goes well, proceed to the well-known *bourrée*.'

Jobert slapped his thigh in good cheer. Most of the women and many of the officers responded with delight, as they were acquainted with these lively dances of rural origin.

'Ladies, do you feel you can accommodate so many well-formed fellows?' asked Inoubli with a devilish wink.

'There are not many times we girls can be paid so well, so early in the evening and later, only complain of how sore our feet are,' said Anissa, a slim, flashing-eyed brunette, with her hands on her hips, creating a laugh and cheers from all.

'If our musicians will take up the tune so we might measure the metre and if our ladies divide into two groups of four,' said Inoubli. 'Then, gentlemen, please separate into two groups so you may dance into one of the ladies' circles, then dance one rotation before departing the circle, allowing another gentleman in.'

The evening began with Inoubli guiding the twirling gentlemen through the steps of the gavotte. The tavern keeper ensured a steady flow of liquor to dancers and musicians. Half an hour into the class, Geourdai, his face flushed from dance and drink, tapped Jobert on the shoulder and jerked a thumb at over a dozen men drinking at tables by the fire.

The men were filthy from toiling outdoors, either local construction or farm labourers, their dirty hair loose, their muscular hands begrimed. Their drunken sneers showed they were taking great delight in mocking the dancers and interrupting the instruction by clanging jugs and drinking vessels on the greasy tabletops.

With a swift appraisal, Jobert spun towards the menacing labourers. 'On me! On me! Duque, Fergnes, Geourdai! On me!'

The men at the tables lurched upright to receive the impending attack, some drawing knives and belts, other changing their grips on wooden beer-mugs. The crackling of the fire in the hearth the only other sound in the now silent room.

'Gentlemen,' said Jobert, 'it is now time you all went home to your wives.'

The labourers looked at each other in confusion. One thickset fellow, beer-stein in hand, stepped toward Jobert, responding, 'And if we do not have wives?'

'But you good citizens must have wives. Otherwise, as unmarried patriots you would be avoiding the levee en masse. Then I would call out the barracks guard to hold you all in the regimental cells until the gendarmes arrive.'

Jobert sensed the men's hesitation. 'Would you like to go home now to wake tomorrow morning besides your wives? Or go to bed this evening in the army?'

The men shrank back, the threatening postures dropped away, knives, belts and wine-jugs returned to their original locations. Draining their mugs, they pressed towards the tavern's front door.

'Monsieur Inoubli,' said Jobert, 'your parade, sir.'

To which Inoubli bowed, the musicians struck up their tune and the girls took up their partners' hands.

Chapter Five

Freshened by the early snow melt from the Alpine headwaters to the east, the cold, dark stream tumbled and raced among the stunted pine to join the larger streams emptying into the Rhône less than five kilometres to the west. Although the Lyon road wound north from Avignon, the road here paralleled the east-west stream. At the top of a long slope running north from road and stream, Jobert and the regiment's officers gathered around Colonel Morin, as horses were led away to pasture by attendant troopers.

'Let me introduce today's discussion with the following news,' said Morin. 'Those district administrators with a modicum of patriotism and integrity are complying with Paris' directions for the raising of recruits in a timely manner. The ... less than responsible district administrators are either delaying their provision of allocated men, or sending in the district's criminals, drunkards and imbeciles. This action both slows the enrolment of men in the local centres and, what is more, decreases the number of recruits who have an ability to ride.

'I have decided to adapt to these circumstances in two forms. First, the recruit batches will now arrive every second day. Second, I shall suspend the formation of 11th and 12th Companies and integrate their current manning into the 5th and 6th Companies, thus reducing us to a five-squadron regiment for the foreseeable future. I have already shared this development with those 5th and 6th Squadron officers affected.'

Many officers rocked back on their heels. Jobert looked about and found downcast colleagues.

'But now for today's tactical study,' said Morin. 'North is in the direction of the road crossing the saddle two-thousand metres hence. We may assume the enemy's main force lies to our north over that saddle. Our own main force lies to the south. For our purposes today, two squadrons of the regiment will camp on the meadow on the opposite, or southern, side of the stream and road. We will focus on the requirements for a two-squadron camp down this northern slope towards the side of the stream.

'The officers of the 1st and 2nd Squadrons, under Major Avriol's guidance, will consider the factors of the camp relating to horses. The officers of the 3rd and 4th Squadron, under Major Spiccard will consider the factors of the camp relating to the men. I shall take the 5th and 6th Squadron's officers and discuss the issue of supply to the camp. In two hours, we shall reconvene and share our learnings before returning to barracks.'

The dozen officers of 1st and 2nd Squadron returned to the stream bank to be addressed by one of Morin's two chiefs of squadron, senior regimental combat leaders capable of independent tasking.

'I am Major Avriol. The chief of squadron for 1st and 2nd Squadrons.' Avriol's low voice caused all to focus on his iron-hard, nonplussed visage. Jobert considered how Avriol projected his ferocity; his intense eyes and thick black moustache, his hair bound back into a queue.

'Gentlemen,' said Avriol, 'the Colonel made it most clear what drives our momentum. The Colonel identified that accelerated individual promotion and rapid regimental expansion in the last three years has created critical areas of inexperience as much as it has allowed fresh ideas to form. Here we are, confronting an essential battlefield requirement, the setting of a camp. As we must always consider the enemy first, how does the enemy affect the sighting of the horses in camp?'

The subsequent eager discussion recognised that the enemy's light cavalry could approach this camp as easily from the east or west. The young officers identified the enemy's objective to either steal or destroy the squadron's horses and advocated for placing the horse lines furthest from the enemy.

'Where on the ground might we see the horses located?' asked Avriol. Due to the lay of the land, this consideration inferred the horse lines would be parallel to the stream.

'Wherever there is cavalry, there are four elements.' Avriol held up four fingers. 'Dust, mud, shit and lots of it. Are we satisfied with the placement of the lines?'

It was acknowledged that the ability of the horse lines to foul the water over a significant length compromised the location. Discussion identified water access for the men at the most upstream limit of the camp, then further downstream, water access for the horses, then even further downstream, a ford for the crossing of traffic from the road into the camp. A piece of ground was identified which, should there be heavy rain, the water run-off, from where the horses stood and defecated, would not foul the identified water access points.

'Two squadrons consist of four hundred horses.' said Avriol. 'What will be the dimensions for the horse lines required? We have enough fellows. Let us pace it out.'

It took Fergnes and Jobert to point out the stream's high-water mark, from evidence of previous storm debris, to mark the minimum safe base of measurement. A solution of four company-strength horse lines was established, extending from the stream's high-water mark far up the slope. Once paced out and marked by the syndicate, the area of two hundred by twenty metres was impressive. Moreover, this was just for two squadrons, not the entire regiment.

Convening once more at the top of the long, sunny slope with the other officers, Avriol had appointed Jobert to present the group's findings to the wider audience.

'In summary, sir, gentlemen,' said Jobert projecting his voice to those assembled, 'our group identified the following considerations for horse lines: protection from enemy raids; relationship to the water source to gain access and to eliminate the fouling of the water due to either movement or rain run-off and to eliminate the impact of the stream rising due to storms; the dimensions requiring both the positions of the horses and lanes allowing men to feed, clear manure and lead horses to and from; and the significant amounts of rope, pegs, hammers, shovels and rakes to cause this all to happen.'

The group who would consider the requirements of the men presented a long list of considerations, which were scribbled into notebooks. Such considerations included flat sleeping areas, access to water, security picquet locations, access to horses, access to timber and sighting of cooking fires, sighting of latrines for both access and rain-induced run-off, access to a dismounted parade ground and the siting of command, medical and supply tents.

Before the 'men versus horses' compromises could be re-solved, the third group provided insight into the need of supply: the location of the ford to allow wagon access from the Lyon road and the ford's relationship to other water access points; the need for a circular one-way route around the outside perimeter of the camp and a centre road through the middle of the camp;

the need to establish unload points uphill so stores could be walked downhill; and a wagon park with subsequent horse lines dedicated to the supply trains.

While small, white butterflies flitted about the meadow, the ensuing debate was of great interest. The junior officers desired a definite solution. The senior officers observed how each junior fellow revealed his character by his participation in the discussion. The robust discussion failed to produce a definite plan.

Morin held up his hand. 'Gentlemen, look at what we have not achieved in three hours in the middle of a sunny day, after a good night's rest, a hearty breakfast and without anyone shooting at us.'

Jobert heard Sergeant Major Koschak before he saw him.

'If you gutless worms ever try that again,' said Koschak, 'I will rip you a new asshole. I will show you royal fucking army.'

Koschak's jacket, helmet and sword belt already lay on the ground as he unbuttoned his waistcoat. The eight corporal section commanders were braced to attention in a single rank, obscured by the dung piles and wagons beside the barrack's wall.

The four platoon sergeants faced the men at one end of the rank. The manner in which the sergeants held their scabbards inferred to Jobert they would draw their sabres and cut the corporals down at the slightest suggestion.

As Koschak removed his shirt the corporals' eyes were wide with fear. At the sight of his muscular torso, the men trembled.

One sergeant jerked as he spotted Jobert approaching. Jobert held up a hand and shook his head. *I want to hear this.*

'I have lost two teeth.' Koschak lifted his lip. 'Broken ribs.' He showed a deep indentation on his side, then flexed a jagged scar on his left shoulder. 'And taken a cut, all from enemy action.'

Koschak then turned his back on the corporals. 'There is the royal, fucking army, you sacks of shit.' Three of the corporals took a step backwards from Koschak's scarred back lacerated from floggings. 'Not enough pipe clay, horseshoe too loose and while putting a wheel on a wagon, not saluting an officer smartly enough.'

Koschak spun and faced the terrified men, his roar mere centimetres from their faces. 'Do not ever fucking royal army me again, you weeping pox-sores. Ever! Men like me killed the royal army, not worthless piss dribbles like you. Men like me massacred our officers to ensure the end of flogging, not putrid snot like you. Men like me fought France's enemies, screaming "Liberty, Equality, Fraternity" at the top of our lungs, while you arseholes tied pretty ribbons on each other's cocks.'

Clenching and unclenching his fists, his powerful shoulders running with sweat at his exertions, Koschak's eyes sought the slightest reason to drive his fist into any, or all, of their throats.

'How fucking dare you shame that uniform with those comments, you clap-ridden turds. As a point of regimental honour, I should reach down your throats and rip your balls out. You have no fucking idea of "Liberty, Equality, Fraternity" until you have killed another man to keep it, you fucking maggots.

'You and your soldiers will not know how to survive Austrian steel unless you obey my experienced instruction. Do you seriously believe your soldiers think you are credible as battlefield leaders?'

The eight corporals shook, their heads wobbled, while eyes flickered from side to side but never leaving Koschak's face.

'Which of you steaming dung balls wants to go? Obviously, this company, this regiment does not understand patriotism like you do, so fucking leave. But if you want to stay,' he now poked each man in turn in the chest with two rigid fingers, 'I demand you scream "I am a corporal section commander of the 2nd Company, 24th Chasseurs". Go on, you spineless bitches, scream it, or I will tear your fucking hearts out.'

They screamed the required phrase for all they were worth. Flecks of their white spittle hitting Koschak's beetroot face, his malevolent green eyes not wavering from their blanched faces.

Koschak stepped backwards from the last man, regarding them all with his hands on his hips. 'If you wish to become a trooper forever, posted to lick my shit for eternity, you even think the expression "royal army", whilst wearing that uniform and your only desire will be the liberty, equality, fraternity you receive from an enemy's blade.'

Blood throbbed against Jobert's high collar. *Bloody young fools. Your arrogance will get us all killed. Or worse.*

'Now, you rancid weeds,' said Koschak, 'on the command "Move" you will gather your sections in column of fours on the square. If any man in your section squeaks or quivers, I will poleaxe you limp pricks, with a single blow right there, on the square. Now, ... move!'

All the men ran as if shot out of a cannon. Four men stumbled, two fell, then scrambled to run after the others.

Koschak noticed Jobert approaching as he pulled his shirt over his head. 'Good afternoon, sir. Can I assist you?'

Jobert studied the bearing of each warily still sergeant. 'Sergeant Major, my observations of the company's preparations for deployment tomorrow appear most positive, but I am keen to listen to your perspective.'

'The men's readiness for deployment to either camp, or war, could not be more perfect, sir.'

A grim half-smile creased Jobert's face.

'I thought as much. Then I will let you get on. Good afternoon.'

Drizzling rain dripped from Jobert's bicorne. He tilted his head to the right to allow the dribbles of rain to bead off. At the front centre of 2nd Company, Jobert looked from one end of the company line to the other. *I should be savouring the moment of a full-strength chasseur company, but ...* His eyes slid to his men's right hips incongruously devoid of scabbard and hilt.

For most souls on parade in poor weather it might be considered a time of discomfort, but Jobert noticed Geourdai's self-righteous smile. At that moment, Geourdai was the right-most person of the regimental line and no-one stood beyond him.

In centuries past, when men fought with shields, the left side of the body was well protected and the right ribs were always open to attack from an opponent diagonally opposite. The natural impulse of the warrior was to press left, which subsequently crushed the sword arms of the men to the left. Hence only the bravest of the brave stood their ground on the right of the battle line. At an individual level, a warlord's champion was referred to as his 'right-hand man'. At an organisational level, to occupy the 'right of the line' was a point of honour, either an individual person or a selected group of soldiers.

As company second-in-command, Geourdai stood on the very right of the 2nd Company's front rank. Today, with 1st Squadron absent in camp, 2nd Company and thus Geourdai, was the right of the regimental line and hence, Jobert assumed, his smugness.

'Second-in-command!'

Geourdai squeezed his horse forward into a trot, halting in front of Jobert to salute.

'March 2nd Company to camp, Lieutenant.'

'2nd Company,' called Geourdai, 'form column to the left, walk, march.' Behind Neilage's lead, Sergeant Pultiere's platoon wheeled out into column of fours, at the walk, across the face of the company.

Jobert heard Koschak's 'whisper' to the men, 'Shine, lads. The whole regiment is watching you.' The chasseurs were rigid in the saddle as Pultiere's two corporals snarled comments out of the side of their mouths to maintain the perfection of the drill movement. Jobert snorted at the corporal's newfound ardour following their recent chat with the Sergeant Major.

His bemusement was cut short when he spotted Colonel Morin and his party by the stone entrance to the barracks. '2nd Company, eyes right by troop, carry on.'

'Troop, eyes right,' ordered Neilage, four horse lengths from Colonel Morin.

The lead corporal's face remained rigidly to the front, to maintain the alignment of the platoon, as the twelve ranks of four horsemen passed the Colonel. All the other fifty men of Neilage's troop had their chins over their right shoulders, eyes flickering to gauge their dressing, where their horses were walking and to look the Colonel in the eye.

'That man!' called the Regimental Sergeant Major mounted beside Morin. 'Do not look at your horse. He will not change colour. Look the Colonel in the eye, lad, and convince him you are the best bloody chasseur in the Republic.'

Unsure to whom the Regimental Sergeant Major's comments were levelled, near fifty heads and associated eyeballs swivelled even further.

'Well done, Sergeant Pultiere, well done, carry on.' Colonel

Morin returned Neilage's salute. 'Horses looking good, Sergeant Bredieux, well done, carry on.'

Morin twisted in the saddle and inspected Bleu's hind hooves. 'You are one of those "shoes on the front feet only" men, are you, Jobert? Let me know how your experiment goes. Major Avriol, do not let his wild ideas cripple my 2nd Company.'

'No, sir,' said Avriol, beside Jobert.

'Smartly executed. Good dressing, men,' called Morin as he received Voreille's salute. 'Good lord, Jobert, another experiment?' Orlande drove Jobert's personal two-wheeled cart, as part of the company's wagon train, past the Colonel's party.

'Yes, sir. Should you so desire, sir, there is a steaming cup of tea moments after the cart pulls up.'

'I look forward to your review of the tea, Avriol.'

Having cantered onto a low rise, Avriol and Jobert brought their horses back to a walk and pushed their horses under the boughs of a dripping oak tree. Avriol watched the walking progress of 2nd Squadron's six hundred metre column, of both Jobert's senior 2nd Company and de Chabenac's junior 8th Company, cross a brook at the bottom of the knoll.

'As my father would say, sir,' said Jobert, 'any bastard can be soldier on a sunny day.'

Avriol smiled as he arranged the folds of his coat over his saddle. 'Yes, my old regimental sergeant major would add, there is a thin strip of skin between a man's anus and his scrotum. When you get that wet, that is when you have leadership problems.'

They both laughed at solid military wisdom.

'You have had the recruits two weeks and the horses ten days. How would you summarise your company's capability right now?'

'They can dress themselves and assemble on parade, sir. They can strip, clean and assemble a musketoon. They can tack up a horse properly. They understand the fundamentals of columns of fours. I have committed sergeants. My second-in-command, sergeant major and myself seem to be connecting well enough.'

'Where do your concerns with your company lie?'

'I am gravely concerned that my men do not have sabres, sir.'

Avriol dropped his eyes to his gloved hands and flicked his reins.

'A quarter of my men are poor riders,' said Jobert. 'Extra equitation is required. Spending time learning to ride cuts into our time to prepare for battle. I am concerned with inexperienced junior leaders. In days past, having nobility as useless troop commanders was never an issue, whilst they were surrounded by veteran sergeants and corporals. I have second lieutenants and corporals far from capable at this rank level.'

'Where does your focus lie in the coming days?'

'We will establish camp today, but it is my intent to break and set camp daily. I want to set solid guard routines and procedures. The officers and senior non-commissioned officers will fence daily. Mounted drill will extend from column of fours to column of platoons and, of course, extra equitation for men and horses who require it. I intend to conduct dismounted reconnaissance patrols by night with the officers and non-commissioned officers, with the wider intent of testing the guard. I will introduce advanced riding techniques across country and jumping.'

Avriol twisted in the saddle to look Jobert in the eye. 'Lieutenant Colonel Raive described to us what you achieved against the Austrians at Jemappes, Jobert. I demand you bring that level of élan to 2nd Company.'

Chapter Six

April 1793, Avignon, France

'Fire!' called Jobert down the line of four officers supervising the four chasseurs.

Four triggers were pulled. Four musketoon cocks struck forward, sparks from flints catching the priming in the pan, issuing a sharp hiss. Then a moment later, the charge exploded in the inner chamber propelling the four recruits' first musket balls fired in the army towards the targets fifty metres away.

'Load!'

This third day in camp for 2nd Company was choked with gun smoke.

'Ready!'

Jobert stood at the right of the line of the firers so he could see the firing mechanism of the chasseur he instructed, as well as kept a watch on Voreille and his chasseur. Geourdai stood next in the line and Neilage on the left with their respective chasseurs.

'Present!'

In an unsupported standing position, with butts thrust into

their right shoulders, the troopers levelled their shorter-barrelled cavalry muskets at the targets. Each platoon had made one horse-sized and one man-sized bag of grass over the last two evenings. Each target had a two-foot and one-foot diameter plate of wood respectively fixed to the bags indicating the vital areas.

'Fire!'

The four muskets exploded in a thick cloud of gun smoke.

'Kneeling, load!'

At the feet of each of the four targets, a small crease on the slope shielded a shallow ditch. In the ditch, on their backs, lay four men of the section and Koschak. They hooted as the first balls zipped unseen over their bodies and peered to see if the target would sway on its stand when hit, or better, if the wooden plates splintered when struck.

'Ready!'

Cocks were pulled back to arm the spring-loaded mechanism. Koschak kept score in the trench. The sections wagered on the outcome. The section with the best marksmanship would earn bottles of brandy.

'Present!'

Of the sixty firers so far, Jobert consulted his notebook tally, less than ten men had hit the wooden plates while standing and less than half had hit the targets at all.

'Fire!'

The musketoons cracked. Kneeling was by far the better stance. Nearly everybody hit the target and a third of the firers hit a vital wooden plate.

'Kneeling, load!'

Even Avriol, Fergnes and de Chabenac had lain in the ditch and were excited by the experience and its application, to the soldiers of the 1st, 7th and 8th Companies. With lungs sufficiently full of white smoke, those gentlemen had since departed.

With four troopers on the firing line and four in the target ditch, the remaining four soldiers of the section were dismounted just behind the firing line, each holding three horses. The horses were slowly becoming accustomed to the noise and the smell of firing.

'Mount!'

Mounting was not yet a fluid action. As each firer mounted, the musketoon attached by a clip to a chasseur's white cross belt thumped mercilessly into his right ribs. The young horse was agitated, both from the ungainly mounting causing the girth to twist on its ribs and stepping away from its mates with whom they nuzzled for comfort. Jobert snorted. *Wait until you attempt to mount with a dragging scabbard.*

'Ready!'

The cocking of the musketoon presaged the loud noise soon to come and many young horses swung their bodies in distress, causing loaded musketoons to be facing anywhere in a three-hundred-and-sixty-degree arc.

'Steady, lad,' said Jobert to each young chasseur. 'Relax your arse and your heels. Let him settle. Now squeeze him forward three steps, ... yes, Present! ... Now back up six steps ... Fire!'

The musketoon fired and the horse jumped.

'Load!'

For the majority of the young riders, the act of mounting with and then discharging, a loaded musketoon on a nervous mount was stressful in the extreme. To load the weapon whilst mounted doubled their anxiety.

Holding reins and barrel in the left hand, the soldier's right hand sought the final cartridge in their cartridge pouches swinging at their right hips yet was confounded by the butt of the clipped firearm. Once gained, the paper cartridge was bitten open, then whilst the chasseur groaned inwardly, the left hand sought to settle the horse and hold the weapon. The right hand held the open cartridge without spilling powder or ball, then half-cocked the mechanism, opened the frizzen to allow a touch of powder to be tipped into the pan and then finally closed the frizzen.

Grim-faced young chasseurs flicked their eyes imploringly to Jobert in the hope this nightmare might end. It did not. They pressed on, tipping the remaining powder and the ball down the barrel, then swapping hands to hold horse, weapon and ramrod. The chasseurs struggled not to bend their wooden ramrods as they packed the charge and returning the ramrod into its sleeve on the barrel, whilst the twirling young horses disoriented them.

'Ready!'

Introduced to mounting, firing and loading, at the end of yesterday's practice, the troopers watched in awe as Jobert, Koschak and Geourdai demonstrated the technique. The mounting and loading movements of all three battle-experienced, senior chasseurs were graceful and precise. Jobert's and Koschak's horses stood like rocks, apparently unconcerned with the activity, but their ears indicated they were locked on to their riders, nonetheless. Even as Geourdai's younger horse swung about, Geourdai made no effort to adjust his horse with his hand, he pivoted like a dancer, his face never leaving the target.

All three men hit the wooden plates with both mounted shots, the second shot within thirty seconds of the first. The audience shook their heads in disbelief.

'Present!'

Behind each officer on the firing line, a sergeant placed five ball cartridges in the cartridge pouch of the waiting trooper holding the horses. Jobert checked the height of the red sun above the smoke-obscured horizon.

'Fire!'

More explosions, more smoke, more distressed horses.

Jobert checked his notebook's scores. So far, only three men had hit the plates whilst mounted and approximately fifteen had caused the target to swing on its stand. *If only I had more time.* 'Dismount! Section, change!'

The meadows on either side of the road steamed in the morning sun, as Jobert watched the column of wagons and chasseurs approaching 2nd Company's ambush.

Morin had ordered the testing of each chasseur company's understanding of the many drills required when escorting convoys. Today, Fergnes' 1st Company undertook the escort duty.

On one side of the road was a walled farmhouse, from which Jobert viewed the impending attack. In the garden beneath Jobert's window, the lady of the house tendered her garden, waving to the horse soldiers passing her front gate. The road between the house and the milking barn opposite was slippery with fresh cow-shit and churned mud. The dairy cows bellowed for lost calves in the surrounding stone-walled enclosures.

Further up the lane just beyond the farm, on a stone bench at the crossroads, Jobert could see, what appeared to be, two elderly women smoking pipes, their hand-barrows full of onions close by. A young officer commanding the escort's advance guard signalled for the convoy to halt and with his sergeant, rode forward through the pungent mud, to confirm directions with the old ladies.

'Excuse me, Captain Fergnes, sir, something is not right.'

Beneath Jobert's window, Colonel Morin pivoted his horse to

face a wagon driver, then observed the response from 1st Company's commanding captain. The young soldier looked to the senior man from his vehicle's seat but pointed across the open meadow toward the haystacks and the stream beyond the farmstead.

Jobert raised an eyebrow. *Has this lad spotted us?*

Fergnes held his sabre in hand and his horse on a short rein. The horse spun on its hindquarters, as he observed the length of the convoy's column. Jobert and Morin could see that Fergnes was not looking where the trooper was indicating, instead he was looking at the milking barn on the opposite side of the road.

With the advance guard halted, the two section-strength flank guards trotted forwards to the outer sides of the milking barn and the farmhouse, one flank guard standing amongst the haystacks observing the stream. The lead wagons halted and the entire company slowed, with the centre of the convoy alongside the hedges and the walls of the farmhouse.

Colonel Morin saluted the lady in the garden and asked if the rain had caused any damage. The woman pushed back her bonnet, politely responded that all was well and then asked to be excused as she had a pot of brandied apricots simmering on the hob in the kitchen.

Morin noted her haste, and with a glance at Jobert, gathered his reins and lengthened his heels to sit deeper in his saddle. For his part, Fergnes squeezed his horse into a trot to get to his halted advance guard.

At the very front of the halted column, a second lieutenant doffed his bicorne to the elderly women, enjoying their pipes in the morning sun at the crossroads. The 'ladies' leapt to their feet, pulling two long cavalry pistols from each onion barrow. Sergeants Bredieux and Huin fired their blank charges at the feet of the lieutenant's horse, the signal to initiate the ambush.

Led by Voreille, there rose about a dozen men from the grass under the hedge and from behind the farmhouse wall. With faces, head wraps and capes woven with grass and caked with mud, the ambushers fired their blank cartridges as one into the 1st Company troopers and wagon horses. Horses groaned with fright as they became engulfed in the smoke cloud. Without pause, the shutters from the farmhouse's upper story beside Jobert also flew open and more blank fire poured from the windows.

With the advance guard spurring horses around from the crossroads to follow a roaring Fergnes, the rear guard pressed forward between wagons and walls to intercept the hedgerow ambush.

The barn diagonally opposite the house exploded with blank fire, gun smoke billowing, gates creaked open and startled cattle trotted out into the crowded lane. Wagon horses leapt aside from the scared cattle and wagons skewed across the slippery road.

Koschak, leading another section of mud-caked troopers from the barn, followed the cattle, bellowing 'Reload! On me! On me!'

Pinned between wagon horses and skittish cattle, Fergnes looked beyond the young wagon driver. The chasseur had slumped in his seat, feet on the buckboard, arms folded, staring downcast at the backs of his horse team. In the meadow beyond the wagon, a line of hay sheaves was assaulting at a run.

'Oh, great heavens! Gather your reins!' Fergnes screamed to the abandoned drivers as the grass hatted, grass caped hay-soldiers presented musketoons to fire a troop volley at forty metres from the convoy. Without pausing to reload their musketoons, but pulling off their verdant headdress, led by Geourdai and Neilage, the hay-men charged the convoy.

Later, as the smoke of the mock-battle drifted away from the farm, both Fergnes' and Jobert's companies reassembled.

'Captain Fergnes,' asked Morin, 'would you attend me?'

Fergnes spun his lathered horse to face his commanding officer. Jobert accompanying the colonel maintained a solemn appearance considering 2nd Company's victory.

Morin looked at the driver still pouting on his wagon seat. 'Chasseur, you said something was not right. What was not right?'

The chasseur straightened. 'Haystacks in March, sir. Nobody cuts hay in early spring. Certainly not green hay, made of bulrushes, then stands the sheaves in ricks in a field of short, uncut barley grass, under the shade of the stream's willows, ... sir.'

'Well done on both your important observations, lad, and thinking to inform your officers.' Morin turned to Fergnes, who was seething at a po-faced Jobert. 'Captain Fergnes, the Republic pays these lads to be the ears and eyes of the army. Despite their rank, I find it of value to consider their opinions on occasion. Do you agree?'

The pleasant, night-time distraction of watching flames dance along the crackling embers of the campfire was broken by the distinct creak of wagon axles across the stream. Jobert checked the camp area and saw Huin standing by his platoon fire looking in the direction of the Lyon road. At the metallic thud of shod hooves above the gurgling of the brook, Pultiere stepped out of his tent in an alert pose and Duque snorted awake from his fireside snooze.

At least two weapons were cocked prior to the clear, firm

challenge of 'Who goes?' was heard from the sentries in the dark. The muffled response from the horsemen was unclear, as was the release of the cocking mechanisms making the weapons safe, but the splashing of hooves and wheels was clear enough as the party crossed over the stream.

At a nod from Pultiere, troopers at the closest fire stood, slung their musketoons over their shoulders and, ducking under tent lines, went out into the darkness and received the incoming horses. Duque resettled himself at the fire once he had poured a little brandy into the coffee mugs of Jobert and himself.

'Good evening, sir,' said Koschak. Koschak and a trooper emerged from the darkness, with saddles and shabraques over their arms and saddle portmanteaus slung over their shoulders.

'Good evening, Sergeant Major. Your sergeants and yourself all home safe from a day's leave?'

'Yes, sir. You will remember Chasseur, now Trumpeter, Moench, sir? I assume he will be in the tent with the quartermaster corporal and the farrier?'

Jobert nodded and looked at Moench, a relaxed man in his late twenties, noting how his curled moustache appeared quite fierce in the firelight. 'Welcome back to the company, Moench. Did the regiment look after you?'

'Thank you, sir, good to be back.' Moench grinned. 'Yes, the headquarters' trumpeters did their best to look after my pay with their card games.'

'Where is your little brother? The Sergeant Major's piper?'

'He is posted to regimental headquarters, sir.'

'Settle yourself in, lad, then come back for soup.'

Moench stepped out of the firelight to follow Koschak to his new lodgings within company headquarters.

Lying on his sheepskin shabraque, Jobert rearranged his cape about him and settled back to stare into the fire, with his laced coffee in hand. Duque placed two thick pieces of timber on the fire and the resultant sparks crackled and wafted up to the sharp stars.

Koschak and Moench returned to the fire; Koschak with his cup and a bottle, Moench with his bowl and his fiddle.

'Sergeant Huin will have soup, lad,' Duque said to Moench, waving his coffee mug in Huin's direction, 'and your fiddle will pay for it easily enough. A gentle tune, mind you, we break camp at four o'clock tomorrow morning.'

Moench drifted over to Huin's fire where he was welcomed with exclamations of delight.

Jobert waited for the passing bottle to return to Koschak.

'The regiment has received over-breeches and sashes,' said Koschak. 'I have stored the sashes in barracks awaiting issue of the dolman jackets, but I have brought the over-breeches with me for issue to the men.'

'Might we issue the sashes as well, Sergeant Major? I know they are a decorative item worn with the dolman jacket, but they act like a truss for the lower back. Many of the men are growing very stiff from the amount of time in the saddle. The sashes may assist.'

'I will have the company quartermaster corporal bring them out tomorrow, sir. I have also purchased one hundred water gourds and the twine to create the slings.'

'One hundred? Did the hogged horses' manes receive that much from Geourdai's mattress maker?'

'That, plus the profit from the dance classes.'

The calming whisper and pop of the flames, supported by Moench's nearby melody, was interrupted by a human sob and the snort of tear-induced mucus. Sergeant Bredieux and three men ducked under the tent line and approached the company headquarters' fire. Jobert took a deep breath, as recruits' tears were an occasional feature of the camp.

'Evening, sir,' said Bredieux clenching his pipe between his teeth.

'Good evening, Bredieux, how was your leave?'

'I have returned to camp ten minutes ago, sir. I cannot remember.'

Jobert recognised the blubbering young man as one of the Tulloc brothers. The elder brother stood behind Bredieux his face quite downcast. Jobert knew the older brother as a competent horseman who schooled the poorer horses with him. Beside him their section corporal shoved the upset younger brother, whispering, 'For fuck's sake, son, shut up.'

'Sir, we had those six lads' riding skills assessed by the Regimental Sergeant Major,' said Koschak. 'He suggested we keep two and the other four are to be sent to 6th Company. Chasseur Tulloc is one of those to be posted out.'

'Sir,' said Tulloc, 'I will do anything to stay with my brother, sir, anything, please, sir.'

'Shut up, you idiot,' said Bredieux.

'Chasseur Tulloc,' said Koschak, 'I know you to be utterly dedicated to your mare, but in the saddle, you have all the balance and grace of a sack of potatoes, without the sack. Having said that, sir, remember Tulloc struck the wooden target plates four days ago with all five rounds.'

'Please let me stay, sir.'

'Chasseur Tulloc,' said Jobert, 'you cannot ride well enough to go into battle with the 2nd Company.' Jobert raised a finger to ensure the trooper's silence, to which Tulloc clamped his lips together with a sob. 'Lad, if you were to remain you would be killed in our first action. Worse than that you would get your horse killed and your brother killed. I am simply not going to allow that to occur. Do you understand me, Chasseur Tulloc?'

'Yes, sir.' Tulloc shuddered and tears ran down his face, to which his elder brother gripped his shoulder from behind.

Duque coughed.

Jobert slid his eyes across to see Duque staring into the fire, hunched over his coffee mug. Maintaining his watch on the fire, Duque barely moved his lips to utter 'Apprentice farrier,' loud enough for Jobert and Koschak to hear.

Jobert considered the option, passing his gaze from Duque to the fire, to Koschak's shrug and back to the agitated Bredieux and the whimpering Tulloc.

'I will continue to consider your situation. Nonetheless, Chasseur Tulloc, you will obey your orders and be prepared to return to barracks with the company quartermaster corporal in the morning.'

'Yes, sir. Thank you, sir.' Tulloc wiped his nose on the sleeve of his tailcoat.

'All right, that is enough, you lot,' said Bredieux. 'About turn, quick march. Goodnight, sir.'

Catching Duque's eye as he turned, Bredieux gave Duque a solemn nod.

Chapter Seven

'An urgent message from General Mouret for the Colonel.'

Jobert and a hussar major, General Mouret's aide de camp, were ushered into Morin's plush apartment, discernible by the light of a cosy fire and a few table-mounted candelabras. The room smelt of cigar smoke and brandy.

Morin rose and greeted them with a wide grin. He and Raive were settled into comfortable armchairs around the Colonel's fire, with crystal glasses of a dark brown liquor, obviously in a most cheerful mood.

'Good evening, sir.' The hussar major passed Morin an envelope.

'I see you have travelled far, sir,' said Morin. 'Follow my valet and he will accommodate your refreshment. Were you escorting the good major, Captain Jobert, or are you here to see one of us?'

'I wish to speak with you, sir.'

'Tonight?'

'Yes, please, sir.'

Morin indicated Jobert toward tapestry-upholstered dining

chairs at an intricately carved table. Morin resumed his armchair by the fire, inspected the seal of the envelope, then removed and read the contents.

The smile disappeared from Morin's face. His eyes flickered toward Raive. Morin passed the note to Raive, then slumped back in his chair and blinked at the dancing flames. 'It has begun. Civil war has erupted in the Vendée. The army is on the move.'

Jobert remembered how the Vendée, a region of France on the Atlantic coast through which a number of major rivers flowed, had erupted in violence in 1789 and 1790. The communities of the Vendée were wealthy from sea-borne and river-borne trade and that wealth was extinguished with the abolition of noble privilege and the flight of the nobility. The Vendéens deeply resented the intrusion of Parisian revolutionary madness, especially affronts to their deep-seated Catholic faith and now the demands of February's levee en masse had tipped them into civil war.

'The infantry of the 31st *Ligne* are to march north. The 24th Chasseurs are to maintain civil law and order along the Rhône valley. As we have seen, from the ambushes of our convoy escorts, our men can canter excitedly in circles and enthusiastically discharge blanks from their musketoons. But without sabres ...' Morin rapped his knuckles hard on the armrest of his chair.

Green timber in the fire hissed and popped as silence descended, the flickering firelight caused the room's shadows to quiver. An ember sizzled out onto the hearth rug, for Morin to extinguish it with his boot.

'Excuse me, sir,' said Jobert, 'I have also received news that I wish to share.'

Morin slid his eyes to gauge Jobert and raised his thick eyebrows.

'I have been reliably informed, sir, that there is an armoury in Valence, three days ride to the north, which contains four thousand sabres. It is believed these weapons are held by the enemies of the Republic.'

Morin and Raive turned slowly to face Jobert, their stares harsh, their mouths open.

'Sir, I request permission to depart immediately, with a small party, for this armoury. I wish to confirm or deny the information I have received. If true, then I propose to lead a squadron raid to secure the sabres for the regiment.'

Having turned in their armchairs, shadows covered Morin's and Raive's faces from the wavering firelight. Unable to gauge their reactions. Jobert kept his own face emotionless in the circumstance.

Morin drew deeply on his cigar. 'You are saying, Jobert, that someone has told you that there are four thousand sabres in an armoury three days ride from here?'

'Yes, sir.'

'Jobert, how might we assess the reliability of this information?'

Jobert breathed deeply in an effort to keep his reply succinct.

'The contents of all armouries in the vicinity of Lyon, which includes this small armoury in Valence, are compiled in a report dated the first day of the month. This report is received in Paris five days later. A review of the Lyon armoury returns for the 1st of November 1792, the 1st of December 1792 and the 1st of January 1793 shows that the Valence report was always included in the combined Lyon return.'

'You are saying your informant has access to the reports of the National Convention's War Committee.'

'Sir.'

Morin leant back in his armchair, drained his brandy and reached for the nearby crystal decanter. 'Continue.'

'Those Valence reports up to the 1st of January 1793 list only edged-weapons. The Valence armoury's reports consistently contained four thousand cavalry sabres, four thousand cavalry swords, four thousand infantry swords, four thousand infantry briquets and four thousand bayonets.'

Morin swayed in his chair. 'Enough for four regiments of chasseurs or hussars, four regiments of dragoons or heavy cavalry and two regiments of infantry.'

'Yes, sir. The Valence return is completely absent from within the Lyon report for the 1st of February 1793. Perhaps a coincidence, it is worth noting that His ..., the King was executed on the 21st of January 1793. Again, on the 1st of March 1793, the Lyon report does not include the Valence return. The War Committee has only become aware of this irregularity in the last ten days. The message was couriered to me within a day or two of revelation. I received the letter today.'

'I am imagining such weaponry is to be delivered to anti-Republican forces erupting in civil war in the Vendée.'

Raive put down his cigar to take up his pencil and notebook. 'Should Jobert depart at first light, sir, he will arrive at the armoury within two weeks of the anomaly's discovery. It is reasonable to assume Paris will have arrived there before, but it would do no harm to know.'

'To confirm the allegation, Jobert would need to gain entry,' said Morin. 'How, Captain, would you gain entry into an armoury, presumably held by our enemies?'

'If my party were to depart at first light, we would arrive at Valence before sundown three days hence. We would observe the armoury, its environs and the routines of its staff. Based on our observations, we would enter the armoury the fourth night or the fifth day from this evening.'

'Who would you include in your party?'

'Fergnes, de Chabenac, Sergeants Huin, Pultiere and Bredieux and my corporal groom, sir.'

'Why those?'

'I have come to trust Fergnes' judgement. De Chabenac's past may open doors that Fergnes' and mine cannot. I value the cunning and initiative of the men in my company. The corporal is well known to me. We served together in Belgium last year.'

'You walk through the front gate, bid the keepers "How do you do?" and confirm the weapons are all there on the racks. Then what?'

'I would send a message to the raiding force, led by Geourdai and Koschak, who I would position less than one hour south of Valence.'

'It is possible,' said Raive, 'to compose a raiding force and set it on the road to Valence behind this reconnaissance party. The raiding force would need to be larger than one squadron, perhaps 1st and 2nd Squadrons, commanded by Major Avriol and include a number of wagons from the regimental train. The raiding force could well arrive at the armoury by dawn of day five.'

Morin tapped his cigar ash into the fire. 'And there we have it.'

Four evenings later in Valence, a boot sole scuffed on the wooden stairs outside.

Jobert's head jerked back from half-sleep. He picked up the two cocked pistols by his side, shoved Duque's boot with his own, without taking his eyes off the dim outline of the door. Duque woke with a grunt, rolled over to sit up from his sleeping position on the floor and took up his loaded and cocked pistols. On this side of the door, the room was warm and silent, the coals in the hearth providing a weak glow, outlining de Chabenac and Bredieux breathing deeply under their blankets.

In the pitch-black Valence tavern corridor, beyond the door, a wooden bucket, deliberately placed, was heard to scrape on the timber floor, its metal handle clanking on its side as it moved.

The bucket scraped again on the corridor floor beyond the door.

With that signal, Duque placed his pistols on the floor, shook out his blanket and returned to sleep.

Jobert stood, slid back the door bolt allowing Fergnes and Huin to enter, then moved to the fire and placed on the kettle and a few small logs.

Fergnes and Huin shivered from their midnight prowling. Fergnes hung his wet cape on a wall peg, sat on a stool by the hearth and extended his hands toward the growing flames. Locking the door behind him, Huin draped his coat over the back of a chair, sat and pulled off his sodden boots.

'Tea? Bread?' asked Jobert, conscious of the sleeping men around the small room.

'Yes, please,' said Fergnes.

'No, thank you, sir,' said Huin. 'I will get my head down.'

With that he reached over and poked the snoring bundle of Bredieux on a nearby cot. 'Shift your skinny arse, Bredieux.'

The poke caused a wet, hacking cough from Bredieux, which dislodge something in his lungs that he noisily swallowed. Bredieux rolled over on the cot releasing a long, odious fart.

'Oh, delightful,' said Huin, pulling his blanket and cape about him and lying down on the cot beside Bredieux.

Fergnes tipped his head toward Huin and mouthed to Jobert, 'Good man'.

'Anything to report?' asked Jobert, pouring a mug of black tea.

'Nothing. You?'

'The local guards on the main gate in the lane changed at midnight, again confirming their six-hour shifts. No-one has entered or departed through the gate since the fat man at seven o'clock this morning. Perched high in the old cathedral, de Chabenac and Bredieux confirmed smoke coming from the leftmost chimney all day, but nothing from the right-most chimney.'

Fergnes screwed up his face as he dunked a crust of bread into his tea. 'Are these gate guards loyal National Guardsmen unknowingly protecting a traitorous secret, or enemy in disguise and thus part of the conspiracy?'

'They will have their skulls cracked and hands hog-tied, no matter what. I will open their throats, if I have to. I do have some good news. At the evening change of guards on the main gate, Bredieux attempted to deliver a barrow of firewood to the armoury. He was told to return in the morning when bread was collected.'

'Ah, our fat man,' said Fergnes, 'who emerged at seven o'clock this morning, ought to re-emerge again?'

'One way in, only at seven o'clock, with five hours before the guard changes.'

Fergnes stared into the embers as he sipped his tea. 'Avriol would have our squadrons with Pultiere by now. Once the signal is given, you feel confident Duque and Pultiere will connect within the hour?'

'Absolutely. How about you? Ready to shave your glorious moustache?' asked Jobert.

'That is not a question that a gentleman should ask a lady.'

'Oh, I beg your forgiveness, madame.'

'Oh, insult upon insult. Mademoiselle, please.'

'Indeed, mademoiselle, then you had best arrange a fine fellow to defend your honour.'

'I was hoping my brave chevalier might attend me at seven o'clock tomorrow morning.'

They both grinned wickedly.

'This Valence stunt and the convoy ambushes,' said Fergnes, swallowing the last of his tea. 'What is the source of your penchant for deception?'

Jobert reflected on his answer.

'What would you do, how far would you go, to get the edge over your enemies?'

Just after seven o'clock, three deep, hollow clicks of withdrawn bolts heralded the creaking of a wooden door set into one of the two iron-embossed gates of the main entrance to the armoury. The door opened and the two scruffy, unshaven National Guardsmen sentries turned from the embers of their small brazier. A portly young man squeezed through the door, out into the dripping dimness of the armoury lane and locked the door behind him.

From his curled sleeping position in the gutter, Duque sat up stiffly. This was the signal to Jobert and the others. Duque wrapped his vile blanket, saturated with stale urine and rancid wine, about his shoulders and waited. He had lain in that position in the entrance to the armoury lane for over two hours and now his hips and knees ached incredibly. Nevertheless, Duque ground his teeth together and pushed into his pain to stay focussed on his vital role.

The thirty-metre-long armoury lane, wide enough for two wagons, formed a T-intersection off the crooked Valence street, now filling with citizens. Enclosed by high stone walls, above the lane was a timber-shingle roof, badly in need of repair, through which too much rain dribbled and not enough light crept.

Seeing Duque sit up in his position just inside the armoury lane, Fergnes and Bredieux, out in the street, stopped sweeping and moved their barrows of dung, bottle shards and leaves towards the junction. Dressed as peasant women, Fergnes and Bredieux swept the street for over two hours, ensuring they were noticed and ignored whilst the guards changed shifts one hour ago. The movement of the barrow was the signal to the final three men who could not see Duque from their concealed positions.

With a large woven-cane basket over his arm, the fat young man from the armoury waddled down the dim lane, skipping around the puddles, cape billowing, golden curls poking out from beneath his green felt hat.

In the dark corner of the lane, a near-fingerless hand extended from a putrid bundle of rags and said, 'Sir, a sou for an old soldier?' The boy skirted Duque's arm and stench to enter the street.

Amidst the morning throng, heads bent in the drizzle, the young man whistled a merry tune, side-stepped a dung barrow and a pipe-smoking street sweeper and proceeded up the street towards the bakery. He paused on the bakery's front step to admire the cut of a rather smart jacket, the fabric of the jacket matching the hatband, worn by a tall, well-dressed young man leading a limping horse.

He then entered the bakery and its cloud of delicious fresh-baked goods for today's provisions.

De Chabenac continued to lead a limping Vert down the street. He halted Vert across from the dim armoury lane and bent to pick up a hoof to examine it. As Vert's hoof was checked, one street sweeper moved to the far side of the T-intersection, whilst the other smaller sweeper entered the dripping lane, frozen fingers tucked under her armpits and broom held in the crook of her elbow and removed leaves from the gutters and puddles.

One guard at the gate, sat on a small, three-legged stool by the brazier's dull coals, wrapped his threadbare blue jacket about him and puffed at his pipe. The other fellow pissed against the iron gate's hinge and watched the comings and goings in the rainy street, framed by the walls of the lane.

A tall, portly gentleman, with an old-fashioned coat, walking cane, battered tricorne and grey, powdered wig wandered into the lit frame and struck up a conversation with the well-dressed toff with the lame horse. Old Powder Wig, as the guard nicknamed him, guided Young Mr Toff and his horse out of the middle of the busy, wet street and, within the relatively sheltered entrance of the lane, inspected the horse's feet. The elderly gentleman bent over stiffly, with the aid of his cane and ran his fingers up and down each of the horse's legs.

Then Young Mr Toff attempted to lead the horse in the middle of the street and lane junction so Old Powder Wig could observe the gait of the horse. Old Powder Wig was unable to move quickly enough to position himself and observe the horse's foot fall. The drunkard was roused from his rancid slumber, induced with a few coins to lead the horse, which allowed Old Powder Wig and Young Mr Toff to evaluate the horse's lameness.

Avoiding the circling horse, one of the street sweeper hags had crossed the street to join her mate who was smoking her pipe in the shelter of the lane. The sweeper had found an old cigar butt in the gutter and was wiping mud off it. The two women placed their brooms against the wall and with a small flint, attempted to coax the wet cigar butt to life.

At that moment, the podgy boy from the armoury ducked out of the rain of the street, avoiding the lame horse, led by the putrid beggar and the two crones fussing over their flint.

The guards smiled when they saw a young trollop on his

arm. The skinny hipped girl, not much more than sixteen, was giggling, tucked up under the young man's cape, kissing him on the cheek and tickling his crotch with her fingers. For his part, the young man's eyes were wide with surprise, perhaps alarm, but a rictus grin was plastered across his face, despite the wavering squeaks of discomfort.

'Oh, my beautiful boy, do not you lose it before I have had you,' said Huin, approaching the guards with his beau, fluttering his kohl-lined eyes from beneath the brow of his tattered bonnet. 'Now, my sweetheart, get out your key so you can stick it in my keyhole.'

Huin winked at the guards, rubbing his inner thighs through his gown suggestively. The four of them clustered at the small door set into the gate, within the cloud of Huin's cheap perfume. The guards laughed while the portly young man grunted with pain from the wristlock Huin had applied within the folds of the cape.

'No matter if you lose it, my darling, I will soon revive you when you see what I can do with this here hard sausage.' Huin giggled and nodded to the sausages and baguettes poking from the cane basket. 'Where does a girl get satisfaction these days? Here, my handsome man,' Huin stroked the chest of the guardsman inside his lapels of his jacket, 'please hold the basket so he can get in and … get in.'

As one soldier took the basket, the lad from the armoury un-locked the door amidst grunts of, it was assumed, anticipatory eagerness. Huin pressed his awkward bulk through the door into the blackness beyond. 'Basket, please?'

As the National Guardsman passed the groceries to the girl, a force lifted him from behind, his forehead cracking the door jamb as he was bodily thrust through the door. His musket, with bayonet fixed, slung over his shoulder, got caught in the door frame, wrenching his shoulder painfully.

Inside the door the soldier spun off balance, only to see the dark outline of Old Powder Wig, framed in the doorway, bringing the butt of a heavy cavalry pistol down upon the bridge of his nose.

The second Guardsman, shocked by his comrade and Old Powder Wig hurtling through the door, followed swiftly thereafter by Young Mr Toff with two pistols in hand, found he was pinned with force to the gate by the two street sweepers and four pistol barrels in his face and throat.

'Silence or die,' rasped one sweeper with pipe firmly clenched between 'her' teeth. 'Through the door. Now!'

The Guardsman ducked his head through the small door sufficiently low enough so as to get his slung musket through as well. As he made out the prostrate form of his colleague, white cross belts gleaming dully from the external light, he heard the swoosh of the pistol, somewhere above and behind him in the inky blackness, just prior to it connecting with the junction of his skull and spine.

Fergnes, pistols in hand, lifted the hem of his skirt and apron and stepped into the black, clammy opening. Bredieux followed, turning inside the doorway to nod his bonnet to Duque. Duque, standing with Vert across the lane's entrance, nodded in return. Bredieux stepped back into the gloom, closed the armoury door and shot the internal bolts.

Chapter Eight

At first, in the pitch-black interior of the armoury, the five chasseurs strained to hear any sounds other than the young man's whimpering from Huin's wristlock, the wings of pigeons high up in the eaves and the graceful, muted tune of a well-played violin. As the startled pigeons exited the roof through broken shingles, so the dull light of the rainy day outside leaked in and everyone's eyes adjusted to the gloom.

Jobert soon made out that they all stood at the base of an empty stone loading dock, in an area large enough for a wagon and team to turn alongside. Should the gates open behind them, one wagon would load or unload from the dock, turn out into the lane to let the next wagon in the lane into the dock.

At either end of the raised dock, two short sets of stairs led up to two heavy timber doors into which a small metal grille was embedded. The door on the right was dark and silent. From the door and the grille on the left leaked warm light, a hint of smoke and the source of music.

'Mozart?' asked Jobert.

'Tsk! Haydn,' said de Chabenac.

'Sentries, take post,' said Fergnes.

Fergnes sprang to Huin's side and shoved the fat youth to his knees, wrenched back his head by a handful of curly locks and held a knife so firmly to his throat that it pierced the skin causing blood to run down the boy's pallid neck.

Jobert, de Chabenac and Bredieux placed their pistols aside. Jobert threw off his jacket, tricorne and wig and released the long rope wrapped under his waistcoat. Released from sweeping and prostitute duties, Bredieux and Huin discarded their bonnets, capes, aprons, clogs and gowns. With the assistance of de Chabenac and Jobert, Bredieux and Huin changed into the jackets, cross-belts and bonnet-de-police of the unconscious Guardsmen. As Bredieux and Huin readied their uniforms and muskets, Jobert gagged and tied the soldiers with strips of linen and leather thongs.

Jobert unbolted the door and the two new Guardsmen, muskets slung over shoulders, stepped back out into the dim, dripping laneway. Duque signalled all was well from the entrance to the street, which Bredieux relayed to Jobert. The door closed and was bolted from the inside.

The young man was hefted to his feet at the base of the loading dock and pushed up the stairs. As they mounted the stairs, Jobert took a handful of the lad's golden curls and rammed his face into the stone wall. The boy moaned and gurgled blood through split lips, as he was pressed to the left-hand door on the dock.

The violin ceased. Footsteps crossed to the door. 'Is that you, lad?'

Jobert grabbed a jacket cuff of the boy's, pressed the boy's pudgy hand to the door, fingers outspread. Producing a small dagger from his cuff, Jobert sliced off the tip of the boy's little finger at the last joint.

The young man screamed as the grille opened. His bleeding, blubbering face was pressed to the grille by Fergnes. Jobert, out of sight, held up the hand with the amputated stump of the little finger to the grille's view.

'Uncle! No! No! Please, no!'

'My lord, boy, what has happened?' The inner man stepped back from the grille, unlocked the door and drew the bolt.

With that, Jobert crouched and threw his shoulder at the door. The door recoiled under his force as Jobert tumbled forward into the inner-guard room. The person on the other side of the door was flung backwards and sprawled on the floor. A heavy ring of keys flew from his grip and hit a writing desk with a loud clang.

'On me! De Chabenac, on me!' Jobert regained his feet and leapt upon the violin player, an elderly fellow, flipped him over, trussed and gagged him.

De Chabenac sprang through the door, pistols extended and searched the guard room. Kitchen fire, kitchen table, two armchairs, violin, writing desk, pantry cupboard, lanterns on a peg, another locked door beyond, but no-one else.

Following de Chabenac, Fergnes threw the moaning young man inside the room, closed and bolted the door, then removed his sodden disguise of filthy bonnet, clogs, shawl and apron. Jobert stepped across to the wailing boy, who losing control due to the severe pain of his finger's amputation had wet his pants, trussing and gagging him as well.

'Only this door and that door,' said de Chabenac, pointing his pistols at the door they had just barged through and the padlocked door on the far-side of the room.

Stepping from his skirt, in his underdrawers, Fergnes kicked the keyring at the base of the desk towards Jobert. The ring had six keys.

Jobert stepped to the door they had just forced and

confirmed one lock and key. Jobert turned to the locked door and unlocked it with a second key. The door opened onto musty blackness beyond. 'Lanterns, please, de Chabenac.'

Jobert stepped into the icy warehouse. Even before de Chabenac brought the lantern, the firelight from the guard room flickered upon rows and rows and rows of silent, glimmering scabbards.

'Good grief! They are here.' Fergnes' words echoed in the vault.

As de Chabenac joined them and lifted the lantern higher, the vastness of the storeroom became obvious. Hundreds and hundreds of swords and sabres were standing in their metal scabbards in wooden racks.

'As we agreed,' said Jobert, snapping back from the trance of the glimmering metal. 'Search for any other access points that allows counter-attack. I will tell Duque.'

Grabbing a lantern from a wall-peg and lighting it with a taper from the fireplace, he noted a mantlepiece clock showed half-past seven. Unbolting the guard room door, Jobert moved onto the landing dock. He descended the stairs and opened the grille embedded in the gate door. Peering through the grille, all Jobert could see was Duque and Vert's dark outlines framed in the misty light in the street. 'Lads?'

'Sir?' Huin stepped into Jobert's vision.

'The sabres are here. Send for Avriol's squadrons immediately.'

'Yes, sir.'

Jobert did not see Huin's signal, but he watched Duque mount Vert and trot away, limp healed, into the foot traffic in the street and out of view.

Jobert closed and locked the grille and by the light of the lantern confirmed the third key locked the gate door. Checking the unconscious Guardsmen were both breathing and their bindings secure, Jobert bounded up the right-most step with his lantern and pistol and unlocked the right-most door with the fourth key.

He entered an identical guard room as the left-most room, but it was dark, silent and dusty. His lantern highlighted the door to the right storeroom in the same place as the other room. The fifth key opened the door. Within this second warehouse, the lantern illuminated more swords and the innumerable leather scabbards containing bayonets and the short, broad infantry swords, briquets.

Jobert returned out through the right-hand guard room and strode across the loading dock and found Fergnes and de Chabenac in the warm left-hand guard room.

Jobert looked at the captives. The elderly man lay trussed face down on the floor and was rocking himself, sobbing. The young man moaned as he writhed, his face pale beneath the bleeding scrapes, clenching and unclenching the hand that had lost the fingertip. The blood pulsed from the open wound with every clench of his fist.

'We searched the walls right around,' said Fergnes. 'There are no external doors. That is the only way in or out of the storeroom.'

'Ah, on this level, yes,' said de Chabenac, 'but we found a locked trapdoor in the floor. It was hidden underneath timber pallets and old weapon racks. It is locked from this side. No-one can enter from the other side.'

'I passed the message to Duque at half-past seven,' said Jobert. 'I calculate trotting and cantering the ten kilometres to Pultiere will take him to just after eight o'clock. I predict Avriol will arrive as late as nine o'clock. I have opened the right-most store and it contains infantry edged weapons. Let us now search that right-most storeroom together for counter-attack access points.'

'You have accounted for all six keys?' asked Fergnes.

'No, only five. The sixth is possibly the trapdoor. Let us confirm we have secured all access points before we investigate the trapdoor.'

Their search of the right warehouse by lantern light confirmed no other access doors existed.

Jobert noted the clock read quarter-past eight as the three chasseur captains passed through the left-most guard room on their way to the trapdoor. At the broad timber trapdoor set into the floor of the left-most warehouse, Jobert knelt and tried the sixth key in the padlock. The key did not fit.

'We have a key without a lock and a lock without a key. A pretty riddle. Time for a gentle chat with our new friends.'

Jobert strode into the guard room and in the flickering light of the fireplace considered the two men lying on the floor. His eyes drifted about the room and rested on the pokers in the hearth. I can do better than branding.

Jobert flipped the old man over on his back. The old man cried out at the stiffness in his joints from lying on the cold stone floor. His hands were crushed beneath his buttocks, arching him uncomfortably. Jobert grabbed the man under his jaw with both hands and dragged him over to the prostrate, blubbering youth. The old man choked from Jobert's hold on his throat.

'Sir,' said Jobert, 'I have two questions. What does this sixth key unlock? And where is the key to the trapdoor? But, please, do not bother yourself to answer! You will only waste both of our time by lying.'

With that, Jobert rolled the young man over and then face down on top of the old man. The old man cried out under the weight of the younger, his bound hands crushed under him. Jobert produced his small dagger and cut the young man's ties. Leaning his full weight on the boy, Jobert grabbed his mutilated hand and placed the bleeding outstretched fingers on the older man's face. The old man, choking from the crushing weight, wriggled to be free of the bloodied hand, but Jobert forced it in place over his mouth and nose.

'Tell me, son, have you ever cupped the soft breasts of a pretty girl with this hand?'

'What ... What?' The young man's face turned green.

'It is a simple question. Have you ever cupped your lover's sweet breasts with this hand?'

'Uh, no, no, ... please, no, ... please, Uncle.'

'What? Not ever pulled her nipples gently with these fingers?' Jobert squeezed the tip of the amputated finger.

'No! No! No! ... please, Uncle, please.'

'Hah, Uncle. Your lad has never felt a young woman's breasts. Never? What a shame. Because the last feeling he will ever receive through this hand will be your face.'

With that, Jobert grabbed the young man's middle finger, lifted his right hand and opened the skin deftly around the wrist in preparation to amputate the hand. The boy screamed as the blood ran. The old man choked on the blood running into his open mouth.

'Look at your hand, boy. This is the last touch you will ever enjoy. Your uncle's face, while he denies me the truth to my questions.'

'No! No! Please, Uncle, please!'

'Oh, stop! Stop! Please stop!' cried the uncle.

Jobert positioned the knife to cut through the outer tendons. 'Oh, hush now, Uncle. I know you are a man who has held a woman's breast. The boy does not have to cup them for himself. You will be able to tell him what it is like.'

'Please! Please!' screamed the boy, his face purple.

'Stop, Jobert!' said de Chabenac. 'I order you to stop.'

Jobert rolled sideways and looked up to see de Chabenac's distraught face.

'Stop! These ... these are our people,' said de Chabenac. 'These men are faithful and loyal servants of His Most Gracious Majesty. They cannot be treated thus.'

'We are!' cried the choking man at the base of the pile. 'My lord, I beg you.'

The young man issued a bestial, high-pitched, incoherent scream.

'Do not stop, Jobert,' said Fergnes. 'I know Jacobin scum when I smell it. Deprive the Republican spawn the sweet, young breasts of France this instant.'

'No, these good, good men are our Royalist brothers,' yelled de Chabenac, his face a deep red. 'I command you, with all that is holy and sacred, in the name of our beloved sovereign lord and master, to stop this foul outrage.'

'Jacobin or Royalist, it does not matter,' said Jobert. 'They will tell us nothing. I have started now. It will not take much. The hand is another for my collection.'

'The desk! Please my dear, sweet lord, the desk! The desk!' called the old man.

'To hell with the desk,' said Fergnes. 'This fat, little bastard probably does not want to feel a woman.'

'No! It is in the desk, my lord.'

'Where? Where, my good man? Speak quickly!' cried de Chabenac.

'The ink well.'

De Chabenac lifted the ink pot from the well on the writing desk. He pounded the desk with his fists, splashing ink on every surface within two metres. 'What about the ink well?'

Jobert inserted the blade into the tendons at the back of the wrist and lifted them clear of the skin. The boy thrashed at the pain.

The old man, face blue, groaned under the shifting weight. 'The hole in the bottom of the ink well. Insert a quill, my gracious Lord. Make your butcher stop.'

De Chabenac fought tears of frustration and fumbled to insert a writing quill, with fingers slick with black ink, into the small hole in the bottom of the ink well.

Something clicked. A panel swung open on the side of the desk.

'Stop, Jobert! Please, stop. He has revealed a hidden panel. There is a locked box within.'

Fergnes leapt to the side of the desk with the keyring. 'The sixth key opens the box.'

As the box opened, Fergnes sat back holding up a small brass key.

The three approached the trapdoor carefully.

Jobert placed the coiled rope beside the lanterns. 'Cover the lanterns. Have your pistols ready. Fergnes, unlock then open the trapdoor just slightly.'

Jobert lay on the floor and extended his face towards the door. Fergnes unlocked the padlock with a smooth click and withdrew the lock from the hasp. Fergnes then lifted the door, shielding himself behind the hinge.

Jobert breathed through his nose, savouring the air coming from the hole in the floor. 'Open fully.'

'What were you expecting to smell?' asked de Chabenac.

'People. Stale breath, body odour, garlic, weapon oil and smoke, either wood smoke, gun smoke or tobacco smoke. A lantern, if you would be so kind.'

Fergnes swung back the trapdoor and the three listened.

A faint gurgling of water was discerned, as well as a strong stench of sewerage.

De Chabenac lit the entrance and revealed a steep timber staircase descending a floor three metres below. Fergnes, with cocked pistols readied, descended the steps. Once he arrived at the bottom of the stairs, he made one pistol safe, tucked it into his waistband and asked for the lantern. Taking the lantern, Fergnes disappeared from the others' view, pistol extended, deeper into the room beneath.

Jobert made ready to descend with pistol and lantern, when de Chabenac coughed to clear his throat. 'In there,' de Chabenac nodded to the guard room, 'is that what it takes to be a soldier?'

Poised at the entrance to the stairs, Jobert scrutinised de Chabenac's shadowy frame. 'To secure fraternity, we require equality. To secure equality, we require liberty. To secure liberty, it takes that.'

'Oh, really? Amputate a man's hand, without a tourniquet, as a form of torture? Would you have taken his hand?'

'I took the boy's finger and someone else will soon take the boy's head. As for the hand —'

The light flickered in the room below. Fergnes appeared at the base of the stairs. 'Gentlemen, I was unaware you both require formal invitations to join me.'

Doubting de Chabenac, Jobert stepped back from the entrance. 'After you, sir.' De Chabenac descended into the room.

'The room is as large as the guard room above and full of shelving,' said Fergnes. 'I have searched this wall for access and found none.'

'What is the water gurgling?' asked de Chabenac.

'The city's sewerage. Only accessible through floor grates you could barely squeeze your hand. So, no, not an entry point.'

'What about the size of the room?' Jobert held up his lantern and searched the ceiling. 'Does any part extend beyond the warehouse above, thus allowing access through the ceiling?'

'Though I have seen no other stairs leading upwards, I will check the ceiling.' The three searched the floors, walls and ceilings for any other entrances.

'Jobert, come and look here.' Jobert moved to his lantern light and found Fergnes, holding up a silken Royalist standard embroidered with the Bourbon fleur-de-lys. 'There must be over one hundred standards, rolled on their staffs, waiting to be rallied to.'

'Indeed.' Jobert's face and voice hardened in the presence of the hated symbol. 'The shelves over there contain hundreds of maps and charts. Quite a treasure. Where is de Chabenac?'

De Chabenac stood at a high bench, his lantern revealing three opened iron-bound chests. He stared at the contents without moving. The bench was long and on top and on the shelves underneath were many such boxes disappearing into the darkness. Arriving across the bench, Jobert and Fergnes saw the three opened chests were full of small calf-skin purses tied at the necks.

'I have opened and counted five purses,' said de Chabenac, not looking up from the neat piles glinting in the lantern light, 'and each contains fifty gold louis so far.'

'Fifty louis is one thousand francs,' said Fergnes, 'or nearly six months' pay for a captain in each purse.'

'Three sacks each makes at least one years' pay for us all,' said Jobert. Without hesitation he distributed purses from one of the opened chests, 'An extra purse each for company funds. Four sacks for Duque, Huin, Bredieux and Pultiere.'

De Chabenac looked at the other two. 'Well, I suppose we have —'

'Stop!' said Fergnes. 'Do not waste time justifying it. Just take it.'

Jobert stepped back into the gloom and soon after the others heard the ripping of cloth followed by lengths of timber poles hitting the floor. Jobert re-emerged into the lantern light with three shredded Royalist standards. 'Appropriate?' Jobert wrapped his eight purses into the white embroidered cloth.

'Do you still have the key?' Jobert asked Fergnes, as he hoisted the now considerable weight onto his shoulder.

'Yes.'

'Why not keep it? You found it.' Jobert took his lantern toward the stairs. 'They are here. I can hear trumpets and banging on the gates. Last man out might consider locking the trapdoor.'

The grille in the door within the gate clacked open. Jobert squinted out from the deeper darkness. Morin, Huin and Bredieux peered back at the silent opening.

Bredieux removed his pipe from his mouth and projected his voice into the blackness beyond the grille. 'Sir, I have with me Colonel Morin, 24th Chasseurs, Lieutenant Geourdai's 2nd Company and Captain de Chabenac's 8th Company, sir.'

The gates screeched on rusted hinges as Fergnes and Jobert swung them inwards.

Morin's eyebrows raised at the spectacle before him. 'Gentlemen, what an interesting morning you appear to have had.'

Fergnes stood in his underdrawers, shirtsleeves, in bare feet and his top lip freshly shaven. In a begrimed waist coat and trousers, Jobert stood with his hands on his hips, his shirt sleeves soaked in blood to the elbows. De Chabenac, up on the loading dock, might be considered presentably dressed if not for his ink-soaked jacket, waist coat and face.

'The cavalry sabres and swords are in this store, sir' said Jobert. 'The door over there, on the right, leads to infantry edged-weapons.'

'It is not my intent to ruin our good fortune today by greed. One thousand sabres will suffice.' Morin noticed the bodies lying behind the opened gates. Morin squinted down at the two trussed and groaning men in only shirt sleeves, their faces in pools of blood and vomit.

As Jobert invited Morin into the left-most guard room, Morin stepped over the face-down bodies of the armoury keepers. The fatter of the two was emitting groans, between laboured breathing, his right hand and the back of his wet trousers, where his hands were tied, covered in congealing blood. The strong odour coming from the wounded man indicated he had recently voided his bowels. The elder of the two, labouring with a wheezing breath, rolled his red-rimmed eyes down towards the floor stones, away from Morin's pitiless gaze.

Stepping through an inner door into a vast, muggy store-room, Morin smiled as Jobert held up a lantern to the thousands of glimmering hilts and scabbards.

Morin reached for the nearest scabbard and drew the sabre. 'Ah, Klingenthal. Excellent. Not more than one thousand past this door. Anything else you wish to report, gentlemen?'

'No, sir,' the three captains replied.

'No? Then, Jobert ... happy twenty-eighth birthday.'

Chapter Nine

During the return escort of the sabres to the Avignon barracks, de Chabenac brought his horse in beside Jobert's mount. 'My word, he is a solid chap and he maintains quite a walking pace. Is he a different horse? I swear in Valence he had two offside socks.'

Rouge's ears flicked at de Chabenac's mount appearing along-side. Jobert scratched Rouge's wither as a form of pat. *I suppose I best get to know the fellow.* 'That was a different horse, but yes, both are very similar.'

'How many do you have?' asked de Chabenac.

'Three.'

'Three? My goodness!'

'I can afford three because my family are horse breeders and trainers. For two or three generations, they have bred horses for artillery and engineer officers. The horses are dependable, sound-footed and hardy on campaign, as opposed to the lighter types, more hot-blooded, preferred by infantry and cavalry officers on the parade ground and about the town.'

'You take three horses on campaign?'

'Yes of course, you understand if a trooper loses his horse in battle, he walks back to the regimental rally point. Since an officer needs to remain on the field in command, he needs successive horses. My three are rotated daily through the roles of my saddle horse, my next saddle horse led by my groom, who is a chasseur corporal too injured for combat duties. My valet drives my third horse in a light cart. They travel easily at the end of the company column, not back in the baggage train.'

'Your horses are trained to harness as well as saddle?'

'Naturally, since a horse can pull more than it can carry, it is a better use of a horse than a packhorse. And these are the attributes desired by artillery and engineer officers, both prior to and post the revolution.'

De Chabenac contemplation drifted from Jobert towards the fields around him. 'I am still learning the trade of soldier. Do you mind if I plague you with questions?'

'I can only share what I know. Did you have a particular question about horses?'

'More so the preparation for campaign. May I ask what you carry in your cart?'

'Prior to my previous regiment marching to war last April, I valued having access to drinking water. By that I mean clearer heads can be maintained by slaking the distraction of thirst and a belly full of water pushes back hunger pangs. After Belgium last year, I valued the ability to get out of the rain. I do not mean staying dry or sleeping dry. Just not having rain interrupt the ability to maintain a light at night while reading, writing or discussing options over a map.

'I now have a light, two-wheeled, one-horse cart, which carries not a tent so much as a rectangular fly, a folding table, two camp chairs and a keg of water. It also carries writing material, a small iron stove in which cooking coals can be permanently maintained and hot tea can be prepared, bucket, shovel, basic cooking and eating utensils and a laundry keg.'

'A laundry keg?'

'Yes, a small keg of water and soap into which a shirt, drawers and stockings neatly fit. By the end of the day's rattling around, the clothes are washed.'

'May I ask what you carry on your horse?'

'Over my time as a sergeant, I have had made an oil-skinned paillasse that doubles both as a mattress and as a waterproof groundsheet. In fact, I can fit comfortably inside it when it is raining. I also have a double blanket sewn such that I can be in between it. It either doubles beneath me on a hot night or about me on a cold night. My servants have the same on each of my horses and we then fold our bedrolls as saddle blankets. As you know, these iron and timber cavalry saddles are less than a perfect fit.'

With that, Jobert lifted a corner of his sheepskin saddle cover, or shabraque, to reveal the saddle pad beneath.

'You do not prefer an officer's leather saddle?'

'Of course I do, but the cost of three officers' saddles is prohibitive. Then the thought of leaving expensive saddles lying around the battlefield on dead horses does not sit well with me. Yet I can always lay my hands on an army standard-issue saddle.'

'If you have this very clever bedroll as your saddle blanket, what lies across the front of your saddle bow under your shabraque?' asked de Chabenac.

Jobert again lifted the woolly shabraque to reveal his pistol holsters and a tightly rolled bundle of green wool and white canvas. 'Obviously, pistol holsters with pistols, pistol tools, weapon oil, spare flints, sharpening stone, hoof pick and spare fitted horseshoes. Then the roll contains my cape and a canvas horse rug. You know, a simple rug as you might have on a stud horse or racehorse. As a young chasseur, I had the opportunity to rug officers' horses and I saw how well these rugged horses did on campaign. Last year I did the same and now I can keep my exhausted horses warm and dry. They hold their condition longer and can go further without succumbing to cold, rain and illness.'

'Do you mind me prying like this?'

'Not at all, if it helps you prepare.'

'Then what is in your portmanteau?'

'Because this weight bounces on my horse's kidneys,' said Jobert patting the long, cylindrical, fabric barrel that was strapped behind his cantle, 'I am very strict on myself, my servants and my soldiers to ensure it carries only the bare necessities. I carry one set of drawers, shirt and stockings, toothbrush, mirror, razor, small flint, candle, soap, cup, spoon, bandage roll and a small bottle of hashish oil as medicine. Does that insight help?'

De Chabenac squinted at the road ahead. 'Yes, thank you, it does indeed.'

Jobert guessed some internal debate furrowed de Chabenac's brow.

'It was arranged for me to join a regiment of dragoons,' said de Chabenac, 'as a troop commander at the age of sixteen, upon completion of my school term. That was mid-1789. Needless, I did not join my regiment.'

A visceral pain creased de Chabenac's face.

'Yes, I now see the folly of those times. I could not imagine having two sixteen-year-olds as troop commanders now, let alone me of any value at that age. When ... when everything changed, Colonel Morin allowed me to join the Chasseur Volontaires eighteen months ago. I joined as a trooper and was elected sergeant by the end of the month. When France declared war on Austria last April, I was elected to company second-in-command. Thus I ... I ...'

Jobert contemplated de Chabenac. *I thought I was rid of useless young noblemen. But since he commands the junior company in my squadron ...*

De Chabenac held his head high but the muscles in his jaw clenched as he sought assistance from the passing farmsteads. 'I have much to learn and a lot of people are relying on me to learn fast. And here I am unsure of what I require in my own portmanteau.'

'How many years on a captain's pay would it take to pay off just one of those?' asked Lieutenant Colonel Raive. 'You know this was the seat of the Comte de Chabenac before the de Rossis acquired it in 1790.'

Jobert turned his head away from the four massive chandeliers which lit the length of the de Rossi ballroom. 'Our de Chabenac's father?'

Raive's face twisted to indicate something very wrong. 'No, his uncle. Noble privilege was already abolished before he was taken to the guillotine, I am told. Quite a different fellow to our man's father.'

Jobert greeted Inoubli, the dance master, who passed close by. Inoubli was resplendent in a coat, trousers and hat of turquoise silk, with matching ribbons on his shoes and queue. 'The dance master the young officers engaged.'

Raive looked over Jobert's shoulder and arched an eyebrow. 'We are about to be introduced.'

Jobert turned and saw de Chabenac approaching with two attractive women on each arm.

'Ladies,' de Chabenac bowed his head to an elegant woman in her mid-forties, 'may I introduce Lieutenant Colonel Raive and Captain Jobert. Gentlemen, may I introduce my mother, Madame de Chabenac and my sister, Valmai.'

Madame de Chabenac, a tall, attractive woman, wore a green gown with pale yellow gloves and matching yellow ribbon woven through her blonde hair. Valmai, in her late teens, was tall and slim, her white gown, gloves and hair ribbon set off by a red waist sash and a thin red ribbon around her throat.

Both men bowed low. Jobert was aware that the thin red ribbon at her throat was the latest fashion with young women, indicating a family member had been sent to the guillotine. Valmai responded with a slight curtsy, her blonde curls dancing on her pale neck.

'There is a gavotte in two dances time,' said Valmai. 'Do you dance the gavotte, Colonel?'

'I do, mademoiselle,' said Raive, 'but I am promised to Madame de Rossi.' Valmai cocked her head on an angle. 'And you, Captain?'

'I am able to make a complete ridicule of the gavotte as any other dance, mademoiselle, but I was hoping I might inflict my rustic actions on you, madame.'

'Oh, no,' said Madame de Chabenac, 'the gavotte is too lively for me. How are you for the next *allemande*?'

Jobert forced a smile. The allemande was the last of Inoubli's dance classes and although Jobert had enjoyed the evening lesson, he not been able to practice due to the company's deployment to camp.

'Madame, if you would be so gracious as to risk injury for France, you would honour me with the allemande?'

'If I must suffer for France, Captain,' said Madame de

Chabenac, 'then so be it.'

'Mademoiselle,' said Jobert, 'you will have ample opportunity to engage another partner for the gavotte once you have appraised the condition in which I return your mother.'

The candlelight weaved in Valmai's eyes. 'Then I will observe you quite closely, sir.'

Upon the allemande striking up, Jobert offered his right arm to Madame de Chabenac and guided her onto the floor. Jobert was relieved that, by the end of the dance, without too much embarrassment, he was able to return the lady safely to the party.

Jobert then escorted Valmai out onto the floor for the gavotte. His hands were clammy, conscious of his average performance whilst dancing with the girl's mother and now in close company with Valmai herself. The gavotte was a widely accepted favourite, with which Jobert felt comfortable. Forcing a relaxed smile, he was aware of the looks his partner was drawing from his regimental colleagues. Demonstrating her excellence in the movements of the dance, Valmai maintained a polite smile to both Jobert and acquaintances dancing close by. As the lively music took hold, Jobert was transfixed by the candlelit, twirling Valmai.

Upon returning to the de Chabenacs, Jobert found that Raive had excused himself and Avriol and Fergnes had joined the party.

Avriol slid hungry eyes off Valmai. 'Jobert, Fergnes requires you as his second. Would you attend him?'

'Ah, certainly, sir. Ladies, would you excuse me?'

'Before you go, Captain Jobert,' said Valmai. 'Since I was prepared to sacrifice my feet for France, may I request that you maintain your study of the art by gracing me with the bourrée before supper?'

Jobert's heart skipped a beat. 'Mademoiselle, I would be honoured. Until then.'

Fergnes, stepping back as well, took two glasses of champagne from a passing silver tray and gave one to Jobert. 'My goodness, those are most striking boots. Wherever did you get them, as I must have a pair?'

Jobert glanced with some exasperation, away from Avriol and Valmai conversing, to his new dress boots, a shade of green Moroccan leather which matched his dress trousers.

'I had them made here in Avignon. I will send my valet with the details. Avriol directed me away from de Chabenac's gorgeous sister to attend you, as a matter of some urgency. Sir, you interrupt the blossoming romance of a regimental brat with a young noblewoman. Was it only to enquire about my boots?'

'Not at all. I am in some difficulty. I would be deeply obliged if you would assist me. Making your observations discreetly, do you see over my shoulder a matron with a striking blue feather in her hair?'

'I do.'

'Then you will see two young brunettes by her side,' said Fergnes. 'One taller, the other with a most ample bosom.'

'I do,' said Jobert. 'The taller girl is looking this way.'

'Oh, very good. I have become acquainted with that lady. Her name is Marguerite. But she refuses to dance with me unless I can find a partner for her cousin, Camille. May I beg of you, sir, two dances with the cousin?'

'Two dances? Then two bottles of very good brandy.'

'What? You scoundrel! The girl is most attractive. Staring down at those magnificent breasts is surely not an impost. One bottle.'

'Agreed. One bottle of very good brandy.'

'Since you are not a gentleman, sir, I intend to provide a flask of cat piss knowing you will not be able to tell the difference.'

The two young officers, dancing in the candlelight with the

young ladies, looked quite smart in their best dress uniforms of their previous regiments; breeches cut in the tight-fitting Hungarian style, braided, snugly tailored dolman jackets with colourful regimental sashes wound around their waists. Once the dances were complete, they all refreshed themselves with champagne.

Marguerite's hazel eyes flashed as she laughed. Fergnes and she exchanged glancing touches of each other's forearms. Jobert found Camille a most pleasant companion, but there was no spark to their conversation as he had found with Valmai. As he glanced around the room, seeking a reason to excuse himself, he noted for the third time Geourdai looking their way and tipping another glass of champagne down his throat. As he reflected on Geourdai, the hurried movement of an unknown hussar major caught his and Fergnes' attention.

'A general's aide.' Fergnes returned his attention to Marguerite.

Jobert watched as the officer joined Colonel Morin by the fireplace and passed him an envelope. 'Ladies, sir, would you excuse me as I promised the upcoming bourrée to another.'

Jobert crossed back to the de Chabenac party, where he found Avriol still attentive to Valmai and she, most at ease, parrying his flirtations with a confident laugh.

'Would you excuse me, sir,' said Jobert, 'but the lady has promised me her hand for the bourrée.' Avriol glowered at Jobert, his thick moustache curling into a sneer as he bowed at the lady's departure.

As Jobert turned toward the centre of the long ballroom with Valmai on his arm, one of Morin's aides de camp was whispering to Madame de Rossi. His face grim and hers surprised.

Perhaps it was the flickering candlelight, the champagne or the music, but Jobert felt Valmai's glances were more intimate as they danced the bourrée. To his pleasure, she brushed against him more than was required of the dance.

As the bourrée ended, a small bell sounded from the musicians' area. The room turned toward the sound and all could see Madame de Rossi, flanked by Colonel Morin and the unknown hussar major.

Madame de Rossi, in some distress, screwed a lace handkerchief in her gloved hands. 'Ladies and gentlemen, the Colonel and I have received important news that is worth sharing with you all. Colonel?'

Jobert, Valmai and the other dancers pressed forward.

'Thank you, madame,' said Morin. 'Ladies and gentlemen, I have just received news from our headquarters in Lyon. A few days ago, General Dumouriez was defeated in a series of battles in Belgium. This loss has allowed Austria to regain Brussels and to advance her armies to the frontiers of France.'

A collective gasp issued from the group. Valmai clutched Jobert's arm. Jobert winced as he and his previous regiment had served under the command of Dumouriez a few months ago. *Another bastard nobleman shows his true colours.*

The assembly looked to Morin for any other news. 'Following his defeat, General Dumouriez defected to the Austrians.'

'No!' The ballroom exhaled in shock. Valmai pressed herself against Jobert, her imploring eyes glancing back to her mother, clinging to her brother's arm.

Chapter Ten

May 1793, Avignon, France

Accompanied by stirring pieces played by the Avignon city band, the 24th Chasseurs paraded its men and horses, their uniforms and equipment.

Jobert considered Raive's extensive guest list. It included the Lyon-based commanding general Mouret, the governors and dignitaries of Avignon and the infantry colonel of a nearby infantry regiment, the 31st Ligne. Taking advantage of the regiment's hospitality were eminent local families, such as the de Rossis and every local supplier of horses, uniforms, equipment and accoutrements.

Jobert's demeanour was enhanced when he learnt he was to host de Chabenac's mother and his stunning sister, Valmai. Arm in arm beneath their parasols, Madame de Chabenac and Valmai maintained serene smiles and courteously bowed to each party that passed. Jobert maintained a gracious military bearing in their presence. It was obvious that the two ladies wished to treat with him at arm's length. There was no hint of familiarity that was enjoyed at the recent de Rossi ball. Even

Madame de Rossi barely acknowledged Madame de Chabenac as she passed.

The recent defection of General Dumouriez to the enemy, Jobert reflected, had reawakened the hatred and suspicion of the nobility, whether aristocratic, such as Dumouriez, or minor nobility, such as the de Chabenacs. Now each family needed to protect itself from any scandalous association with the nobility who remained within the community.

Second Lieutenant Neilage took the opportunity to present his parents to his company commander and the attendant de Chabenac women.

'Tell me, Captain Jobert, what am I looking at here?' asked Neilage senior.

'Sir, the fellows walking and leading horses are exhibiting what our soldiers wear whilst performing barracks maintenance duties. You will note the comfortable bonnet-de-police, the simple, short, woollen stable jacket, again simple, hard-wearing hemp stable trousers and wooden stable clogs which saves a trooper's feet and boots from deteriorating in freezing mud.'

Neilage senior, hands on hips, admired his business' handiwork in transporting so much of the raw material on display in his Rhône barges. 'Yes, I remember the load of hemp we delivered from Marseille.'

'The two hundred fellows mounted on the chestnut horses are parading the uniform we might expect to wear on an everyday basis. The new bicornes with regimental plume, the simple, single-breasted, woollen tailcoat and waistcoat, white, linen trousers over long boots with spurs. Note the dark orange, or capucine, regimental facing throughout the uniforms; on plume, jacket collar and piping on jackets and bonnet-de-police.'

'Where is our lad's troop?'

Jobert sought 2nd Company amongst the six hundred soldiers circulating around the square. 'There, sir. You will identify

2nd Squadron mounted on bay horses in our full-dress uniform. Those are the fellows in the fur-crested helmets, the more intricately patterned, double breasted full-dress tailcoat and waistcoat, the whitened, leather cross belts for sabre, musketoon and cartridge box. You will note the new campaign over-breeches, a pair of trousers which can be buttoned down the side of the leg, with an under-boot strap and robustly made of linen and leather to protect the standard linen trousers.'

'Excuse me, Captain Jobert, look there,' said Valmai. 'Why do only a few soldiers wear a capucine jacket with green piping? Their jackets' colours are completely reversed from the colours of the other men's jackets. And they ride grey horses?'

'Well observed, mademoiselle, for those are our trumpeters. The regiment is reliant on those fellows transmitting the orders of the officers to the rest of the soldiers. Their distinctive jacket and horses make them immediately recognisable and they signify that an officer is within their vicinity should anyone be seeking that officer.'

Neilage's party moved on.

'Ladies,' said Jobert, 'you will note the fellows in the helmets have a solid sky-blue pompom at the base of their plumes. That is my 2nd Company. But of greater interest, madame, do you see those that have a white and sky-blue pompom?'

'Oh, yes, I see,' said Madame de Chabenac, 'but there are quite a lot them.'

'Yes, madame, that is the one hundred chasseurs of the 8th Company. Your son's command.'

The ladies exchanged smiles at his revelation.

'Ladies, might I seek glasses of cordial for your refreshment?'

'Yes, thank you, that would be most welcome,' said Valmai taking her mother's arm to drift closer to the passing 8th Company.

Jobert turned towards the milling guests and host officers in the middle of the square, seeking any soldier bearing a tray of drinks. Spotting one, he raised his hand and attracted the trooper's attention. Not only did the soldier obey his summons, but Geourdai and Fergnes, from different locations in the crowd, converged on Jobert as well.

'Jobert, a moment of your time?' asked Fergnes. 'I have the most pleasurable honour of hosting Mademoiselle Marguerite's party. You will remember her and her cousin from the ball? Her father is a supplier of bulk metal. Anyway, I am invited to call upon the family, but again, Marguerite insists upon me bringing a partner for her cousin.'

'Camille?' asked Geourdai.

'Indeed, sir,' said Fergnes. 'Jobert, may I coax you with further good brandy to attend the party?'

'No, my friend. As lovely as Camille is and as good as your brandy was, I am just not of a mind at this time to pay court to young ladies. I am sorry, no.'

'Sir, may I offer myself to your service?' said Geourdai. 'I would be honoured to complete the group. If you feel it appropriate?'

'Indeed, sir, yes, I would be obliged. Allow me to inform the ladies and I will return with further details. Obliged indeed, excuse me.'

Geourdai wobbled his head smirking his lop-sided smile and jigged on his toes.

'That would go some way to explaining you inhaling trays of champagne at the ball,' said Jobert. 'Here was I thinking you were looking across the dance floor at Camille and I so as to admire my new boots — Good grief! What is that?' Jobert scowled toward the official party. 'Another hideous version of a trumpeter's uniform? Can you see it?'

'Oh, yes,' said Geourdai, 'the silk capucine trousers, coat and hat. No, that is not a trumpeter. That is Inoubli's homage to our regimental facings.'

'Inoubli? The dance-master? Invited to the regimental party?'

'As I understand it, Inoubli arrived as a member of the Governor of Avignon's party.'

'How curious! Oh hello, stand to arms. The official carriages are coming forward signalling an end to this circus. I had best attend my ladies.'

Jobert arrived back at the side of the de Chabenac women, just in time to receive their empty glasses, as de Chabenac himself joined the group.

De Chabenac bowed. 'Ladies, sir, as the guests are now departing, I am released from attending the General. Thank you, sir, I am obliged as to your kind attentiveness towards my family.'

As de Chabenac took his mother's arm and moved to depart, Valmai turned to Jobert. For the first time today, she looked him in the eye and placed one gloved finger on the back of his gloved hand. 'Thank you,' she mouthed silently. With a slight smile, she turned to follow her brother and her mother.

A flare of heat scorched Jobert's chest.

Upon entering Morin's office, Jobert saluted.

Morin turned his head from the window, teacup and saucer in hand, and nodded without looking at Jobert. Raive sat by Morin's polished timber desk, his notebook opened on his knee and pencil ready.

De Chabenac sat immobile on the edge of his chair in front of Morin's desk. De Chabenac's face wax drawn, his eyes sunken, as he viewed a point on the long curtains above Morin's head.

Not turning from the window, Morin looked down into his teacup. 'Captain ... Chabenac's family were assaulted and grievously injured in the town yesterday evening by assailants unknown. The family believe the attack was connected to the latest wave of anger and violence towards those of previously noble class.'

Jobert eyes flicked with alarm to the rigid de Chabenac. By removing the 'de' from his name, de Chabenac was renouncing publicly any connection with his family's former noble ancestry. Chabenac had not moved a muscle during this introduction, continuing to stare at a point above Morin's head.

'Not believing he has the loyalty of his company, due his family's past,' said Morin, 'Captain Chabenac has offered his resignation from the 24th Chasseurs. Naturally, based on the Captain's sterling service to date, I have not accepted. I have countered with an offer of the role of regimental aide de camp, to which Captain Chabenac has delighted me with his gracious acceptance. Thus, the command of 8th Company has become vacant. I seek your views on the prospect of Geourdai promoted to the post.'

Jobert's mind raced. *No! I cannot afford to lose ...* 'I would fully support such a selection, sir. Geourdai would be an excellent choice of company commander.'

Looking toward Raive, Morin nodded before turning back to his view out onto the square. Raive brushed his moustache with the back of his knuckle. 'Jobert, with Geourdai's promotion, do you have a view as to his replacement?'

Jobert's eyes narrowed as he contemplated Morin's back. *I doubt his readiness, but since you have backed him thus far ...* 'I strongly recommend Lieutenant Neilage for company second-in-command, sir.'

Morin grunted approval from the window. Raive made a note. 'In that case, would you recommend a suitable candidate for troop commander?'

'I would recommend, without hesitation, Sergeant Huin, sir,' said Jobert.

A further nod from Morin prompted Raive to scribble. 'Do you then have a candidate for platoon sergeant?'

'Sir, I request an opportunity to consult with Sergeant Major Koschak before putting forward a name.'

Morin turned from the window with a strong wave of his hand dismissing any further conversation. 'There are many strong candidates throughout the regiment. Bring in Geourdai, if you please?'

Geourdai stepped into the room, stopping beside Jobert and with a tight mouth and jutting chin saluted his commanding officer.

'Yes, good morning, Lieutenant,' said Morin. 'Captain Chabenac has accepted the position of regimental aide de camp. I wish to offer you the command of 8th Company. Do you accept?'

From his rigid position of attention beside Jobert, Geourdai's eyes flicked from the Colonel's steady gaze to a frozen de Chabenac, to the regimental second-in-command poised over his notebook. 'Sir, I would be honoured to accept the command, sir.'

'Then congratulations, Geourdai, the post is yours. But, gentlemen,' Morin raised a warning finger to both company officers, 'I demand your absolute confidence in the matter for the next twenty-four hours, as I have a little deception of my own to weave. I will make the appropriate announcements on parade tomorrow morning.'

'Have we all received our soup?' Without undue ceremony, Morin waved the attendant officers to sit. 'Then allow me to relate the news I have just received from Paris.'

Morin cleared his throat from his stance behind his chair, looking at the young faces down the length of the table. 'Last week, Austria, Prussia and Sardinia have felt it necessary to re-issue their declarations of war. The states of Naples and Portugal have also declared war against the Republic, joining Britain, the Netherlands and Spain. Of particular significance to ourselves here in Avignon, the Pope has declared war against France.'

As Morin named each state declaring against France, discomfort grew in each breast. The news that France was at war against the Pope was a heavy blow to the audience.

'The forty thousand strong Army of the North operating against the Austrians, Prussians, British and Dutch near Conde have met with defeat and considerable loss.'

Mouths opened in disbelief. Movement in chairs was minimised. Soup spoons were placed on the table. Anxious looks were exchanged.

Morin patted the back of his chair. 'In Paris, with the intent of placating the competing political factions, the National Convention has formed a select group of three men to execute government policy. The new organisation, to which the War Committee is directly answerable, is known as the Committee of Public Safety.'

Jobert stirred his soup slowly and stroked his stubbly jowl. *Power has taken a step from an assembly of hundreds to a cabal of three.* The three men selected for the new organisation were known as the most extreme voices of their opposing factions.

'In the face of increasing internal and external enemies to our Republican ideals, one of the first requirements of this new Committee has been to authorise an even wider confiscation of church property to increase the Republic's revenue. This exhaustive program comes with the decree that all churches be known immediately as Temples of Reason. We, in this room, are blessed with the enviable opportunity to observe how our local communities and the majority of our local soldiers, will react to this policy directive.'

Jobert watched his brother officers. *All of Europe is marching to destroy us. The closest armies are only two hundred and fifty kilometres from where we sit. Civil war rages six hundred kilometres to our north-west. Embers of local prejudice are fanned into a flame of hatred by Paris. Paris will demand the 24th Chasseurs extinguish those flames. Yet the soldiers we have striven to form into companies, are goaded to mutiny by Parisian madness.* This was too much for many, whether they still maintained their religious faith or not. Hands went to mouths, eyes were downcast.

'Gentlemen, finish your soup,' said Morin. 'Our soldiers have worked hard to provide it.'

The audience wriggled and sat upright in their seats and, by scribbling notes with purpose, refocused their energies.

'There is much work to be done to which our regiment and our chasseurs are ideally suited. The 24th Chasseurs has been ordered by General Mouret to provide escorts for all military movement in the three hundred kilometres between Lyon and Marseille.

'Due to the impending, dispersed nature of regimental operations, I am establishing a third regimental aide de camp position on my staff. I invite nominations for the post to me in writing by six o'clock this evening. I shall announce my decision on parade tomorrow.'

'Tell me what happened?'

Sitting beside Jobert at lunch, Chabenac had merely picked at his food. Having completed their meals, the others departed to their companies with hearts heavy from Morin's news.

'De ... Chabenac,' said Jobert, his hand on Chabenac's forearm, 'what has happened to your family?'

Chabenac turned his head toward Jobert. Both men held each other's gaze for an extended moment.

'My parents were visiting old friends. Their visit extended into the early evening. Their route home was too near the theatre district. One of ... those ... those new ... plays had just completed. The audience was emptying out of the theatre into local taverns.'

Jobert slumped. *Propaganda endorsed by Paris, where the execution of the King, the vilification of the nobility and the supposed thrill of the guillotine was overacted to fuel the illiterate audience's drunken hatred.*

'A group of men, inspired by the theatre, gave my father a beating, breaking his ribs, fingers and cheekbones. These ... fellows having struck my mother repeatedly, breaking her nose, then attempted to ... have her. Valmai escaped. By screaming "Fire! Fire!", she attracted passers-by to the scene, causing the assailants to flee.'

Memories of another back-alley murder were awoken in Jobert. He clenched his teeth and flared his nostrils to subdue his rising nausea.

Chabenac wiped his nose on his lunch napkin. He cast his sunken eyes down as soldiers cleared their plates.

'They know,' said Jobert. 'Not the details, but the whole regiment knows. Where is your family now?'

Chabenac placed his hands flat on the table and closed his eyes to steady himself. 'My father is gravely ill in bed. My mother is working through her own pains to attend him.

My sister runs errands fetching medicine and food.'

'What is your intent concerning the attackers?'

Chabenac opened his eyes to face Jobert. 'What can I do? How would I find them? And if I did, what could I do? The magistrates would release them to laugh in our faces.'

Jobert blinked in a moment of misunderstanding. 'What is your company doing?'

'My company?'

Jobert looked away, clenching his jaw. 'How does your company feel about your former nobility?'

'My second-in-command was from outside the old Chasseurs Volontaires, so he feels distinctly uncomfortable with my family. My sergeant major and I served together before the 24th Chasseurs was raised. His respect fades as time passes and Parisian propaganda increases. I am treated as an old friend with an infectious disease. Previous regimental friends now wisely keep their distance.'

Jobert reached out and gripped Chabenac's shoulder, at which Chabenac closed his eyes and dropped his head. 'Is there somewhere your family can go to feel safe?'

'Emigrate?' Chabenac jerked his head erect, his nostrils flaring.

'No, brother, no. Family, I mean, friends, like the de Rossi.'

'The de Rossi? Hah! No ... no ... no-one. Anyway, my father is too injured to move. The attack has done greater injury to his broken heart than his brittle bones.'

'If a safe place was found, would your mother consider it?'

Chabenac searched Jobert's eyes, then pushed himself back from the table and stood. He shook his head and walked to the door.

Contemplating Chabenac's back as he walked the length of the dining room, Jobert lounged back in his chair, fingering the handle of the small dagger he kept concealed in his cuff.

Chapter Eleven

'24th Chasseurs à Cheval, stand at ease!'

Jobert watched Morin.

Mounted on his charger in the middle of the long, dusty square, Morin looked about him with deserved pride at the one thousand mounted warriors of his regiment. Twelve weeks ago, such an organisation did not exist.

'Flexibility is the basis of our regiment's success in battle. Flexibility is our regiment's ability to change our formation, to change our operations, in the face of a changing battlefield situation. Flexibility to change from one activity to another activity requires excellence in communication. One form of communication that serves our regiment well when we are too far away to speak, are our trumpeters. Another form of communication that serves our regiment well when we are spread apart, are our regimental messengers, or aides de camp.

'Because of your demonstrated excellence in recent weeks, France requires your services far and wide. For me to keep you informed, so that you can do what you do best, I require more aides de camp. Today, I am announcing, with great pleasure, that Captain Chabenac is posted to our regimental headquarters as an aide de camp.

'I have selected Captain Chabenac because I trust him. I trust him implicitly. Since he volunteered to fight for the Republic by joining the Chasseurs Volontaires two years ago, he has impressed every chasseur he has met with his deep sense of patriotism and integrity. Captain Chabenac has proven time and again his determination to do the right thing for our regiment. This is exactly the man who will overcome any obstacle to bring us the information we all need to do our duty to the best of our ability. Captain Chabenac!'

'Sir!'

'Captain Chabenac, on behalf of 8th Company, thank you for your untiring efforts in raising a fearsome company of chasseurs. Now, to regimental headquarters, take post!'

Chabenac squeezed his horse and trotted across the square to the line of regimental headquarters officers.

'I made mention just now of your individual and collective excellence,' Morin continued, 'so it disappoints me when I see some of you incorrectly dressed. I will call out the names of those offending chasseurs who have caught my eye. They shall fall out from the ranks and parade before me. Lieutenant Geourdai, 2nd Company!'

'Sir!'

'Second Lieutenant Neilage, 2nd Company!'

'Sir!'

'Sergeant Huin, 2nd Company!'

'Sir!'

'Corporal Yinot, 6th Company!

'Sir!'

Each chasseur trotted his remount from his position in the ranks, into the middle of the square, where they formed line to the left of Geourdai. Once formed in line, each man sat rigidly to attention, pressing on the ribs of their horses with alternate calves to distract them from the now unfamiliar mounts close on each side of them.

'These chasseurs are incorrectly dressed because they are wearing the incorrect rank insignia. I shall correct that situation here and now. Captain Geourdai, company commander, 8th Company.'

Morin pressed his mount forward and passed across the strips of embroidered silver ribbon, to be sewn above Geourdai's jacket cuffs.

'Lieutenant Neilage, company second-in-command, 2nd Company.'

'Second Lieutenant Huin, troop commander, 2nd Company.'

'Sergeant Yinot, platoon sergeant, 2nd Company.'

As well as presenting Yinot with his strips of ribbon, Morin passed across a new feathered plume for his headdress, topped with capucine, with the sky-blue woollen pompom at the base.

'Gentlemen, congratulations. Fall in.'

'Come with me. Immediately!'

That is all that Jobert said to Chabenac in the dining room. As Chabenac accompanied him, Jobert strode across the square, out of the barracks, through the marketplace and down an alley beside the tavern where the 2nd Company officers had taken their rooms. Jobert pounded the tavern's stable yard's closed gates with his gloved fist.

The internal bar lifted and the tall wooden gate swung open.

The tavern yard was silent. No chickens. No dogs.

One of 2nd Company's sergeants, Yinot, closed the gate behind them, a half-cocked musketoon held tight in the crook of his arm, his sabre hanging by the sword knot from his wrist. Jobert crossed the yard and Sergeant Pultiere removed the bar from the stable gate.

Jobert passed into the stable. Chabenac followed him. Within the dim barn, they joined fourteen solemn men. Four men in civilian waistcoats and shirtsleeves sat on the floor, all looking up at him and Jobert. One began to whimper.

Spaced around those sitting, stood Neilage, Koschak, Voreille and Huin, all stripped to their waistcoats and cradling either pickaxe handles or long coach whips.

Against one wall were Geourdai and his 8th Company second-in-command and sergeant major. Geourdai leant relaxed against a post with his arms folded. The other two stared at the floor, avoiding Chabenac's, their previous company commander's, eye.

The last three silent men were identifiable, by their blue jackets, white leather aprons and long-handled broad axes, as infantry sappers from the 31st Ligne. One fat, one tall, one with a crushed nose, all with thick beards, all smoking pipes, all with hard, scarred faces. At their feet lay chains and leg irons.

The stable door closed behind Chabenac and the external bar clunked into place.

'Stand up,' said Jobert to the four men sitting on the floor. Three did so. 'This is the son of the parents whose bones you broke behind the theatre three days ago. Chabenac, remove your jacket and sword. We have found the men who attacked your parents. Three of them have confessed to the four's involvement. This is the man who broke your father's nose, ribs and fingers. This is —'

Having dropped his bicorne, tailcoat and sword belt in the dust of the barn, Chabenac stepped forward and struck out.

His punches came without warning. The first was a left jab that spun the head of the first thick-set man, then a right cross followed striking the side of the chin. The jaw cracked. The man gurgled, swayed and fell to a knee, spitting blood.

The three infantry sappers stood erect from their slouched positions. Well balanced over his feet and driving his punches through from his hips, Jobert acknowledged that Chabenac had been schooled to fist fight.

The second tall, ginger-haired thug stepped around the fallen first assailant. His teeth were gritted, his nostrils flared, his eyes were dead. He was not afraid. The man drove a powerful left cross towards Chabenac's face.

Following his first two punches, Chabenac's fists had withdrawn back to a defensive posture, fists close to his face, elbows close to his ribs, his stance wide and hips dropped. Chabenac tipped his body to the right and his adversary's powerful strike swung just over his left ear. Chabenac pivoted and drove a right hook into the man's ribs. The audience gasped as the ribs were heard to break and the fellow was lifted by the blow. Chabenac followed with another right hook across the man's shoulder, his fist finding the point of the chin. Again, bringing the force of the hit through from the hips, the power of the hook snapped the man's jaw. Before he had time to gurgle on the blood entering his punctured lungs, Chabenac's third strike was a pivoted left cross to the nose. The tall man's head snapped back, he buckled backwards to have his head crack on the dung-smeared cobblestone floor of the barn.

The first thick-set thug wasted no time getting to his feet, as Chabenac's swift blows felled his mate. Chabenac's last left cross left his ribs unguarded. The man dropped his hips and drove his punch into those vulnerable ribs. Again, with a cheer from the sappers and Koschak, Chabenac brought his last punch back into a defensive block and with a balanced skip, deflected the new strike on his left elbow. Then stepping back inside the outstretched arm, Chabenac dropped his hips to power two ferocious upper-cuts, one into the man's sternum and one into the man's jaw. As his winded opponent was unable to take in air though a mouth of teeth and blood, Chabenac rolled his shoulders to bring his full weight through his left fist down onto the man's nose. With the gurgling noise of a split water-skin, the big fellow melted to the floor.

Through trained instinct, Chabenac resumed his defensive posture and stepped past the two fallen bodies to the third standing man. Chabenac dropped his guard when he saw who it was. 'You?'

'I am sorry, sir …' The third man lowered his eyes, his hands by his side.

'My mother had just come from your mother's house! You scoundrel! My mother had just made soup for your mother!'

'Sir, I am so —'

Chabenac drove a right uppercut into his jaw. The crushing blow severed the tongue. The man's scream sprayed Chabenac with bright red blood. Reaching out behind him, the man arced backwards down, and thudded onto the stable floor, where he writhed against the flow of blood and splintered teeth into his airways.

Hands by his side now and sucking in air, Chabenac stared down at the final man, moaning in fear, cowering on his knees, his hands over his head. 'You! Every time my family suffers, there you are in a shadowy corner nearby. Your unseemly obsession with my sister is unconscionable. Get up!'

'Please, sir.' His boyish face had been raked with fingernails. 'Get up!'

Jobert stepped forward and offered a coach whip. Chabenac looked Jobert in the eye, then took the whip, flicking its vicious length behind him.

Chabenac flogged the man on the floor. The man's ear-piercing screams were directed into the dung and dust of the barn floor, as the whip sliced through his shirt and bit deep into the flesh of his back. Lash upon lash opened previous welts and the man's back was pulped. After fifteen or twenty such lashes, the screaming stopped and the cringing back relaxed into unconsciousness.

Chabenac stopped his wild swings, his breathing laboured, his body quivering, his face purple from rage and effort.

The room returned to silence, apart from horses stamping in their stalls, pigeons resettling in the hayloft and the third man still scratching in the dust to breathe.

Jobert held out to Chabenac his jacket, bicorne and sword belt. Chabenac adjusted his uniform and departed the barn.

Geourdai stood erect. The second-in-command and the sergeant major of 8th Company braced to attention to face his expected wrath.

'The 24th Chasseurs fight for France and her families,' said Geourdai, 'but we die for our regimental brothers. By failing Chabenac, your 8th Company brother, by your deliberate inaction, you have dishonoured 8th Company. By doing nothing to relieve the suffering of Chabenac's parents, one of the Republic's families, you have dishonoured the 24th Chasseurs. 8th Company is shamed that 2nd Company has done what you ought to have done. The shame and dishonour of 8th Company is heaped upon you both. You have much to do to put it right. Take your dishonour from this place. Now!'

Both men hurried from the barn across the yard. Geourdai nodded to Jobert as he departed.

Jobert turned to the stout infantry sapper smoking his pipe. 'Your parade, Sergeant.'

At a nod from their scar-faced sergeant, the two other burly sappers picked up the leg irons and attached them to the injured men spread across the floor. 'Put your mind at rest, sir. The 31st Ligne will turn these bastards into soldiers. Then, if they want to have a swing at someone, they can swing away for France.'

'My father is dead.'

Sitting on one of Jobert's folding camp stools, Chabenac pulled the cork out of a bottle of brandy with his teeth, then spat the cork into the flames of the campfire. The cork hissed with green flame. Chabenac poured two mugs of brandy and passed one to Jobert.

'My sincere condolences for your loss.' Jobert put down his empty soup bowl to rub his tired eyes. 'To ... to your father, may he rest in peace.'

'My father.'

Both drank deeply. Jobert returned his mind from long buried memories that the toast had aroused. 'Forgive me, I cannot think clearly. When did he pass?'

'Three weeks ago.' Chabenac examined the depths of his cup. 'Thank you for apprehending those vile culprits.'

Jobert not lifting his eyes from the fire, finished his brandy then passed his mug back across to Chabenac. 'Where did you learn to fight like that?'

'One of the masters at school secretly trained us to fistfight, based on old English publications. My father purchased extra tutoring for me since I was destined to serve in a regiment of dragoons.'

The small fire sizzled and popped as the air gradually chilled. The snores of exhausted men in the surrounding tents blended with occasional croaks, squeaks and clicks of local frogs.

Chabenac poured more brandy. 'Are your parents still with us?'

'Ah, no ... no, my mother died in childbirth when I was a boy.'

Chabenac looked up for the other half of the answer.

Jobert's jaw trembled, his eyes searched the flames. 'My father? My father also died in a back-alley attack. Nearly ten years ago.'

Chabenac reached forward with Jobert's refilled brandy, then poked the ends of a few thicker branches deeper into the fire. 'Sorry, ... I am sorry.'

'Have you been on the road long, Chabenac?' Chabenac's fair hair was thick and unkempt, a raggedy blond moustache drooped over his upper lip, begrimed stubble covered his sunken cheeks. Chabenac's boots were dull from a lack of polish and his over-breeches were black from horse sweat, saddle oil and dust.

'Not as long as you. Ten days, maybe. Yours is the last company I had to find. I have news and orders.'

'Have you seen ... Geourdai?

'Yes, I have visited good old 8th Company.' Chabenac's handsome smile darted across his face. 'I have sighted them a few times now. The latest was whilst they were passing through Valence of all places. I knew the first time would be the hardest. And it was. But all that is behind me. 8th Company is Geourdai's now.'

'Valence. When were we there?'

'Early April. Two months ago. You will not have heard that the swords were destined for uprisings here in the south, not the Vendée as everyone expected. What is more, the orders to release the weapons were to come from Royalist agents operating from Avignon.'

Jobert opened his sore eyes to focus on the dancing flames. 'I am aware that Lyon is now in revolt against the government. Are the 24th Chasseurs to march to Lyon?'

'The 24th Chasseurs have orders to concentrate in Avignon. That is all I know.'

Exhausted by the litany of military disasters and too tired to understand the implications, Jobert wobbled his head. *Sleep, wake and rejoin the regiment.* Jobert shifted his position on his shabraque and cape laid out beneath him, and avoided the smoke wafting his way.

A grunt in the dark behind Chabenac announced Voreille ducking under a tent line.

'Ah, Voreille, you have reminded me.' Chabenac rummaged in his sabretache. 'I have letters for you both. Voreille, you must receive a letter every week. It is incredible. It must be love.'

'No, it is nothing like that, sir.' Voreille blushed in the fire light. 'We are just friends.' Voreille stepped away from the fire cradling the perfumed envelope.

Jobert broke the wax seal. 'Would you allow me to read my letter quickly? There may be some news pertinent to our conversation.'

Chabenac rolled the brandy around his mouth and gritty teeth as he watched the flames dance along the burning sticks. Draining his cup, Jobert wriggled into a sitting position, with his shoulder to the flames, angling the letter to the wavering light.

'Aha! You remember Morin's lunch the day after your parents were attacked? Do you remember me asking you if your parents had anywhere safe to go and you said "No"?'

'Yes, I remember.'

'Do you remember me asking if a safe place was found would your mother consider it?'

Chabenac watched Jobert over the top of his brandy mug.

Jobert shook the letter emphatically. 'As you know, the men of my family have a background in horses and saddlery. The family's women have a long tradition as regimental seamstresses. Due to France's incessant wars, my wider family has become quite comfortable as a result. I am close to my cousin, Michelle. She is a seamstress and quite a capable businesswoman, who operates at least two or three workhouses, producing military headdress accessories. Michelle lives in a pleasant, if not fashionable, home in Paris, with Michelle's and my great aunt. She is, as yet, unmarried, but is well connected into Parisian society —'

'One connection to someone who has access to the War Committee's armoury reports.'

'So it would appear. After that lunch I wrote to her asking if it were possible to support your family. She writes back that your family would be most welcome in our family home in Paris. Michelle reasons that since your family is relatively unknown in Paris it would add to your safety. Also, with our family's military contracting, our wagons can move your family's effects at no cost to yourselves.'

Jobert squinted through the drifting smoke to gauge Chabenac's reaction. Impassive Chabenac watched the flames.

'Michelle includes a letter of introduction to be passed to your mother.' Jobert held up a sealed square of parchment. 'She believes there are number of advantageous situations that your mother and sister might consider, once agreeably settled in Paris.'

Jobert passed Michelle's letter of introduction to Madame de Chabenac across the embers. 'A genuine offer of aid to your family, Chabenac. Why not?'

Chapter Twelve

June 1793, Avignon, France

A pleasant morning breeze ruffled the long curtains of Morin's tall office windows. With chasseur companies away on task or training, little noise or dust drifted in from the square. The chat from the desks of the regimental clerks was subdued beyond the Colonel's door. As Jobert and Geourdai entered, Morin and Raive pored over maps on a small table by the unlit hearth.

'Gentlemen,' said Morin, 'the survival of liberty, equality and fraternity hangs in the balance. Paris is in utter anarchy. Different factions struggle for power, in the face of foreign invasion, civil war and consistent military defeat. Each opposing faction fiercely proposes their own solution for ensuring the Republic's existence.

'The new Committee of Public Safety, now completely under Jacobin control, has placed France under a "revolutionary dictatorship". The National Convention is now dominated by the Jacobins and the *sans-culotte* mobs. They have used the uprising in Lyon to enact legislation that eliminates any Federalist opposition. About thirty Federalist members have been arrested and will likely be executed.

'The majority of opposition members arrested represent departments here in the south, such as Lyon, Marseille, Toulon and Avignon. This political blow added to ongoing Jacobin policy towards the Church, plus the Pope declaring war against the Republic, drives the regional towns to rebellion.

'I have received news this morning, the port of Marseille is now in open revolt. Marseille Federalists seek to leave the Republic. The city's Jacobin administration has been overthrown and the National Guard garrison overwhelmed. To hold France together, the regiment needs to act immediately.'

Morin tapped on a map with a pair of navigational callipers.

'I am expecting immediate orders from General Mouret in response to the Marseille situation. Yet I am keen to anticipate the general's intent. Raive and I have studied the maps and I feel it imperative to place a surveillance screen around Marseille. Jobert, your 2nd Company has just returned from escort duty to Toulon and Marseille, I feel comfortable sending the full 2nd Squadron the three days march to Marseilles. Questions, gentlemen?'

'Yes, sir. Where will the other squadrons be deployed whilst we undertake the screen?' asked Jobert.

'Fergnes' 1st Squadron will remain in barracks to respond to General Mouret's orders. 3rd Squadron is to escort a powder convoy from Avignon to Nice. 4th Squadron is still escorting convoys to the siege of Lyon. 5th Squadron, not yet battle capable, will secure our barracks here.'

'3rd Squadron has a powder convoy on the roads to Nice, sir? Do you foresee that impacting on 2nd Squadron screening the roads around Marseille?'

'The 4th Artillery Regiment, based in Nice with the Army of Italy, has a consignment of forty tons of powder to be delivered to their batteries. The 4th Artillery has sent one of their captains to oversee the convoy. What is his name? Bonaparte? 3rd Squadron will utilise routes initially covered by 2nd Squadron up until Aix-en-Provence. Any further thoughts?'

Jobert leant over the chart on the table. 'Sir, I see Geourdai's 8th Company approaching Marseille from Senas and screening the north around Les Pennes-Mirabeau. I will take 2nd Company via Aix-en-Provence and Aubagne and screen Marseille from the east. Does that fulfil your intent?'

'So be it, Jobert,' said Morin. 'Have 2nd Squadron ready to march within the hour.'

In the valley of Aix-en-Provence below them, ragged volleys of musket fire punched the air. Having parted with 8th Company before dawn, 2nd Company had marched for eight hours until the sound of musket fire halted the company moments ago.

Jobert checked the readiness of the company column three hundred metres back. Neilage and Huin rode the length of Huin's troop, checking charges were tamped and musketoons cocked. Duque tucked the four wagons and Jobert's cart into a defensive circle. Koschak confirmed the company's all-round defence.

The sharp cracks from the exchange of musketry continued unabated. Left and right of their company commander, Voreille's dismounted sentries darted glances inwards towards Jobert, Chabenac and Moench. Jobert passed his telescope to Chabenac and checked his watch. Midday.

'Chabenac,' said Jobert, 'bluecoats at the gates of Aix are

the town's National Guard. The near two hundred fusiliers in civilian dress attacking the Guard are, more than likely, Marseille Royalists. Agree?'

'Hmm, Royalists or Federalists?'

'Rebels! Is that better? Lieutenant Voreille, 2nd Company will charge the rebels, Huin's troop leading. Bring in your flank and rear guards, reform your troop behind Huin's troop line. When Moench sounds Charge, extend the battle line on the right, aim for the Marseille road to the south to cut off or cut down as many as you can. Understand?'

Voreille's eyes were wide, his face pale.

'Voreille!' said Jobert. 'Our action is to stop these rebel bastards returning to Marseille. By any and every means. Is that clear?'

'Yes, sir, ... yes!'

'Chabenac, sir, would you be so kind as to pay our compliments to the commander of the town's Guard.'

Moving back to the horse-holders, at Jobert's direction, Moench waved a hand-signal for Neilage to advance in column of fours. Voreille cantered away and waved in his rear and flank guards. The chasseurs squeezed their tired horses forward. Moench signalled Neilage to form column of platoons, then Moench now signalled 'Trot, column of troop'.

Despite the hoof beats of one hundred horses around the advancing company, the firing beyond the crest grew louder,

Jobert, on Vert, stood in the middle of the road facing his oncoming soldiers. An inner crescendo prepared him for the fight. He knew he confronted his chasseurs with eyes fierce, nostrils flared, teeth bared.

Chasseurs with musketoons on thighs, shortened their rein lengths in their left hands and extended their battle line. The company became four wavering ranks, the twenty-four men and horses of the front rank compressed by the verges of the road. Huin's troop comprised the front two ranks with Voreille's troop the third and fourth rank.

Jobert peered down toward the farm buildings on the perimeter of Aix-en-Provence. The firing had fallen away in the nearest out-buildings, the gun smoke cleared, rebels and Guardsmen looked toward the dust on the slight ridge.

Jobert raised a gloved hand and halted the ranks. 'Lieutenant Huin, is your troop ready for battle?'

'Yes, sir!' Huin's parched throat croaked.

'Sergeant Yinot, is your platoon ready for battle?'

'Yes ... yes, sir!' cried Yinot.

'Sergeant Pultiere, is your platoon ready for battle?'

'Absolutely fucking yes, sir!' Pultiere's eyes bulged.

Jobert stood in his stirrups. '2nd Company, are we ready for battle?'

'Yes, sir!' roared back the men.

'2nd Company, will advance, walk, march! Moench, sound *Advance!*'

Jobert pivoted Vert over his hock. He drew his sabre, before heading down the slope at the trot. As the line of chasseurs crested at the walk, musketoons on thighs, with Moench's trumpet screaming the *Advance*, the four hundred National Guardsmen, hunkered down behind the stone walls of the outer homes of the town, let out a thrilling cheer.

'2nd Company, sabres! Trot, march.'

One hundred musketoons, attached to cross belts, clunked onto right thighs on their release from one hundred right hands. One hundred blades hissed metal-on-metal from their scabbards. Four hundred hooves beat a deafening thunder down into the vale of Aix-en-Provence.

Jobert cantered forward and set the direction of charge. The rebels fired at the advancing cavalry. Three hundred metres, well out of effective range, the closest rebels fired wildly and too early. *Under pressure, the idiots fire too high.* The National Guardsmen renewed their fire with vigour. Pultiere and Yinot on either end of the front rank called, 'Hold! Hold the line, boys, hold!'

With his trotting company covering the distance in moments, Jobert noted the Guard on his half-left, leaping over the walls, bayonets fixed and charge forward in a raggedy line.

Jobert pointed his sabre. 'Huin, forward on this line. Charge!' Jobert brought Vert to the right of the line. 'Moench, sound *Charge!*'

Moench's trumpet screamed with urgency. Huin's men screamed in desperate conviction, extended their sabres, elbows locked, blades and hilt guards turned out to the right, as those that could, crammed as they were, lifted their horses to a canter.

Few rebels fired, many ran away, most screamed but no-one could hear. One young fool, having failed to slide his ramrod away within its sleeve on the musket's barrel, shot his ramrod at Jobert. Jobert skipped Vert smashing the man down with the horse's shoulder, Jobert's iron stirrup catching his face. The man rolled away in the dust only to be crushed underfoot by the ranks of horsemen behind.

Voreille yelled at his troop, emerging from behind Huin's at the trot, extending the company battle line. At this fast trot, the lines of horsemen sped at fifteen kilometres per hour. Yet to Jobert, his chasseurs seemed to wallow, whilst the rebels flashed in and out of the dust, smoke and buildings.

'On me! Voreille! On me!' Jobert's sabre pointed at nearly one hundred rebels, throwing away muskets, cross-belts with cartridge pouches, satchels, jackets and hats, running down the road, away from Aix-en-Provence, south to Les Pennes-Mirabeau.

Crossing the Les Pennes-Mirabeau road now, Jobert checked Vert, as rebels ran in blind panic, seeking the trees lining the road as a haven from the flashing hooves and sweeping blades. Voreille and his fifty soldiers burst into view between the roadside trees, knocking or cutting terrified rebels to the ground.

'Voreille, block this road. Let no man escape.' Voreille's flushed face gave a grim nod to Jobert, before yelling orders to the chasseurs on his right.

Colliding with oncoming rebels, Jobert spun Vert to the left of the troop line. Bredieux roared into view, his blade catching a man who crossed his path with an appalling cut to the shoulder. The man dropped to his knees, screaming, as Bredieux's nimble bay mare and other fleeing rebels leapt across him.

'Bredieux, on me!' Jobert squeezed Vert back into an extended canter and noting Bredieux's sword salute, burst out of the tree-lined road, though the fleeing fugitives, toward the eastern road leading out of Aix-en-Provence to Aubagne.

Bredieux bellowed to his platoon. Jobert looked back to see a swarm of Bredieux's chasseurs, their extended line melting into a thundering pack, sabres held high, hacking through frightened rebels, as if riding through tall reeds.

Jobert's new objective was the other rebel avenue of escape, the road to Aubagne some two kilometres, or at a slow canter on weary horses, some five minutes distant. Jobert led the hunt through the jumble of small holdings and worker's cottages on the outskirts of the town. The laboured breathing of the twenty-odd horses and the drumming of their iron-shod feet rebounded off the stone walls and wooden out-buildings.

As Jobert and Bredieux's men pressed their exhausted horses towards the Aubagne road, Jobert saw that a company of the town's Guardsmen had captured a large group of prisoners. Attempting to avoid the converging groups of horsemen, both Bredieux's as well as Huin's troopers, who appearing through the buildings having followed Neilage from the Aix-en-Provence's western gate, the rebels crowded close to their captors.

'Moench, sound *Rally*!' Jobert let his sabre swing down his leg on its sword knot over his wrist and plucked at his watch. Moench's trumpet piped the long notes of the *Rally*. The watch read half-past-midday.

Emerging from the dust behind Huin's chasseurs, Koschak cantered on a tight rein, alert in the saddle for a quick cut.

'Sergeant Major! Prisoners! Wounded! Trains!'

Koschak saluted with a blood-soaked blade.

Chapter Thirteen

June 1793, Aix-en-Provence, France

Dawn's cool glow lit up calm clouds beyond the Alps to the east. Horses stamped, tossed heads and flicked tails at the morning's lazy flies. A quiet crowd from Aix-en-Provence woke early to send off their Guardsmen to Marseilles.

At the civic reception the previous evening, Jobert was delighted that the Mayor of Aix-en-Provence and the local National Guard commander had placed a battalion of six companies at his disposal. Jobert had 2nd Company salute the two National Guard companies who were to march ten kilometres south to the village of Les Pennes-Mirabeau to join Geourdai's 8th Company.

With the cheers to their Guardsmen dimming as the one hundred and fifty local infantrymen marched south, Jobert and Chabenac sat and watched Neilage, with a platoon escort, pass the front of the company and join the procession. The chasseurs, in good spirits, called nonsense to each other as the platoon departed on its mission south.

Jobert gripped Chabenac's hand. 'Even with rebel scouts on

the road, you ought to be with Geourdai well before ten o'clock. 2nd Company and I should arrive at Aubagne by midday and be observing both Marseille and the Marseille road east to Toulon. Tomorrow, as you return to Avignon, Neilage and I will link up, confirming a trail that skirts Marseille.'

Chabenac squeezed his horse into a trot to follow Neilage's platoon.

Jobert lifted Bleu into a one-hundred-and-eighty-degree pivot to face the company. The chasseurs smiles left their faces, all eyes focussed on their captain. 'Lieutenant Voreille! March the 2nd Company to Aubagne. Guards out!'

The column of horsemen clip-clopped along the road to the east. The three hundred men of the four remaining National Guard companies followed 2nd Company, waving goodbye to families and taking into their ranks fresh loaves and skins of wine passed from the crowd.

Jobert joined the column beside Koschak. Having spent the evening in the town at the invitation of the Mayor of Aix-en-Provence and the commander of the town's National Guard, Jobert was eager to catch up with his company's senior soldier. 'Satisfied with 2nd Company's first combat, Sergeant Major?'

'Indeed, sir,' said Koschak. 'How lucky we were that our first taste of blood was smashing a gaggle of dockworkers and masons' apprentices in the flank. As opposed to walking into an ambush by Prussian jaegers, or to meet a wall of Austrian dragoons. Very fucking lucky, indeed, sir.'

'Exactly! I intend to grasp this opportunity to school our men in battle against such an amateurish foe to the full. How are our wounded this morning?'

'Chasseur Millone is suffering acute embarrassment, as he rides a wagon with Duque, due to breaking an arm falling off his horse. I have reassigned Millone's horse to the lad of Pultiere's who lost his horse. As to the other, young Dalmuz is certainly proud of his musket ball graze across his shoulder.'

'What was the outcome for the horse that took a ball through the knee?' asked Jobert.

'The horse was given to the farrier to destroy. Your Orlande had other ideas. He led the horse into the town and traded him with a butcher for two sides of pork.'

'Hah! How did the lads take the loss of their first troop horse?'

'Obviously quite melancholy, a few sniffles. Pultiere had the whole section parade around the horse and salute her as she was led away.'

'As we know, there will come a day soon that the loss of remounts, even butchering and eating wounded horses, will become as mundane as cleaning musketoons.'

Koschak grunted in acknowledgement.

Jobert tickled Bleu's shorn mane, appreciating this moment of partnership before a bullet, either an enemy's or his own, took any one of his own beloved horses away. 'What is your impression of the company's reaction to their first combat dead?'

'Like all of us when we saw it the first time, sir. The hushed deference. The expectation of punishment. The priest and the crowd of townsfolk arrived with a feast and absolution, so it was put quickly from their minds. The women passing out hot bread and roasted chickens reminded the lads what they are here for.'

'I never heard the final tally. How many were found dead by the evening?' asked Jobert.

'About thirty rebels and five Guardsmen, I understand,' said Koschak. 'Fifteen rebels were found shot at the limit of their attack. Not more than ten were found with cuts and the rest were trampled underfoot.'

'Were you happy with the lads' drills?'

'Shit yes, sir! Bredieux's flank guards responded well on hearing the initial fire. No musketoons were fired mistakenly.

The lads slid from column of fours all the way out to company battle line under fire, albeit paltry fire, yet on a tight road, mind you. Horses had not lost any shoes. Neither galled backs nor mouths by the time we set camp. No, the men did well first-time in. How about you, sir? What impressions do you have of the affair?'

'The Mayor and the National Guard commander were delighted with the three hundred prisoners. Aix-en-Provence is an old university town so cherishes the ideals of the Republic and were always going to stand firm. I am delighted with having our ranks increased with a battalion of five hundred local infantry. We might even retake Marseilles ourselves?'

'Steady, sir, steady,' said Koschak. 'Shall we first see if these lawyers' clerks and bakers' boys can march for six hours straight with muskets on their shoulders?'

For many of the chasseurs of 2nd Company, today's Battle of Aubagne was eagerly anticipated. The six hours slipped by under the endless blue of the warm Mediterranean sky, for the march-fit horsemen at least. Jobert watched the young chasseurs smoke, laugh and boast to their section-mates of impending prowess in the upcoming battle.

For their part, the local lads of the Aix-en-Provence National Guard struggled to complete the march of thirty kilometres. The infantry's first two hours of marching were full of merry stories, building on their martial achievements of the previous day. During the second two hours of marching the long, dusty columns were silent, apart from the expletives that came with stepping in fresh horse manure. In the final two hours, with water gourds and wineskins drained, the infantry column had tripled its length from the initial one thousand metres including baggage train. The grumbling and cursing caused a long, low hum within the beat of six hundred shoes.

At one thousand metres, Jobert studied Aubagne through his telescope. 'Time, Voreille?'

'Just on midday, sir.'

Through Jobert's telescope, Aubagne seemed quiet in the midday sun. Lying in a small valley, the town of Aubagne was surrounded by orchards and cottages and the occasional large farm with its internal yard surrounded by a walled cluster of buildings. Shaded lanes crisscrossed between the households. The hum of flies and bees dominated, punctuated by the call of a distant goose or calf.

Jobert turned to Voreille, Huin and the mounted infantry major, commanding the four Guard companies strung out on the road behind them. 'You will note, gentlemen, the rebels have not set outposts at a visual distance from the highest town rooves or spires. No rebel sentries are posted at musket, or cannon, range from the walls of the old town. No-one, neither rebel nor citizen, can be seen moving on the streets. No church bells, shots, drums nor bugles sound in warning.'

Jobert collapsed his telescope, placed it away in his coat pocket and turned in the saddle to address the Guard's chief of battalion, a major in his sixties, astride a stout farm horse. 'Sir, with your permission, I do not plan to use the time as a period of instruction for my troop commanders, but I wish to align our thoughts on the action before us.'

'Please, proceed, Captain Jobert,' said the major.

'From the information we are receiving from this reconnaissance, consider the options available to the enemy. The enemy is either not in possession of Aubagne, or the enemy garrison is indeed sleeping after lunch, or the enemy is waiting in ambush. The greatest threat to us is an enemy in ambush.

'With all local artillery pieces deployed with the various Republican armies and the horses absorbed into the levee en masse, the likelihood of a small enemy cavalry force, or even a cannon, facing our force is possible, but unlikely. That the rebels mounted an infantry assault onto Aix-en-Provence yesterday supports my contention. Most likely ambush would be an infantry attack from the cover of the stout buildings in the narrow lanes of the town.'

Jobert pointed a gloved hand to a tree-lined roadway to the west.

'My objective is not to secure Aubagne, but to secure the Marseille road. To that end, 2nd Company shall depart the Aix-en-Provence road, circling west of the town towards the Marseille road, via these hamlet lanes. Huin, your remaining platoon and the company train will wait for the infantry here on the Aix-en-Provence road. Place yourself in support of the infantry's entrance to the town.'

Second Lieutenant Huin twisted in the saddle and searched for the head of the infantry column.

'Voreille, upon reaching the Marseille road, I shall leave Bredieux's platoon to secure the road against any threat from Marseille. With Pultiere's platoon, we shall enter Aubagne from the west. If we set out now, our column from the west should enter the town as the infantry enter the town from the north.'

'Eminently sound. I approve,' said the National Guard major, wobbling the sparse plumes of his faded tricorne that must have dated from his last combat thirty years ago.

Leading a patrol, Koschak joined the group. 'Gentlemen, having just spoken to local farm hands, it is confirmed that Aubagne has a garrison of one hundred men up from Marseille.'

'Then we have no time to lose,' said Jobert. 'Voreille, column of fours, follow me, trot, march!'

Voreille's troop trotted along the two kilometres of local pathways towards the tall poplars outlining the Marseille road. In distant meadows on the higher slopes of the shallow valley, men and women stood stiffly from their field labour and watched the column of horsemen weave amidst the thatched-rooved cottages and the stone barns. Milking cows, tethered close to their owners' crofts and restless from the sudden arrival of the horses, bellowing for their stray calves. The troop slowed to a walk only once to allow a small girl the opportunity to move her gaggle of geese off the path.

Fifteen minutes after leaving Huin and the infantry major on the Aix-en-Provence road, the fifty chasseurs brought their horses to a walk and formed up in two ranks in the shade of the Marseille road.

Jobert's eyes scanned the shadows. Leaves danced in the breeze. Above, a single crow flapped across the cloudless sky. Swallows twittered in nearby haylofts. The occasional bark of a farm dog. *Something is not right.* 'Sergeant Major, with Sergeant Bredieux's platoon, secure this road and deny enemy movement toward Aubagne.'

'Yes, sir,' said Koschak. 'Sergeant Bredieux, have your platoon fall out to that hedge, dismount, commanders to me.'

A few of Pultiere's weary horses took the opportunity of the brief halt to urinate.

'Sergeant Pultiere,' said Jobert, 'dismount your men in line where you are. You have five minutes to drink, adjust girths and check musketoons are loaded.'

'Right, lads,' called Pultiere, 'focus on saddles, not water. Corporals, check your musketoons. Platoon, dismount!'

With the jangle of sabres, musketoons and spurs of dismounting horsemen in front of him, Jobert's watch indicated twenty minutes past noon. Jobert stepped down from Bleu, checked his girth and accepted a swig of water from Moench. 'Platoon, mount! Musketoons ready, follow me back to Aubagne. Column of fours, trot, march!'

A few troopers emitted a low moan in the proximity of their captain.

Jobert's head jerked around, his nostrils flared, his jaw clenched.

'Shut your guts, you idle pricks,' roared Sergeant Pultiere. 'You heard the Captain, get ready to fight, or get ready to have your throats opened.'

With a renewed sense of urgency, the platoon urged tired horses from the halt to the trot, forming column with musketoon on thighs, and followed their officers up the leafy road to Aubagne.

Ten minutes later just out from the town's western gates, the column of horsemen broke to a walk.

There in the shade, two rebel sentries reclined against a cool stone wall and, with their muskets tucked into the crooks of their arms, snored. Under a large tree nearby, women stopped clearing a lunch table of cups and platters and watched the chasseurs.

'Shall I wake these gentlemen, sir?' asked Pultiere.

Jobert scowled at the sleeping sentries. *Has the footfall of thirty horses not roused you, you useless bastards?* 'No, Sergeant.'

Jobert turned in his saddle to face the platoon of soldiers. 'Men, this is why sleeping on sentry duty is such a serious military crime.'

Jobert dismounted Bleu, drew his sabre and placed the blade tip at the base of one man's throat. With his left hand, Jobert then held the barrel of the sentry's musket. Jobert thrust his blade deep into the chest of the sleeping man, cutting his aorta. The sentry coughed, jerked his eyes open, thrust out his quivering legs, released the contents of his bladder and then slumped back.

The other sentry stirred awake. Jobert repeated the execution of the second man. Jobert wiped his blade on one sentry's soft cap and remounted Bleu. Jobert looked across Voreille, Moench and the troopers, their mouths hanging open in appalled shock. 'Do not let that happen to you. No bastard gets to "play" soldier.'

The dead sentries farted and twitched at their horses' feet. Pultiere grinned. The young men exchanged looks of dread.

Jobert and Pultiere passed the shady lunch table and the silent, wide-eyed citizens. Pressing further into the town, the small column of chasseurs noticed the noise level of a crowd starting to build. The group of horsemen turned a corner and entered the main square of Aubagne.

In the square, over three hundred footsore, grumbling National Guardsmen rounded up, with their bayonets, one hundred bewildered Marseille rebels, surrounded by at least one thousand murmuring citizens of the town.

Noting Jobert's entrance into the small square, the old Guard major doffed his ancient tricorne in salute.

The Battle of Aubagne was complete.

Bleu flicked his ears back to his rider as Jobert slipped his feet out of his stirrups, stretched his legs and rotated his ankles to relieve aching muscles. 'Voreille, lead the company back to Bredieux. We need to determine the outer-most limit of the rebels before we set camp tonight. And, Voreille, … had I chosen to take those sentries prisoner, I would have had them shot as traitors.'

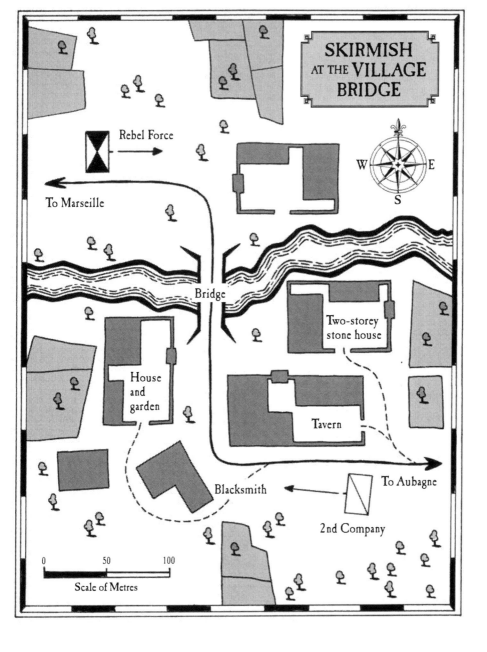

SKIRMISH AT THE VILLAGE BRIDGE

Rebel Force

To Marseille

Bridge

W E
S

Two-storey stone house

House and garden

Tavern

Blacksmith

To Aubagne

2nd Company

0   50   100
Scale of Metres

Chapter Fourteen

Jobert watched the firefight develop rapidly.

Leading a vedette, Sergeant Bredieux had fired first at a fleeting target. By the time the yelling in the old timber tavern beside the stone bridge had converted into return fire, Bredieux dismounted his chasseurs and took up positions in a split-log blacksmith's shed on the opposite side of the Marseille road. Bredieux and his men hit two rebels attempting to depart the tavern by the front door.

As fire intensified from within the tavern, the remaining chasseurs of Bredieux's platoon dismounted, leaving the fourth man in each squad to hold the horses. Following Voreille, with his sabre drawn, the chasseurs surrounded the tavern yard and directed their fire at the rebel musket barrels protruding from the shuttered windows.

The shallow valley in which Aubagne lay was formed by a small river which flowed west, entering the Mediterranean Sea south of the city of Marseille. For the one-hour trot-march from Aubagne, the Marseille road ran on one side of the brook.

As the road now turned towards the visible outskirts and spires of Marseille, it crossed the river at a narrow point spanned by an ancient mossy-stone bridge.

Musket fire rang out from across the stream.

As musket balls zinged in the air about them, Jobert assessed a band of Marseille rebels, about thirty-strong, approaching the bridge at three hundred metres.

'Lieutenant Huin,' called Jobert, pointing his sabre at a two-storey stone posthouse, 'rebel column approaching the bridge. Secure that stone building beyond the tavern. Have Yinot's fire dominate the bridge.'

Yinot's platoon changed direction down a village lane and disappeared towards their objective.

Although the fire faded from the tavern, the musketry across the narrow, swift stream increased.

'Moench,' said Jobert, 'find Voreille in the smithy. Tell him of the enemy approaching the bridge and that Huin has secured the stone house beyond the tavern.'

Twisting his trumpet's lanyards so that the horn was behind his back, Moench dismounted. Handing his reins to Duque, Moench cocked his musketoon without unclipping it from the broad, white cross-belt, before departing on his errand.

Jobert's watch read half-past four o'clock, less than three hours until dusk. Musket fire continued to be traded by opposing individuals. Bleu pawed the gravel road with impatience.

'Tulloc. Duval. With me,' called Koschak. The three men dismounted, with Tulloc and Duval cradling their newly acquired long-barrelled rifles and followed Koschak along the back wall of the forge towards their sniping destination.

Over two months ago, during the confusing receipt of the regiment's initial firearms issue, Lieutenant Colonel Raive kept twenty rifles in the regimental armoury. For those company commanders desiring the weapon be issued to their companies, the rifles were available. Jobert secured two rifles.

Tulloc and Duval had won the company prizes for the best shooting results, with their short-barrelled musketoons, during their training in Avignon. The two proved themselves deadly accurate at the standard fifty metre range, from the ungainly mounted position, but were uncannily accurate at one hundred metres when dismounted. Armed with the longer, rifled-barrelled weapon, Tulloc and Duval impressed their company mates with consistent strikes on 'man-sized' targets at an incredible three hundred metre range.

Running back from the forge, Moench cringed as musket balls from the other side of the stream chipped stone walls and thudded into tree trunks.

'Sergeant Pultiere,' yelled Jobert, 'dismount your platoon. Draw sabres and pistols. Clear the tavern of the remaining enemy. Fortify the tavern against assault. Duque, once Pultiere clears the tavern, bring the train into the tavern yard. We will set camp there.'

Duque jerked his chin in compliance and trotted his four led horses four hundred metres back up the Marseille road, towards Aubagne, to the five waiting wagons.

The rebel musket fire was decreasing. Jobert peered across the bridge towards his rebel opponents. *You are running out of options now we have the bridge.*

One of Bredieux's section corporals waved to Jobert from the blacksmith's shack. Jobert squeezed Bleu towards cover by the shed's wall, dismounted, leaving Bleu with Moench and followed the corporal into the workshop.

The smith's deep-timber, iron-lined, coal-filled forge and a series of different sized iron anvils, all mounted on massive oak stumps, provided excellent cover for the three groups of chasseurs. Two chasseurs maintained steady fire, as the third man loaded their musketoons. The fourth man of the squad was somewhere outside with the other horse-holders of the platoon.

In the gloom behind the large leather bellows, Jobert found Bredieux and three wounded men, one of them Voreille. Voreille gripped a blood-soaked handkerchief to his gloved left hand, ashen yet determined.

Bredieux's unlit pipe was clenched hard between his yellow teeth. 'Sir, I do not know what to do.'

Jobert knelt and squeezed Bredieux's shoulder before he assessed the wounded. A chasseur sat against the wall, rocking back and forth in pain, moaning to himself, cradling a blood-soaked arm. He was shot through the elbow. *My friend, you will lose that arm by nightfall.*

A second chasseur lay on the dirt floor of the workshop, the front of his braided dolman jacket open, the chest of his white waistcoat and shirt now dark from his blood loss. His blue lips gurgled a bloody froth down his begrimed cheeks. His hands scratched the floor and his boots scraped back and forth, as he worked hard to breathe. With a glance, Jobert knew this young chasseur would die soon.

'Sergeant, see to the ammunition across your platoon. The enemy fire is decreasing as they are unable to cross the —' A roar of human voices exploded across the street. 'That is Pultiere clearing the tavern. They will soon provide crossfire over the bridge.'

'What about these men, sir?'

'Focus on your platoon, Sergeant, and your task of stopping any enemy crossing the bridge. Now go!'

The weary creases on Bredieux's powder-blackened face set themselves in determination.

'Voreille, cross the street to Pultiere. Have your wound bound so that you can use your sabre. Coordinate the fire from your two platoon positions so that no-one crosses the bridge.'

With a knitted brow, Voreille flicked his eyes to the man shot through the lung, then looked at Jobert. Jobert held Voreille's eye and shook his head imperceptibly. Voreille gritted his teeth, his eyes watering, stood with the assistance of his sabre and left the forge.

Weapons fired somewhere outside. Jobert observed two rebels, two hundred metres across the bridge towards Marseille, collapse attempting to cross the road. *Our rifles.*

Jobert spun surprised to see Neilage and Moench enter the rear doorway. 'Welcome, Lieutenant. I was not expecting you until tomorrow. But there is no time for chit-chat. Moench, dismount the platoon escort who accompanied Lieutenant Neilage. Lead them behind the garden wall of the house next door. I intend to lead them in a flanking attack across the stream.'

Neilage's smile evaporated as he stepped across the outstretched legs of the two wounded soldiers.

'Neilage, the bridge is the company's focus. I am now taking your escort platoon across the stream to push the rebels back. I want our vedettes on the far side by nightfall. Send some of Pultiere's men to have these two wounded taken to the tavern. Send a rider back to Aubagne for the town's surgeon. I will return to the tavern by dusk. Do not lose the bridge, Lieutenant.'

In their smoky corner of the low-beamed tavern, Geourdai's 8th Company headquarters on the Mirabeau-Marseille road, Chabenac poured wine into Jobert's wooden cup. The liquid twinkled deep purple in the sputtering candlelight.

Chief of squadron Avriol watched Jobert empty his cup.

'To what do we owe the pleasure of your visit to our scruffy little war, sir?' asked Jobert.

'One week ago,' said Avriol, 'Avignon followed Marseille's example by erupting in open revolt.'

Geourdai jerked at the news. Remembering his friend's growing romance with the local girl, Camille, Jobert's innards spasmed at a memory of Valmai de Chabenac. *Good grief, surely there is enough to occupy the mind than romantic connections.* He remembered his father's words that if the regiment wanted you to have a wife, the regiment would have issued you with one.

'Then what is required of 2nd Squadron, sir?' asked Jobert.

'No change to your current task, Jobert. 2nd Squadron is to remain screening Marseille. As of three days ago, General Carteux in Lyon ordered a concentration of three thousand troops in Valence.'

'Forgive me, sir. General who?'

'Carteux. Mouret has been replaced. Committee of Public Safety'.

Jobert sought any sign of clarity. A frown from Chabenac warned against it.

'Three thousand troops are not a great deal of force,' Avriol continued, 'but more than enough to recapture Avignon and Marseilles. Around four battalions, a battery of foot artillery plus the 24th Chasseurs. Colonel Morin has Fergnes' 1st Squadron screening the southern half of Avignon while 4th Squadron screens the northern half. 5th and 3rd Squadrons remain in barracks protecting the forty tonnes of powder. All the while 2nd Squadron is lazing in the sun around Marseille.'

'Surely, sir, the powder convoy has not remained in Avignon for two weeks?' asked Geourdai.

'It has not been a simple affair to find the eighty bullocks to pull the twenty drays required,' said Avriol. 'Engaging forty bullock-drivers whose loyalty to the Republic has been vouchsafed has been another challenge. The artillery captain who commands the convoy, and it is 4th Artillery Regiment's powder after all, has decided to leave the convoy where it is. This Captain Bonaparte has departed for Valence to offer his services to General Carteux's headquarters claiming the roads are not open to the convoy due to rebel activity.'

'Does Colonel Morin require 2nd Squadron do more to maintain safe passage to Nice, sir?' asked Jobert.

'No. It is not the security of the roads that holds Colonel Morin's attention, but the security of information. Your recent report described rebel prisoners speaking of two hundred chasseurs escorting a large powder convoy. The Colonel believes agents in the city of Avignon would have known of its arrival and, possibly, its destination as Nice from the barge wharves. But only sources inside the 24th Chasseurs would have known of the number of troops in the escort. Lieutenant Colonel Raive has reasonably assumed there are enemy informants within the regiment and is seeking any other instances of compromise. A reasonable assumption since our soldiers have been recruited from districts around a city which has just revolted.'

Jobert took a mouthful of cheese and dried fish from a central platter. *Spies within my squadron?*

'Speaking of the dismissal of Mouret,' said Avriol, 'and of agents intent on compromising the regiment, be aware of yet another emerging threat.'

Jobert's chewing slowed at the rising anger in Avriol's voice.

'The Committee of Public Safety has created a new breed of animal, the People's Deputies,' said Avriol. 'Such Deputies are young, driven individuals, well connected within the Jacobin Club, on a frightening crusade of liberty, equality, fraternity in the Jacobin style. These Deputies have been assigned throughout the army to dismiss, arrest and execute whomever it takes to ensure both the army's loyalty to the Republic and identify appropriate talent to overcome the woeful string of battlefield defeats. Hence the dismissal of Mouret and the promotion of Carteux. Carteux was a dragoon twenty years ago and now paints landscapes. A very keen Jacobin, but from all accounts from Lyon, a poor general. We will see how well he effects the re-capture of Avignon and Marseille.

'The key point is these citizen-Deputies will visit the 24th Chasseurs in due course. The advice is if you disappoint them you will be executed. If you impress them you will be forced to accept promotion to high command and in due course, be executed. Heed my words, Jobert, these are very dangerous people.'

Chapter Fifteen

July-August 1793, Marseille, France

'Sir, wake up.'

Jobert sat up, blinking at the meagre light from the candle. He craned his face away from the light to see the messenger. 'Who is it? What is it?'

'Chasseur Dalmuz, sir. A message from Lieutenant Huin, sir. It is now four o'clock.' The soldier counted his fingers as he recited the message. 'Inside Marseille there is excited cheering, beating of drums and light … torch light, sir, not a bonfire.'

Other men lying nearby rolled over in the darkness to listen. Chasseur Dalmuz looked at his little finger. 'Something is happening inside Marseille, sir and Lieutenant Huin requests your presence, please, sir.'

Jobert groped for his boots. 'What time is it now?'

'Half-past four, sir,' said Duque, further back in the shadows. 'Saddle Bleu, sir?'

'Sound *To Arms*, sir?' asked Moench, another voice in the darkness.

'Please, Duque, and no, Moench, as we are not in any im-

mediate threat. Sound *Reveille* then *Commanders In.*' The sound
of metal scraping on floorboards followed as Moench sought
his trumpet.

Within five minutes of the trumpet sounding, the room,
glowing from the small fire in the hearth, was crowded with
men in various forms of undress, but each without exception
wearing boots and sword belt.

'Huin is on outpost duty with Yinot's platoon,' said Jobert.
'Huin reports something is happening in Marseille. I am riding
there now. Sergeant Pultiere, stand to, prepare your platoon to
depart immediately. Go now. Lieutenant Neilage, have one of
Voreille's platoons ready to depart to my location, should I
send a message. Prepare to defend the bridge here. Prepare to
withdraw the train to Aubagne.'

Thirty minutes of trotting through the pre-dawn gloom later,
Dalmuz and the three other chasseurs from his squad, brought
Jobert, Moench and Pultiere's platoon to the edge of a long
field sloping down towards the eastern outskirts of Marseille.
Visible just over five hundred metres away through the light
Mediterranean mist, Huin and Yinot observed the city.

'Good morning, sir,' said Huin. 'You can see that column of
rebels departing the farthest gate. I estimate up to two thousand
men marching north.'

Jobert reached into his jacket for his telescope. 'With back
packs on and satchels bulging, no less. Marching to drums and
tricolour, not Royalist, standards.'

'I took the opportunity to take prisoners before first light,
sir, sentries from the eastern gates. The prisoners were eager to
inform us they are advancing to Avignon.'

'Of course, march to Avignon to link with the revolt there.'
Jobert remembered the issue of spies. 'How would they know
of the revolt if we hold the roads?'

'Couriers may possibly have come from routes west of the

Rhône, sir, via Nimes or Arles, then via the Rhône's mouth, across the short stretch of sea to the port.'

'Said the son of a Rhône bargeman. But their current route north could take them to Aix-en-Provence.'

'The prisoners did not say the destination was Aix-en-Provence,' said Huin. 'If I may say, sir, Aix-en-Provence repulsed the initial attack. The National Guard there stands firm and the town is not in revolt as Avignon is. Why would the rebels wait three weeks to stage a second attack within a day's march that requires such a train?'

Jobert lowered his telescope from the horse- and man-drawn wagons, the small flock of sheep and women pushing handcarts that were now departing the city behind the column, to consider the slight young officer beside him. 'Why would the column not approach Avignon west of the Rhône, as the couriers had done?'

'That would require them to travel by sea and then upriver, sir. The route west of the Rhône is at least two days longer and the roads to Arles run through the marshy country at the river's mouth. Every local knows the diseases that lurk there in summer.'

'Ignore local knowledge at your peril.' Jobert reset his glass to his eye.

'The rebel column will be in 8th Company's location in two hours. The prisoners said they were aware only one hundred chasseurs stood between them and Avignon.'

'What?' asked Jobert. 'How would they know that?'

'They were told by their officers that only one hundred chasseurs stood before them on their three-day march to Avignon.'

'But no rebel informant in Avignon would know only 8th Company stands on the road. That information is coming from within either 2nd Company or 8th Company. Someone is talking.'

'Indeed, sir, for someone is listening. Do you want to question the prisoners further?'

'No, not now. I need to get a message to Geourdai and Neilage. Would you assist me by taking dictation?'

Jobert blinked into the middle distance as he arranged the information in his mind.

'To Geourdai, Marseille's east gates, five o'clock, 2nd of July. Enemy. Up to two thousand strong column of rebel infantry is advancing on Avignon. Most likely to move on shortest route via Senas. Rebel prisoners confirm this. Rebels aware only 8th Company blocks the route to Avignon. Rebels have a scarcity of horses. No cavalry. No mounted commanders. Some wagons in their train horse-drawn, some man-drawn. No guns seen at this stage. Artillery unlikely, but possible. Due to inexperienced rebel infantry, enemy column will become over-extended and be most vulnerable in the day prior to arriving at Avignon.'

Jobert watched Huin complete the sentence in his notebook.

'Huin, a disciplined company of regular infantry would be fifty metres long. Four companies would be two hundred metres long. Do you remember the volunteer National Guard setting out from Aix-en-Provence? The four companies from Aix-en-Provence were one kilometre soon after stepping off and had extended to three kilometres in thirty kilometres. These rebels have the same negligible campaign experience and have ninety kilometres to travel.'

'Indeed, sir. They ought to be caught at the Durance.'

'More local wisdom, no doubt. Do tell?'

'The Durance River, sir, flows west from the Alps and enters the Rhône just south of Avignon. A bridge at that point has been a natural defensive location since the Greeks advanced north from their Marseille landing sites over two thousand years ago.'

'But will our commanders have a force assembled to take ad-vantage of such a position? ... Back to my messages ... 8th Company. Your primary task is to maintain contact with the head of the enemy's column. Enemy may advance on multiple routes to Avignon, east of the Rhône. Be prepared to cover all routes east of the Rhône towards Avignon. Inform Colonel Morin immediately of rebel movement north. Liaise with 1st Squadron currently screening south of Avignon.'

Jobert paused to allow Huin to finish.

'I will need to inform Geourdai of what we are doing. So, ... 2nd Company will observe rebel departure from Marseille, screen any movement toward Aix-en-Provence and screen the rear and east flank of the rebel column. Could you read back what we have so far?'

Huin re-read the message.

'Yes, send that message now. Then take a message for Neilage.'

'Yes, sir,' said Huin. 'Sergeant Yinot, I have an immediate message for 8th Company.'

'For Neilage, ... Second-in-command. Five o'clock, Marseille east gate. Enemy. Two thousand rebels departing Marseille, north for Avignon. At this moment, no rebel movement eastward to Aubagne. Abandon current defence of village bridge. Bring Sergeant Major and ready-to-march platoon to company commander's location. Be prepared for 2nd Company to screen enemy column east flank for four to five days to Avignon. Be prepared to be without company trains for two days.

'Task Voreille with escorting the trains with final platoon to Aix-en-Provence via Aubagne. Collect all company wounded in Aubagne. Inform the chief of battalion in Aubagne and the National Guard commandant in Aix-en-Provence of the situation. Would you read that back?'

Huin re-read the message.

'Very good, Huin,' said Jobert. 'Now, tell your men to save the food they have and fill their water gourds. It is going to be a long day.'

The Marseille Federalist commanding general stood with his back to the tall barricade of overturned wagons, rubble-filled barrels and heavy timber beams, which reinforced the southern gate of Avignon. On his right, the evening sky was a dull violet as the twilight faded in a cloudless sky.

The general's gaze moved from the near-black line of enemy chasseurs à cheval to the three hundred of his 'rebel' fusiliers, in three packed ranks, preparing to fire their last volley as rear guard then run for the barricade. Around the final fire line, the previous three hundred were ordered to break and, leaving dead and wounded behind, they now raced past their commander at the barricades, desperate for the safety of Avignon.

The general reflected that he had achieved his mission. His Marseille 'rebels' had advanced four days to reinforce Avignon. Those four days were a challenge for his two thousand inexperienced troops; blistering July days, enshrouded in the chalky dust of the Rhône valley roads, water scarce despite the proximity of the river.

The price of achieving his first objective, Avignon, was twenty percent of his force dead, severely wounded or prisoner and twenty percent marching with minor wounds. The cause of those losses was over eighty hours of near continual enemy action.

His men referred to the Republican chasseurs à cheval that shadowed his force, every hour of every day since departing Marseille's gates, as 'the vipers' and 'the wolves'. His advance guard spoke of the 'vipers' to the front of his advance, striking out from under every rock and tuft of grass. The rear guard referred to the omnipresent 'wolves', to the rear and flanks of his column, killing swiftly should anyone lower their guard.

The commander was not surprised. His force had no light cavalry of its own to keep these Republican chasseurs at bay. As horsemen, the enemy were simply faster. They protected nothing, so could come, kill and go at will. The enemy knew the ground in front of his advance, so time and again, prepared sound ambush positions that were difficult to counter-attack. But, he reflected, without artillery the Republican light cavalry were never going to stop his advance.

Although equipped with the shorter-barrelled, thus short-range, cavalry musketoon, the enemy used captured muskets and even long-range rifles, in volley-fire to deadly effect. The volleys, by day or by night, were focused, so the kills were concentrated. Any movement after such a violent attack provoked a second volley, usually from a concealed, unexpected quarter. Then, the dismounted horsemen would be re-absorbed into the shadows of the scrubby hills. Their impact created more fear in his ranks than dead.

Every moment of the march was a struggle. Attempting to collect water at the river's edge required harrowing assaults into well concealed ambushes. The three nights during the march were sleepless, as hour upon hour, volleys hit their mark. Any attempt to ambush the Republicans at night resulted in a counter-ambush as his troops eventually withdrew.

Pushing out skirmishers created further casualties and losses of muskets and ammunition, as the chasseurs were better skirmishers. Since the third day, not one of his soldiers would skirmish too far beyond their own front rank for fear of bringing the focus of accurate rifle fire upon themselves.

His junior leaders removed their feathers from their hats and avoided waving their swords and calling out orders or encouragement to minimise a marksman's ball tearing their chests open. Standards would only be borne aloft in the third rank, not the front rank, to avoid the inevitable bloodshed that came with that duty.

Only at one point could the men from Marseille claim battlefield success.

This morning, a large group of local National Guardsmen blocked the rebels' advance at the bridges across the Durance River. The commander recognised fear, the fear of having to spend one more night stalked by the merciless cavalry, as the impetus that drove his men to crush the opposing Republican Guardsmen and force the crossing of the Durance bridges. The general was grimly thankful that the Republicans had not assembled a larger force at the Durance this morning.

Even now, the general soured, two hundred metres from the safety of the Avignon, it took a fire line of three hundred fusiliers to keep the two hundred wolves and vipers at bay. Cavalry snipers, out of musket range at over two hundred metres, firing dismounted, rifles cradled across their saddles, maintained a slow rhythm of fire and could not fail to hit someone within the one-hundred-metre-long target of the fire line.

The rebel fusiliers cringed as the dead and wounded fell within the fire line. Those same fusiliers in the line, seeing the dead and wounded from the previous abandoned line, screamed at their retreating mates to run faster for the barricade.

There, forever just beyond range of the fire line, the Republican chasseurs edged their battle line forward, sabres in hand, poised for any slip in concentration.

Jobert squirmed in his saddle. *Fucking lawyer! This arsehole needs his throat opened.*

As the Federalist rebels disappeared within the barricades of Avignon and violet twilight darkened to purple night, the Deputy of the People arrived in a blaze of theatrical glory. Waist and chest wrapped in tricolour sashes, long, fluffy tricoloured feathers bobbing from his over-sized bicorne, accompanied by Colonel Morin and Major Avriol and surrounded by a torch-bearing guard from the regiment.

Jobert's men and horses were exhausted, filthy, parched with thirst and one hour from dismounting in barracks. Weary horses urinated where they stood, creating an all-pervading stench within the two ranks of the squadron. Some horses, keen to roll in the dust, or simply lie down to rest, were kicked and slapped to remain standing.

We do not need our patriotism inspired at this particular moment.

Yet the Deputy maintained his harangue, praising their supposed 'victory' over the rebels. The man, Saliceti, was slightly older than Jobert, thick black-brown hair framed a thin face and a sharp nose. Saliceti raved that all nobles were traitors and encouraged the men to denounce their officers. He cited the city of Lyon recently declaring separation from the Republic and yet another defeat in the Vendée, where the Republican prisoners were slaughtered by the Vendéens.

Jobert doubted any of his chasseurs, coated in four days of chalk dust, aching from a long day in the saddle, desperate for water and one hour from barracks and the many hours of chores before bed, had the energy to implicate their officers as traitors to the Republic.

When the Deputy's diatribe turned to describing non-commissioned officers as tyrants should they attempt to enforce drill, Koschak emitted a grunt from the rear rank to deter Pultiere from drawing his sabre. The ideal non-commissioned officer should be elected, lectured Saliceti, not educated, to maintain the patriotic fervour of the troops. Bredieux and Yinot exchanged a shake of their heads in the flickering torch light.

To his credit, the Colonel reminded the numb chasseurs how the chief of squadron and the two company commanders had all risen from the ranks. Saliceti took that lead to extoll the warrior virtues of Avriol, as chief of squadron, in leading 2nd and 8th Company in the relentless hunt of the fugitive rebels to their temporary lair in Avignon. This sparked murmurs amongst the men, indignant that some non-cavalry dandy would confuse the obvious difference between a major with the appointment of chief of squadron and a senior captain with the appointment of squadron commander.

Saliceti droned on how General Carteux's brigade would soon sweep down from Valence and cleanse Avignon and Marseille of anti-government filth. Pultiere issued a few dry comments on the usefulness of that force at the Durance River this morning, as opposed to remaining the last two weeks in Valence. Koschak rumbled him to silence.

The monologue closed with encouragement for any man to approach the Deputy, at any time, so that he might listen to any concern they have. Jobert was beyond care, concentrating on the long list of tasks that the company must complete before collapsing on their mattresses of straw many hours hence.

Bone-dry throats were encouraged to scream 'Long live the Republic' into the warm night air, over and over, until Saliceti rode amongst the puddles of horse piss and putrid men, waving his arms to orchestrate an impromptu *La Marseillaise* ...

Arise, children of the fatherland,
The day of glory has arrived ...

Chapter Sixteen

August–September 1793, Avignon, France

At a regimental lunch in late July, Colonel Morin addressed Jobert and the regimental officers.

'Gentlemen, Avignon is now back within the Republic. The 24th Chasseurs are to Marseille. The second-in-command will provide the details in a moment.

'Other news from Paris. Of concern, the fortress of Valenciennes, under siege for four months, has finally fallen to the British and Austrians, opening the route to Paris. As a result, Robespierre, that most ... energetic Jacobin gentleman, has been elected to the Committee of Public Safety.

'Of immediate issue to us here in the regiment, two infantry officers with the 31st Ligne have been denounced to the People's Deputies. I am told that it is common in such matters that the officers are denied any defence and the judgement is either death or imprisonment. Such denouncements are driven by activities of undercover agents within the ranks of the regiment, disgruntled men hoping to gain from the Jacobin opportunity. To that end, at some cost, I have arranged Certificates of Citizenship from the authorities in Paris for all our officers.

'As you are aware, last evening, I asked the sergeants of the regiment, none of them old Royal army, led by dependable rogues such as Bredieux and Pultiere, to hold elections amongst the men to determine if there are any officers to be denounced. I prompted this action to see if any undercover agendas might be revealed. Although there were some interesting nominations, from some predictable, disgruntled quarters, I am pleased to announce, the regiment's sergeants, corporals and troopers did not vote to have any officer denounced.

'Are there any questions? No? Then, may I have your attention for the details of the regiment's march to recapture Marseille.'

'Ah, Bonaparte,' said Raive to the captain of artillery, as Jobert joined them, 'have you met Jobert who commands our 2nd Company?'

'Yes, indeed, I have had the pleasure,' said Bonaparte with a brief bow. 'Good to see you again, sir.'

'The pleasure is mine, sir,' said Jobert. 'Travelling again, I see.'

'Yes,' the sharp-faced, young captain smiled. 'With Marseille falling back into our hands this week, I have been discharged from General Carteux's staff. I am now on my way to your barracks in Avignon to collect my powder convoy and your 3rd Squadron.' Bonaparte swished a document to emphasise his mission.

The two chasseur officers watched the captain's brisk stride towards his waiting horse.

'Sharp fellow, that Bonaparte,' said Raive. 'Have you read his pamphlet that he wrote during Carteux's tedious recapture of Avignon?'

'*The Supper at Beaucaire*? Yes, I have. He makes simple, but powerful, point.'

'Did you also know his close friend and ours, citizen-Deputy Saliceti, passed it to Robespierre's brother, no less. Who in turn passed Bonaparte's essay to the Dictator himself. Bonaparte is another clever young man on the make.'

A carafe of straw-yellow wine arrived at their table.

'Shall we toast the return of Marseille firmly back within the Republic?' asked Raive.

'Why not, sir? I would expect the recapture of Marseilles ought to be well received in Paris.'

'Especially if the news is delivered by our friend Saliceti. Yet Paris' viewpoint will remain grim. You will have heard of our recent, embarrassing defeat near Lille, no? In essence, three battalions of British Guards basically cuffed twelve battalions of our boy-soldiers around the ears, our lads were so ridiculously easy to defeat. The British now have Dunkerque under siege.'

Jobert drained his wine glass in a gulp.

'With the rebels in Lyon now under bombardment,' Raive continued, 'Carnot, another fierce Jacobin as we know, has been elected to the Committee of Public Safety, as the Minister of War. Carnot has barely sat at his desk when he has declared yet another levee-en-masse.'

'If the fortress Valenciennes fell one month ago,' asked Jobert, 'and the road to Paris declared open to the allies, why has Paris not been attacked? With this constant news of French defeats, why have the allies not destroyed the Republic?'

'Because the Republic is blessed with fools for enemies. Each of our enemies is ruled by a single tyrant, who is advised by men of noble houses, each nobleman in turn most keen to replace the current despot with themselves. Our enemies are incapable of a clear national approach. Multiply that inbred selfishness across the sovereigns that oppose the Republic and the allies are incapable of working together. Their incompetence assists France following each of our defeats. No, the advance from Valenciennes now waits for the British to secure the Channel ports, hence the siege of Dunkerque.'

Jobert's head jerked at movement in the crowd. 'Sir, it appears Captain Chabenac seeks you out.'

Chabenac's grim face was flushed. Raive opened the slip of paper handed to him, his merriment evaporating as he scanned the note.

'It appears Royalists in Toulon have invited the British and Spanish fleets to secure the port. It appears Fergnes' 1st Squadron is in contact with Spanish troops. The Colonel has just received orders from General Carteux to screen Toulon. Local rebels are one thing, gentlemen, but British and Spanish regulars are another. Jobert, have 2nd Squadron ready to march to Toulon within the hour.'

'Gentlemen,' said Colonel Morin to Jobert and the assembled officers, 'having just returned from General Carteux's headquarters, I can provide further information as to the situation developing around Toulon. I direct your attention to the chart before us. We are here, on the western edge of this chart, on the Aubagne-Toulon road, at the northern head of the Ollioules defile. Toulon is in the centre of the chart. Mount Faron dominates the landscape to the north of Toulon, as does the Inner Harbour to the south-west.

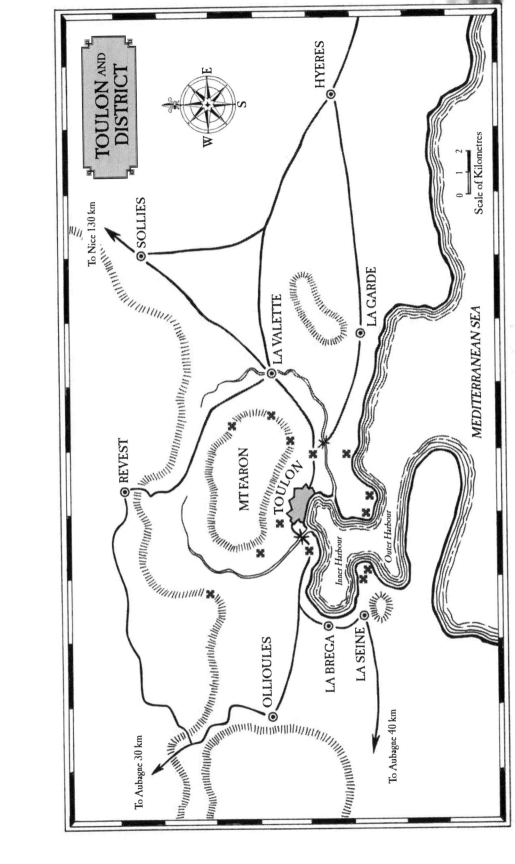

TOULON AND DISTRICT

Scale of Kilometres
0 1 2

To Nice 130 km

SOLLIES

REVEST

LA VALETTE

MT FARON

TOULON

OLLIOULES

LA BREGA

LA SEINE

Inner Harbour

Outer Harbour

To Aubagne 30 km

To Aubagne 40 km

LA GARDE

HYERES

MEDITERRANEAN SEA

'Some comments on our enemy. On the 27th of August, Federalist and Royalist factions, having overthrown the port's government and National Guard, invited a combined British and Spanish fleet into Toulon. The enemy fleet is currently about twelve ships-of-the-line. That fleet has discharged a force of about four thousand men. One battalion of British infantry is now holding the city and a Spanish brigade, of approximately four infantry battalions, secures the outer fortresses. A combined British and Spanish force, supported by foot artillery, has reinforced the rebel militia and currently holds the head of the Ollioules defile.

'I now wish to highlight the seriousness of the situation. It is understood that the British and Spanish have captured sixty French vessels in the port, or one-third of the Republic's navy. Consider the significance of this act. For eighteen months, our foreign enemies have consistently failed to link with Royalist forces in the Vendée and have no Royalist support in Belgium or on the Rhine. Here, for the first time, the Royalists and Federalists fight side-by-side with foreign enemies, what is more, from a major supply centre. In the same stroke, France has lost one-third of her naval power. A most serious situation, gentlemen.

'Our operations are not solely dependent on General Carteux's forces here on the western side of the port. It is anticipated forces detached from the Army of Italy will approach Toulon from the east, through the towns of Sollies and Hyeres, here on the chart. Knowing the distance to Nice, for a courier to get a message there and for an infantry force to immediately depart, I cannot see that force arriving before the 4th of September.

'General Carteux has accepted our proposal to widen the 24th Chasseur's screen around Toulon. Yet the regiment is spread thin. 5th Squadron still maintains our regimental barracks in Avignon. 4th Squadron continues with escort duties from Avignon north to the Army of the Alps' siege at Lyon. 3rd Squadron is escorting the artillery powder convoy to Nice. That leaves Fergnes' 1st Squadron and Jobert's 2nd Squadron to operate around Toulon.

'Captain Fergnes, your 1st Company will operate west of Toulon and the Inner Harbour to observe enemy movement on the Ollioules-Toulon road. 7th Company will maintain escort duties from here back west to Marseille.

'Captain Jobert, your 2nd Company will operate east of Toulon. From there, the company will observe the enemy-held fortresses south-west of La Valette. 2nd Company is also to support the advance of forces from the Army of Italy approaching from Nice. Major Avriol, who will travel with you, has been tasked with placing himself at the disposal of the commander approaching from Nice, as General Carteux's liaison officer.

'Captain Geourdai, your 8th Company shall remain with me, in reserve, at the head of the Ollioules defile. Gentlemen, take a moment to consider in greater depth your options, before briefing me as to your intentions.'

Avriol and the four company commanders from 1st and 2nd Squadrons gathered around the chart to discuss their courses of action. Raive moved between the two groups adding aspects of logistics that could be provided by the regiment. After an hour of discussion, Fergnes presented his plan operating west of Toulon, then Jobert presented the 2nd Company plan to conduct reconnaissance east of Toulon.

'Sir,' said Jobert, pointing to the chart with his small dagger, 'once on the valley floor beyond Revest, 2nd Company shall continue the advance to La Valette. From La Valette, three platoon patrols will set out.

'First, Major Avriol and Lieutenant Voreille will move with one platoon to observe Toulon's eastern fortresses, south-west of La Valette.

'Second, I will advance towards Hyeres, with two platoons

and the train, crossing the high country north of La Garde. Unsure if local paths are capable of supporting wagon traffic, the company column will include a train of twelve pack horses. I will leave a platoon and the train to establish camp in the high-country east of the fortresses, whilst I proceed to Hyeres with the other platoon.

'Finally, Lieutenants Neilage and Huin will move to identify enemy between La Valette and Sollies, with the remaining platoon. I foresee a further two or three days of observing the enemy before the anticipated arrival of forces from Nice. With your permission, sir, Captain Chabenac might accompany us. He shall return to you tomorrow evening with the results of our initial reconnaissance. I shall also send word Major Avriol is in contact with the detachment from the Army of Italy.'

Morin looked up from the chart to appraise Jobert. 'I approve your scheme, Jobert. Good luck.'

The narrow Revest-La Valette road wound down towards the floor of a tight valley which encircled the northern slopes of Mount Faron. As the first dull pink and grey clouds over the distant Alps heralded dawn, Pultiere and a vedette of four troopers led the company along the stony track through the brittle, twisted scrub. The near-vertical northern flanks of Mount Faron rose on 2nd Company's right. Further back from the lead patrol, Jobert, Avriol, Chabenac and Moench rode with the remainder of Pultiere's advance guard platoon.

'Sir, riders,' said Moench.

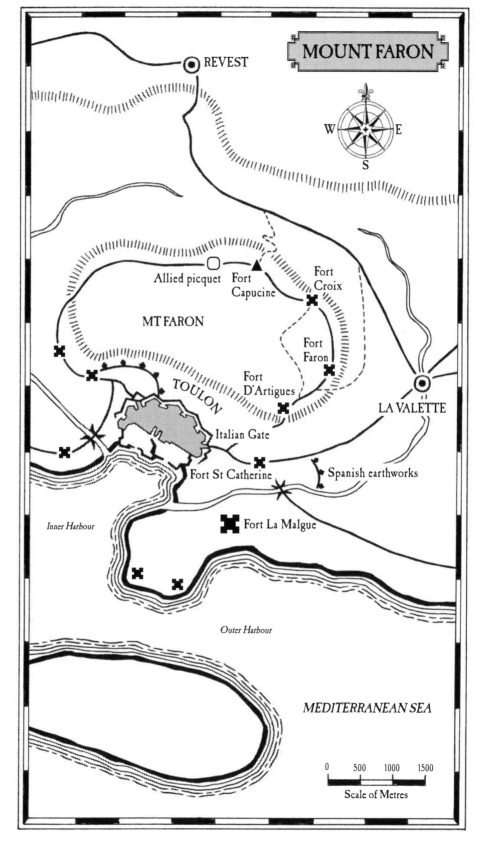

Jobert turned and saw Koschak approaching at a fast trot, his right hand holding his musketoon and his reins. In his left hand he carried a tin cookpot. Following the Sergeant Major was a chasseur who had a threadbare peasant boy clinging to his back behind the saddle. The child wore the soldier's crested leather helmet.

'Breakfast, gentlemen?' asked Koschak. 'Fresh goats' milk.'

Avriol removed the lid and drank before passing the hot, creamy milk to Jobert.

Childhood memories raced through Jobert's mind as he drank. Barefoot children milking cattle and goats, the heat of the animals' great bodies and the sweet, cut-grass odour from their steaming dung in contrast to the icy cobblestone floors of his grandfather's mountain stables.

'I have just had an interesting conversation with a goat herder,' said Koschak. 'An elderly chap from Revest, Quandalle is his name, with two dozen goats was trying to hide in the scrub as we passed. He and his grandson here,' Koschak indicated the child of about ten, 'were coming down off Mount Faron and returning to Revest. I have promised to purchase all his goats' fetta, as he does not want to sell it to the Spanish. In return I have borrowed his grandson as a guide to La Valette.'

Jobert passed the milk urn to Chabenac and wiped his chin with the back of his gloved fist. 'So, there are trails up onto Mount Faron from the northern —'

A cannon fired in the clear morning air caused roosting birds to erupt in noisy flocks. Unsure of the source of the fire through the scrub everyone looked around. The three veterans, Avriol, Jobert and Koschak, tightened reins and froze waiting for the fall and bounce of the plunging shot.

'Sir, up on the hill.' Koschak's chasseur pointed, translating Provencal from the agitated child.

Three consecutive blasts were fired. Jobert searched the

slopes for the fort but only a wisp of gun smoke could be seen, the dissipating cloud wafting over the crest on the morning's warming air.

'Huh! No ball. Fort Croix is signalling,' said Avriol, consulting a sketched chart of Toulon's defences. 'We must assume they have seen our column's dust.'

As the column continued its march to La Valette, the scrub thinned and became olive groves heavy with ripening fruit. Pultiere and his leading chasseurs disturbed a small herd of goats. Filthy children tending the bleating stock emerged from the scrawny bushes, animated when they saw one of their own riding in the column. They jabbered at their friend crowned with a chasseur's helmet.

'Sir, there are Spanish in the town and militia just over the rise,' said the young chasseur, translating the children's squeals.

Two muskets fired from beyond the crest, accompanied by short, flat 'barps' from a hunting horn. Jobert, Avriol and Chabenac leapt to the canter, scattering children and goats, to join Pultiere's vedette.

Eight hundred metres away La Valette appeared dull within shadowy groves and low-lying smoke from morning kitchen fires. Six armed civilians sprinted down the road toward the town. Within the town, drums beat *To Arms*. Through their telescopes, Jobert and Avriol watched Spanish grenadiers, wearing white jackets and cross belts, tall, slim, mitre-shaped caps and above-the-knee gaiters, forming in a three-rank fire line, amongst the outer stone walls and fruit orchards of the town.

Jobert closed his watch. Seven o'clock. 'Moench, sound *Commanders In*.'

'May I ask your intent?' asked Avriol, without taking his eye from his telescope.

'Only to pay our compliments, sir.'

Jobert, Avriol and Chabenac trotted forward, with snipers Duval and Tulloc and their two 'seconds', until they were over two hundred metres from the Spanish line. Obeying the trumpet call, Neilage, Voreille and Koschak reined in beside Jobert and the young officers drew out their telescopes from their pistol holsters.

Jobert passed his telescope to Koschak. 'Spanish infantry, gentlemen. Observe the enemy forming a company fire line, thirty men wide, three men deep. The tall, fur caps indicating a grenadier company, the best of their battalion. The battalion headquarters may well be in the town. The company was alerted by a rebel patrol with musket fire and horn blasts. Note how platoons are marching from other sections of the town to reinforce the line. There is good reason to assume Spanish fusilier companies may be holding posts in Sollies and Hyeres. With your permission, sir, I intend to threaten to charge the fire line to observe how the Spanish react.'

Huin arrived in a flurry of white dust from his post with the northern flank guard.

'Lieutenant Huin,' said Jobert, 'call in your guards and form troop line. Moench, sound *Form Line*. Lieutenant Voreille, bring up Bredieux's platoon. Form platoon line with the intent of flanking the Spanish line from that field of wheat stubble to our left.' Jobert noted Voreille's wide-eyes and slack jaw. 'Neilage, accompany Voreille. Questions, gentlemen? No? Then to your posts.'

'Here is an opportunity to observe your marksmen in action,' said Avriol, 'I see no standards but there is a company pennant on the end of their line. Snipers, dismount, ready. Duval, Tulloc, present. Drop the mounted officer, then the pennant bearer. Do you have the range?'

Duval and Tulloc took aim with their rifles supported across their saddles. Both rifles fired.

The Spanish officer was punched out of the saddle. His men could be seen rushing to support him. Duval's and Tulloc's 'seconds', chasseurs who had been christened 'snipers' mates', passed their marksmen their loaded, second rifles, then raced to load the first rifle.

The rifles fired again. The Spanish pennant bearer and a grenadier beside him jerked back as the balls struck home.

'Duval,' said Avriol, 'see the junior officer with his sword drawn, red sash, white feathers in his hat? Drop him.'

Duval's rifle fired.

'Tulloc, drop any man who picks up the pennant.'

Tulloc's rifle fired.

Huin's troop trotted down the slope to form a battle line fifty metres behind Jobert.

'Skirmishers!' called Chabenac over the shrill notes of the trumpet call. Chabenac pointed to about fifteen Spaniards darting and weaving one hundred metres forward of their line, to take up sharpshooting positions to bring Avriol's and Jobert's group under fire.

'Advance parties, fall in,' said Jobert to Avriol, Chabenac and the marksmen, then drawing his sabre, turned to Huin's troop of nearly fifty men in two ranks, '2nd Company, ready, present high.' The chasseurs aimed their musketoons at a forty-five-degree angle from their shoulders. 'Royal Salute to His Hispanic Majesty, fire!'

Fired at forty-five degrees, the fifty-odd musketoon balls barely made two hundred metres, enough to fell one or two skirmishers, but the fire was sufficient to send the others to ground.

'Company, sabres!'

The Spanish skirmishers seeing the preparation to charge, raced head-long back to the safety of the fire line. The Spanish drummers beat out an order, as grenadier non-commissioned officers moved among their soldiers bellowing out instructions, as they prepared to receive cavalry.

'Aha! We have their measure. Due to the groves and walls around them,' said Avriol, 'they feel comfortable not to form square to repel us.'

'Moench, sound *To Mess.*'

The chasseurs roared with laughter as the trumpeter played the unexpected meal-time call. The galling laughter was heard by the solid line of Spaniards. The introduction of 2nd Company to the invaders complete, the company prepared to march around La Valette to separate into the three platoon patrols.

'2nd Company, form column of fours, left turn, walk, march! Sergeant Major, trains in.'

Chapter Seventeen

Three blasts caused great puffs of white smoke to billow out from the gun embrasures.

As Fort La Malgue fired her 'salute', Avriol and Voreille observed through their telescopes the towers and spires of Toulon, lit by the early morning sun. Being only six hundred metres distant from newly raised enemy earthworks, half-section vedettes were set around the dismounted officers.

'If we take our observation from the left, or south,' said Avriol, connecting his sketch map, held by Voreille, to the ground in front of them, 'we can see the imposing bulk of Fort La Malgue on the slight knoll. Our observations confirm our assumption that the fort has fields of fire south across the Outer Harbour and east along the shoreline approaches to the port and north-east across the stream to cover the flank of Fort Sainte-Catherine. Note the British flag flying from the fort. Moving our view to the right, or north, we see a stream. It appears from the white jackets, that the Spanish are developing the earthen breastworks.

'Sir, is that the Spanish colours by the group of wagons right of centre?'

'Well observed. Moving right again, we observe Fort Sainte-Catherine, north of Fort La Malgue, covering the approaches from La Valette, the northern flank of La Malgue and the breastworks and the lower slopes of Fort D'Artigues. Again, Spanish colours hoisted on Sainte-Catherine.

'Halfway up the slopes of Mount Faron, Fort D'Artigues, providing flank fire in support of Sainte-Catherine to the south and the lower slopes of Fort Faron and fire across the approach from La Valette. Again, Spanish colours hoisted. Higher still, Fort Faron covering Fort D'Artigues and La Valette. Out of view from us here, Fort Croix on the north-east crest of the mountain, who saluted us earlier this morning.'

Avriol took a swig from his Prussian water canteen.

'Voreille, let me share with you a thought. We see that the British hold Fort La Malgue and the Spanish the breastworks and Fort Sainte-Catherine. Not only two distinct units, but two distinct national forces, language difficulties, ripe for exploitation along their boundary. Do you see the boundary that exists between them?'

'Yes, sir. The stream.'

'Quite so. Wooded, low ground. A defined boundary for the defenders. A clear route for infiltration by ourselves, their enemies. I would assume it well patrolled by both parties, thus removing the threat of exploitation.'

Voreille became confused at Avriol's initial offering of leverage over the enemy only to withdraw it.

'If any future situation required it, I propose a reconnaissance adventure, disguised as a lost Spanish patrol, moving between the walls of La Malgue and the stream, in the area patrolled by the British.'

'What would occur if the lost Spanish patrol met with a

British patrol?' asked Voreille.

'I foresee their officers conversing in the language our enemies have in common.'

'That being French, sir.'

'Madame Duhamel, gentlemen.' The attractive brunette, in her late thirties, bobbed her head. 'Wife of Commodore Duhamel. My husband is out with his squadron defending the Republic's interests. How might I assist you?'

A slow smile created a dimple in one cheek, as Madame Duhamel appraised Jobert and Chabenac, a raised eyebrow indicating that she liked what she saw. A glare flickered across Jobert's face towards a smiling Moench.

'Madame, as you would be aware the enemies of France have taken the port. The Republic has armies converging on the invasion as we speak, from Marseilles and Nice. I am conducting a reconnaissance of the area. My generals require your farm as temporary base camp.'

Madame raised her hand to her throat, glancing at an elderly maid standing just behind her. 'What shall become of my staff and I, Captain?'

'My company will occupy your barns and fields, madame, neither your home nor your servants' quarters, I assure you. My patrol must depart. I shall leave Sergeant Major Koschak and over twenty men to set the camp, but I shall return here this evening. Captain Chabenac and I shall be accompanied by my chief of squadron and three company officers.'

Madame's green eyes lingered on Koschak's thick chest and

deep neck, before indicating, with a theatrical flourish her tall, stone farmhouse. 'I shall prepare a supper for you. Six cavalrymen to dinner is not a burden at all. I shall look forward to it, Captain. As a naval wife I understand that supper shall be served whenever your labours for the day are complete. Perhaps we can discuss the details over tea?'

'Thank you, madame, but my business awaits. Perhaps Captain Chabenac might attend your welcome hospitality?'

Madame Duhamel's small tongue darted to her upper lip as she took in Chabenac's blond curls and steady blue eyes. 'I would very much appreciate the company. I hear so little of the news in the wider world. Before you go …,'

She took a few quick steps forward saying something in Provencal. The child sitting behind the chasseur responded. Jobert twisted in the saddle to get a sense of the exchange.

'The lady asked is the boy in any harm, sir,' said the chasseur doubling the boy on his remount. 'The boy said he was fine and that we are heading to Hyeres.'

'Captain Jobert,' said Madame Duhamel, 'there are no Royalists in Hyeres. A company of Royalist militia passed through our manor yesterday on their way to Hyeres. The fools spoke of securing the approaches to Nice. But the National Guard in Hyeres informed them that they were not welcome. The company returned to Toulon yesterday evening.'

'No British or Spanish regulars with them, madame.'

'Not with this attempt, sir.'

'How far is it to Hyeres?

'Two hours.'

'I am obliged, madame.'

'Oh, I am very much at your service, sir.' Madame Duhamel curtsied and with her maid, returned to the house.

Jobert exchanged looks of surprise with Chabenac and Koschak.

'And you take that smirk off your face, Chasseur Moench,' said Koschak, 'or I will kick you so hard you will be wearing your arsehole for a hat.'

Two musket shots rang out, four hundred metres away, further north along the road from La Valette to Sollies. Huin and his three flankers appeared from the orange grove to join Neilage on the road.

Pultiere pointed at Corporal Duflot and his three chasseurs two hundred metres further north along the road, on the lip of a small rise. 'The advance guard are signalling "infantry", sir.'

Muskets fired at a much closer range. Neilage and Huin looked down the road to see the advance guard return fire from the saddle.

Neilage drew his sabre. 'Stand fast, Sergeant Pultiere, await my signal to follow. Huin, on me.' He wheeled his broad-chested mare into a canter, lengthening her stride towards the leading chasseurs.

With Huin's horse thundering behind him, Neilage was astounded to watch Duflot draw his sabre and gallop further down the road towards Sollies. Two of the men followed their corporal, pressing their horses to the faster gait, without drawing their sabres. The third chasseur, remembering his drills of drawing his sabre before moving faster than a walk, followed at the gallop soon after.

'Duflot, stand fast! On me! On me!' cried Neilage.

As he crested the rise, Neilage could see the four chasseurs charging down on two white-clad Spanish infantrymen. Duflot scorching ahead, the next two, tugging on reins to slow their horses and scrabbling to find their bouncing, undrawn sabres, with the final chasseur twisting in the saddle to look back at Neilage.

Only two hundred metres in front of them, were two white-coated Spanish fusiliers, with their characteristic knee-high gaiters and their black bicornes. One Spaniard sprawled in the road and the other assisted him to stand. The mounted men bore down on them swiftly.

The Spaniard on his feet, seeing the closing horsemen, dropped his mate and his bicorne hat and ran away at full tilt towards Sollies. The remaining fellow sprawled in the dust, scrabbled in panic and pulled himself to the shallow gutter at the side of the road. Then, without panic, came up on one knee, musket into his shoulder and aimed at Duflot.

The Spanish ambush was sprung on the six French horsemen at less than thirty metres. At least ten Spanish line infantry rose from shrubs, tree trunks and walls and fired as one volley. With each musket ball impacting on the body like the blow from a powerful man wielding a sledgehammer at full-force, French men and horses crashed to the ground.

Duflot's throat received a musket ball which ripped out his neck vertebrae, flicking his skull back. He never knew his horse took a ball through the knee, missed its step, hit the road at full-stride with its chest and snapped its neck, only to crush Duflot's limp corpse as it rolled.

Millone, the chasseur behind Duflot, slammed painfully forward into his saddle bow, as three balls thudded into the face and chest of his horse. The horse's head disappeared somewhere beneath its knees, then somersaulted on the unyielding gravel road. Chasseur Millone screamed as bones in his shoulder and upper arm snapped as he smashed into the road. Rolling clear, despite having broken the same arm three months ago at the charge at Aix-en-Provence, Millone bellowed through the excruciating pain to scurry forward on hand and knees towards the Spanish fire line, knowing his cartwheeling horse's hindquarters were still somewhere above his head. As the horse's body crashed to rest, Millone, overwhelmed with pain, vomited into the dust.

The third chasseur was hit simultaneously with two balls, one ball ripping though his lungs and a second through his liver. As the chasseur's body was punched out of the saddle by the force of the balls, he ripped on the reins. His horse, its head tugged to one side, ceased its galloping stride and slid on its hindquarters to a halt, alarmed as the rider thudded into the gravel beside it. Seeing the ungainly outlines of the two other dead horses, the horse wheeled away, tugging reins from dying fingers, seeking the horses approaching from behind, leaving his chasseur face down in a widening pool of bright-red bubbles.

The fourth chasseur, hearing Neilage screaming at him from behind and the Spanish fire line disappear in a wall of white smoke, tried to shut down his bolting remount. His horse was side-on to the Spanish fusiliers, when balls thudded home, one ball striking the arm of his spur, shattering his ankle, but not entering the foot and another ball tearing into his horse's chest for a perfect heart shot. The horse folded to the ground. The chasseur, jerked from the saddle, bent double with pain, sat astride the ribs of his groaning horse, looked up through his tears to see Neilage swirling above him.

Huin kicked his feet clear of his stirrups, leapt from the saddle of his sliding horse. As he reached for the wounded soldier, he was wrenched backwards. His terrified horse would not take another step towards the awkward thrashing and grunting of the dying horse.

The road was silent. Huin was having difficulty calming his

horse to remount.

'They are reloading! Quickly!' called Neilage.

His little chestnut mare pivoted over her hocks and sprang to the dazed soldier astride the wheezing carcass. Neilage dropped his sabre, allowing it to swing on its sword knot on his wrist, leant out of the saddle, thrust his hand through the chasseur's cross-belt and grabbed the bow-straps across the front of his saddle.

'Hold on! For fuck sake, hold onto me! Huin, let go of your horse, we will follow him home. Huin, grab my stirrup. Now!' Huin released the reins, his horse turning and bolting back to Pultiere's platoon.

Having lost his right arm securing the soldier to his saddle, Neilage was unable to shorten his reins to guide his horse. Huin stumbled to grab Neilage's left, or nearside, stirrup leather, knocking Neilage's foot clear of the stirrup iron. Punched in the face by Neilage's scabbard, Huin tucked up his knees and managed to throw his arm across Neilage's thigh to dig his fingers into Neilage's portmanteau straps.

Without reins and only one stirrup, Neilage screamed in determination to stay on, as his red mare extended her stride to a gallop and follow Huin's horse and the surviving chasseur's horse in a mad race home.

The second volley from the Spanish ambush exploded.

Neilage bellowed as he was rocked clear of the saddle, as the balls thwacked into his mare's hindquarters. She screamed from the intense pain and leapt forward. Neilage screamed again, as he barely remained seated, his right arm on fire with the weight of the wounded chasseur.

Within moments, clear of Spanish musket range, all three horses descended rapidly to a halt eager to snuffle with their waiting mates in Pultiere's platoon. Huin released his grip and crunched to the ground, sprawling under horses' hooves.

Chasseurs leapt from their mounts to catch the loose horses and help the returned men.

Neilage looked down into the dead eyes of the chasseur he had saved. The man had taken a ball from the fusiliers' second volley through the ribs. Neilage released his aching grip on the bow-straps and the young soldier folded to the dirt at his mare's feet.

Pultiere watched the Spanish move amongst their kills before dismounting. He set his jaw as he watched the Spanish fusiliers dispatch a wounded horse with a pistol and a dying chasseur with a bayonet.

Jeering obscenities at the French, the Spanish lifted Chasseur Millone gripping his broken shoulder and directed him towards Sollies with a musket butt to the kidneys. Millone had been one of 2nd Company's first battle casualties and now had the dubious honour of becoming 2nd Company's first prisoner-of-war.

Whilst Huin unsaddled his friend's horse, Neilage inspected her wounds. One ball had cut the vital femoral artery in the groin on the inside of her nearside hindleg and blood gushed across the mare's teats and abdomen to pool thickly at her hooves. Another ball had smashed her offside hip joint. She held her head low as she kept all her weight off that leg.

Pultiere could see Neilage's trembling eyes flickering in shock.

'Here and now, sir.'

Huin, with a sour face, tugged one of Neilage's pistols clear of its holster under the dusty shabraque. He opened the pistol's frizzen to check there was powder in the pan and withdrew the ramrod and confirmed paper, ball and powder were well tamped. Huin cocked the pistol. 'Here, I will do it.'

Pultiere cast a quick look back to the Spaniards who waited in a loose skirmish line three hundred metres distant. Five hundred metres beyond them, a white column of thirty to fifty Spaniards marched to reinforce the fight.

'Through the temple, sir, aim for the base of the opposite ear.'

Neilage's vision swam with tears. 'No, no, I will.' His teeth clicked as his jaw spasmed.

His knuckles gripped both the reins and the pistol's butt. Neilage searched his mare's face for any option but this. Her black eyes and perked ears focussed on him. She snorted and prodded his belly with her soft muzzle.

Neilage gripped the trigger of his pistol hard.

The last sunlight of the day filtered through the dust and cobwebs into Madame Duhamel's barn. The faint notes of a mournful melody, from Moench's fiddle, drifted in from the yard. Swallows twittered as they fluttered into the eaves to roost.

Reflecting on the report of the ambush near Sollies, Jobert reclined against an empty manger, shifting his eyes slowly from the downcast Neilage and Huin to Pultiere who held his eye. Jobert and Koschak exchanged a sombre look. Avriol checked his watch. Jobert frowned and blinked as he took in that Cha-benac was freshly shaved, his face and hair clean, his boots and uniform brushed. Chabenac supressed a grin at Jobert's review.

'I have prepared an initial report for the Colonel,' said Avriol. 'Chabenac will be on the far side of La Valette by nightfall and back with the regiment in three hours if he leaves now. See to your men, Jobert, before attending madame. Should you and your officers not be able to attend supper, I shall make your apologies to the lady.'

The officers exited the gloomy barn. In the barn yard, on barrels, planks, bales and boxes, sat 2nd Company. A lit brazier blazed in the dusk, illuminating four saddles arranged on barrels in the centre of the silent men. Every face was turned to the display. No-one spoke. Moench picked a homely tune on the strings of his fiddle. Blank eyes showed that every thought was far from this place. Some men sat with arms around each other's shoulders, a few wiped eyes and noses on jacket sleeves.

'Today,' said Jobert, '2nd Company met in combat the well-trained and disciplined infantry of France's enemies. Tonight, we mourn the loss of four brothers. Six months ago, we all formed 2nd Company. Sergeant Major and I watched your hard work in those early months, caring for your horses, mastering the musketoon and the sabre and finding your place in the regiment. Every man, without exception, impressed us.

'Three short months later, we, as 2nd Company, obeyed the orders of France to confront those who would do France harm. As brothers, we stood against men who would strip liberty, equality and fraternity from our families. Between Avignon and Marseille, we buried two brothers, farewelled three due to wounds and have watched many return to us with the scars of battle. We have seen the passing of seven of our beloved horses. Today we met with an enemy of a much higher standard than before. That enemy ripped our four brothers from us and four of our faithful horses.

'As chasseurs à cheval, we shall seek the moment patiently, then we shall strike. As 2nd Company, we shall avenge our brothers.'

Over ninety throats breathed a guttural growl in assent.

Chapter Eighteen

'That, sir, gentlemen, ends the orientation of Toulon's eastern defence.' Avriol projected his voice over the wind to the two dozen officers about him. 'Do you have any questions, sir?'

Standing where Avriol and Voreille had evaluated the Toulon fortresses three days ago, Jobert scanned the near horizon for any undue movement or signals from his chasseurs. With so many senior French officers in close proximity to the breastworks between La Malgue and Sainte-Catherine, 2nd Company was dispersed in an arc of protective vedettes.

'Do we have any questions for Major Avriol as to the fortresses before us?' asked General Lapoype of his assembled brigade commanders and staff, the wind whipping his cape about his legs. 'No? Then I do. What do you make of the enemy, Avriol? A raid to destroy our fleet? Or securing the port to support further operations? Should we strike at them? Or prepare to lay siege?'

Jobert watched People's Deputy Saliceti, tricolour plumes thrashing in the Mediterranean breeze, twist forward to hear

Avriol's response. In the last few days, General Carteux's division remained unable to force its way down onto the coastal plain. Nevertheless, the link between the regiment and 2nd Company had allowed the People's Deputies, to be escorted north of Mount Faron to meet with the infantry division arriving east from Nice.

'Sir, if it is a raid,' said Avriol, 'from a light cavalryman's point of view it is conducted poorly. The enemy have been in location now nine days, lost the element of surprise and have neither destroyed nor removed the fleet they have captured. On the other hand, efforts to strengthen Toulon's defences and reinforce the enemy garrison by sea have been negligible. I suspect, sir, our enemies are bickering most fiercely at the dinner table each evening and inaction prevails.'

Avriol contemplated the reaction of those senior gentlemen around him. The divisional commander from the Army of Italy and his four brigade commanders remained stern, whilst Saliceti smirked.

'Excellent fellow, well said.' Saliceti slapped Avriol on the shoulder. 'I told you, Lapoype, he was good. Avriol here led a regimental raid to secure a Royalist armoury in Valence a few months ago. He was then instrumental in whittling away the recent Marseille Federalist advance on Avignon.'

Avriol bowed to Saliceti's compliments yet drilled a grinning Jobert with an intense glare.

'Remember, citizens, the directive fresh from Paris,' Saliceti continued. 'Make terror the order of the day. Hah! With the execution of hundreds, if not thousands, of the Republic's enemies in Marseille and Avignon recently, I know the fools who hold out in Lyon shit themselves as the walls crumble under our guns. I expect those traitors who allowed the fleets of foreign tyrants into Toulon are anticipating similar swift justice. I am keen to see you launch yourselves at their throats in the coming days.'

The commanders shuffled in their discomfort.

Lapoype turned his back on Fort La Malgue and Saliceti. 'What enemy lies between here and Hyeres, Avriol?'

'None, sir. The enemy expects your advance from Sollies.'

'How is the enemy disposed between Fort Sainte-Catherine and Sollies?'

'Two companies of the second battalion of His Hispanic Majesty's Cordoba Regiment, sir, have been identified so far. A company of fusiliers in Sollies and a company of grenadiers in La Valette. Those outposts have not ventured far from the respective towns' outer wall since my chasseurs arrived three days ago.'

'Gentlemen,' Lapoype addressed his brigade commanders, 'the division shall advance in two columns. One column will secure Hyeres and La Garde. One column shall secure Sollies and La Valette. La Valette shall be ours by tomorrow evening.'

'Excuse me, sir?' asked Avriol. 'May I suggest my company of chasseurs guide your assault forces down the Sollies road?'

'Well done, Avriol.' Saliceti delivered another delighted slap to Avriol's shoulder.

Jobert's scan of his vedettes was interrupted by a cough close by his shoulder.

'How do you do, sir? Cobereau of the 15th Dragoons, at your service.'

Jobert turned to see a major of dragoons in a shabby uniform. The soles of the man's tall boots were peeling off, his green tailcoat was threadbare, missing buttons, patches over the elbows desperately in need of further patching. His white trousers and waistcoat were a deep brown with filth. The mane that ought to flow down from his battered bronze helmet was reduced to scruffy tufts.

'Captain Jobert, 24th Chasseurs, and I at yours, sir.'

'You must forgive my bold approach, sir. The Army of Italy

has had a hard time in securing resupply since the Marseille revolt closed the routes to Nice and the cavalry is the poorest cousin in that Army. I am in desperate need of horseshoes for my squadron. Do you have any to spare, please?'

Jobert winced and sucked his teeth. *Opportunity! We have three full sets of shoes.* 'Sir, my company is only able to shoe the front feet, such is our want of shoes. Perhaps my company farrier might visit you tomorrow and my quartermaster corporal have a quiet look around my regiment for anything spare. How many horses do you have, sir?'

'Two hundred. I too need only shoe the front feet. I would appreciate any kind consideration, Captain Jobert. You will be aware of the new law requiring all farmers to surrender their grain. My squadron's current tasking is to take grain from farmers to feed the division and muster in the division's deserters. I cannot complete my mission without horseshoes. Your farrier will find my bivouac on the eastern side of Hyeres. Forgive me, the commanders are departing and I must go.'

The dragoon major strode away to a knot of thin, scruffy horses and an equally shabby escort.

'Do not stare so, Moench,' said Jobert. 'If this siege continues through the winter, that is what we will look like soon enough. But, my friend, an opportunity to trade on favourable terms has arisen. Return now to the Duhamel manor with a message for Sergeant Major Koschak. Get our company farrier to travel immediately to the dragoons this very afternoon to evaluate their horses. Tell him that the dragoons seek two hundred pairs of shoes. Have Duque sniff out what they have that is worth trading. We need to enter their camp before they hide, eat or drink what they have of value.'

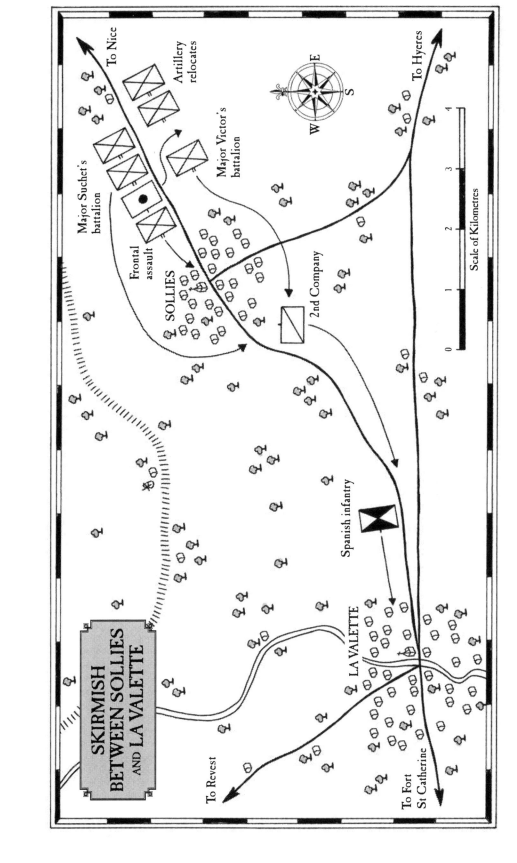

SKIRMISH
BETWEEN SOLLIES
AND LA VALETTE

To Nice

Artillery relocates

Major Suchet's battalion

Major Victor's battalion

Frontal assault

SOLLIES

2nd Company

To Hyeres

Spanish infantry

LA VALETTE

To Revest

To Fort
St Catherine

Scale of Kilometres

0   1   2   3   4

The next day, across the four hundred metres of rye stubble surrounding the outer farmsteads north of Sollies, Jobert searched for movement behind the thick, low stone walls and within the olive groves.

'You are satisfied there is no movement, Jobert?'

Jobert glanced at the white-coated infantry captain who led the regular infantry skirmishers ahead of the blue-coated volunteer battalions.

'Captain de Beaussancourt, if my chasseurs move forward to the treeline, will your skirmish line cross the meadow and clear the walls? If so, from that point the chasseurs will depart on their next task.'

De Beaussancourt gave a surly nod and turned to shake out his company into the two lines of skirmishers, half on either side of the road. The incessant drumming reminded Jobert that the head of the infantry brigade was closing on the heels of his screen.

'Lieutenant Neilage, trot forward to the walls to draw Spanish fire. The infantry skirmishers will follow. Once across, leave the advance to the infantry.' Neilage swallowed hard as he contemplated the silent walls.

One hundred metres behind the leading skirmishers rode a gaggle of senior officers accompanying divisional commander General Lapoype. Jobert squeezed Bleu into a trot towards the approaching, blue-coated infantry column. Moench, Duque leading Rouge and the four chasseurs of the sniper party followed.

'Sir,' said Jobert to General Lapoype, 'the outskirts of Sollies just ahead. The skirmish line is crossing the last open area to deploy the guns before the town. We have not sighted the Spanish, sir.'

'Then the lead battalion need not wait for the guns,' said Lapoype. 'Brigade commander, send your lead battalion into the town immediately.'

Infantry drums thrashed out a new rhythm. Fifty metres behind the command group the battalion deployed for the attack. Over seven hundred fierce-eyed volunteers had marched in road column, six men wide and one hundred and twenty men long. Now those eight companies spread outward, like great wings, sixty men wide on either side of the road and twelve men deep. Seven hundred throats roared *'Vive République!'*. The general and his staff scurried to clear the front of the battalion.

Jobert and his six shadows trotted east on their next task of intercepting the battalion of Major Victor.

Once Lapoype's lead brigade had closed-up to assault Sollies, the follow-on brigade would step off the Sollies road and bypass Sollies to the east. The follow-on brigade's leading battalion, Major Victor's 5th Battalion, Volontaires Bouches-de-Rhône, were guided by Voreille and Pultiere's platoon through the network of farm by-ways. Within four hundred metres of the Sollies road, Jobert found the long line of blue-coats weaving through the groves, led by a knot of officers, with a company of white-coated 'old army' skirmishers, jogging to keep up with the mounted chasseur screen.

Jobert saluted Lapoype's follow-on brigade commander. 'There has been no contact with the Spanish, sir. If they lie within the town, General Lapoype has ordered the lead battalion to assault into the town without artillery support. The battery is now redeploying to your brigade, sir. Further, sir, if the Spanish have evacuated the town, then they may well reinforce La Valette.'

The brigade commander grimaced at Victor. Both men now anticipated a more difficult assault against the Spanish regulars for their objective of La Valette.

'With your permission, sir,' said Jobert, 'may I take a patrol forward to identify the current location of the Spanish?'

'I would be obliged, sir.' The brigade general turned toward Victor.

'Continue to advance your battalion to La Valette without delay.'

Victor gave Jobert a wink, as he spun his horse to attend his battalion. 'Find them, Jobert and block them this side of La Valette. We will be there soon enough. We will eat them in the open.'

Jobert, stepping Bleu off the path, waved to Voreille and Pultiere to join him and checked his pocket watch. Ten o'clock. 'It is highly likely that the Spanish are no longer in Sollies and are on the road south to La Valette. 2nd Company needs to find them. Voreille, continue to guide Major Victor's battalion to the La Valette road with one section. Give me Pultiere and his other section to find the Spanish. As soon as Victor's infantry find the road, press south at best speed to find me.'

Collecting Pultiere and a section of ten chasseurs, Jobert, Moench, Duque and the marksmen party trotted through the silent farmsteads with gates, doors and shutters bolted against the drums' growing intensity. After fifteen minutes, they emerged from the orchards and vines onto the La Valette road south of Sollies.

An open gate at a large farm caught Jobert's eye. He saw that the gate bar was forced. Signalling to halt his small column, Jobert, Moench and Duque rode through the open gate to find themselves enclosed in a fragrant orange and lemon grove. Jobert saw many recent shoe prints in the puddles around the central well and troughs.

'Sir,' called Duque, 'there is a lot of fresh piss against this wall.'

With his suspicions confirmed that the Spanish had stopped here in the last hour, Jobert squeezed Bleu back to the trot, out the gate and the column proceeded down the road.

Jobert heard the Spanish before he saw them.

Fort Faron fired one gun from the sheer slopes four hundred

metres above their heads and one thousand metres from where the Spanish column stood. The iron ball falling from great height struck the field of cut stubble like the single beat of a monstrous bass drum, sending up a cloud of chalk dust and straw. *A ranging shot.*

Three hundred metres distant, the Spanish column was strung out on the road, attempting to identify themselves to the fort above by yelling, beating drums, blowing bugles and waving company pennants.

Jobert's eyes widened in alarm. *This is not a column of one Spanish company. This is a column of two companies within half-an-hour's march of reinforcing La Valette. How will we get in front of them to block them?* One option was to canter in a wide arc across the mown meadows. Jobert saw another option.

'Musketoons, ready. Snipers, unsling rifles. Pultiere, the marksmen and I will charge down the left of the column. Count slowly to five then charge your section down the right side of the column. Lads, ride in single file, fire into the Spanish and scream your fucking heads off.'

Jobert pulled back the shabraque covering his pistols then cocked one pistol in his left, rein hand.

'Lads, listen, rally on me at the head of the column. Duque, take Tulloc's rifle, he will need both hands to gallop. Drop Rouge's lead rope and let him follow. Pultiere, ready? Snipers, on me!'

Bleu sprang into a flat gallop.

A horse walks at approximately five kilometres per hour and essentially doubles its speed each gait thereafter; trotting at ten kilometres per hour, cantering at twenty kilometres per hour and galloping at forty kilometres per hour. At the gallop, Jobert closed the distance to the Spanish column in thirty seconds.

Spanish fusiliers tasked with watching the rear of the column were distracted by Fort Faron's ranging gun and the noise of their comrades around them. Those Spanish fusiliers attentive to their duties, screamed their warnings, some raising their muskets to fire. As balls zipped wide, Jobert leant forward, low in profile, musketoon outstretched like a sabre, his knees guiding Bleu into the gap between the column and the roadside gutter.

Jobert fired his musketoon into a wide-eyed Spaniard. *My first Spaniard.* Jobert and Bleu continued to thunder down the column's one hundred metre flank in ten seconds.

Dropping his musketoon onto its clip on his cross belt, he fired the pistol in his rein hand into the mass of open-mouthed faces darting by his knee. The fusiliers found it awkward to bring muskets on their right shoulders to the 'present' on the left side of their bodies.

As Jobert looked down to his right holster to grab his remaining pistol, a moustachioed face, framed by a black bicorne, appeared at Bleu's shoulder and then just as rapidly disappeared, probably somewhere under Bleu's pounding hooves.

Jobert fired his remaining pistol by the time he cleared the head of the Spanish column. Looking back to judge whether he had cleared musket range, the crescendo of musketoon fire from the galloping troopers built.

With hands full of empty pistols, Jobert dropped his hip, put one heel to Bleu's flank and spun his warhorse to disengage the powerful stride, descending to a trot, then halt, facing back to the head of the Spanish column. Jobert scanned for loose horses as the chasseurs raced to join him, faces flushed, eyes wide, swearing and laughing at their escapade. No empty saddles, except for Rouge.

'On me! On me! Form line. Reload. Snipers, dismount, ready. Sergeant, parade state.'

Marksmen and their 'mates' sprang from their saddles and prepared the rifles to fire. Horses blew hard through square nostrils.

'Section, all present and accounted for, sir.'

'But, Sergeant, I have been shot,' cried a chasseur.

Jobert saw the soldier was shot through his boot into the calf. There was blood on the horse's ribs and girth, but the horse was not coughing blood nor blood coming from the horse's nose. The horse was fine.

'Shut up, son,' said Pultiere. 'Reload. We will take good care of your scratch in a moment.'

Jobert watched the Spanish column milling in place and calculated that not more than twenty-five rounds were fired by the eighteen chasseurs. Fusiliers knocked down were lifted up. Spanish non-commissioned officers raged to reform ranks. A knot of four dismounted officers conferred at the head of the column.

Duval squinted along his iron sights, his rifle cradled across his saddle.

'Fire!' called Jobert. Both rifles spat flames. Two Spanish officers reeled backwards.

The marksmen received their second rifles from their mates, aimed and fired. Another officer and a fusilier in the ranks just behind him spun and collapsed.

Twenty fusiliers were dispatched as a skirmish screen to push the chasseurs away from the column. The Spanish skirmishers were swift in their movements, as they approached Jobert's patrol across a mown field without cover.

'Snipers, mount. Section, about —'

'Sir, chasseurs on the far ridge,' cried Duque pointing at a troop column of French chasseurs eight hundred metres north up the Sollies road.

'Snipers, stand fast, enemy skirmish leaders, fire! Section, sabres! Moench, sound *To Mess*. Give them a cheer, boys.'

Moench found it difficult to set his lips to blow the call due to his grin. The trumpet call *To Mess* had become 2nd Company's catch-cry. Yet the call had a double effect; it halted the enemy skirmishers at their one hundred metre limit of safety from their column as well as raising a clear cheer and waving of blades from the far chasseurs.

Tulloc and Duval fired again at the skirmish leaders.

'Moench, sound *Form Line*. And keep sounding the call until they do.' Someone got the message on the opposite rise. The chasseurs on the far side of the fields extended into company frontage.

'They are all there, boys,' said Pultiere. 'That is our 2nd Company!'

As the cheers erupted about Jobert, the Spanish drummers thrashed out a beat to change formation. *Will the Spanish form fire lines to the north and the south or form square?* The skirmishers turned and ran to their column, dragging one man and leaving another where he lay.

'Moench, sound *Advance*. Snipers, mount, form second rank. Section, trot, march!' The trumpet's note rose clear in the midday air.

Spanish drums rolled. Spanish sergeants roared to complete the manoeuvre. Dust rose from the chasseurs on the far side of the meadow.

'The Spaniards are forming back-to-back fire lines. Idiots!' said Jobert. 'Hold, boys, hold. Moench sound *Charge* twice.'

'Shorten those fucking reins, lads,' called Pultiere, from his position on the right of the line. 'Up around their fucking ears.'

Moench's trumpet screamed. The far line screamed in response, sabres extended flat, a ripple of reflection from the overhead sun, their second rank disappearing in a hoof-driven thunder of yellow-white dust. Over their drums the Spanish screamed as well and the half-formed fire line was engulfed in gun smoke as they fired a ragged volley.

Jobert saw his chance as the Spanish reloaded. Bleu's powerful body launched from trot to gallop in a singular, muscular stride. 'On me, lads! On me!'

The section roared behind him. Musket balls zipped somewhere near him. Bleu moved so fast his hoof beats were no longer discernible. Jobert guided Bleu to the left of the Spanish towards a line of stragglers being forced into place in the hasty formation by their sergeants using the shafts of their long spontoons.

A man's back. Jobert's eye aimed his sabre tip for the base of the neck, so as not to catch the backpack's straps. Hit. Jobert let his shoulder roll down with the weight of his enemy passing under and behind him. Blade clear. Jobert swept his blade back to give point.

Spanish fire was slackening. Dust billowed. Bayonets were raised.

Then backpacks, backpacks everywhere. The Spaniards turned, pushing back into the ranks behind them, nowhere to run.

A young Spanish officer stood forward of the mass in the swirling dust, his blade en garde, his feet shuffling backwards. Without his hat his clay-whitened queue and the neat curls above his ears were yellow-grey with dust. Jobert skipped Bleu to shorten his stride, then trotted sideways, Bleu's heaving body angled obliquely at the Spanish officer. 'Surrender, sir, surrender.'

The Spanish officer threw down his sword. His fusiliers watched him. Muskets clattered to the ground like branches in a storm.

Jobert glanced at the sound of demented laughter. Voreille thundered past, just one of many black-green spectres, waving his blade in the air, throat filled with raucous joy. Dust swallowed vision.

'Moench, sound *Rally*.' Moench struggled to drop his sabre onto his sword knot then scrabble for his trumpet.

A cannon fired from the fort above them. Everyone looked up into the choking yellow cloud. Bleu shuddered as the single beat resounded through the earth from somewhere close by. Moench's strident call caused the Spanish infantry to look back in fear.

Jobert pressed Bleu and his blade tip towards the Spanish sub-altern. 'Form column, march your men back to Sollies. Now!'

The young officer nodded, turning towards his fusiliers, not knowing what to do next. Those fusiliers who he could see crowded together, listening for the guns above.

Somewhere drums were beating. French drums. Yinot emerged from the settling dust, standing in his stirrups, shrieking in Spanish.

'Sergeant Yinot, what are you saying?'

'Ground arms, form column, sir and follow the fucking drums, sir.'

Chapter Nineteen

September 1793, La Garde, France

'Ah, Captain Chabenac,' said Jobert, 'how smart you appear this evening. Well-groomed and highly polished. Another bath, I take it?'

'Most refreshing, I assure you. Have you not tried … the bath?'

'With reconnoitring an invasion force whilst investing a substantial fortress, sadly I have not yet found the time. But I am ever thankful that there are some officers who are able to attend to the vulnerable citizens whom we are dedicated to protect.'

At one of the troop fires across Madame Duhamel's barnyard, Moench's fiddle played a lilting tune accompanied by a few subdued singers.

'Gentlemen, I am distributing one of Major Victor's jars now,' said Koschak. 'It is a fair drop, so here is a bottle for you.' Sitting on a small timber crate, his back against a stone wall, Jobert shielded his eyes from the brazier's flames to find his cup somewhere at his feet.

'Victor?' asked Chabenac.

'Major Victor, commander of the 5th Battalion of the Volontaires Bouches-de-Rhône, a volunteer battalion in Lapoype's division. He has thanked us for the capture of the two Spanish companies the day before last with two stone jars of wine.'

'How decent of him. Whatever for?'

'Victor was tasked with leading the assault to capture La Valette. Those two Spanish companies from Sollies would have reinforced La Valette, making the task for Victor most difficult and producing a much higher butcher's bill for his battalion. Volunteer battalions are ever fickle beasts.'

A tethered cow defecated close by in the shadows. Two calves peeked from behind their mother's hocks towards the brazier.

'Is there a need for madame's cattle amongst our horses?' asked Chabenac.

'No, sir, the cow and her babies are ours. We received them and one hundred rations of grain as a trade from the 15th Dragoons.'

'Indeed! What occasioned such commerce?'

'They sought two hundred pairs of shoes. We had shoes to spare.'

'Fresh milk and a feast of veal in due course. The 2nd Company has not lost its entrepreneurial touch, I see.'

'That is not all.' Jobert passed Chabenac a captured fusilier company pennant, before drawing out three sacks of coins from a satchel to thump them on the bench. 'The proceeds of sale of our prisoner's belongings.'

'What was your prize?'

Jobert stoked the brazier with a log before adding a pot of water to the small blaze. 'We kept the Spaniards' purses, which was a tidy sum for company funds and distributed their two hundred blankets and water bottles amongst the men. The infantry are ever desperate for shoes, bicornes and shirts. We sold them two hundred each thus our reward. Unfortunately, muskets and bayonets were claimed by the divisional staff.'

Chabenac nodded into the fire and drew his boots away from the heat. 'Did you get your man back?'

'No. The Spanish told us Chasseur Millone was taken to Toulon for questioning. He was their only insight into both our cavalry and our eastern approach. As our first day on this side of the port, Millone would have known nothing of Lapoype's division.'

'How does 2nd Company stand following this latest affair?'

'Three killed. Six wounded, one of whom will not return to the company. Eight horses lost. Our parade state is now less than ninety.'

The coals in the brazier popped, embers drifted upwards, steam rose from the pot and hot ash tumbled out of the brazier's vent holes into the dirt. At a nearby fire, the wine worked its magic as Moench played a lively tune and the chasseurs clapped and sang along.

'How are your horses?'

'Fine. All fine.' Jobert superstitiously tapped his wooden wine cup.

'Why do you name them with colours?' asked Chabenac. 'Come now, the mystery requires revelation.'

'Once I was elected an officer in my previous regiment, I had to supply my own horses. My family furnished me with three. I named them Rouge, Blanc and Bleu after the tricolour. I lost Blanc at Jemappes last year ... a year, my word. Anyway, on my way south to join the 24th Chasseurs I received a replacement. I decided to continue the tradition, hence Vert. It also makes it easy for Duque and I to speak of them, when we are in the thick of it. Anyhow, enough of me. What news do you bring?'

'The road down the escarpment to Ollioules is now open.'

'Good grief. That has only taken twelve days,' said Jobert.

'Having observed Carteux's speed at Avignon and Marseilles, are you surprised? General Carteux has established his head-quarters at Ollioules, as has Colonel Morin. Major Avriol reports to Carteux that Lapoype is also expecting reinforcement from Nice.'

'That is fortunate, as Toulon was reinforced by the enemy. Nine ships-of-the-line brought in another one thousand British and another four thousand Spanish.'

'Do not expect a swift resolution to the dilemma,' said Chabenac. 'It is becoming obvious that there is bad blood between our two esteemed generals.'

Jobert folded one of his thick leather gloves to take the pot of water off the brazier. 'Huh! I will be happy when the company is reunited with our baggage in Revest.'

'Revest? Why ever Revest?'

Jobert poured a handful of finely diced tea leaves from a small tin cannister into the boiling water. 'Avriol's doing, I am pleased to say. General Lapoype has two attack options. Take the coastal approach and attack Forts La Malgue and Sainte-Catherine. Or attack over Mount Faron and flank Forts Croix, Faron and D'Artigues. Lapoype's cavalry currently combs the area for deserters and is engaged in appropriating local grain stocks. To avoid those dreary duties, Avriol has suggested that 2nd Company, based in Revest, patrol Mount Faron on foot. Lapoype accepted the proposal, hence, we return to Revest tomorrow. My dear friend, greater becomes my reliance on you to pay the regiment's respects to Madame Duhamel.'

Chabenac stood, bowed with great solemnity and poured the tea.

A week later, in the early hours of the morning, a thick Mediterranean fog clung to the southern slopes of Mount Faron, the slopes that faced Toulon. On the northern slopes, the mist dissipated and the stars shone through the gaps in the clouds on the chill, moonless night. The light breeze that carried the cloud caused the stunted pines that covered the mountain to mourn.

Jobert was the last man to descend into the hidden path, feet first on his bottom. Waiting chasseurs blocked the entrance behind him with thorny branches. The path followed a slight gully that the chasseurs had converted into an access way to the track system that laced across the mountain.

Deep in the gully, a cramped ten-man camp was established. Ten small nests were scraped into the chalky stone. Yet, at that moment, twenty filthy, weary chasseurs waited silently in the cracks and crevices of the camp. At the lowest point of the camp, a small pine-branch lean-to obscured the light from the embers of a nearly spent fire which slowly burnt behind a rock screen.

Jobert joined Koschak bent over a single candle illuminating a pencil-sketch chart of the track network of Mount Faron. 'Anything to report on the tracks west of Fort Croix, Sergeant Major?'

'There was no movement on the tracks tonight, sir. Neither in nor out.'

'Same for my patrol between Fort Croix and Fort Faron. Nothing. Fourth night in a row and no movement out of the forts by night.'

A whisper moved along the waiting chasseurs until it found Jobert and Koschak. 'Patrol coming up the face.'

'What time is it now? Four o'clock.'

Neilage squeezed into the tight space, breathing deeply to recover from his five hundred metre ascent of the northern face of Mount Faron. 'My section is now all in, sir.'

By the flickering candlelight, Jobert regarded the two men in their hard-wearing, but unremarkable, uniform. All three wore their green stable jackets, white, hemp stable trousers, white cross-belt with cartridge pouch and shoes and bicornes taken from Spanish prisoners.

'Prepare your section for descent, Sergeant Major,' said Jobert.

Picking up his musketoon, Koschak squeezed past the group out into the darkness. Soon the soft footfall of shoes on the dark rocks sounded as the platoon began the twisting, moonless, hour-long descent off Mount Faron.

'Neilage, welcome to Fort Capucine.' Jobert rubbed his tired eyes. 'Since I arrived up here four mornings ago, we have established this camp four hundred metres from Fort Croix to allow patrols to come and go, carving sleeping hollows, paths and latrines within the camp. It appears the routine of rotating section patrols is working well enough.

'We have just completed the fourth night patrol. So far, there has been no movement by the enemy on the tracks by night. Upon dusk, the forts bar their gates until dawn. Night patrols need to continue to determine that this routine is maintained.

'Day patrols move out in darkness, establish a quiet place to observe the tracks, then return to the camp after dark. Our observations of the tracks by day are that enemy relief columns, of not more than company strength, march up the mountain from both the south-east and the west, departing the lower forts after six o'clock in the morning. Only twice have we seen supply wagons and only one on each occasion, accompanying the relief column. The wagons remain within the forts through the day, presumably to rest the oxen, then depart by four o'clock to be secure within the lower forts by dusk. No wagons have yet remained overnight, I assume, due to no forage and insufficient water for the oxen within the forts.

'Here on the chart, six hundred metres from here, is an outpost camp of company strength. The piquet was British when we arrived but is now Spanish as of yesterday. Dependent on the company commander, the piquet may patrol the tracks by day. But at night, the enemy have not strayed far from their fires.

'The constant message to the patrol commanders is to remain unobserved. If we are discovered, then Mount Faron will be reinforced making an attack over the mountain near impossible. We have not yet encountered anyone by day, but should we, our uniform identifies us as royalist militia from the port.'

'Very good, sir, I have it. You need to get going or Koschak's platoon will descend without you.'

Jobert slapped Neilage on the shoulder, picked up his musketoon and departed for the descent to Revest.

The door clicked closed behind him.

Jobert drained his merlot then refilled his glass from the crystal decanter before looking about the bathroom. Madame Duhamel had been insistent that Jobert relax with a bath before supper, whilst her maid brushed his uniform and boots.

The room was lit with many small candles and smelled of lavender and lilac. The bath was not a simple tub by a fire. It was deep and square, approximately two metres along each side. Large pottery urns of steaming water stood ready to add to the water already in the bath. Thick green towels were folded on the tiled rim. Around the edges of the room, ferns in pots obscured statues of nymphs, satyrs and naked youths cavorting in the Roman style.

Jobert downed his glass again, smiling as he removed his clothes, placing his uniform in a basket by the door as requested. He stepped into the bath's warm water, lay back taking his head below the surface, allowing the heat to relax his muscular frame. He sat up to pour another glass of merlot and pondered on the curves of the female statues.

The door clicked open.

Jobert expected to see the basket of dirty clothing withdrawn. It was.

Before the door closed, Madame Duhamel entered the room with a silver tray and another steaming salver. She wore a see-through shift, again in the Roman fashion, pinned at the shoulders, with splits down the thighs. The lady wore nothing beneath the gown.

Resisting the desire to cover himself, Jobert leant back against the tiled rim to admire her barely concealed nude form through her diaphanous gown. Madame stepped into the bath, the material clinging to her calves. She bent over him, her breasts swinging freely and placed the tray on the rim beside his head.

Jobert saw the tray contained hot water, a razor, a pot of shaving soap with a small, thick brush embedded in the froth. Madame lifted the hem of her shift and squatted down across his groin, the water causing the sheer material to cling to her body up to her ribs.

Jobert took a gulp of wine and then tipped the glass towards her mouth. Madame sipped the merlot before proceeding to lather his face with shaving soap. Jobert closed his eyes as the blade glided across his cheeks. His mind raced as he imagined how he would detect whether this was a seduction or an assassination. *I suppose Chabenac had survived.*

Although Jobert worked hard so that his facial expressions did not betray him, there was nothing he could do about his erection pressing hard into her buttocks. Jobert opened his eyes as she wiped the froth from his face with a small towel.

Madame cocked her head to admire her handiwork. 'Now, roll over onto your hands and knees. I am going to wash your back.'

One evening in 2nd Company's camp in Revest, after another two weeks of patrols stalking the goat tracks of Mount Faron, Jobert sank exhausted onto a folding camp stool. Orlande placed beside him a steaming cup of tea, a bowl of thick vegetable soup and a large chunk of olive bread with garlic butter.

Jobert was too tired to think of what to do next.

'Eat,' said Chabenac.

On this recent foray onto the mountain Jobert had ascended Mount Faron, after dusk yesterday evening, with a section patrol, the men alternating the porterage of small casks of wine, sides of smoked goat and boxes of salt and feta cheese.

Once within the cramped gully of Fort Capucine, his patrol maintained the camp's security, whilst a night patrol crept along the mountain paths. Jobert had rested fitfully through the night wrapped in his double-blanket and cape against the drizzling fog. At four o'clock in the morning, after the night patrol returned and descended and another patrol arrived to take over security duties, Jobert took his chasseur section patrol to observe, by day, the enemy's company-strength outpost camp on the northerly point of Mount Faron.

A British company occupied the post this day. The British gathered firewood and maintained a watch on the valley floor far below. The enemy company were visited by a water wagon on both its ascent to and descent from, the Spanish at Fort Croix.

A sophisticated undertaking had grown out of a simple idea. If Huin and Yinot spoke fluent Spanish, then how might the company learn more by conversing with, or eavesdropping on, the Spanish. Thus, the latest of 2nd Company's commercial ventures was born. Patrols lugged wine, meat, salt and cheese up the mountain, as Jobert's patrol had this morning. With Morin's blessing and Raive's resourcing, the company's 'Spanish water-cart', accompanied by the niece of old Quandalle, the Revest goat herder, and Moench's younger brother, Koschak's piper during recruit training, conducted trade from a small donkey-cart.

It was well known that the forts were poorly supplied, some going two days without rations. When revictualled the garrisons were issued with rotten meat and fly-blown bread. The Spanish and British relief columns on their way to and from the forts paid well for the items supplied from the cart.

With Madame Quandalle's assistance, a backstreet tavern became the party's overnight Toulon base. During the day, Jobert's hidden patrol had observed the enemy troops relaxing with a bawdy madam, enjoying a welcome cup of wine and a merry tune, then paying the loyal French entrepreneurs handsomely for the goat meat and cheese, salt and wine, supposedly brought up from secret caches in Toulon. Yet the French militia sentries at Toulon's eastern Italian Gate watched three Spanish supply soldiers and a local French cantiniere, press their donkey for a daily load of water casks to the forts.

It was to Morin's advantage to inform Saliceti of the scheme, as Saliceti already had other merchants within Toulon providing him invaluable intelligence on the invaders. Soon a reliable supply of information began to move from Toulon to

Carteux's headquarters via 2nd Company's, expanded now to 24th Chasseur's, patrols on Mount Faron.

After dusk, Jobert's patrol returned to the cramped shelter of 'Fort Capucine'. There, once the night patrol had departed and Geourdai and an 8th Company patrol arrived, Jobert descended with his chasseurs. The eleven fatigued men arrived back with 2nd Company in the yard of Quandalle's goat farm, by nine o'clock this very evening.

There, under Koschak's strict arrangements for returning patrols, Jobert and the men stripped and bathed, ladling hot water from large basins to rinse off the lathered soap. Whilst bathing, a duty section pounded their filthy shirts, stable trousers, underdrawers and stockings, then hung them undercover to dry.

Now dressed in clean drawers, over-breeches, shirt, waistcoat and stable clogs, Jobert could not keep his eyes open as he slurped his soup.

Chabenac sipped his tea. 'A squadron of eight enemy ships entered Toulon bringing eight hundred Sardinians and two thousand Neapolitans. Their arrival has initiated much discussion.'

'Discussion that might become action?' asked Jobert, his mouth full of soup-soaked bread.

'Do you remember the artillery powder convoy fellow, Bonaparte? It appears Bonaparte has abandoned 3rd Squadron and the powder convoy in Aubagne, reassigned himself to Carteux's staff, built himself a battery on the western side of the Inner Harbour and has commenced to bombard the enemy fleet. Colonel Morin has reassigned 3rd Squadron to assist Bonaparte in his endeavours. You would have heard the bombardment of the fleet and the fleet's return fire over the last week?'

'Yes, I have watched it from up there.' Jobert waved his spoon toward the mountain.

A horse, approaching at a fast trot in the darkness, was challenged by a sentry. A nearby fire illuminated a grey horse entering the company horse lines and a regimental trumpeter dismount. Jobert and Chabenac watched the soldier stride towards them. Both captains recognised the man as Avriol's trumpeter. *A message from Lapoype's headquarters, not from Morin.*

'Major Avriol sends his compliments and requests that you, Captain Jobert, sir, attend General Lapoype's headquarters tomorrow morning at eight o'clock.'

'Certainly. For what purpose?'

'General Lapoype intends to attack Mount Faron, sir.'

'When?'

'The day after tomorrow, sir.'

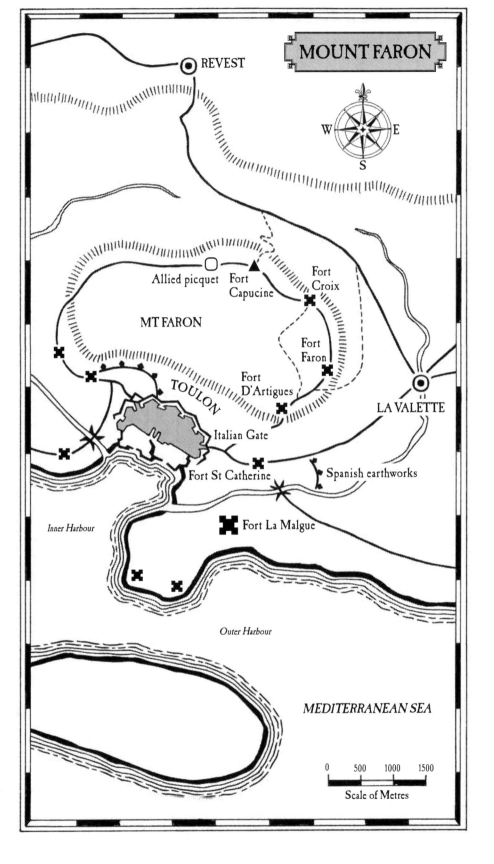

MOUNT FARON

REVEST

W E
S

Allied picquet Fort Capucine Fort Croix

MT FARON

Fort Faron

Fort D'Artigues

TOULON

LA VALETTE

Italian Gate

Fort St Catherine Spanish earthworks

Inner Harbour

Fort La Malgue

Outer Harbour

MEDITERRANEAN SEA

0   500   1000   1500

Scale of Metres

Chapter Twenty

October 1793, Mount Faron, France

In the black, clammy fog, over a dozen men, slipping on the uneven, slimy boulders underfoot, clustered around Jobert and Geourdai's lamp.

'Three o'clock, sir,' said Geourdai in response to Victor's question. 'Gentlemen, my lamp is the final station in the path up from the valley floor. You are now on Mount Faron. Two paths, marked every fifty metres with pairs of chasseurs à cheval, depart from this location. One path runs west to the British piquet. The other path runs east to Fort Croix. Captain Jobert is your command guide and is now connected to the path guide. Should you wish to proceed to the British piquet, six hundred metres west, sir, you are now able.'

Jobert watched Victor's shadowy form pause in the dark, pine-scented mist. Victor's battalion of seven hundred men were in one long single file, rattling, cursing, slipping and clinging to the chalky boulders on the trail twisting away in the darkness down the sheer face of Mount Faron. Victor's plan was to take the first three companies and attack the British outpost, leaving the other seven to gather in the dripping, muddy gullies, until he could lead them to assault Fort Croix. *So much could go wrong assaulting fortresses on a mountain on a foggy, moonless night.*

'Jobert, take us to the British,' said Victor.

Jobert set out toward the next pair of chasseurs. For Jobert, it was not difficult to find the next pair of guides. The challenge lay with single file of over two hundred infantrymen climbing the path to keep up with one another. On a paved, level street by day, a distance that would be strolled in seven minutes took thirty minutes on this particular morning.

Having glided along Mount Faron's trails for three weeks now, the chasseurs of 2nd Company were uncomfortable with the amount of noise the infantry made in assembling their company columns. Voices and equipment were the culprits. Musket stocks cracked and rattled against the handles of briquets and other loose-hanging metal pots and flasks. Bayonets fixed to the musket's muzzle, clinked and scraped against other bayonets and low pine branches, resulting in an unappreciated shower of dew onto the soldiers beneath.

Swearing and surnames were the key words and phrases hissed in the fog, as non-commissioned officers grabbed and pushed men, exhausted and unsteady from their hour-long five hundred metre climb, by their cross-belts and backpacks, into company columns.

Although the fog muffled much of the noise, four hundred metres west of Jobert and two hundred metres from the enemy, Koschak watched a pair of British sentries, silhouetted by their campfire, peer into the blackness attempting to identify the direction of the growing number of metallic clanks. Pultiere's platoon was posted at the end of the path to the piquet camp, with the task of securing a sheltered gully that would allow the infantry to move from column to line prior to assaulting the British camp.

'How much Spanish can you speak, Pultiere?' asked Koschak. 'What is the word for 'friend'?'

'*Amigo*, Sergeant Major.'

'Captain Jobert will be at the head of the column. Send a runner. Tell him the British are beginning to react to the noise. Tell him to move quickly as the game is up.'

With that, Koschak removed his distinctive fur-crested helmet, reached into his waistcoat and fished out his bonnet-de-police. Placing it on his head, Koschak cocked his musketoon, drew a broad-bladed dagger from his belt, stood and walked towards the enemy. '*Eh, ingles amigo. Espagnol amigo, per favor, eh?*'

The British sentries parted. One trotted back to the fire to warn, the other brought his musket to the shoulder.

'*Vino, ingles amigo, eh? Espagnol amigo, gracias.*'

The British fusilier looked to camp, then back to the black figure approaching him in the gloom, the light from the campfire insufficient to illuminate his target clearly. The approaching shape did not wear the characteristic bicorne, nor the blue tailcoat with white lapels over a white waistcoat, nor white trousers and held his musket away from his body with one hand. The sentry lowered his musket and considered the offered gourd.

'*Eh, ingles amigo, vino, eh? Espagnol fortaleza Croix, per favor. Croix, eh?*'

As the British sentry held his musket in one hand, pointed west along the ridgeline, saying something about Croix, his eyes on the gourd, Koschak pivoted and thrust his dagger through the sentry's voice-box. The British soldier hissed and sagged.

Koschak shuffled to both open the flesh of the man's neck and grab his musket barrel. The soldier dropped to his knees his head resting on Koschak's thigh.

Koschak's hands were full with musketoon, musket, gourd and bloody knife. With difficulty he laid the coughing man face down and watched the camp one hundred metres away. Other sentries were moving, pointing. The unmistakeable noises of a column of men was clear to Koschak, standing midway between the camp's nearest fire and the sheltered gully. '*Eh, ingles amigo, espagnol amigo, eh?*'

Someone was pointing towards him to assist the understanding of a man with a sword. An officer.

Koschak strained to confirm he could hear the noises of rushing, clanking men over a wide area behind him, hoping to identify the lead company assembling in line. The officer and six silhouetted British infantry moved towards Koschak, sword and pistol drawn, bayonets lowered. Koschak dropped to one knee and took aim with the musket.

'*Ingles amigo!*' called out two familiar voices somewhere in the fog behind Koschak.

The muted metallic bustle and muted commands grew louder. The British drew nearer.

'*Ingles amigo!*' cried Koschak, as he aimed for the officer at fifty metres.

'Koschak, return now!' Jobert's unmistakable command gave Koschak the bearing he needed. Koschak fired the musket.

Hit low in the belly, the British officer emitted a bovine bellow and leapt backwards. His legs folded to roll amongst the dew-laden rocks and spiky grass. Koschak dropped the musket, turned and strode toward Jobert and Pultiere, both grunted his name into the mist.

The British presented their muskets and in the moment they hesitated, since they had no targets, simultaneously British drums beat *To Arms* around the campfire, as French drums beat *Charge* from the gully.

Victor stood on the thorny lip of the sheltered depression and identified the British fires. Brandishing his sword, Victor roared over his shoulder, 'Forward with me, lads. On me!' The white-coated line company, from the 59th Ligne, attached to Victor's blue-coated volunteers, surged forward screaming, slipping on rocks and mud. With enemy campfires guiding them the company rushed forward with the bayonet.

The British sentries fired at the dull white figures emerging from the mist. The British roared with alarm, struggled out of their blankets and into their boots. Most grabbed their muskets, fewer grabbing their backpacks. Then they ran disordered down the sloping track to their camp's rear, south-west to the lower forts some three kilometres distant.

Victor halted his infantry line, thirty men wide and three men deep, beyond the furthest fires and stared into the shifting fog. He turned to find the one hundred and twenty men of the two volunteer companies, in the second line, breaking ranks to scavenge the camp. Volunteer soldiers slung their muskets to investigate cookpots and barrels, grabbed sacks, casks, satchels, blankets and backpacks. In a moment, before the 'old army' line infantry could about face and look about them, the British camp was cleaned of anything of, or suspected of, value.

'Jobert, now take me to Fort Croix.'

'It is now four o'clock, sir,' said Geourdai. 'Gentlemen, we could hear the musketry, the drums and the cries of your charge.

Our chasseur vedettes observing Fort Croix have reported hearing the Spanish beat *To Arms.*'

Victor had returned to the point in the ridgeline track system, which connected to the paths leading off the mountain to the valley floor below,

'Captain de Beaussancourt?' said Victor to one of his company commanders.

'Here, sir. My company is ready to move to Fort Croix, sir.'

'Good. Jobert, let us proceed.'

Again, the movement over two hundred metres of slimy rocks and through the pines' low branches slowed the column of over four hundred and fifty men of the remaining seven companies of Victor's battalion. The fog seemed to dissipate under the denser woods as Jobert and Victor followed the path. Within thirty minutes the command group stood beside Neilage, who was stationed with chasseurs observing the fort, looking across three hundred metres of cleared ground, hugged by thick mist, to the forbidding bulk of Fort Croix.

Built of stone, the walls of Fort Croix rose five metres above ground level. A three-metre-deep and five-metre-wide ditch surrounding the fort caused the walls to be difficult to surmount. The four sides of the fort were one hundred metres long with bastions projecting beyond the face of the wall so defensive fire could be directed into the ditch at the base of the wall. The gate and bridge, over the ditch, was protected by a walled compound on the far-side of the ditch, through which ran the road from Fort Faron, eight hundred metres distant across cleared fields of fire. At eight hundred metres, guns within Forts Croix and Faron would be in mutual support of each other.

'Sir,' said Neilage, 'the Spanish garrison beat, I assume, *To Arms*, after the firing to the west was heard. Since then, at least two companies have departed. There is neither light nor movement on the walls and the compound gate on this side of the ditch appears open. I believe the Spanish have withdrawn to Fort Faron.'

Victor drew his sword. 'De Beaussancourt, 35ᵗʰ Ligne, follow me. Sappers, scaling ladders to the front. Jobert, hold the follow-on blue-coats until I return.' In a clatter of slung equipment, the infantry shuffled forward, each holding the cross-belts of the man to his front.

'Neilage,' said Jobert, 'do we have observation of the road to Fort Faron?'

'Yes, sir. Voreille has a platoon observing Fort Faron, as well as vedettes observing beyond Fort Faron towards Fort D'Artigues.'

The white-coated company had disappeared into the fog and no noise had come from the fort. The final six companies of volunteers marched the three hundred metres to the squat, brooding fort. With a fusilier holding a pitch-soaked torch aloft, Victor looked at his pocket watch, then at the mist around him. Fog still squatted on the cleared apron around the fort, but the air had taken on a translucent quality as first light crept into the eastern sky.

'It is now five o'clock. Fort Croix is ours. The enemy has abandoned it. I require the next two fusilier companies in the column to move into the fort and secure it. The fog is lightening with dawn in one hour. De Beaussancourt, the grenadier company and the remaining four fusilier companies, prepare to march to Fort Faron —'

A gun roared in the mist.

Five hundred faces turned east along the wagon-rutted ridgeline road to the Fort Faron. Two further guns fired consecutively.

'Fort Faron, sir,' said Jobert. 'The fort is signalling Toulon she is in contact with us. Guides await, sir. May I describe the ground around us which mist and night currently cloaks? A wide, cleared space, over which this road runs, lies around both forts. It allows the batteries of both forts interlocking arcs of fire. In essence, sir, if we are in the open, as we are now, albeit hidden by fog, we are under the enemy's guns. The ground falls away to the west of Fort Faron, towards the port, in which we might assemble before the assault.'

'Take me to this covered ground, so I might consider my assault.'

Voreille's guides led the three hundred metre crunching, clinking, cursing infantry column off the road and down a slope, until the soldiers once again came under the dripping boughs of the stunted pines, where the sticky mud reverted to slippery boulders.

'Guns are preparing to fire!' Stooping black figures loped down the slope towards the column. From within the enclosing fog, the battery from the Fort Faron fired near simultaneously.

The wet grass hissed with shot. The upper boughs of the pines rattled and swayed with the blast. The cringing column's long flank, heard but not seen by the fort's gunners, was the target of the fire, but their march had taken them down the slope and under the full-effect of the case-shot. Nevertheless, a few cries and moans were heard from within the last two companies.

'Guns to fire,' called a lone voice out in the fog. Jobert recognised the voice as Voreille's.

'Lie down, lads, lie down,' called de Beaussancourt.

The fort's artillery fired again. The case-shot swept gravel and grass within its sizzling wave, the mist danced and swayed in the dull, grey light, the branches groaned as the trees leant back to receive the cannons' blow.

'Twelve pounders, sir,' said de Beaussancourt.

'At least five twelve pounders, sir,' said Victor. 'What is your understanding of the garrison, Jobert?'

'I believe Fort Faron had a garrison of four hundred prior to the addition of Fort Croix's two hundred.'

'We have cleared the ridgeline piquet and captured Fort Croix. My companies have done good work. As for Fort Faron, our surprise is gone. Dawn is with us, as will be enemy reinforcement from Fort Sainte-Catherine below. I would have with me now less than five hundred. To assault over open ground without artillery, the guns will not leave me the manpower I need to secure the top of the walls, let alone to clear the walls. But with the other two battalions of the brigade it could be done. Jobert, my aide de camp needs to inform General Gardanne to send up the remainder of the brigade. Can he be escorted back along the path?'

Jobert had been watching black figures in crested helmets, distinctive due to their single white cross-belts, moving purposefully, surefooted, amongst the heavily laden, clattering lines of infantry. Jobert noted two crouching dark shapes scurry over the lip of the slope. As Victor stopped to speak with the battalion surgeons attending at least a dozen groaning, writhing men, Jobert discovered Voreille kneeling over a wounded chasseur.

'He has been hit, sir,' said Voreille.

'Here, chasseur, take my water flask,' said Jobert. *The shock will make him thirsty.* 'Lieutenant Voreille, listen. Leave the observation of Fort Faron to the infantry. You are their guides, not their skirmishers. Do you understand?'

'Yes, sir.'

'Well done on keeping a watch on the guns, lad. Now, give me a guide to take me back to Fort Croix.'

Just after dawn, the brigade commander for Lapoype's attack, General Gardanne and the two remaining battalion commanders arrived at the fort at half-past six. The remaining eight hundred infantrymen of the brigade were now either strung out along the path or still climbing 8th Company's trail up the northern face of the mountain. On the upper terraces of Fort Croix, General Gardanne looked up to see the morning sky through the thinning fog. 'Major Victor, how is your battalion arrayed?'

'Sir, I have eight volunteer companies and two line companies with me. I have three companies holding the enemy's ridgeline piquet covering the western route to the lower forts. I have two companies securing Fort Croix. I have five companies securing an assault location just west of Fort Faron. Fort Croix and Fort Faron have cleared fields of fire between them allowing the forts to provide mutual support to each other. We are currently within range of at least five twelve pounders confirmed within Fort Faron.'

'Observing the construction of this fort, is Fort Faron constructed similarly?'

Victor looked to Jobert.

'Yes, sir,' said Jobert. 'Fort Faron is constructed in the same manner as Croix and with the same approximate dimensions.'

Gardanne turned to consider the chasseur officer before retuning his focus on Victor. 'The enemy has a garrison of six hundred, yes? My brigade has your battalion of seven hundred, Major Victor, plus two further battalions of four hundred each. In your opinion, it would require the entire brigade to successfully carry Fort Faron without artillery support?'

'Yes, sir.'

Gardanne looked into the mist now beginning to waft and swirl, disturbed by the heat of the unseen sun. 'If the brigade captures Fort Faron, will I have the strength remaining to hold both Faron and Croix should we be counter-attacked? That is, two fresh battalions of four to five hundred each?' Gardanne held up his hand to counter any argument. 'I think not.'

Gardanne reflected upon the brigade's situation by leaning through the gun embrasures and peering down into the wide ditch below. Jobert watched the commanders and staff officers shuffle to compose their conflicting inner thoughts into a patient stance.

'Here is what shall be done. Aide de camp, inform General Lapoype of our situation and request reinforcement. In the meantime, the 1st Battalion du Var shall take up our western post holding the western road to the lower forts. Major Victor, your 5th Battalion Bouches-de-Rhône shall concentrate its companies in order to invest Fort Faron in preparation for assault. The 4th Battalion Montagne de Marseilles shall occupy Fort Croix and prepare it for defence. There we have it, gentlemen.'

With that, the assembled officers broke away to their duties.

Jobert checked his watch. Seven o'clock. 'Moench, we have been on the trot for four hours. Have you had a little bread?'

'Not yet, sir, I can wait. But I want to refill my flask while we are here.'

'No, do not! Do not touch the water in the fort. I hesitate to take water from wells the enemy has recently abandoned. We will find some more somewhere else.'

Jobert strode over to Major Victor's side. 'Sir, it is my intent to visit my vedettes, beginning in the west, if that meets with your desires.'

'It does and further, I would be obliged, Jobert, if you would oversee both the guiding of the 1st Battalion du Var to the western piquet and the return of my companies to our assembly camp west of Fort Faron.'

'Does General Lapoype have a follow-on brigade ready to support this attack?'

'Not that I am aware of. Knowing the division's dispositions, it will take considerable time to assemble such a force.'

'Indeed, sir.' Jobert saluted. 'Would you excuse me?'

Chapter Twenty-One

With the fog having burnt off, Jobert sat beside Moench on an exposed pine root, removed his helmet and wiped his brow. Moench reached into his waistcoat, brought out a crust of bread, tore it in two and passed half to Jobert. The soldiers filing into Victor's sloping assembly area, the infantry companies Jobert had just guided from the western outpost, were interrupting his view of the outer harbour and the Mediterranean. Jobert knew there were crestlines further south towards the port from which there were stunning views across Toulon and its harbours. On one day patrol, he had the good fortune to watch the enemy's fleet exchange fire with Bonaparte's batteries far across the Inner Harbour.

A flustered chasseur jogged towards them through the infantry bivouac. 'Sir, from Lieutenant Neilage at Fort Croix. Sergeant Major Koschak has reported enemy advancing up the western road at nine o'clock. Two companies of British and a battalion of Sardinians. Blue tailcoats, sir, with red lapels.'

Victor, sitting nearby, snapped his watch shut. 'Half-past nine.'

A single musket fired. Six hundred heads jerked south-west towards Fort D'Artigues. Then a volley of twenty muskets fired. 'Beat *To Arms!*'

Jobert slurped his tea and scoffed his soggy crust as the eight men of the battalion's drum corps thrashed out a violent, high tempo beat. An infantryman raced through the campfires, every soldier pointing the way to their battalion commander, as they grabbed their muskets, shrugged on their backpacks and formed in company line.

'Spanish, sir,' reported the soldier to Victor. 'Captain de Beaussancourt says two battalions of white coats, sir.'

'Let us observe their advance, Jobert.'

The musket fire crackled the abrupt signature of skirmishers, continuous and lacking any pattern.

Jobert, Moench, an aide and a small party of burly regimental sappers trotted after Victor. Once one hundred metres beyond the assembly area, it was clear de Beaussancourt's one-hundred-man company, deployed in two lines of skirmishers, held the handful of Spanish skirmishers. The lead Spanish battalion marched up the slope to their skirmishers. The second battalion wheeled off the road into the low ground.

Musket balls zipped close to where they stood.

De Beaussancourt strode up to his commander and saluted. 'I will not be able to hold the enemy, sir. To bring my line back up the slope will expose the line to case-shot from the fort. I also note the enemy's second battalion is flanking my line, but also your assembly area. What would you have me do, sir?'

'Look!' said Victor. 'The first battalion is also wheeling into the low ground to flank us. Then look further down the road, by Fort D'Artigues, a third battalion. British possibly?' Victor spun towards his aide de camp. 'Inform General Gardanne of this development. Confirm to him that we have one enemy battalion from the west and three battalions from the south-west. The enemy is flanking us with two battalions through the low ground and the final enemy battalion is advancing on this road from Fort D'Artigues. Go! De Beaussancourt, remain in skirmish order, move on the Spanish flank above them, stay between them and the battalion.'

They returned to Victor's eight companies of blue-coats and one of white, arrayed in line on the boulder-strewn slope under the pines. Six hundred anxious eyes followed Major Victor as he joined a knot of company commanders awaiting their battalion commander's orders.

A dragoon captain, with the armband of a brigade commander's aide, stepped forward to salute Victor. 'General Gardanne extends his compliments, sir and says he finds it unwise to fight his brigade in two places. He requests that you withdraw your battalion to Fort Croix, at your earliest convenience and draw up in front of the gate house, facing the south-west. You will find the 1st Battalion du Var withdrawing to Fort Croix to take up a position facing west.'

Jobert bent to whisper to Moench. 'We must return to Fort Croix. Once there, I need you to run a message to Captain Geourdai. Inform him the enemy are now converging on Fort Croix. General Gardanne's brigade is concentrating on Fort Croix. The 8th Company path up the face is redundant. 8th Company need to form up on the valley floor and return to Revest. Repeat that message.'

With Neilage, Voreille, Bredieux, Duque and Moench standing around him, Jobert replaced his watch in a pocket within

251

his heavily braided dolman jacket. Ten o'clock. *Seven hours on Mount Faron.* 'As we understand it, four enemy battalions are converging on Fort Croix. One British along the road from Fort Faron, two Spanish coming up the slight valley and one Sardinian through the scrub from the west. We also know Fort Faron, over there, has the gun range to where we are standing. They have not fired yet, either to conceal that fact from us or saving their ammunition for whatever this day holds. Are there any questions on the enemy?'

The two officers dropped their eyes, brows furrowing, searching for appropriate questions as if they were quizzed at one of Colonel Morin's instructional rides. The other three clenched their jaws to shut out their fears.

'Our three battalions are concentrating their efforts here. One battalion within the fort and two forming line, here, in front of the gate house, one facing down the road to the south-west and one facing the paths west along the wooded ridgeline. We need to get 2nd Company in a position to boost the brigade's strength. Remember we are guides and vedettes because we know these mountain paths so well. Lads, we are not the infantry's skirmishers, certainly not with musketoons. We have nothing to protect us, neither sabres, nor fog, nor night, so do not get caught in the middle of two battalions exchanging volleys.'

Jobert looked up as the drumming grew louder to watch Victor's 5th Battalion march towards Fort Croix.

'Sergeant Bredieux, bring in your path guides and reform your platoon. I require you to hold a position on the paths that lie underneath this fort on the face of the northern slopes. If we need to evacuate the brigade off the mountain, I shall send the battalions to you. Do you have any questions?'

Bredieux shook his head once and tapped the ash from his hooked pipe on his musketoon stock.

'Lieutenant Voreille, you have a platoon and the marksman Tulloc with you, yes? Major Victor's 5th Battalion will form up facing down the road. Maintain contact with the 5th Battalion from a position to the left of his line and the north-eastern face of Fort Croix. From there you will be able to warn him of any flanking attack or guide him over the lip and under the fort to Sergeant Bredieux.'

Firing crackled through the woods to the west.

'That will be the 1st Battalion du Var withdrawing, guided by Koschak and Pultiere. Neilage, Pultiere's platoon will be the last to enter the brigade fire line here at Croix. Pultiere needs to position his chasseurs to the right of 1st Battalion's line so that he can warn them of flanking attack and guide them to Bredieux on the north-western face of the fort. You need to make the connection from Pultiere's platoon to Bredieux's platoon.'

Neilage brought up his chin, shrugged back his weary shoulders and in a display of dramatic confidence, swept back his blond-red moustache with the back of a gloved finger.

'Duque, in Yinot's absence with the water cart in Toulon, you have his platoon, yes? You, Moench and I will be at the most vulnerable point of the brigade formation.'

Moench gave a snort as he rolled his eyes.

'The point of the triangle is where 5th Battalion faces down the road and 1st Battalion faces towards the woods. It is the point of that triangle, the flanks of both battalions, that the two Spanish battalions will emerge from the low valley over the lip. The only force that stands beyond the triangle's tip, over the lip of the slope between the brigade and the Spanish is a line company from the 35th Ligne. They are dressed in white tailcoats and black bicornes. The Spanish are dressed in white tailcoats and black bicornes.'

Duque raised his eyebrows as he looked at Jobert, blowing a long breath out of his nose as he tightened his mouth.

'Duque! I require you to take your chasseurs out over the lip of the ridge, find this company of the 35th Ligne and guide it, at Captain de Beaussancourt's convenience, back to Moench and I, waiting for you, at the tip of the triangle.'

Duque flashed a quick, humourless smile to a fearful Moench.

'Twelve o'clock now, sir.'

The battery within Fort Faron fired as ordered.

Rear-Admiral Gravina, of His Spanish Majesty's Royal Navy, counted the explosions, delighted the fort's battery squeezed the sixth of their seven pieces onto the ramparts.

The six twelve-pound balls flew the first seven hundred metres then skipped, striking the hard-packed earth, underlain with ancient boulders, like giant drumbeats. The bouncing iron tore through the French battalion which faced down the road, ripping away three men at a time, casting aside their torn bodies like discarded dolls. The balls continued to bound through the empty centre of the French triangle to slice through the other French battalion, with its back to the guns, facing the western woods.

The French brigade erupted with screams. Not so much from the wounded, but the non-commissioned officers bellowing at the men to close the gaps.

The second and final round fired as ordered. Ammunition was low within the fort and no-one knew what the day would bring. Six more bouncing iron balls. Another twenty or thirty ripped corpses. More gaps in the line. More screaming.

The Admiral nodded for his Spanish brigadier to advance

his line. The drums rattled out Advance as the three hundred and fifty fusiliers marched up the hill. The brigadier-general's force was a mixture of Spanish, Neapolitan and Sardinian and they were keen to drive off the waiting French skirmishers who had dogged their march so far. The French fired from their concealed positions in the rocks and thorns above them. Officers leading the front rank were punched into the earth. Men within the front rank reeled back with strangled gasps.

Riding tall in the saddle, Gravina set his teeth as the balls zipped about him. The French skirmishers broke and ran. Gravina's fusiliers crested the top of the gully's edge.

Gravina, with his telescope opened and passed to him by an aide, surveyed the scene, beginning with the squat, grey block that was Fort Croix. He noted the upper terraces of the fort were manned with infantry. No artillery. He smiled.

To his left, or north, he saw Lord Mulgrave's force of a Sardinian battalion, supported by a few British companies, standing well back in the treeline, taking refuge from blue-coated French skirmishers. Behind the skirmishers was a small, blue-coated French battalion, not more than four hundred men, in three ranks.

To his right, or south, beyond his fusiliers, stood a wide, empty space and in the distance Gravina could see the tops of Fort Faron. Beyond the space which allowed the artillery to play their part, the Admiral could just see the edge of Captain Elphinstone's British companies. Elphinstone, a naval officer, was supported this morning by a company of Toulonais royalists, from the newly raised Royal Louis Battalion. In front of both the artillery and Elphinstone stood a larger French volunteer battalion.

Gravina smiled to the second brigadier within his force mounted beside him, a Sardinian, as they both noted the weak point in the French line.

The ends of the two outward-facing French battalion lines formed the tip of a triangle, covered by a single company of white-coats. Gravina nodded to the brigadier and waved his telescope. The Sardinian general gave the order for the second line of Gravina's force, two hundred elite Spanish and Neapolitan grenadiers, to advance to a position where they might assault into the flank of one, or both, French battalions.

The drums rolled, the grenadiers came into line and halted.

Around three thousand combatants stood before Fort Croix in the spring sunshine. With throats bone-dry with fear, they, British, Spanish, Sardinian, Neapolitan and French, waited for the next command.

Jobert stood within the 'tip of the triangle. He noticed the beads of perspiration running from the brim of General Gardanne's bicorne.

'The enemy have paid us their compliments,' said Gardanne. 'It is now after midday, gentlemen and there is no sign of movement on the valley floor indicating reinforcement will reach us. We have a fort with no artillery, no ammunition beyond the sixty cartridges per man, no water and no food. But we do have a goodly supply of Spanish turds floating in the fort's well and carpeting every room, so disease marches to join us.'

Enemy drums thrashed out another command. The officers turned to look out between the exposed flanks of 5th Battalion and 1st Battalion and over the heads of de Beaussancourt's company.

'Spanish and Neapolitan grenadiers coming up, sir,' said the general's aide.

'I need to withdraw. I need to withdraw now. I need to conduct that withdrawal in an orderly fashion.'

The officers shuffled in an uncomfortable silence. Victor squinted at Jobert.

Jobert brought his shoulders back and took a step forward. 'Sir, there is a way down the mountain. On each face of the fort there is a fortified door, a sally-port, which leads out into the surrounding ditch, accessible by companies already within the fort. With scaling ladders, the companies might then exit up and out of the ditch on the northern face. There beneath the lip of the ditch on the northern side, I have a platoon of chasseurs, waiting on the maintenance paths which circle the fort, able to guide your companies down the face of the mountain.'

'I am obliged, sir. Then, gentlemen, let us withdraw our companies in good order.'

'Sir!' Victor stepped forward. 'May I have the honour of standing as the rear guard, bringing my battalion in through the gatehouse last, sir?'

'As you wish.'

A battalion volley was fired by the enemy.

'The enemy have chosen to advance, sir,' said the unflappable dragoon aide de camp, as musket balls zipped overhead.

Chapter Twenty-Two

The night sky was clear. There would be another thick fog in the morning as there was yesterday morning up on Mount Faron.

2nd Company feasted. Soldiers came to Koschak to refill their bottles from Major Victor's large stone wine jars. Hoping for more, a line of chasseurs approached Orlande carving veal from the roast calf turned on a spit. The tang of roast garlic, wine and herbs poured across the carcass blended with the burning pine-cones glowing within the crackling platoon fires.

Jobert stared up at the stars, drank deeply and listened to the spinning of fireside tales.

'After that long silence,' said Pultiere continuing his story of this morning's battle, between licking his greasy fingers, 'the Sardinians in the western woods fired a battalion volley and then came out through their smoke with drums beating and bayonets lowered. The 1st Battalion du Var's skirmishers fired and retired to their battalion line. The Sardinians paused, both due the fire and waiting for the British companies to come up on their left. When the British emerged from the timber, fuck me, Duval pumped so many rounds into those bastards, I thought his barrel would melt. Here, fill us up, brother.'

Moench reached across to pour the remnants of the wine bottle into Pultiere's cup.

'The Sardinians came on again,' Pultiere continued, 'but the British are starting to lag because they have no officers remaining out front and their left flank is open to us in the low ground. I order the platoon to stand up and fire and the Sardinians and British halt and look at us. And there you have it. The 1st Battalion fire their only volley of the battle, to which the Sardinians recoil from the hit. 1st Battalion, covered by their own smoke, turn and run. When the smoke clears, like a conjurer's trick, where a battalion of blue-coats once stood, a company of white-coats now stands. That pause is enough for the flanking company of British to charge us. I called it a day and we slid past Bredieux and back down the path home.'

Duque emptied his arms full of firewood onto the existing blaze and a shower of sparks and curses leapt up into the night air.

'Keep your chemise on, ladies,' said Duque, silencing the group by waggling a bottle in front of their faces. 'It was us in the centre who provided you the pause to fuck off, while we were shitting ourselves. Captain Jobert had pulled the platoon I was with back behind Victor's 5th Battalion. Major Victor was on fire. He wheels his battalion around to face the Spanish cresting the lip —'

'And Neapolitans,' said Moench.

'Oi! Who is fucking this cat? The Spanish and the Neapolitans see the change in formation and advance. The captain commanding the company from the 35th Ligne, de Beaussancourt — now that bastard is hung like a rogue elephant — fires a company volley and marches the company forward seven steps. The fucking Spanish stop in their tracks, so de Beaussancourt backs his boys up seven steps. Now Major Victor has his eight-hundred-man battalion facing six hundred Spanish and fucking Neapolitans.'

Duque slurped from his cup.

'That is when we notice that the 1st Battalion has gone,' said Moench.

'Oi! Thank you! Fuck me, 1st Battalion has gone in a puff of smoke. De Beaussancourt wheels his company to face the Sardinians. Major Victor orders fifteen paces rearwards march. My platoon is forced backwards. We can see the Spanish fusiliers and grenadiers are following us up, bayonets lowered. Victor orders fire and, with their only volley of the day, the blue-coats turn and run into the fort.'

Duque reached forward into the fire and retrieved a smouldering twig to light his pipe. 'There are, the two white-coat companies standing shoulder to shoulder, backs to the gatehouse wall, Victor, Jobert and us, balls swinging in the breeze. The officers look up to see why there was no support fire coming from the ramparts above our heads.'

'No bastard there, brother.' Bredieux exhaled an indignant cloud of tobacco smoke. 'The battalion in the fort ran when the others came streaming through and started entering the ditch from the sally-ports. The whole lot of them were pouring down the slope. Useless pricks. They ran all the way to Revest. Utter fucking chaos.'

'That is when we received fire from our left from the British,' said Duque. 'Not a lot of fire, mind you. Young Voreille and his platoon were tearing the arse out of those British companies towards Fort Faron. Young Tulloc did a brilliant job. He even knocked a senior Spanish officer out of his saddle, the bastard. No, while young Voreille held the eastern flank popping up over the lip, the British would not move forward. Those dirty little fucks, the royalist militia, backed away quick smart.'

'Those British were so far away,' said Moench, looking to Duque to see if he had permission to speak. 'The Spanish grenadiers were squeezed by the Spanish fusiliers and the Sardinian battalion, so they halted to adjust their line. That is when the company from the 59th Ligne fired, turned and ran.'

'It was the same time that Captain Jobert told me to go,' said Duque. 'We all jumped down into the ditch, ran around the fort to the scaling ladders, found Bredieux and headed home.'

'There we were,' said Moench now controlling the story. 'The captain and I, Victor and a group of infantry sappers, wringing the handles of their broad axes, they wanted to carve up the Spanish so much and of course, de Beaussancourt's company.'

Moench, aware of the power of the dramatic pause, looked up to see all eyes on him, as he was one of the last men to depart the field alive.

'The Neapolitan grenadiers charge. Victor orders fire. De Beaussancourt's company fires and we all stream through the gatehouse. It was not until we found Sergeant Bredieux did we realise de Beaussancourt and his company had not followed. De Beaussancourt stayed and held the gatehouse.'

'Slaughtered or captured?'

'We do not know.'

'I have just come from visiting the commander of the 35th Ligne,' said Victor. 'We drank to the health of Captain de Beaussancourt and his company.'

Jobert poured two tall brandies, not in balloons but in glasses none the less.

Victor savoured a mouthful before swallowing. 'Mount Faron cost us seventy dead, sixty captured and three hundred wounded. How many did you lose?'

'Only three wounded, sir. Thankfully. Two will return to the company.'

Victor gulped down his remaining brandy then poured himself and Jobert another. 'Gardanne has been relieved of command. I learnt that Lapoype had no follow-on brigade. In fact, he never received our request for reinforcement. Indeed, General Lapoype was entertaining citizen Deputy Saliceti the whole day at his chateâu in Sollies.'

'To absent brothers, sir.'

Paris
1ˢᵗ of October 1793

Jobert shrugged. *Three weeks late.*

Darling André,

'Make terror the order of the day' was the Committee of Public Safety's proclamation on the 5ᵗʰ of September. My friends who know such, tell me that the recently passed Law of Suspects is executing over three hundred and fifty 'enemies of the Republic' a week.

The reported slaughter that came with the recapture of Avignon and Marseilles beggars belief. There are those of us most saddened at what might eventuate when Lyon and Toulon are regathered within the bosom of the Republic. I do so hope that you have been and will be far from such determined restoration and firm enforcement of Republican ideals.

No news comes to us from the south. All Paris cares for is the progress of the enemies' sieges of our border fortresses, holding our destruction at bay. We are all so pleased that you and Captain de Chabenac ought to be far from danger as there would be little utility for cavalry in a siege.

The new law forcing farmers to surrender their grain is beginning to provide some relief to the mood of Paris as bread is available in larger quantities. I dread to imagine the state of the streets if the desperate hunger of the sans-culottes was to be extended.

For wont of flour for cake, we celebrated Aunt Sophie's 75th birthday with small cups of egg custard. Our darling Aunt remains a fierce beacon of strength for our women and their children. Madame de Chabenac has won Aunt's heart by demonstrating her devotion to improving the living conditions within the workhouses.

On the other hand, Aunt senses that Valmai is a little too wild. Only in my company does Aunt refer to Valmai as 'that mischievous mare.' What delicious irony that these days allow the peasant daughter of a soldier, raised in a mountain barn to sew, to cast such matronly scorn on a young woman of genteel birth, raised with such fashionable comforts, reduced now to poverty and fear and prey to depredation. For my part, a deep feeling of friendship is blossoming between Valmai and myself.

But I do have one mote of good cheer. Our beautiful Didier is now a Chief of Squadron in the famous 1st Hussars, no less. Yes, your brother! You will remember the 1st Hussars defected to the Austrians *with General Dumouriez in March this year. The resultant scandal would have meant the disbandment of the regiment. But, in light of its exceptional battle honours since the fall of the Bastille, the 1ˢᵗ Hussars is to be reraised. Didier writes that his squadron of volunteers replenishes the kernel of Republican virtue in the legendary regiment.*

Write to me this minute,
We love you very much,
Your loving cousin,
Michelle

P.S With this evening's mail Father writes that Grandfather is ill. I shall set affairs straight here and depart …

A spasm squeezed Jobert's heart as he remembered his grandfather's words. *They say you have all the time in the world. They are wrong. You do not have a second to lose.*

'Mail from Avignon,' said Jobert. 'Your ladies are well. I had the honour of dining with Marguerite's family.'

Jobert dropped perfumed envelopes in front of both Fergnes and Geourdai, each fellow quite snug in their seats by the fire avoiding the bitter late-November wind whipping the dust in the lanes outside. Jobert stepped over Chabenac's long legs stretched towards the hearth to pour himself a cup of coffee from a pottery jug.

'Dining with young ladies' families?' asked Chabenac. 'I do so hope you found the time to 'bathe' in Avignon?'

'Hah! I must report to the regimental second-in-command. Is Raive about?'

'The second-in-command now works from General Dugommier's headquarters. From there he is able to drive the army's resupply since he coordinates all the convoys' escorting cavalry.'

'Dugommier?' asked Jobert. 'Did not Saliceti replace Carteux with General Doppet, the doctor?'

'Indeed, Doppet was our erstwhile commander for a few weeks, but Saliceti has since replaced Doppet with Dugommier a week ago.'

Jobert raised his eyes to the smoke-begrimed rafters and took a deep breath.

'Imagine if the Colonel replaced a company's commander with that regularity,' said Geourdai. 'That company would be useless.'

Fergnes' eyes furtively swept nearby tables. 'Is not that exactly what the army is now, with every man and his dog taking a turn at army command at the whim of the Deputies? Anyway, Jobert, Raive is unavailable today. Dugommier's headquarters is hosting a council of war. Our superiors are discussing how we might prepare the army for winter.'

'Where are the squadrons located presently?' asked Jobert.

'1st Squadron patrols Mount Faron,' said Fergnes, 'and 8th Company is in reserve. With 2nd Company's return from convoy escort we may well be re-tasked. 3rd Squadron continues to support Major Bonaparte on the western shore of the Inner Harbour.'

'Major, indeed?'

'Yes, since his return to the army's staff two months ago, Bonaparte has conjured nine batteries of forty guns on the western shore out of thin air. Bonaparte has grown a force of over one thousand officers and men in his batteries and eighty artisans, converting naval artillery to field artillery, out of nothing. Deputy Saliceti is backing him. So then is Colonel Morin, by placing 3rd Squadron at Bonaparte's disposal, escorting to his batteries whatever guns, men, powder, ball and timber can be scrounged.'

'The gentleman is impressive,' said Jobert.

'That is all well and good,' said Fergnes, 'but the enemy outnumbers us in artillery ten to one, which includes their fleet and three hundred French guns captured within the port and the upper forts.'

'But we have the numbers in infantry,' said Geourdai. 'Lapoype has received another ten thousand men from Nice. With the recapture of Lyon, fifteen thousand men are marching south.'

'Speaking of Lyon,' asked Chabenac, 'is it true that two thousand were executed in Lyon following its recapture.'

Jobert's downcast eyes were solemn. There were no overt reactions from the others.

'But the enemy continues to reinforce Toulon,' said Fergnes. 'Not just three thousand more Spanish and British reinforcements, but six thousand Sardinians and Neapolitans as well. The enemy now boasts a squadron of Spanish dragoons. Even the royalists in the port have formed the Royal Louis Battalion. Do we truly wonder at the extent of executions when we recapture these cities?'

The wet logs in the fire popped and hissed, a shower of embers spraying out onto the filth-encrusted mat in front of the hearth.

'What of the wider world, Jobert?' asked Chabenac. 'Has there been further developments since the Committee of Public Safety executed Her ... Marie Antoinette?

'Apart from Russia joining the coalition's war against us, no, not really. Have I heard correctly that we have lost La Valette?'

Chabenac leant forward after a cautious look about the room.

'Sadly, the fool Lapoype has lost La Valette. Lapoype ordered firing at the enemy shipping passing through the Outer Harbour. The enemy landed a small contingent at a point south of La Garde and established a battery to protect their seaward movement. With his impeccable sense of timing, after a week, Lapoype sends in a brigade of two thousand and crushes the battery. With their impeccable sense of timing, the next day, the enemy counterattack. A column from Fort La Malgue drove us back to La Garde. Another column came down from Fort D'Artigues and drove our brave volunteers out of La Valette.'

Jobert hung his head. 'There is much to be said for remaining on the road and ignorant. Did you know the Committee of Public Safety are guillotining failed generals "to encourage others"? The broadsheets report that over six hundred general officers have been dismissed in the four years since the fall of the Bastille. Further, at least half of them have been executed.'

'Then it must be our turn soon,' said Geourdai. 'To command the army, I mean, not to be executed.'

Jobert snorted. 'Does not the latter follow in the trains of the former? But before we assume command of the army, as it is late November, and there appears no end to this siege, ought we first prepare our chasseurs and horses for the winter ahead?'

Chapter Twenty-Three

December 1793, Revest, France

Jobert looked across the campfire at which all the troop commanders and platoon sergeants had gathered, bar Huin and Yinot with the 'Spanish water-cart'.

'I have inspected the company, sir,' said Neilage. 'I can confirm everyone now has, at least, two shirts, two pairs of underdrawers, two pairs of stockings and two blankets, with each item serviceable for the coming winter. But the company purse is near empty.'

Jobert's scowl lifted from his soup and pinned Neilage and Koschak. 'What? Have we spent all the money from the prisoner's purses and the sale of their clothing?'

'I purchased only what was agreed, sir,' said Koschak. 'Only enough clothing to make good that which was unserviceable. Marseille is in a very grim state. I had the quartermaster corporal press on to Aix-en-Provence to search for what was needed. Prices were steep, despite the volumes sought.'

Jobert's ill humour settled on the evening's fire. 'We must seek any opportunity to refill the company coffers.'

'Could we sell horseshoes to the artillery batteries?' asked Bredieux.

Jobert gave Koschak an enquiring look.

'Since the horses have been at rest here in Revest, sir,' said Koschak, 'we have reshod two hundred shoes and the chasseurs hold two hundred spares within their saddle frames. The company farrier has two hundred spares in his stocks.'

'One-hundred pairs. Do not touch them. Keep them for winter.'

The fire blazed resinous smoke from a pine branch catching alight.

'Winter, sir,' said Koschak. 'Knowing that rugging a horse at night is as good as feeding it a ration of grain, as they say. How might we go about gaining horse rugs like yours, sir, for the company.'

'It is a good idea. We have no money, but I am happy to think it through.'

'Most chasseurs have three blankets,' said Voreille, 'one from their initial regimental issue and two taken from the Spanish outside Sollies. Nearly all the chasseurs have sewn a double blanket and the other, if they have it and it is serviceable, is used as a horse blanket.'

'Blankets are no good in the rain, sir,' said Koschak. 'The re-mounts need to be under canvas, like Captain Jobert's.'

'How much canvas?' asked Neilage.

'Two metres by two metres.'

'Where would we find it?'

'Perhaps the fishing fleet in Marseille. But we have no money for canvas, sir.'

'There is canvas in Toulon. Naval stores have sails.'

'You will not get anywhere near sails,' said Bredieux. 'Like powder, sails, masts and rope stores demand the heaviest naval guards.'

'Tents?' suggested Voreille.

Neilage sneered. 'In the navy?'

'No, sir. Spanish and British tents, sir.'

'Those tents currently full of Spanish and British soldiers, sir?' asked Koschak. 'Unlike the rectangular tent-flies we sleep under, regular bell tents are made up of triangular pieces to create the bell shape. There would be a lot of unpicking and resewing to make a rectangular horse rug.'

'Hammocks,' said Bredieux. Everyone looked at Bredieux exhaling blue tobacco smoke into the heat of the fire and considered this source of canvas. 'The navy would have hundreds of hammocks. Hammocks are kept in general stores which do not require a guard.'

'A hammock would be two metres long,' said Koschak, 'but would it be two metres wide?'

'We will probably need one and a half hammocks per horse,' said Neilage. 'One hundred and fifty hammocks.'

'How are hammocks stored?' asked Jobert.

'Probably like blankets, sir,' said Koschak. 'Folded in bales of ten, trussed with twine.'

'How heavy would they be to lift?'

'One man could lift a bale.'

'Could one man carry a bale from Toulon to Revest?'

'Ah, no, sir. In that case, two men or a wagon,' said Koschak.

'How many wagons?' asked Neilage. 'Fifteen bales, one wagon?'

'In Toulon, we know draught horses and bullocks would be under tighter guard than powder. We would do well to find donkeys.'

'Then seven bales a wagon, two wagons, four donkeys,' said Neilage.

'A cart for a pair of donkeys, sir, not a wagon,' said Koschak. 'Fifteen bales, three small carts, six donkeys. Find six draught animals in Toulon? Impossible.'

Everyone looked at each other across the fire in acknowledgement of the extreme improbability. Neilage shrugged, accepting his previous suggestion unworkable. 'Then thirty men to carry fifteen bales.'

'How would you get thirty men in?' asked Jobert. 'Patrol? Thirty uniforms? Language?'

'The Royal Louis Battalion wear old royal army white, sir, like the line battalions,' said Koschak.

'Risking the loss of thirty men, three sections from eight, is unacceptable. How else?'

2nd Company's command group stared into the fire.

'Could we find thirty men in Toulon?' asked Neilage.

'Who?' said Jobert.

'De Beaussancourt's company,' said Duque, as he moved around the outside of the group gathering the empty soup bowls. Everyone exchanged glances at Duque's suggestion.

'Where are they kept?' asked Koschak. 'Or have they been transported out? Like the five-thousand Republican sailors removed from Toulon by the British.'

'Our Spanish water-cart needs to answer that,' said Jobert.

'How long have they been there?' asked Koschak.

'De Beaussancourt's company? Since the 1st of October. Two and a half months.'

'If they are there,' said Koschak, 'they would be very sick, if not dead. Yet, if we freed sixty of them, we could alternate the porterage. How many of us would it take to free them? Five? Ten?'

'How do you get five to ten men in?' Jobert squinted for a solution in the flames.

'As a lost Spanish patrol via the British at Fort La Malgue,' said Voreille. Every face turned towards him at the suggestion. 'Ah, ... Major Avriol and I discussed it once.'

'No, ... good suggestion,' said Jobert considering Voreille a moment. 'A patrol of one Spanish officer, one Spanish sergeant and four men. Uniforms?'

'Spanish prisoners' jackets are easy to come by,' said Koschak, 'which can then be switched into Royal Louis militia, if we had to.'

'And a naval officer,' said Bredieux. 'Someone with the appropriate authority to request the release of naval items from the naval general stores, sir.'

'Captain Duhamel might have a spare uniform at home.' Koschak smirked into the glowing embers. 'A trip to Château Duhamel, sir? If you are too busy, sir, I could manage that.'

Jobert ignored the innuendo. 'Why would a naval officer take one hundred and fifty hammocks out of the city in the middle of the night?'

'Naval gunners at the forts?' said Neilage. 'Deception? Moving by night so the French do not see what they are transporting? To obscure preparations of freshly dug gun positions in forward redoubts?'

'A Royal Louis prisoner escort takes the bales to the outer forts,' said Jobert. 'In through La Malgue and out through where? Fort Sainte-Catherine?'

'Fort D'Artigues is smaller,' said Koschak, 'and not far up Mount Faron's slopes.'

'Is not La Valette now in enemy hands?' asked Neilage. 'Will it not be difficult moving down the slopes of D'Artigues, past La Valette to Revest? A mounted troop would be needed, at least, to get anywhere near Fort D'Artigues.'

'We still have to go in and out through the Toulon's eastern gate,' said Jobert, 'the Italian Gate. Go in before and go out after the guard changes. Who will be the seven?'

The crackles of pinecones in the flames filled the silence.

'Me,' said Jobert. 'Which excludes the second-in-command

and Sergeant Major Koschak. If I am lost, 2nd Company maintains her commanders.'

Neilage exchanged a glance with Koschak. 'Lieutenant Huin or Sergeant Yinot as the Spanish officer? Sergeant Bredieux as the naval officer?'

'Slow down.' Jobert held up a hand. 'If Huin is the Spanish officer and Bredieux is the naval officer, then all other officers or sergeants are excluded.' Voreille slumped at his exclusion.

'Four troopers, one from each platoon,' said Koschak.

'Include marksman Duval,' said Jobert, 'but not Tulloc. That is seven men. I am risking the loss of seven men to maintain our horses through winter. Very well, when?'

'There is another brigade marching in from Nice to join Lapoype on the 14th of December, sir,' said Neilage. 'We would do well to complete this raid before there are any adjustments to Lapoype's line.'

'Then that gives us two nights,' said Jobert. 'Tomorrow night or the night after? Since we need information from the 'Spanish water cart' as to where the prisoners are held, if they exist at all, it will be the night after. The evening of 13th of December. We also need Lieutenant Huin back with us, for him to be ready as a Spanish officer.'

'With Château Duhamel our only source of naval uniforms and the base for our lost Spanish patrol,' said Koschak, 'we will also need tomorrow to support Madame Duhamel becoming 'abreast' of our plan and allowing her to fully 'grasp' our 'firm' intent of 'inserting' our —'

'Yes, thank you, Sergeant Major.' Jobert suppressed a grin. 'Let us talk through the plan again, seeking any risks and listing what we need.'

Thick, low rain clouds covered the moon. The intermittent, soft splats of heavy raindrops on the clods in the abandoned fields around Fort La Malgue, accompanied the careful footfalls of Huin's silent patrol as they approached the low hill on which sat one of the largest fortresses in Toulon's defences. As the patrol moved forward toward the dull glow of torchlight on La Malgue's ramparts, Jobert identified the torchlight of parties moving on both sides of the stream which separated the British Fort La Malgue and the Spanish breastworks eight hundred metres distant. Although the breastworks were not discernible at this range in this light, Jobert discerned the lit tents at the stream's crossing point, which acted as a point of coordination for the two forces.

Two torches flickering in the increasing breeze moved down the slope from La Malgue towards the lost patrol cloaked in the darkness. The rhythmic sound of clanking, ever present with a body of marching troops no matter the size, was heard approaching above the wind.

'Ready, lads. Here we go,' said Huin. '*Quien va alla?*' The patrol kneeled on the bare earth and cocked their muskets.

'*Britanico, amigo, ingles, ingles.*' The rattling marching became whispered commands and muskets brought to the ready. 'Do you speak French?'

'Most certainly, sir.' Huin stepped to change his position in the darkness. 'This is His Hispanic Majesty's Mallorca Regiment. Who goes there?'

'His Britannic Majesty's 30th Regiment of Foot, sir. I would be obliged, sir, if your party might approach our torchlight, please.'

'I have a patrol of myself and six others. I shall approach you now.'

Huin, followed by his patrol, moved carefully across the field, until they were outlined in the gloom ten metres apart. Jobert counted the British officer with a sergeant beside him, two torch-bearers and four other soldiers.

'Make safe,' said Huin in Provencal. The Spanish patrol un-cocked their muskets.

'I am Major don Carlos Valdes, sir and I am at your service.' Huin bowed, performing an admirable imitation of Chabenac.

'Sir, I am Ensign Horace Torkington and I am at your service. Are you aware you are within the British area of responsibility? Did you not cross over the stream from the Spanish redoubt?'

'No, we have come along the shoreline from Cap Brun. Would you care for some brandy?'

'Just the thing for a night such as this. Was that your patrol firing?'

'Yes, we saw off a French vedette,' said Huin.

'Are you making for Fort La Malgue, sir?'

'No, Fort Sainte-Catherine. I have with me a messenger I need to deliver to that fort. May I introduce Captain don Jeromino Moreno Frias, sir, of His Hispanic Majesty's Royal Navy.' Huin stepped back to introduce a naval officer in a befeathered bicorne, dark jacket, dark waist sash, white trousers and tall, cuffed riding boots.

'I am at your service, sir.' Bredieux, clutching at his wind-ruffled hat, bowed low.

'And I at yours, sir. Then, Major, may I assist you and the Captain by escorting you to our coordination point with your countrymen at the stream.'

'You are too kind, but I must get to Sainte-Catherine as quickly as possible,' said Huin.

'But the shortest route to Sainte-Catherine is via that redoubt, sir.'

'I am embarrassed to admit, sir, the commanding colonel of the earthworks will insist on us joining him to dine. However at-tractive that might seem, sadly, it will cause much delay on such a night. The nature of the Captain's dispatch demands alacrity.'

'The only other path, sir, is through Fort La Malgue.'

Huin turned to Jobert. '*Sargento, La Malgue o murallas?*'

Jobert guessed at the nature of the question. '*La Malgue, senor.*'

'Excellent, then we will escort you,' said Torkington. 'My Colonel speaks Spanish and would be delighted to receive you as guests. He is tired of the simpering French frauds within the Royal Louis battalion posted to the fort.'

'Your generous offer is too kind, sir. We have no wish to inconvenience your good selves. Another time, perhaps?'

The British sergeant made a small coughing noise to attract his officer's attention. Torkington turned and spoke curtly to his sergeant. The British sergeant mumbled in response, his face turning to the increasing cold rain. Torkington cut him short. Jobert saw the man's face quivering. *Did he just say 'colonel'?* Whatever the sergeant had said, Torkington squirmed with indecision.

Jobert looked at the two Englishmen under the spluttering torchlight and hatred warmed his chest. *How I remember the banalities of teenage nobility at the expense of the assigned task and without any concern for the men. If I ever doubted Jacobin methods, then this young arse-wipe removes any concerns.*

Torkington spat out a quick command without looking at his sergeant, then resumed his mask of gentility. 'Yes, gentlemen, the rain has become most insistent. I too have duties that await. May I provide two fusiliers and a torch to escort you to my colonel?'

'Your kindness in this matter, sir, is deeply appreciated. I shall certainly commend you to your colonel informing him of your generosity and dedication to duty.'

After parting pleasantries were exchanged, the two patrols stepped off once again. The 'Spanish' patrol followed the two British soldiers, one with a spluttering torch, up a slight track towards the forbidding outline of Fort La Malgue.

The icy rain began to pelt down not far from La Malgue's eastern gate. The walls soared above the group. From under lean-to shelters across each gun embrasure and each window in the stories above the ramparts, candle and torch light illuminated the fortress, hinting at the shadowy paths under the walls and around the fort towards its western gate. Such paths were preferred by Huin and Jobert rather than present their patrol within the fort.

Huin asked the British fusiliers whether they spoke French or Spanish. They spoke neither. Huin used sign language to indicate he wished to take the paths around the fort. The soldiers, becoming more and more agitated in the pouring rain, insisting on moving inside the gate. Jobert considered the options and withdrew his dagger from his cuff. Saved by Huin, the two British fusiliers were presented a heavy purse in exchange for their pitch-soaked torch.

Once the soldiers departed for the fortress' shelter from the increasing deluge, Jobert took the torch, hissing and spitting in the rain and led the patrol under the walls, around Fort La Malgue and found the road leading toward Toulon.

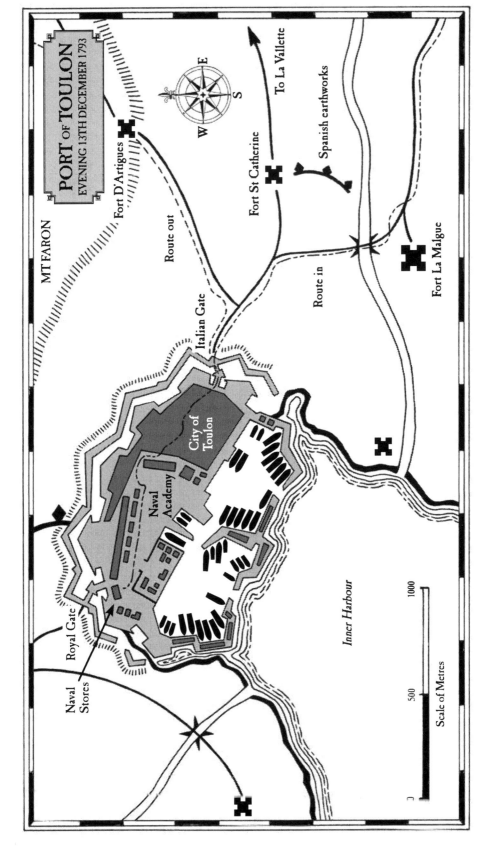

PORT OF TOULON
EVENING 13TH DECEMBER 1793

MT FARON

Fort D'Artigues

Route out

To La Vallette

Fort St Catherine

Spanish earthworks

Route in

Fort La Malgue

Italian Gate

City of
Toulon

Naval
Academy

Royal Gate

Naval
Stores

Inner Harbour

Scale of Metres

500   1000

W   E   S

Chapter Twenty-Four

Hunched in their saturated tailcoats, the patrol pressed through Toulon's eastern portal, the Italian Gate. The Italian Gate was a series of barriers leading to a major internal check-point. The sentries at the main gate were French, British, Neapolitan and Spanish. Heavily influenced by the stakes at risk with their next hand of cards beside the guard room's glowing hearth, the Spanish sentries allowed their countrymen to pass, satisfied that the patrol was escorting a Spanish naval officer to the docks.

Slipping through the gate and into the city, the patrol was greeted by whistles and calls from tattered whores braving the freezing rain.

'Our Madame Quandalle,' said Huin. 'Her disguises are Mount Faron cantiniere by day, whore of Toulon by night. She watches our exit and signals all is well.'

The patrol strode through the empty, muddy streets, their torch now extinguished, blustering past idle French loyalist sentries, into the naval precinct.

Within Toulon's naval precinct, the 'Spanish water-cart' learnt that the chapel attached to the Naval Academy held de Beaussancourt's company. At the bleak, rain-streaked entrance to the chapel, the patrol removed their Spanish bicornes and donned their bonnets-de-police from deep within their warm, but sopping wet waistcoats.

Huin marched the patrol across the small courtyard in front of the chapel, then stepped forward up the broad stairs and pounded on the thick wooden door. The chapel door opened inward to reveal a respectably dressed, middle-aged man, unremarkable except for a bored sneer that twisted his mouth and hooded his eyes.

'I am Lieutenant Huin, Royal Louis battalion. I have here orders requiring me to escort naval stores to Fort Sainte-Catherine.'

'This is not the naval stores.' The gaoler began to close the heavy door.

Huin stepped forward placing his hand on the door. 'I know that. I have authority to collect a prison work party of seventy to carry the stores.'

'We do not have seventy.' The gaoler again attempted to shut the door.

Huin took up the hilt of his sword. 'You attempt to shut this door on me again and I will remove your hand. I am wet to the skin, and I am in no mood for bullshit.'

The gaoler shifted his stance, his malevolent eyes evaluating Huin. He pouted before stepping back from the open door into the vestibule.

'I am told the prisoners captured on Mount Faron are capable of porterage,' said Huin.

'Them? There is only sixty, at least ten are too ill to walk.'

'I need seventy. Let me see how sick they are. Sergeant, with me. The rest of you wait here until called.'

Jobert smiled. *No longer playing de Chabenac, Huin. Now an uncanny likeness to Koschak.*

Inside the chapel vestibule, a thick odour of sewerage, vomit and rotting meat struck Huin and Jobert. Huin and Jobert coughed at the stench and attempted to control their breathing.

The gaoler let out a mocking laugh. 'Oh, my delicate petals. May I see that your authority is correct, sir?'

Huin took out the damp parchment from a sodden leather satchel. The gaoler walked to a tall, writing lectern on which stood a candle, where he examined the document. 'I will need to keep this until the work party has been returned.'

With a heavy set of iron keys, the gaoler unlocked an inner door to the nave and took a lit lantern from a bracket mounted in the wall.

Once inside the black stench of the nave of the chapel, lit only by the lantern in the gaoler's hand, Huin squinted into the dark shapes on the floor. 'Where is the company commander?'

'There. As I told you, too sick to stand.'

'Where is the next senior man?'

'Sergeant!' The gaoler kicked the groaning bodies huddled together on the slimy flagstones. The light faded as Huin and the gaoler turned into a transept, seeking the senior, still capable person in the prison.

Jobert knelt beside de Beaussancourt in the darkness of the chapel. 'Can you hear me, sir? Do you remember the battle of Mount Faron?'

'Yes,' said de Beaussancourt.

'On Mount Faron you were guided by chasseurs à cheval. Do you recognise my voice?'

De Beaussancourt grasped at Jobert's face with a clammy hand. 'Ah, yes, Jobert, 24th Chasseurs, was it not?'

'Very good, Captain de Beaussancourt. It is I, Captain Jobert. I am here to make good your escape. I need you and your men on your feet and prepare to be disguised as a work party.'

'Sergeant! Assemble the men for the work party.'

'Wait!' The gaoler waded amongst the bodies emerging from shadows on the floor. 'Chain them first.'

'Chains?' asked Huin. 'These cadavers cannot walk to Fort Sainte-Catherine in chains.'

'My prisoners are not walking out of this cage without leg-irons.'

'Team them in four even gangs,' said Jobert.

'I beg your pardon, Sergeant. You will chain them, not me.' The gaoler kicked at the prisoners struggling to their feet. 'Leave your blankets, you will be back soon enough.'

With Bredieux waiting in the chapel's vestibule, Jobert had his soldiers sling their muskets, press the prisoners into four gangs of about sixteen men each and fit the leg-irons to emaciated legs, nearly all with festering, rancid wounds. What was occurring was whispered from prisoner to prisoner, causing fevered eyes to glow with reignited determination.

The gaoler hoisted his lantern. 'There is none sick on the floor now. My, my, the dead can walk.'

'I would imagine the storm tonight would be their first bath and first fresh water in ten weeks,' said Huin.

The guttural murmur of assent came from the ragged soldiers about him.

'Royal Louis battalion, eh?' The gaoler leant against a pillar and ran his hooded eyes over each of the soldiers in the escort. 'I have never seen green bonnets-de-police before in the battalion. Why are you wearing green bonnets?'

'That was all there was left in the clothing store,' said Huin.

'What company do you belong to?'

'Battalion headquarters. These men are clerks.'

'He is not a clerk.' The gaoler pointed at Jobert.

'The sergeant is new. He has just escaped from Marseille.'

'And 'he' holds the rank of sergeant,' said Jobert, 'so, watch your mouth, gaoler.'

'Ooh! Very Jacobin, thank you very much. You are absolutely convinced of his loyalty, sir?'

The soldiers stood from their task of chaining legs, grimacing from the stale stench of the chapel. Jobert posted the four guards at key points around the prisoners before moving them out into the rain.

'That is a rifle.' The gaoler pointed at Duval's weapon. 'Let me see that.' Duval stepped back from the reaching hand. 'A clerk does not need a rifle.' The gaoler stepped forward with his hand outstretched for the weapon. 'Give it to me now'.

Jobert stood up and swung a spare leg chain in a low arc. 'Leave my men alone as we are a little busy. But I can always make time to cuff one more leg.'

'Do it,' breathed sixty voices in the darkness.

Jobert advanced. The gaoler emitted a strangled squeal.

'That is enough, Sergeant,' said Huin. 'Our duty awaits. I will take the keys.' Huin stuck out his hand.

With Huin's reprieve, the gaoler's ugly sneer and malevolent eyes fixed on Jobert. 'Keys? Huh! I do not think so. You can unchain them on their return.'

'And if they collapse in chains?'

'They can carry themselves. Or you can remove the limb.'

Huin regarded the man with contempt. Jobert approached the gaoler and reached towards his face with the grimy torch handle. As the gaoler cringed against the wall, Jobert wiped wet pitch-soot down the front of the gaoler's clean jacket, before taking a spare, unlit torch from a wall bracket.

The blinking French naval quartermaster sighed. 'One hundred and fifty hammocks at this time of night, sir?'

Bredieux spread his arms wide, showing the pool of water he stood in, that dripped down from his coat, then slowly turned toward the sixty-odd chained, wretched prisoners and the squad of soaked, shivering guards standing in the pouring rain. 'Sergeant, we are not doing this as a joke. Not on a bastard of a night like this.'

The quartermaster squinted again at the damp parchment request, with its smudged ink, in the flickering candlelight. 'Could I ask why, sir?'

'Of course, you may, son. The stores are for the sappers and gunners at Fort Sainte-Catherine. The sappers are taking advantage of the rain to prepare extra earthworks for our naval guns. The canvas, when covered in mud and grass, conceals the new gun emplacements from the Republican patrols. We are moving the stores by night to deny the information to the enemy.'

'Huh, Army!' The quartermaster shook his head and took an oil-lamp from his desk. 'Come with me, gentlemen.'

Bredieux, Huin and Jobert followed the quartermaster into the naval stores warehouse. The lamp illuminated a long, vaulted room, divided into timber stalls, not unlike stables in a barn.

'There are your hammocks, sir.' The quartermaster raised the lamp to show a wide stall, stacked with hundreds of bales of hammocks.

Jobert lifted out fifteen bales into the aisle between the stalls of supplies.

'My gangs are in teams of sixteen, quartermaster,' said Huin. 'May I bring in two gangs to carry the bales out?'

'Certainly, but you ought to wrap the bales in old, waste canvas from that bin, to protect the bales becoming sodden with rain.'

As the quartermaster moved the lamp to illuminate the canvas waste bin for Jobert, the soft light glowed briefly upon a stall full of large kegs and many small casks.

'What is in the kegs, quartermaster?' asked Bredieux, when Huin had departed to bring in two of the prison gangs.

'British rum from the Caribbean, sir.'

'Mmm, I have not had rum since my squadron was last in Guadeloupe.'

'It tastes like shit, sir, I do not know how you drink it.'

'Ooh, with banana juice, of course.'

Jobert converted his unexpected snort into a cough. *What would an ex-fisherman from Saint Nazaire know of tropical fruit?*

'I have heard of them,' said the quartermaster, 'but I have never had a banana.'

'Would it be possible for a small sip of that liquid sunshine to warm my bones?' asked Bredieux.

Jobert frowned at Bredieux.

'I am sorry, sir, no,' said the quartermaster.

'Not possible at all, quartermaster? On a miserable night like this? Just a sip?'

'But I cannot get the bung out, sir.'

'Quartermaster, you are speaking with a naval captain. Really? No cooper's tools in a naval store?'

'We have what we came for, sir,' said Jóbert.

'Now, now, I am making a genuine request.' Bredieux produced a heavy purse from an inner pocket of his waistcoat and hefted it in his right hand.

'That is not necessary, sir.' The quartermaster's eyes glinted at the purse in the faint light.

'Absolutely not. From one sea-mate to another, I appreciate your succour on a stormy night. Quick now, grab those tools.'

The quartermaster rocked his head indecisively, turned around thinking where the tools might be. Bredieux swung his purse in a swift, low arc and brought it up hard on the quartermaster's skull just under the ear. The sailor collapsed.

'Sergeant Bredieux!' said Jobert. 'What the fuck are you doing?'

'Ten little casks of rum, sir. We could raise money for company funds.'

'Sergeant Bredieux, stop this bullshit, or we will all end up in the naval chapel.'

Huin's thirty-odd prisoners were approaching, chains clanking across the stone floor. Huin started when he saw the body on the floor.

'Sir, someone is coming,' hissed a few prisoners.

'Quickly! Cover him in bales,' said Jobert to the prisoners.

'Good evening there, what are you people doing?' a high-pitched voice called out from behind the glow of a lamp. 'Oh! Good evening, sir.' An elderly, bespectacled French naval lieutenant stammered upon seeing Bredieux's rank. 'Where is the quartermaster? How may I help you, sir?' The lieutenant looked about him with concern, placing his hand to his nose due to the unwashed and rotting stench.

The prisoners wrapped bales of hammocks and then, with some difficulty, hoisted one bale between two prisoners.

'Good evening to you, sir,' said Bredieux. 'I am required to take fifteen bales of hammocks and ten casks of gin out to Fort Sainte-Catherine. The quartermaster has gone off somewhere looking for coopers' tools.'

'Sir, that is not gin. That is rum.'

'I do not want rum, sir.' Bredieux flapped his authorisation documents. 'My requisition says gin.'

'But we do not have any gin, sir.'

'But I must take gin to Admiral Hood's dinner.' Bredieux punched his fist into his palm.

'If I had gin, sir, you would be most welcome to it, but I simply do not.'

'Then what am I going to do?'

The lieutenant recoiled at the ghastly appearance and stench of the prisoners around him.

Huin glanced at Jobert. 'Perhaps we might take the rum, sir.'

'Do not be an idiot, man,' said Bredieux. 'The Admiral specifically stated gin.'

'Should you take the rum, sir,' said Huin, shaking his head imperceptibly to an alarmed Jobert, 'if the Admiral does not care for it then we will bring it back.'

'What? Bring it back tonight?' asked Bredieux. 'Are you mad, sir?'

'I will bring it back tomorrow, sir.' Huin bowed his head, exchanging looks of alarm with the naval lieutenant.

'Have you tasted the rum, sir?' The naval lieutenant winced. 'It is an acquired taste.'

'You have a point. Oh, I do not know what to do.'

'Please, sir, your men need to clear my warehouse.' The lieutenant coughed. 'Please take the rum.'

'Oh, very well. If you insist.'

'How will we carry the casks, sir?' asked Jobert through gritted teeth.

'Bloody landlubbers.' Bredieux rolled his eyes to the stores lieutenant. 'In a sling of waste canvas, of course. Do you have a bin of waste canvas?'

'We do indeed, sir, just there.'

'Get on with it, Sergeant. I do not have all night.'

Jobert breathed to contain himself. Then he created ten slings, hung them around the necks of the stronger prisoners and nestled a small cask into the folds of the sling. With the twenty litre casks weighing about twenty-five kilograms, Jobert knew his soldiers, not the prisoners, would need to carry such a load.

'Now here, the requisition forms.' Bredieux flicked the

papers at the lieutenant. 'I am not happy, sir. I insist on signing a separate form declaring that I was forced to take rum from the store and not gin.'

The storm clouds snagged on Mount Faron, unable to move further inland. The lightening illuminated the mountain's slopes, the thunder boomed down from the shadowed valleys, yet the freezing December rain emptied on the town.

For the laden column of prisoners and guards, trudging back through the slippery cobbled streets to the Italian Gate, the discomfort of saturated woollen tailcoats for the lucky, or simply shirtsleeves for the majority, was bearable in comparison to the thought of returning to the naval chapel.

A shrill whistle sounded. 'Halt!' ordered Huin.

A slim, barefoot feminine figure, dressed in rags, with a scarf about her head and a tattered blanket about her shoulders, materialised from a dark lane.

'They are looking for you,' said Madame Quandalle, her torch-lit face framed with wet curls. 'A British patrol has just come in from La Malgue and reported to the Italian Gate sentries. They seek a Spanish patrol with a slim, aristocratic officer, a naval officer and a big sergeant. The sentries have shut the Italian Gate and the patrol has pressed onto the wharves.'

'Then we need to eliminate who they are looking for,' said Jobert.

'I am able to remain here in the town,' said Huin. 'Bredieux, take my uniform and command the column.'

Bredieux struggled to shrug off his saturated woollen naval

jacket. 'What about you, sir?'

'Give my sergeant's tailcoat to one of the soldiers' said Jobert. 'I will strip to my drawers and join a gang. We also need a way to pick the locks of these leg-irons.'

'I can pick locks.' Madame Quandalle peered at the clinking chains on emaciated legs. 'Do you need to unchain them now?'

'No, not now. We have to get outside first.'

Huin folded his arms across his slim chest since reduced to his shirtsleeves. 'You cannot be seen taking a woman out through the gates.'

The four saturated figures fought the exhaustions that overwhelmed their minds.

'We could take a sergeant.' Jobert held out his tailcoat.

'Then queue my hair.' Quandalle passed her blanket and scarf to Huin. 'Use Huin's ribbon.' Jobert ground his teeth as he willed his numb fingers to undo Huin's queue ribbon and then braid Quandalle's thick, wet hair.

Once complete, and with Jobert having taken his place between some prisoners, Quandalle slapped Jobert's buttocks and squeezed hard. 'You will pay a pretty fee for my extra services, my lovely lad.' The surrounding prisoners whistled softly.

The column adjusted their hold on their burdens and groaned forward through the slimy puddles and the dripping eaves towards the Italian Gate. The light and the laughter spilling from the guard room guided their shuffling, clinking steps.

'Can we pass?' asked Bredieux to the eight raucous men at the card table by the fire. The two British and two Spanish sentries looked up at the sodden Royal Louis subaltern in the doorway.

'Coming, sir.' A French militiaman in plain clothes with a white, Royalist cockade on his bicorne, pushed himself back from the table and crossed the warmth of the room. 'Good evening, sir. Bastard of a night.'

Bredieux stepped back out under covered gateway, adjusted a heavy weight slung about his chest and fumbled with his flint as he attempted to light his pipe. 'Wet flint.'

'We cannot have that, sir. Here, sir, allow me?'

'Thank you, my friend. Here, have the tobacco.'

'Well, thank you, sir. Now, how can I help?'

'I have bales of canvas for the sappers at Fort Sainte-Catherine.' Bredieux jerked his head at the morose, shivering prisoners and drew on his pipe.

'Your papers, please, sir.'

'I gave my requisition for prisoners to the gaoler, and my requisition for stores to the navy. I have no other paperwork.'

One of the two British sentries, a corporal, stepped out from the guard room, into the chill, wet breeze racing through the gateway. 'Who is in your party, sir?' asked the British soldier in halting French.

'This lot.' Bredieux jerked his thumb.

The Briton exchanged a pleading look with the French sentry. 'Do you have a Spanish naval officer travelling with you, sir?' asked the militiaman.

'I beg your pardon. Not unless he is in chains.'

'Do you have any sergeants in your escort, sir?'

The sentries looked the length of the column and a short sergeant stepped into the torchlight. The corporal snorted a laugh and returned into the heat of the guard room.

'Sorry about that sir. I really ought to see your passes. I could send a runner to the Royal Louis duty officer?'

'What?' asked Bredieux. 'To battalion headquarters in Fort La Malgue? These miserable Republican bastards will be dead by then.'

The sentry sucked his teeth as he looked at the wasted men in chains in the shadows of the gatehouse. A call from behind him urged him back to the card game beside the guard room's glow.

'Have you lost your money to these foreigners?' asked Bredieux.

'Yes, sir.'

'Maybe the British Navy can help us both to have their canvas delivered? Here, I have stores for Admiral Hood's dinner party.' Bredieux pulled back the edge of the canvas sling to reveal the iron-bound cask. 'Caribbean rum. As you said, it is a bastard of a night for it and I have to deliver these stores then get these poor mongrels back to their shit-hole.'

'Very good, sir. But we will confirm your passes on your way back, sir, yes?'

Bredieux struggled out of the sling and passed the barrel to the sentry. The sentry placed the barrel behind an overflowing rain butt, stepped to the gate and unlocked the mechanism which allowed the gate's heavy bar to be withdrawn.

The gates opened.

With their loads hefted back upon aching arms and shoulders, the grim column shuffled through a series of outer gates, over Toulon's defensive ditch to set foot on the Fort Sainte-Catherine road. After half-an-hour of marching without torchlight the rain slackened to a light drizzle.

Upon finding the road to Fort D'Artigues, the column pressed up the slope until well off the Toulon-Sainte-Catherine road. Very soon after, the prisoners exhaled a thankful moan as they collapsed on their wrapped bales and unslung the heavy casks from their chests. The sodden escort were dispatched into the darkness as pairs of sentries, as Quandalle unpicked over sixty chain locks.

'Captain Jobert,' hissed the prisoners, 'there are horses out there in the dark, sir. Someone is whistling the trumpet call *To Mess*.'

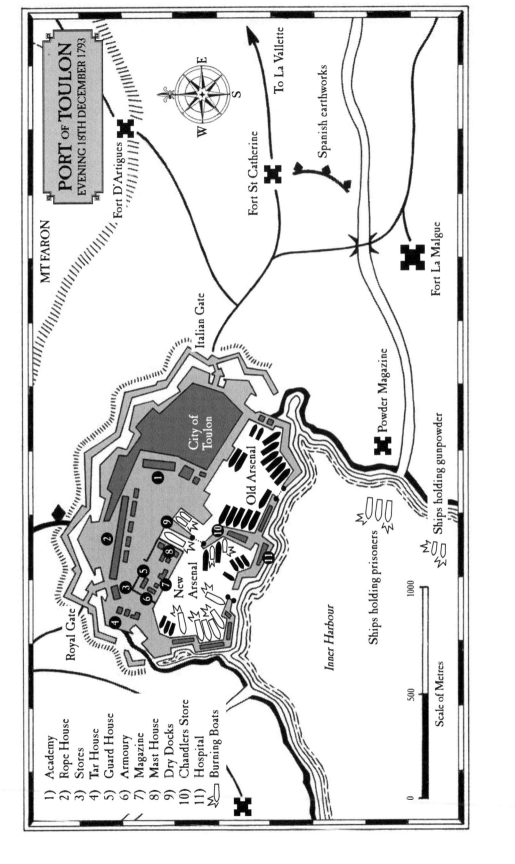

PORT OF TOULON
EVENING 18TH DECEMBER 1793

MT FARON

Fort D'Artigues

To La Vallette

Spanish earthworks

Fort St Catherine

Fort La Malgue

Italian Gate

City of Toulon

Royal Gate

Old Arsenal

New Arsenal

Powder Magazine

Ships holding gunpowder

Inner Harbour

Ships holding prisoners

Scale of Metres

0   500   1000

1) Academy
2) Rope House
3) Stores
4) Tar House
5) Guard House
6) Armoury
7) Magazine
8) Mast House
9) Dry Docks
10) Chandlers Store
11) Hospital
⌐ Burning Boats

Chapter Twenty-Five

Apart from a long dining table, the château's wide drawing room was stripped of furnishings, paintings, curtains and carpets. The near-empty room amplified the sound of many spurred boots criss-crossing the bare floorboards. Dust from the tracks of dried mud, highlighted by the low-angled morning sun, swirled to waist height. The poorly attended fire in the great hearth smouldered, wafting a burnt tang of pine resin and rank hay in the air disturbed by bustling staff officers.

Avriol beckoned Jobert to follow. 'The army is preparing to attack Toulon. General Dugommier conducted a reconnaissance on the 14th of December, the same day that General Masséna's brigade arrived. In fact, the same morning you returned from your recent escapade. The attack is planned for tomorrow night, the night of the 17th and 18th of December.'

Jobert saw Colonel Morin and Chabenac standing within a knot of senior officers consulting a chart at the closest end of the dining table. General Lapoype led the discussion, surrounded by Lapoype's brigade commanders, including the recently arrived Masséna.

'At two o'clock this morning,' said Avriol, 'Bonaparte started his bombardment of the enemy's outer fortresses.'

In a sun-lit corner of the vast room, General Dugommier, Lieutenant Colonel Raive and Major Bonaparte sat on high-backed dining chairs. Bonaparte jabbed at a map spread on the coffee table between them.

Avriol indicated to Jobert, through the darting couriers and aides, a group of three men, Deputy Saliceti and two naval officers, at the far-end of the dining table. 'I am going to introduce you to Admiral Brueys d'Aigalliers and one of his staff officers attending General Dugommier's headquarters. As for the Admiral's staff officer, naval Captain Saint-Joséph is the equivalent of an army colonel.'

Jobert maintained his solemnity with a curt nod.

'Excuse me, sir, gentlemen,' said Avriol. 'May I present Captain Jobert, the chasseur officer who led the raid into Toulon two days ago.' Jobert saluted the sour-faced admiral in his early forties.

'I believe you entered Toulon,' said Brueys. 'What was your intent in entering the city?'

'To take one hundred and fifty hammocks, sir.'

'Why?'

'To create one hundred canvas horse rugs for my chasseur company prior to winter.'

'Hammocks stolen from the French navy.' Saint-Joséph, a wiry, hard-faced man with his thick black hair swept back in a tight queue, shuffled in agitation.

'Not at all, citizen,' said Saliceti. 'Hammocks that were possessed by the Spanish and British navies. Spoils of war'.

Brueys ignored the interjection. 'And you released several prisoners-of-war?'

'We had fought alongside these men, sir,' said Jobert. 'There was a mutual advantage. We needed a work party and they needed a disguise to escape.'

Saliceti chuckled. 'The rumours have it you took an amount of rum.'

'An unintended consequence, citizen.'

'How did you get in?' asked Brueys.

'We passed through the enemy's defences as a lost Spanish patrol in the British sector, sir. We passed through the gates as the escort to a Spanish naval officer. Finally, we modified our uniforms and became royalist militia to secure the prisoners and the stores.'

'Satisfied?' Saliceti beamed at the Admiral. 'Then would you excuse me, gentlemen, as I am keen to join General Dugommier's conversation.'

As Saliceti departed across the drawing room, the four remaining officers rearranged their stances, averting their eyes to conceal their opinions of the People's Representative.

With a nod from Brueys, Saint-Joséph continued the exchange. 'The Army have a plan to attack the enemy fleet and force the enemy to evacuate the port. The plan is sound and may well work. If it does, the enemy would do well to destroy the forty French naval vessels and vast number of stores before departing. As the only representatives of the French Navy hereabouts, we are bent on minimising that destruction. Rumours of your infiltration two days ago reached us here at headquarters. Citizen Saliceti suggested we seek your thoughts on how we might insert a party to affect our desires.'

'Forgive me, sir,' asked Jobert, 'may I ask questions?'

'Of course.'

'How many men are you considering moving into the city?'

'We believe a force of one to two hundred men will be required.'

A flash of alarm passed between Avriol and Jobert. 'For what purpose, sir?' asked Jobert.

'To defend the vital areas that will certainly be targeted by the enemy,' said Saint-Joséph.

'What enemy action do you wish to defend against, sir?'

Saint-Joséph's lip curled in irritation. 'Demolition parties.'

'For the destruction you foresee, sir, how might an enemy demolition party be composed, sir? What tasks would it be required to undertake?'

'One officer and about four men would move kegs of gunpowder to the point of detonation. Then run the fuses, either trails of powder or lengths of rope-match, to an ignition point. When authorised, the party light the fuses. Why is this of any importance, captain?'

Jobert's eyes narrowed as an idea started to form in his mind. 'What if we bluffed the enemy instead of opposed them?'

'How so?' asked Brueys.

'Imagine we inserted our own demolition parties, sir? To all external appearances, the enemy would see our parties have the task in hand. Might that work?'

The naval officers looked at each other. 'We would need the appropriate authorities prepared, in French, Spanish and English,' said Saint-Joséph.

'How might such a bluff be called, sir?' asked Jobert.

'By the deceivers not igniting the fuses when the enemy orders it.'

'If something had to burn, or appear to be burning, could the detonations be set to appear as if some element of our task had been achieved?'

The naval captain turned to his admiral. They both were unsettled by the question. Eventually Brueys nodded.

'Thank you, sir,' said Jobert. 'In the disguise of which nationality would suit our approach the best?'

'Spanish. We all speak Spanish, but none of us speak English.'

'I understand, sir. How many of our demolition parties would be needed?'

'I refer you to this chart of the layout of Toulon's port,' said Saint-Joséph, indicating a number of maps and sketches laid across the end of the dining table. 'There are three key areas within the naval precinct. Buildings within the precinct, ships alongside the internal wharves and a powder magazine outside the city's wall, on the shoreline behind Fort La Malgue. Three parties of one officer and four men, a total of fifteen.'

'Let us say one officer and six, a total of twenty-one,' said Brueys. 'How might twenty-one be inserted, Captain Jobert?'

Jobert cast about for a solution. 'The enemy needs to be focussed on some form of external diversion, sir.'

'Such as a divisional attack on Mount Faron's forts?' said Avriol. 'General Lapoype's party is discussing that very course of action at this moment.'

'That would certainly divert the enemy at both their outer defences and at the city's gates. Perhaps enemy wounded coming down from the forts? A surgeon and wounded in a cart. The cart will allow any extra items that will be required within the port. The cart pulled by walking wounded, no draught animals.'

'Wounded would work very well.' Saint-Joséph pointed to the chart of Toulon. 'The ruse would guarantee us passage all the way to the hospital at the outer wharves, before transforming into demolition parties.'

'Who do you suggest comprises the twenty-one, sir?' asked Jobert. *Are my men about to be sacrificed by the navy?*

Brueys and Saint-Joséph shuffled uncomfortably. 'There is only ourselves here on General Dugommier's staff,' said Brueys. 'There is no time to raise a force from naval personnel in Marseille. One of the three leaders will be Captain Saint-Joséph.' Saint-Joséph bobbed his head in acceptance of the task.

'May I be of service, sir?' said Avriol. 'I speak a little Spanish. With Captain Jobert, might I offer us as the other leaders?'

Brueys grimaced.

A stone thumped in the pit of Jobert's stomach. 'Then, myself,' said Jobert, 'and the best men from my company will constitute the other nineteen required. What is the intended time for the divisional attack, sir?'

'General Dugommier intends to attack in the early hours of the 18th of December.'

'Then my company of chasseurs have only today, tonight and tomorrow to prepare.'

'The army is to attack the port tomorrow night,' said Jobert. 'The attack is designed to threaten the enemy fleet and cause the enemy to evacuate their garrisons and abandon the port. The attack to threaten the fleet will be conducted by General Dugommier's division on the western side of the Inner Harbour. General Lapoype's division will conduct diversionary attacks up onto Mount Faron.'

Jobert scanned the grim faces of 2nd Company's command group, illuminated by the only light in the gloomy barn, the brazier's crackling embers and pinecones. Discomfort twisted their faces as memories surfaced of 2nd Company's participation in the Mount Faron attacks eleven weeks ago.

'The 24th Chasseurs will be supporting these attacks. 3rd Squadron is to guide and escort the forces of General Dugommier in the west. 1st Squadron is to guide General Lapoype's forces up onto the mountain as we did over two months ago.'

Around the fire, a silent exchange of relief.

'As for 2nd Squadron, 8th Company is acting as guides. 8th Company is responsible for ensuring the recently arrived brigade, under General Masséna, the main effort of General Lapoype's attack, arrives in its assembly area.'

Hold your nerve. Let them see nothing but conviction. Jobert's lips curled into a half-grin. 'As for us, 2nd Company is to insert a group of twenty-one men into the city. Nineteen of the twenty-one men will be from 2nd Company. The other two will be Major Avriol and a naval officer.'

The men shuffled in the warm light, glancing at Avriol, attempting to predict the possible implications, before returning their attention to Jobert. *Should we fail, we will not be shamed.* Jobert's eyes appeared to burn with encouragement.

'The senior naval officers at headquarters are expecting the enemy, prior to abandoning Toulon, to destroy the French vessels and the stores housed within the port. First, this group of twenty-one is to move to the enemy's defences as part of General Lapoype's diversionary attacks, specifically within General Masséna's brigade. Second, disguised as wounded from the attacked forts, move inside the city and the naval precinct. Third, disguised as Spanish demolition parties, prepare the stores for destruction, thus bluffing the enemy's demolition parties that the task is already in hand.'

The jaws of the audience clenched in trepidation.

'Take heart, my friends. Since the company works as four platoons, consider the group of twenty-one as one of those platoons. A second platoon will be dedicated to transporting and supporting the twenty-one to a position somewhere on the flanks of Mount Faron in the middle of the night. The remainder of the company will then wrap a protective screen around the twenty-one and the support platoon. The twenty-one can depart towards the city, for all intents and purposes, looking like a cart full of wounded attended by a surgeon.'

Jobert stood from his bench seat, so he could look individuals in the eye.

'The nineteen from 2nd Company within the group of twenty-one will be myself, Lieutenant Voreille and Sergeant Major Koschak. Both two-man sniper teams will be included. Sergeant Pultiere and Bredieux, yourselves and the best ten chasseurs from your platoons as well.

'As I am included in the twenty-one, Lieutenant Neilage, you will command the company in my absence. You will be assisted by Duque, Moench and the section corporals and you will create the support platoon and the screen troop, allowing for the removal of the men earmarked for the twenty-one.'

Neilage looked up from his notebook to nod at Duque and Moench.

'The operation is tomorrow night. There is much to be done, including actions this very evening. We will not wait for dawn.'

Everybody squirmed on their seats, adjusting their notebooks in anticipation of the tasks ahead.

'Lieutenant Neilage, send a warning to the 'Spanish water cart' in the city. That will require a messenger to climb to Fort Capucine tonight.' Neilage nodded slowly as he digested the implications.

'Sergeant Pultiere, you will assist me preparing the demolition parties. We need twenty-one Spanish uniforms of which three are officers' uniforms and at least three sergeants' uniforms. Those uniforms require backpacks, as well as muskets and slung equipment. All that, by dusk tomorrow night.'

'All that can be arranged, sir,' said Koschak, 'but it will cost.'

'Sergeant Major, inform me of the investment required,' said Avriol, looking across the fire. 'I shall put forward a loan which the navy will repay. With interest.'

'Sergeant Major and Sergeant Bredieux,' said Jobert, 'you

will both prepare the wounded. We will need a small cart or trap, a surgeon's uniform either Spanish or French, with tool satchel and sufficient bandages, blood and butcher's offcuts to create the disguise, without compromising the follow-on demolition ruse.

'I foresee ball, bayonet and sword wounds that, should they receive immediate medical aid, the soldiers might rejoin their battalions. Do not fill the cart with casualties with such grievous wounds that questions might be raised as to why those close to death were evacuated from the forts. Plan on all the ten chasseurs with leg wounds in the cart and the remainder of us officers, sergeants and sniper teams as walking wounded pulling the cart.

'Now, lads, refill your cups with rum, gather in your three groups, demolition, wounded and support and talk it through. We will reconvene to smooth out any lumps in the dough.'

Chapter Twenty-Six

Beginning at dusk on the 17th of December, the constant icy rain falling throughout the night flooded the land. Every crevice on the dark, brooding slopes of Mount Faron issued a slippery river of grey, chalky mud, which slithered into the northern valley. Thousands of saturated men groped their way forward in the inky downpour, the columns squelching and slipping in the freezing slime, creating a quagmire for those who followed. Wearied by every step through the channels of slurry up the steep slopes, columns became disconnected in the dark. Precious time was devoured as infantry commanders and chasseur guides, hunched against the squalling rain, pushed themselves and their horses, to re-establish the momentum forward.

As the dawn's dim light penetrated the thick storm clouds, Jobert squinted at the slim hands on his watch. It was after seven o'clock. Masséna's lead troops, in their disconnected companies, were still an hour's mud-drenched upward slog from their attack positions. The information from Geourdai's guides reaching

2nd Company, at the tail of Masséna's straggling battalion columns, did not bode well. No message had been received from the brigades fighting on the crest of the mountain, although the occasional weak rattle of musket fire and roll of drums was discerned in lulls in the sheeting rain.

The morning air shook as five cannons roared. Jobert's and Saint-Joséph's faces jerked toward the sound in the mist above them. In the silence that came from hundreds of men ceasing to struggle in the mud, all could hear the cries of the French infantry charging. 'Masséna is attacking Fort Faron with his lead battalion,' said Jobert.

Commanders bellowed to get the frozen columns moving forward again.

The battery of five cannons roared again into the mist near simultaneously. 'Shit! Battery fire,' said Jobert. 'That is not good.'

'Why?' asked Saint-Joséph.

'The enemy battery will fire their first rounds near simultaneously as the infantry begin their charge, sir. As individual gun crews serve their guns as we scale the walls, the sound of fire becomes irregular. A simultaneous second round of battery fire could well mean our attack has stalled well out and the enemy are seeing the infantry off.'

'Is it always like this in the Army? It can be tediously uncomfortable waiting to bring a squadron of ships into battle line, but there is always something to occupy the mind, the weather, the sea, the rigging, the signals, the guns. Something more than whether I will need my frozen toes amputated before, or after, this attack.'

'No, sir, it is not always this good. We are at the back of the lead brigade of one-and-a-half thousand men. The infantry brigades in Belgium and on the Rhine can be five-thousand strong. We might find ourselves with the last brigade in the last division of a three-division column. It could be worse.'

'I thank my blessings I am a sailor, not a soldier,' said Saint-Joséph.

'I thank my blessings I am a cavalryman, not an infantry-man,' said Jobert.

Avriol joined them, slumping his horse to a halt. 'General Lapoype has received news that we hold the heights of Mount Faron,' said Avriol. 'Masséna has been ordered to attack Fort Faron from underneath. The gun-fire indicating he may well have been repulsed.'

Jobert grimaced upwards into the mist. 'If the same seven twelve pounders stand on the walls of Fort Faron as they did last October —,'

Five cannons roared above them again. Yet Masséna's depth battalions maintained their laboured step as they wound their way up into the mist. The Fort Faron battery roared again.

'What now?' asked Saint-Joséph.

Avriol swore fiercely under his breath. 'I am concerned a second attacking wave has failed, sir.'

'But we are not seeing blue-coat volunteers routing down the slopes, sir,' said Jobert, pointing to the columns advancing up into the drizzle. 'What is more, the follow-on battalions have not checked their march.'

2nd Company's 'twenty-one' and their support platoon branched off the paths following the infantry up into the swirling mist towards Fort Faron and took fresh paths towards Fort D'Artigues. The slopes above the village of La Valette towards Fort D'Artigues were still very steep, but the paths allowed horses, with chasseurs dismounted, to carefully wind their way up. A light, two-wheeled cart, without a horse in the shafts, was pulled along the precipitous tracks with sidechains attached to six remounts.

Forty-five minutes after Fort Faron discharged its last murderous volley, the chasseurs now higher up the mountain's slopes heard a battalion bellow as they charged the walls. The patient twelve pounders fired into the French assault.

Avriol fumbled under his cape to open his watch case. 'Nine o'clock. What? Masséna's third attack?'

The enemy artillery fire now boomed as individual guns. Based on the change in fire from the guns it was assumed the attackers were scaling the walls in the downpour. The chasseurs grunted and hissed their encouragement to their comrades obscured in the cloud. As they plodded and skidded along the narrow paths, Jobert no longer saw the tail of the final infantry company column that 2nd Company had followed up Mount Faron. The thick, low clouds combined with the gun smoke from the battle had consumed the entire brigade.

The Fort again fired a simultaneous battery salute, it was reasonably assumed, at the withdrawing attackers. Each horse and soldier saturated in frozen rain, feet and legs heavy with sticky mud, most having slept at Koschak's command for a few hours at dusk twelve hours previously, stopped and stared upwards at their officers.

'Do we assume the third attack has failed?' asked Saint-Joséph. 'Without the night attack allowing our entry into the city under the cover of darkness, are we too late to affect our plan?'

'Surely, sir,' said Jobert, 'the enemy will only commit to their destructive efforts if the defence here is crumbling. Currently, the defence holds, so there is no inclination yet for the enemy to evacuate the port.'

'Your concerns are not unreasonable, sir,' said Avriol, 'but like Captain Jobert, I too feel confident pressing on. The city, if not Fort Sainte-Catherine, would be aware of the gunfire on the mountain for well over an hour now. We have the story we require to release our wounded Spaniards. Do you feel comfortable in proceeding, sir?'

'I am utterly determined to proceed, sir. How far away are we from the road that links the upper forts to Fort Sainte-Catherine and Toulon?'

'Gentlemen, a messenger from Lieutenant Neilage approaches.' Jobert watched a caped Moench on his grey pick his way carefully down the glutinous path.

Moench saluted. 'Gentlemen, you are currently two hundred metres from the Fort Sainte-Catherine road, but it will take you thirty minutes to travel the distance due to the mud and the slope. There, Lieutenant Neilage has secured a sheltered gully which will allow the 'twenty-one' to be prepared prior to departure for the port. Also, from Captain Geourdai, Fort Faron has withstood three attacks, so General Masséna is swinging south to attack Fort D'Artigues.'

'With your permission, sir,' said Avriol, 'let us press on without delay.'

The column of morose chasseurs and their horses jerked into life once more.

Moench squeezed in beside Jobert. 'Captain Jobert, sir, my brother is with the water cart in the city.'

Jobert faced the drenched, mud-smeared soldier. *I know too well the dread of not having my brother beside me in combat.* 'Moench, stop!' Jobert squelched forward and gripped his trumpeter's shoulder hard. 'Your brother has been in the heart of an enemy fortress for two-and-a-half months and escaped any detection. With his fife as part of the 'Spanish water cart', he has done more than any other man in the 24th Chasseurs to recapture this city. As one of four regimental brothers, he is about to be joined by another nineteen. Whatever happens, we will all do our very best. Yes?'

Moench's eyes welled with apprehension. Gripping Moench's cape, Jobert shook him gently and pushed him a step up the slope.

Before long, the twenty-one 'Spanish' and their support mates plodded into the pine-protected gulch. The spirits of the chasseurs lifted as they leapt to action. The wounded's capes were rolled under shabraques and horses led away. With bandages in place, blood was liberally applied from goatskins. The support platoon manhandled the cart into position, bundled in backpacks, muskets and slung equipment then assisted loading those chasseurs with leg wounds and Avriol, the surgeon. The remaining senior members of the twenty-one and the two sniper-pairs were walking wounded.

As they gathered around the cart to haul it down the mountain, the air was rent with a thousand-throat roar. As the rain continued to disallow musket fire, the defensive fire from the enemy guns was only a few rounds and of a much lighter calibre. 'Ten o'clock,' said Avriol. 'There is Masséna's attack on Fort D'Artigues.'

Jobert noted the morale in the group was high due to being underway and no enemy gunfire from the upper forts indicating that Masséna's attack on Fort D'Artigues had stalled. Progress down the rutted track leading to Fort Sainte-Catherine and Toulon was slow. The roadway bubbled with flowing mud and the cart slid in the chalky slime. The surgeon and the rest of the wounded struggled to manage the cart, with only four chasseurs remaining in the cart due to the restrictions of their bandaging.

Well after eleven o'clock, large groups of Neapolitan and Spanish soldiers swarmed around the cart as they retreated from the upper forts. Offers to assist wounded comrades were politely refused, as 'surgeon' Avriol encouraged the enemy troops, in Spanish and French, to press on to the defences of Toulon. As the path to the upper forts joined the lower road network, the twenty-one wounded and, by now, hundreds of soldiers retiring from Mount Faron were joined by columns of soldiers from all nations, but predominantly Spanish, marching to Toulon.

The tide of retreating men from Mount Faron swept the wounded and their cart through the multiple bastion gates and bridged ditches of Toulon's eastern Italian Gate. Once in the streets, the rain stopped.

'Twelve o'clock, Major Avriol,' said Saint-Joséph. 'What now?'

In the press of formed bodies of soldiers and stragglers, four well-dressed, anxious citizens gathered around the cart to give succour to its occupants. Lieutenant Huin, Sergeant Yinot and the younger Moench assisted the wounded into a nearby alleyway. Madame Quandalle, in the jacket of a British sergeant, bustled about the men distributing cups of gin from a slung cask and matronly good cheer. Bemused by their conspicuous white royalist cockades, Jobert found it curious how dry they appeared.

'Our regiment maintains a 'Spanish water cart', sir,' said Avriol, 'which moves between Toulon and the forts on Mount Faron. The water cart is a conduit of intelligence. Allow me to introduce the commander of the water cart, Second Lieutenant Huin of the 24th Chasseurs. What news, Huin?'

'The enemy admirals here have decided to evacuate the city, sir. The attacks on the western side of the Inner Harbour have succeeded. The enemy's western forts have been falling since dawn. Instead of redeploying their force of six thousand within the defence, the Neapolitans and Sardinians have embarked their troops and sailed beyond the Outer Harbour.'

'Good grief!' said Saint-Joséph. 'We have not a moment to lose.'

Hundreds of enemy troops moved past the cart. A column of Spanish coming into the city, pressing past a column of British forcing their way through to the gates, surged the crowd against the group of wounded.

'The British and Spanish have been transporting their troops across the Inner Harbour from their western forts,' said Huin. 'The Spanish are concentrating their seven thousand within the city. The British are concentrating their two thousand at Fort La Malgue, so they can evacuate from beaches on the Outer Harbour.'

'We need to press onto the hospital, Huin,' said Avriol. 'Do you know a back way?'

'The naval hospital at the end of the Inner Quay, sir?' Huin shook his head. 'You will not get there, sir. The city is in panic. The civilians are filling the streets close to the quays seeking to board whatever is alongside.'

'Belay there, Lieutenant!' said Saint-Joséph. 'Get us to the naval precinct immediately.'

'Yes, sir, but you will get through as a formed body, not as wounded.'

Moving the twenty-one wounded to an abandoned backstreet storeroom, then changing disguises and loading pistols, muskets and rifles, did not take long. Marching the demolition guard of twenty-one and their four civilian 'camp-followers', through the increasing crush of humanity the closer they came to the docks was as frustrating as their muddy night march. The fear of separation from the column caused surges of adrenalin to purge the chasseurs' exhaustion.

The naval-port precinct occupied two-thirds of the walled city of Toulon. The naval quays along the front of the port were divided by a great stone island, called the Inner Quay, into the western New Arsenal and the eastern Old Arsenal. The residents in the remaining third of the city easily accessed the Old Arsenal. It was here that a great mass of agitated civilians pressed into any available craft to be transported to the ships standing at anchor in the Inner Harbour.

One-quarter of the precinct itself was a walled inner compound which faced out onto the New Arsenal. Outside of this inner compound lay such buildings as the tar house, the general store, the timber store, the naval academy and its chapel-cum-prison. Moving across the outer precinct, Jobert noticed the crowds of citizens and columns of troops thinned considerably. The 'demolition guard' had taken the opportunity to draw themselves up smartly and march with great aplomb through the unmanned gates of the inner compound.

Within the walls of the inner compound was where the most vital stores were housed in the armoury, the magazine and the mast house. It was here, within an eerie calm, the demolition guard came to a cracking halt.

Saint-Joséph took in the state of the docks and vessels alongside. 'Gentlemen, would you attend me? It is now two o'clock. We have just sailed into the centre of the enemy's position to find it unguarded. We need to set a guard. I need to get stock of our situation.'

'*Oi! Disculpe, senor.*' The shout came from the docks.

The group turned to see a Spanish officer, in the uniform of the Spanish supply trains, running across to meet them. Jobert turned to judge where the guard were facing and where any other threat might emerge. The supply officer saluted Saint-Joséph and blurted out a long message, frightened eyes bulging from a sweating face.

'*Si somos!*' said Saint-Joséph.

The supply officer's shoulders drooped in relief and with a blissful smile and animated speech, he reached into a satchel and handed over to Saint-Joséph two large iron hoops of keys.

'*Gracias, senor*,' said Saint-Joséph, passing the keys to an open-mouthed Avriol. The supply officer saluted Saint-Joséph, turned on his heel and departed at the run.

Saint-Joséph shook his head in bewilderment. 'There you have it, gentlemen. The keys to each building in the precinct. That may be our only good luck of the day and we have much to do.

'Jobert, first, set a guard on the gate and establish an orderly room within the inner-compound's guardhouse, where we all might pass information. Second, place a watch in the heights of the hospital to maintain observation of the Inner Harbour. Third, secure a boat to take a demolition team to the outer magazine. Avriol, would you accompany me on my inspection. We shall discuss what we observe and plan accordingly. Any questions?'

'Yes, sir,' said Jobert. 'We have two marksmen with us. May I suggest they occupy the observation post and establish a sniper's position in the hospital from which to cover the entry points into both arsenals?'

'Make it so.'

'Also, sir, the employment of our civilians? May I suggest they observe both the eastern Italian Gate and the western Royal Gate?'

'Very good. Pipe the orders to hands and set sail.'

Jobert marched back to the demolition guard, still ramrod stiff at attention and the lounging clique of Huin's 'Royalists'. His eyes took in each face. *We have come this far. I can doubt them no longer.* 'Sergeant Pultiere, with three chasseurs, establish a guard on the gates of this inner compound.'

'Sir.'

'Lieutenant Voreille, establish an orderly room at the gate house. You are the central point to which will send all messages.'

'Sir.'

'Sergeant Major Koschak, with the two sniper teams, from the upper floors of the hospital, observe shipping movement into the Inner Harbour. The snipers are required to target the arsenal exit passages.'

'Sir.'

'Lieutenant Huin, take Sergeant Bredieux and five chasseurs, secure a boat, move to the powder magazine on the shore behind Fort La Malgue and set deception demolitions.'

'Sir.'

'Madame Quandalle, might I call upon you to observe the Royal Gate? Sergeant Yinot, take young Moench to observe the Italian Gate.'

'Sir.'

'The remaining two chasseurs will accompany Captain Saint-Joséph, Major Avriol and I on our inspection. To your duties, fall out.'

Chapter Twenty-Seven

With deep regret, Saint-Joséph looked down the eastern shore of the Inner Harbour at five French ships-of-the-line standing at anchor. Jobert glanced at the furrows on Saint-Joséph's brow. *He feels he is single-handedly saving the French Mediterranean Fleet.*

'Gentlemen,' said Saint-Joséph, 'fleet reports from August state that ten vessels were at sea and about sixty in port when Toulon was lost. I have counted thirty-six in port and a further five vessels sitting out in the roads. I assume the enemy have taken the other twenty. Perhaps you cavalrymen might relate to my pain in losing one ship-of-the-line not dissimilar to the destruction of a regiment's worth of well-trained and beloved remounts.

'Sadly, I do not have the resources to safeguard the five ships who lie beyond the walls of the arsenals. As for the thirty-six that lie alongside within the port, the ability to deny entry to the port is the key to saving the remainder of the fleet. Thus, the challenge we face is considerable.

'First, gentlemen, I bring your attention to the state of the three booms capable of blocking movement on the water's surface into and around the port. One passage into the Old Arsenal, one into the New and one between both at the top of the Inner Quay.

'You will note each boom is comprised of a series of pieces. Two shackles are bolted into the stone pillars of the wharf passageways. The great chain is shackled to one of the wharves. A lighter chain, attached to the end of the boom chain, which, with the use of a capstan, could bring the free end of the chain up to the surface and allow the boom chain to be shackled to the opposite wharf.

'Perhaps from that description you may determine the challenge we face. First, all the capstans for raising the submerged ends of the five-hundred-kilogram chains have been removed.

'Second, here at the exit to the New Arsenal, the two-hundred-kilogram shackle which ought to be bolted to the opposite wharf is missing. Even if the chain could be raised, there is nothing to which it could be connected to set the boom and close the passage. I must resign myself that this passage is to remain open to the enemy.

'Solutions to the missing capstans for the other two booms are either a search of the various stores or forming a gang to haul it up. I shall search the stores as my inspection continues, but I would prefer focusing your physical efforts on the preparations for demolition. As an interim, upon sunset, we shall pull the drawbridges across the passages. That will allow us to move quickly about the quays, as well as hinder the movement of masted vessels.'

Saint-Joséph's despondent gaze drifted across the monstrous ships berthed alongside, oblivious of their desperate situation.

Jobert and Saint-Joséph strode to inspect the guards at the inner compound gate. Sergeant Pultiere had set a fire in the guard room's hearth. The cheery blaze did much to comfort the men gathered out of the harsh breeze blowing in from the sea.

Saint-Joséph rubbed his weary eyes. 'The guard is set on the gates, yes? Lieutenant Huin has departed for the outer magazine? Marksmen on watch in the hospital?'

Jobert rocked his head from side-to-side to stretch an aching neck. 'Yes, sir.'

'But, sir,' said Koschak, 'the hospital is an excellent location for observing the Inner Harbour, but as for a sniper location, it can only cover the two external passages from the arsenals, not the passage at the head of the Inner Quay. A better position that covers all three passages is the Inner Quay ships' chandlers' store.'

'I defer to your greater knowledge in this matter,' said Saint-Joséph. 'When the moment comes that one post is a greater priority than the other, may I ask you to effect the change?'

'Yes, sir.'

'Gentlemen, I have been unable to locate the boom capstans. I will leave that conundrum momentarily and discern a solution in due course. What else? Does the hospital on the Inner Quay provide a threat?'

'No, sir,' said Jobert. 'The patients are triaged for evacuation. The surgeons and their orderlies are loading those chosen to depart into long boats on the harbour side. Only those close to death due to wounds, or those with any sign of contagion, are abandoned in the wards. They are of no threat to us.'

'Then we need to focus on preparing our demolitions. How many hands do we have on deck?'

'Huin and six have departed to the outer magazine. I shall reduce the gate guard to three and the hospital observers to three. Including yourself, sir, we have nine available to set the demolitions.'

'Good. Our fires, should they be lit, must satisfy two audiences. The primary audience is those far from the precinct, whether out in the harbour, on the far shores, Mount Faron, even in the residential suburbs of the city. For this audience we will light the tar house in the outer precinct and the powder magazine in the inner compound, as they are simply stone store houses and can readily be replaced. We shall remove most of the stocks but leave sufficient to create a grand theatre. We shall also build two deception fires behind the inner compound wall; barrels of tar with a few casks of powder all wrapped tightly with sails from the mast house.

'The second audience is those within the naval precinct or on the docks. Those who get too close. For this audience we shall set fire to the rope house in the outer precinct and the mast house in the inner compound. We cannot ever hope to move the vast stores within these vital buildings. We must set timber fires right at their very entrances, so it appears the buildings are burning. Should anyone notice the fire has been poorly set and desires to rectify the mistake, the fires will dissuade anyone to re-enter the building with powder in order to reset the fire. There are also three vessels in the dry docks, one laid down and two in the slipways for refit. Alas, these also will be set to burn.

'There is a third audience who will not require to see fire. Should any enemy demolition authorities demand to inspect our work, we must set deception powder trails. Finally, I shall place a supply of ships' pumps and buckets from the general stores aside in the foolish hope that ...' Saint-Joséph's lips trembled as he stared onto an unseen horizon. 'Hah!' Saint-Joséph slapped his thigh and returned to the moment. 'I shall take Jobert and three men to start on the powder magazine. Avriol, you and three empty the tar house. It is approaching three o'clock, we have two hours until dark. Let us hop to it.'

'Jobert? Jobert!' Avriol's voice rumbled down the stone central corridor of the dank magazine.

'I am here, sir.' Jobert and Pultiere were appreciative for the opportunity to stretch their backs from the heavy work of tipping two-hundred-kilogram barrels of powder ready to be rolled outside. Jobert wiped clammy sweat from his charcoal-smeared face with a sulphur-smelling hand. In the dark bowels of the magazine, there was barely any ambient daylight, a place where no-one illuminated the squat, cold contents with flame.

'Jobert, you will not believe this,' said Avriol. 'A squadron of Spanish dragoons has just ridden their horses into the Naval Academy and left for the docks without them. They include general's and aides' mounts from Naples and Sardinia. You can tell by their saddlery and livery.'

Jobert was too tired to appreciate the implications.

'Just as Captain Saint-Joséph despairs at the thought of the loss of ships,' said Avriol, 'I will not allow two hundred Spanish war horses to burn. I want them sent back to the regiment. The infantry will win all the glory for retaking the city, possibly even the bastard artillery. The chasseurs will be remembered only for taking grain from farmers. Shit, no! We need these horses.'

'Indeed, sir. Can Voreille get word to Yinot at the city gates to get a message out of the city? Young Moench could take one of the horses? Would Geourdai or Neilage be the closest chasseurs? Are they still close to La Valette? Or have they returned to Revest?'

'Very good. I will get Voreille —'

A powerful drumbeat sounded that seemed to emanate deep

in the earth. Their heads jerked. Their eyes widened with alarm. The thick stone walls of the magazine shook. The beat resounded again. A cannon ball, a huge cannon ball, was skipping into the port.

Avriol, Jobert and Pultiere raced for the entrance. The next skip of the cannon ball smashed into masonry somewhere in the city. As the gun that fired the round could be heard far across the harbour, the population of the city started to scream.

'Sir!' cried Voreille from the guard house, as Avriol and Jobert appeared from within the powder magazine. 'Gunfire from the forts across the Inner Harbour.'

'What gun could possibly have that range?' asked Jobert.

'Thirty-two pounders,' said Avriol. 'Either coastal or siege artillery.'

'Thirty-two pounders?' Jobert had seen four and six pounder devastation at Valmy last year and was disconcerted at the destructive power of twelve pounders at Fort Faron two months ago. The thought that someone was firing thirty-two-pound balls at a phenomenal range of over one thousand five hundred metres was overwhelming.

'Captain Jobert, sir,' said Voreille, 'I have a message from Lieutenant Huin. He reports that the powder store on the shore behind Fort La Malgue is now secure.'

'Very good. Inform Captain Saint-Joséph.'

'Yes, sir, but there is more. There are three French ships-of-the-line at anchor in the roads, just off the magazine. They are full of French prisoners. Sir, there are hundreds of them.'

Jobert swallowed hard to concentrate. 'Oh, very well.'

Another ball skipped into the city to collapse a townhouse in the residential sector. The high-pitched wailing increased across the city.

'Why are the enemy firing on the city, sir?' asked Pultiere.

'It is not the enemy who fires, Pultiere, but us. We must have captured the western forts and have now turned the guns on the fleet.'

In the docks of the Old Arsenal across from the inner compound, the cacophony was intense. Men of every nationality bellowed and roared to cast off from their various moorings and pull for the open water and the safety of the fleet. Other men shrieked as they saw the various squadrons of battleships unfurling sail in the Inner Harbour and making for the Outer Harbour and the sea beyond. The civilian men and women on the dockside howled to be taken away with troops. The horses stabled in the Naval Academy screamed.

As Jobert looked up to the thick clouds, threatening rain, a thought struck him. 'Voreille, find Sergeant Major Koschak. Teams of those Spanish horses could pull up the booms. Surely, we can close two of the three. We have one hour of light to harness two teams of six. Find Koschak, then tell Captain Saint-Joséph.'

Voreille sprinted out of the gate.

'Pultiere,' said Jobert, 'we need to finish this work before it is dark in one hour.' Jobert re-entered the inky depths of the magazine. Pultiere dutifully followed him.

Chapter Twenty-Eight
March 1793, Avignon, France

Many tipped and rolled barrels later, a series of rolling cannonades were fired from the now-French held forts across the harbour.

'Surely, not again?' said Pultiere.

Jobert scrambled along the dark, slimy walls. 'No. We ought to hear the strike of the ball before we hear the sound of the gun. The batteries are firing at a target other than the city.'

Out of the magazine, the thick clouds crushed the last of the orange sunset onto the western horizon. As Jobert and Pultiere made their way to the glow from the guard house, Saint-Joséph emerged with his telescope extended. 'Vessels are returning. Fifteen of them in two columns. The shore batteries are taking them under fire.'

'Is it a final evacuation, sir?' asked Jobert.

'No, they are not longboats under oar. They are cutters under sail, flying both Spanish and British colours. They are towing fireships. These are the enemy's demolition parties.'

The clip of women's shoes on cobblestones approached the

spitting torches in brackets on the gate. 'Madame Quandalle,' said Jobert, 'to what do we owe this pleasure?'

'The last of the British have departed the city to Fort La Malgue, sir. I felt you ought to know that only a company of British fusiliers hold the Royal Gate.'

'What of the Spanish, madame?'

'There are many stragglers in the streets, sir, but there are no formed bodies of Spanish troops. There must be hundreds of abandoned soldiers, sir.'

'Where are all these Spaniards now?'

'They are looting the taverns, sir. With dusk and no more longboats, the citizens have locked themselves in their cellars. The streets are deserted.'

'Who holds the Italian Gate?'

'No-one, sir.'

'Nevertheless, we must keep working,' said Saint-Joséph, looking to the dark water of the Inner Harbour. 'The powder magazine is now too dark to extract more barrels and we have sufficient barrels in the deception locations. We will prepare the magazine for demolition.'

Jobert stepped into the warmth of the guard room and found Koschak, Voreille and marksman Tulloc sharing bread and wine, quivering with exhaustion. 'Sergeant Major, did you raise the booms?'

'Yes.' Koschak smiled through his fatigue. 'Yes, we did.'

'Are the drawbridges across the passages?'

Koschak nodded.

Jobert closed his eyes in appreciative relief. Then he considered the two younger soldiers, Voreille and Tulloc, beside Koschak: one second lieutenant and one chasseur. Despite their youth, their faces were no longer rounded. Instead, tar and gunpowder lodged in the crevices of their sunburn. Hands were gnarled not smooth; one hand, Voreille's, had a finger amputated from combat. Their sweat-soaked, filth-blackened shirts and waistcoats clung to their lean, muscular bodies, conditioned by hundreds of kilometres in the saddle, ascending and descending Mount Faron every second day for months and unrelenting hours of sabre drills and fencing.

'Ready to go back at it, lads?' asked Jobert. Voreille's and Tulloc's eyes slid to hold their captain's gaze. They nodded assent, their confident smirks creasing their filthy cheeks. *My horse soldiers are boys no more.*

The clatter of nearly four hundred hooves resounded through the silent streets, amplified by the cloud-encased night. Spanish horses tethered in the offices and classrooms of the Naval Academy whinnied. Heads jerked up in reaction from tying down canvas sails over barrels of tar and powder in the deep shadows behind the mast house. Jobert willed aching muscles to join Saint-Joséph under the pitch-soaked torches by the precinct gates.

Geourdai rode forward from his dark legion, flanked by two chasseurs holding two torches aloft. 'Good evening, gentlemen.' Geourdai's smile was characteristically lop-sided. 'Jobert, I return your messengers.' From behind the torchbearers Yinot and the younger Moench brother slid off the horses' rumps and stepped forward into the light.

'Captain Jobert, sir,' said Sergeant Yinot, 'Lieutenant Neilage sent us to join Madame Quandalle at the Royal Gate.'

'No, Yinot, remain here with us. Geourdai, where is Neilage and 2ⁿᵈ Company?'

'They are holding the Italian Gate. Why? Where is everybody? Out there in the dark, the entire French army is preparing to storm the walls.'

'The lull before the storm,' said Jobert. 'The building across the court holds two hundred Spanish horses. You are to take them back to Revest.'

'Good grief!' Saint-Joséph threw up his hands. 'How can one hundred cavalrymen ride into a city to steal horses, but the army cannot press forward to capture a port with open gates we have fought four months for?'

The merry confidence slid from Geourdai's face. 'I know for certain that the message has been received by General Lapoype, sir.'

Jobert rolled his eyes in his blackened face. 'Once out of the city with the Spanish horses, Geourdai, ensure General Masséna and Colonel Morin are fully aware that the eastern gate is held by us.'

Shoes pounded along the stone wharf. 'Sir! They are coming.'

'Tulloc! Come to the guard house!' called Jobert.

'The enemy's cutters, sir. They are coming in fast.'

The biting wind coming in from the open sea, brought the faint rhythmic splash of many oars. As Saint-Joséph and the chasseurs heard the approaching enemy cutters somewhere out on the black water, adrenalin surged through their aching bodies and cleared their foggy senses.

Saint-Joséph broke their stupor. 'It is now eight o'clock. The enemy commanders are comfortable that the port has been evacuated. They have signalled the authorisation to destroy our fleet. Jobert, I will deal with the commander entering the New Arsenal. You deal with whomever attempts to cross the boom into the Old Arsenal. Beat to quarters, gentlemen.'

'Geourdai, get the horses out of here,' said Jobert, 'and sing the *La Marseillaise* at the top of your lungs as you pass through the streets. 2nd Company, stand fast. Listen in. Pultiere, man the gates and the orderly room with your lads. Remember there are hundreds of enemy stragglers within the town who may come looking for loot. There is also a company of British fusiliers three hundred metres away at the Royal Gate.

'Voreille, Yinot, with me to the Old Arsenal. Have a chasseur bring torches from the guardhouse. Sergeant Major, now is the time to relocate the marksmen to the Inner Quay chandlers' store to cover all passageways. I need you beside them to direct their fire. How many rounds would you all have?'

'Five cartridge boxes, sir,' said Koschak. 'Three hundred rounds.'

Jobert closed his sore eyes to calculate. 'One round per minute for five hours. With all five muskets and the two rifles, fire one round every two minutes, so it appears a number of Republicans are taking back the port. Fire high and wide with the muskets. Only kill with the rifles. If you are unsure of the target do not fire.'

'I understand, sir. Come on, Tulloc. Run!'

Jobert's lungs stung as they sprinted down the quayside, before clattering over the drawbridge onto the Inner Quay, towards the entrance of the Old Arsenal basin.

The Inner Quay was shaped like a capital-letter T. The body of the T divided the two arsenal basins. Along the body of the quay was a tall ships' chandlers' store. Jobert knew Koschak and Tulloc raced on his men's heels to take up that alternate firing position.

Across the head of the T the three-storey hospital squatted, oozing its putrid smell. The simpering of the abandoned who lay in darkness within mixed with the groans of the sullen, shadowy battleships alongside. At the ends of the head of the T were the sea passages, the entrances to both arsenal basins.

Jobert's burning lungs sucked in the chill air. 'Torches ... lads ... quickly.' Voreille and the chasseur that had accompanied them had one, then another, torch flare into life.

Yinot, doubled over from his exertions, flapped towards the pitch-black Inner Harbour. 'Sir, outwards from each passageway runs a channel. You can hear one group of boats coming towards us up the channel and another group well over to our right heading for the New Arsenal.'

Jobert strained to hear anything over the wind, the slap of water against the rock breakwater at the base of the quay and the groans and creaks of the massive battleships moored in the basin. 'Lads, one torch either side of the drawbridge.'

The chasseur trotted over the drawbridge which spanned the great stone-flanked passage wide enough for the girth of the mammoth ships-of-the-line to slide through. The waves in the passage sizzled as they broke upon the slimy links of the boom chain just proud of the inky surface.

Jobert saw a dark cutter's bow emerge from the gloom. '*Amigos, amigos, espagnol, amigos.*'

The response from the crew was an elated burst of Spanish.

'Sir,' said Voreille, 'we are Royal Louis battalion. Speak French.'

'Good man! Yinot, tell them we are French. Ask for an officer. Warn them of the boom.'

A musket round was fired from the chandlers' store. Yinot instinctively ducked as the ball zipped high. The voices in the leading Spanish cutter cried out, followed by the clatter of muskets readied. Yinot yelled a few sentences to the crew.

More shouting ensued and the oars splashed to arrest the forward motion of the vessel.

'Ahoy there,' cried a voice from the cutter, 'I am the commander of the demolition party with authorisation from Lieutenant General don Juan de Langara y Huarte himself. Identify yourself.'

Jobert crouched by the negligible cover provided by the open-sided handrails of the drawbridge. 'Good evening, sir, I am the commander of the demolition party for the Royal Louis rear guard. Is it clear to you, sir, that the boom is lowered in the passage?'

Another musket fired. Another ball zipped through the wind.

'It is, sir, but who is firing?'

'French republicans, sir. They occupy quite a few buildings around the Arsenal. They have raised the boom and then sabotaged the capstan. I am unable to lower the boom. I have set the ships ready to fire in the Arsenal, sir, but I do not have sufficient men to hunt down the fugitives.'

Onboard the cutter, someone held high an oil lamp. A rifle shot cracked in the darkness behind them. A scream emitted from the boat. Spanish expletives exploded.

'If you cannot lower the boom,' the Spaniard continued, 'then I can land my party on the outer quay at the hospital steps.'

'Voreille, run to Koschak,' said Jobert. 'Focus his fire here and now. Tell him we are under the torches and the Spanish will be coming up the steps.' Voreille stepped back into the shadows before running down the spine of the quay.

'That would be excellent, sir,' Jobert said to the wavering shadows in the rocking cutter, 'but the ships in this basin are ready to fire. We have been preparing the demolitions since midday. I need to fire them now, sir, as the Republicans are closing in.'

'Please confirm you need no support from us. I have fireships under tow.'

The musket fire from the chandlers' store increased to two rounds. Balls zipped past to strike water or hull beyond.

'That is correct, sir. No, not in this basin, thank you, sir as your fireships will not clear the boom, sir, but there are French ships-of-the-line out in the roads that —'

Three rounds of rifle fire. Groans and cries of pain from the cutter.

'Come on, you dumb bastards, fuck off!' said Jobert under his breath before calling, 'My duty calls, sir, good luck.'

'Good luck, my friend, and farewell.'

Insistent Spanish commands caused the five cutters to turn back into the darkness of the Inner Harbour. Musket fire sent balls to chase the yawing vessels.

'Quick, lads, back to Captain Saint-Joséph.'

Back to the drawbridge across the New Arsenal they trotted.

Muskets clicked in readiness from the shadows ahead. A foreign challenge was bellowed from a large group of dark-clad men.

'*Amigo, espagnol, amigo,*' called Yinot holding his torch high.

'*Amigo, ingles, amigo.*'

Another musket ball zipped through the darkness. Stone splintered. A shrieking of timber on stone.

'British, sir,' said Yinot. 'They are withdrawing the drawbridge from over the sea passage.'

'Yinot, tell them to cease. We must get us across to Saint-Joséph. Voreille, inform Koschak there are British at the New Arsenal passage beyond the hospital.'

Chapter Twenty-Nine

As the British sea captain approached Saint-Joséph, Jobert reckoned the man, with pointed nose and receding hairline, about his own age.

'Good evening to you, sir. I am Captain Sir William Sidney Smith, of His Britannic Majesty's Royal Navy. I hold the authorisations from Vice-Admiral Sir Samuel Hood instructing me to set the demolitions for the port.'

Saint-Joséph swept off his bicorne in a low bow. 'Good evening, sir. I am Major José de Andrade, commander of the demolition guard authorised by Lieutenant General don Juan de Langara y Huarte. I am at your service. I have been at work since midday and my preparations are nearly complete. I have a few more ships to prepare before I light my fires. Would you care to inspect my work?'

'Indeed? That is wonderful —'

Two muskets fired. Both officers and the few men around them spun to face the source of the fire across the New Arsenal basin. Both commanders cringed as a ball zipped somewhere in the darkness.

'As you see, sir,' said Saint-Joséph, 'the French Republicans are closing in.'

'My goodness, I had no idea. How advanced are your preparations?'

'I have the tar house, the rope house, the mast house, the armoury and the magazine ready to fire. As for the ships, sir, I have all the ships in the Old Arsenal ready to burn as well as the ships up in dry-dock. I was just completing the ships in this arsenal as the Republican fire started to hit my men.'

Smith took in the black filth of tar and powder besmeared on Saint-Joséph's uniform and the weariness of the grimy Spanish soldiers standing behind. The muskets fired like clockwork. 'I have four fireships with me. Let us complete what you have begun.'

'If I may be so bold, sir,' said Saint-Joséph, 'might I alert you to certain factors. The sea wind blows directly onto the docks. It would be my preference to fire the powder magazine last. I would hesitate for the embers of the fireships to light the magazine before its time. Perhaps, if we place the fireships, then remove your cutters from the basin, I can light my fires in an order that will ensure the effect our commanders desire.'

The drawbridge squealed on the stone as it was withdrawn to allow the entry of the British cutters.

'May I also alert you, sir,' said Saint-Joséph, 'to the fact that I am aware the eastern gate to the city, the Italian Gate, has been lost to the Republicans. The Royal Gate is still held against the enemy. An erudite company of British fusiliers has that honour, but I am unaware if they know of the loss of the former gate. I only raise the matter, sir, as your cutters may be the only form of evacuation for those troops, assuming their evacuation should not compromise your directed tasks, of course.'

'Good lord, man. No! We cannot leave those fellows to the predations of the abominable French.'

'Then allow me to alert those British fusiliers, sir and guide them to you. For their passage to your cutters will take them directly through the middle of my demolitions.'

'I am obliged, Major de Andrade. You look to your duties most carefully. I would say you were a sailor, were it not for the fine uniform of your regiment.'

Saint-Joséph straightened his begrimed lapels. 'You honour me, sir.'

Two muskets fired, the balls zipping close enough to shower the group in a haze of timber splinters. Smith's face tightened with alarm as he sought his pocket watch. 'Half-past eight. The tide runs at ten o'clock. Might I take your advice on the placement of the fireships?'

Two muskets fired, followed by moans and shouts erupting from the British cutter clearing the inner wall of the passage. The relentless muskets fired again. Cries and shouts sounded from the British on the Inner Quay. Balls cracked into the stone-work close by.

Saint-Joséph gestured with a wave that the filth-encrusted chasseurs gather around, away from the distracted British. Jobert had a splitting headache and removed his bicorne to rub his powder-matted fingertips through his greasy hair. He looked at the faces in the torchlight who had gone thirty hours without sleep. Red-rimmed eyes blinked slowly, mouths hung open, breathing was laboured, everybody shuffled to maintain their balance.

'The Spanish have not attempted to cross the boom into the Old Arsenal, sir,' said Jobert. 'They have departed back toward the Outer Harbour.'

Saint-Joséph pushed the heels of his palms deep into his eye sockets. 'Men, we have a naval battle on our hands. I, a humble captain, with thirty-six vessels at my disposal, have command of over half the Republic's Mediterranean Fleet. My orders are to keep the fleet clear of a superior enemy. I have one squadron, the Old Arsenal squadron, of sixteen vessels, well clear. We are already succeeding in our mission and the enemy is currently failing in his. Now, our New Arsenal squadron must fight a rear-guard action with seventeen ships here in the basin and three ships to be sacrificed, as our fireships, in dry dock.

'First, I must hinder the enemy's operations by causing the inconvenience of embarking the British gate company. Second, we must start to ignite our fires, the embers will threaten their fireships and force them to depart the basin. Finally, I must stay abreast of the placement of the enemy's fireships. Gentlemen, I seek your counsel on how this might occur.'

The chandlers' store marksmen fired once more. Cries and bellows came from the cutters towing the fire-ships into the arsenal.

'Sir,' said Avriol, 'I will take a British liaison officer with me to the Royal Gate to convince the British company to abandon their post.'

'Sir,' said Jobert, 'I will have Koschak increase the fire into the cutters and make the snipers aware of the British fusiliers moving on the quayside. I will take Sergeant Yinot and light the fires. What is your priority for ignition?'

'Ah, yes. Set your fuses and light them as the tide turns at ten o'clock. First, fire the two frigates in the slipway which should illuminate the basin and threaten the British fireships. Second, the tar house and the deception fire behind the mast house. Third, wait for Avriol to move the British fusiliers through the inner compound. Finally, fire the second deception fire behind the armoury and the ship-of-the-line laid down in dry dock. The entrances to the rope house and the mast house will only be lit on my explicit command. We will blow the magazine last.'

Jobert inhaled deeply and blinked blood-shot eyes, if only to clear his mind and re-energise his aching body.

'I know we are all utterly spent,' said Saint-Joséph, 'but this is the crux of the battle. We sail now close under the enemy guns to deal with these fireships. Every man to his station and good luck.'

A fog descended over the basin. The crack of the rifle fire caused sleepy heads to twitch. Koschak's fire was becoming more insistent.

As Jobert and Sergeant Yinot strode towards the gates of the inner compound, two chasseurs on guard put on determined faces. 'You are doing a good job, lads,' said Jobert. 'Keep talking to each other. Stay focussed.'

'You would do an even better job, Chasseur Arbod,' said Yinot, 'if you fastened your cartridge box and did up your waistcoat. Shit, man, you are a disgrace to the whole Spanish army.'

The young men snorted with laughter and hurried to fix their dress.

Jobert, leaning against the door jamb, wilted in the seductive warmth of the guardhouse. 'Spanish stragglers, Sergeant Pultiere? Were they the first enemy stragglers to approach the gates?'

'No, sir. Groups of about ten, or so, came prowling about but we saw them off in basic Spanish. No, that last lot were at least thirty to fifty strong. They were all armed but they returned to the city.'

Jobert watched the torchlight of Avriol and a British liaison officer disappear beyond the naval general stores building towards the great bastion of the Royal Gate. With his fizzing torch, Jobert looked about him in the dark plaza between the many storehouses of the precinct. *How long ago had we taken the chain gangs into the store for the hammocks? Was it four or five mornings ago?* He looked to Pultiere and Yinot to ask but was unsure if they had accompanied him.

'Fuses, sir?' asked Yinot.

'Yes, of course. Our first three targets are separated by the street which the British will march through. I will stay on this side of the street and light the frigates and then the mast house deception bundle. You run a trail from the tar house towards the guardhouse. If the fusilier company marches between us, I cannot think how I will give you the order to light the trail.'

'How about ... how about if you light any one of your fires, I will light mine.'

'Yes, good, that will do.' Jobert slapped Yinot's shoulder. 'Come, brother, onto our next targets. You have the deception fire behind the armoury and I have the ship laid down in the dry-dock.'

Somewhere, drums thrashed out a quick roll, followed by another. Jobert and Yinot spun towards the Royal Gate. The drums set a marching beat and torchlight, diffused by the fog, illuminated the far-side of the distant buildings.

'The British are coming.' Jobert's drowsiness dissipated as the drumming quickened his heartbeat. 'Sergeant Yinot, run both your fuses. Stand by the tar house. Go!' Jobert moved into the fog only to turn back to the guardhouse. 'Chasseur Arbod, tell Sergeant Pultiere, from this moment forward, all of us must gather at the guardhouse. Yes?'

'I heard you, sir,' called Pultiere from the guardhouse door. 'It is a quarter-past-nine. Go!'

The musket fire rang out so consistently that it had become a dreadful clock.

Jobert ran to the rear of the mast house where he found

barrels of tar interspersed with kegs of gun powder all wrapped tightly in sail against the rain. He ran back to a place which he thought was safe and placed the torch on the cobblestones. Jobert then shuffled back to the fuse cask, removed the bung and, walking slowly, laid out a thick trail of black grains towards the torch. As the cask emptied, he placed the cask at the end of the powder trail to mark its location.

The musket fire in the basin reminded him of the minutes passing. Jobert checked the time by the torch on the ground. Half-past-nine. He felt as if the drums were right upon him.

Running through the wisps of sea fog reaching its clammy tendrils into the streets, Jobert arrived in the deep stone trench of the dry-dock. In here the infantry drumming was dull and the sniper fire was barely noticeable. Silently above him there stood the massive timber hull of a seventy-four-gun ship-of-the-line. Jobert held up his torch, the towering behemoth rose far up into the fog, the ship's name, *Spartiate*, chiselled but not painted on the stern.

'I have not ever burnt a seventy-four-gun battleship before. I will need a memento of the occasion.'

He attempted to unplug the cask and found the bung had been forced into the vent hole and was unable to be removed. Freezing in the dark fog, alarm gripped his exhausted mind. *Where is the closest cask? Is there anything I could smash it with? If I break the cask open powder would spill everywhere and I will be unable to create a fuse trail.* 'Fuck, Jobert!' he screamed at his clouding brain. 'Do your best! Just do your fucking best!'

He raced to the torch and held it high. Jobert saw a hammer. Picking up the hammer and putting down the torch, he scrambled back and set the cask on its end. He then struck the cask with the hammer staving in the baseplate. The powder burst at his feet. He poured a trail from *Spartiate's* incendiary bundle a short distance towards the torch. Not far enough.

He moved the torch and checked the time. A quarter-to-ten. He still had one target to prepare.

Jobert struggled to run up the stone steps to the slipways only to have his shoes slip on the treacherous fog-wet cobblestones. He fell, cracked his knee, dropped his torch, sobbed, and rolled in pain.

As he rolled, his shoes, caked in wet gunpowder, flared into life. He gasped as he backed away from his burning feet. His feet followed him, but soon sizzled into an acrid cloud of gun smoke. He rolled over moaning, wiping tears from his eyes and stood up with his torch. The torch flame was spluttering out of life.

The sound of muskets firing reminded him of his desperate task.

Jobert limped into the slipways and stood between the hulls of the two thirty-two-gun frigates undergoing refit. Again, two incendiary parcels were packed against the keels, from which Jobert created another thick trail and marked its end location with the empty cask.

The dying torch flame showed ten o'clock. *Should I really burn two frigates that an entire army was dying in the mud attempting to save? Was ten o'clock the right time? Would this fire destroy the rest of the moored fleet?* Jobert turned around and around on the spot.

Musket fire woke him from his stupor. He shook his head vigorously, stepped forward, gritting his teeth at the pain in his knee and placed the embers of his dying torch down on the powder trail.

The powder squealed to life. A sparking flame raced hissing and spluttering, towards the incendiary package. The powerful explosion lit up the slipways and the frigates above, throwing Jobert backwards to fall heavily on his side. He moaned in pain, yet the roar of the flames forced him to fight through his injuries, roll over and watch the burning tar blazing up the sides of both ships.

Another fierce explosion rocked the air causing the fog to shudder. Yinot's tar house? As he stumbled out of the roaring heat of the constricted slipways, Jobert heard a keening wail throughout the city as the remaining citizens believed they faced imminent immolation.

Another explosion ripped the night air and reverberated off the low hanging clouds. *Yinot's armoury deception fire? Had the British fusilier company passed through? Had Avriol and his chasseurs returned safely to the guardhouse?*

Jobert limped back to the guardhouse, his path lit by the slipway flames, to find a screaming mob of civilians and uniformed stragglers held back from the gates by a wall of red-coated British bayonets, interspersed with a few near-black Spanish.

'Jobert! Captain Jobert!' The thick body of Pultiere punched and crushed men and women, stragglers and civilians. Fighting his way through the crowd, Pultiere grabbed Jobert forcefully.

'No, stop. Stop!' Jobert screamed as his swollen knee twisted in the cobblestones. 'I need another torch. My fires are not done. Is Avriol back?'

'Yes, we are all in the compound. Wait, sir … Arbod, throw me a torch. Chasseur Arbod, throw me a bloody torch, now!'

The thick torch shaft, its flaring head spinning above the crowd, landed with a scorching thud on someone's shoulder. Someone screamed. The crowd parted, roaring at the offense. Pultiere brought his great fists down on anyone who stood in his way until he held the torch aloft.

'Yinot!' called Jobert above the bedlam, grabbing the fresh torch. 'Light the deception fire behind the mast house. I will see you back at the guardhouse.'

Jobert took the torch and limped back towards the *Spartiate* in the dry-docks. The fog had evaporated with the intensity of the frigates' blaze. The light may have reflected off the heavy clouds above, but the intense tar smoke burnt his eyes and tore at his throat.

In the deep dry-dock, the light from the fire in the slipways illuminated the sides of the immense *Spartiate*. Jobert trembled as the roaring, leaping flames from the frigates released his last stores of adrenalin. His mind was like a guttering candle about to snuff out. He shook his head and swallowed mucus against a sand-dry throat.

What souvenir should I keep from burning my first battleship? He coughed a tearing laugh at the thought there would be more than one.

Another explosion, but its ferocity was muted in the deep stone dry-dock. Yinot had lit the mast house deception fire.

Jobert focussed on the little cask marking the trail to the vast timber hull. A trail that was far too short, due to him smashing the cask's top. Jobert put the torch down beyond the reach of the flame-ravenous black powder. He picked up the cask and spread the powder thinly in a large area with his foot. Then stepping well back, threw the torch and limped away, the broken cask tucked under his arm.

The torch tipped end over end as it flew through the air, landing on the end of its handle on the stone of the dry-dock floor. Balancing momentarily, it fell. The flaming head igniting the arc of dispersed gun powder in a harsh smoky crackle. The sparks flew to all corners of the spread mess and soon found the short, wavering trail leading under the folds of the sail-bound incendiary barrels.

This time, Jobert was well clear when the explosion erupted.

Super-heated tar sprayed outwards, up the keel and rudder, splattering the super-structure and the stern. Jobert turned on the dry-dock steps to see the word *Spartiate* written in devilish flame.

Chapter Thirty

From the middle of the Inner Harbour a phenomenal explosion erupted.

Everyone stopped speaking.

Everyone stopped moving.

Except every bird roosting in a ten-kilometre radius of Toulon. They all leapt up into the air as one huge cacophonic flock.

On Mount Faron and all around the Inner Harbour, everyone, every soldier, every civilian, of every and any nationality, turned and looked up at the huge plume of flame erupting from the surface of the Inner Harbour two kilometres away from the New Arsenal basin. The massive flame rose all the way to scorch the underbelly of the clouds.

Captain Smith, of His Britannic Majesty's Royal Navy, slumped as he put his watch away. Doffing his bicorne, he bowed to Saint-Joséph. 'The *Isis*. A French thirty-two-gun frigate storing two hundred tonnes of powder. Your Spanish naval colleagues have set her off, de Andrade. I am sure she will leave a pretty ripple on the pond and produce an interesting wash against our sides. Eleven o'clock and an ebbing tide signals my departure, dear sir.'

As the deadly irritation of musket balls continued to zip out from the chandlers' store, Jobert faced Saint-Joséph directly. 'The prisoners, sir. Our sailors in the harbour?'

'Excuse me, Captain Smith, sir,' said Saint-Joséph. 'I know for a fact that there are a large number of French prisoners held on ships in the roads. *Isis'* flames mark out the three ships to which I refer. Can you not see them clearly, sir? I would take it as a point of honour if those men were released prior to the firing of the ships.'

'Ah, yes, indeed, sir.' Smith licked his lips, as he glanced at three of his seven cutters racing to exit the arsenal.

Two fireships were tied alongside their intended targets. The remaining two cutters attempted to secure the final two fireships, heavy with tar and gun powder. All four fireships were perilously close to catching alight from the embers from the fires ashore.

With an all-mighty roar, the magazine exploded, showering the basin with large chunks of masonry. Several men in the cutters were sliced open by the whirling debris.

'I repeat, Captain Smith, sir, leave the bow lines of the fireships to my men,' said Saint-Joséph, 'and we will pull them to their target ships.'

Embers from the magazine's explosion set off the powder in one of the towed fireships with a massive whoosh. Sailors in the escorting British cutters screamed. The two fireships not yet secured were cast off. The crews of their escorting cutters leapt to their oars, desperate to move to the arsenal exit. Smith bellowed at his subordinates. They in turn raced to the quayside, roaring at the cutters, motioning for all British vessels to leave the arsenal.

The high tide which had brought the British and Spanish demolition cutters into the Inner Harbour had peaked. As the tide now ran out it drew water out of the arsenal basin, causing it to rip through the narrow stone-wharf passages between arsenal and harbour. The cutters were now chased by two loose fireships, one of them aflame. A fireship tethered astern of three great warships issued a powerful explosion, ignited by the flames billowing out from its loose mate.

'Certainly, sir,' said Smith. 'I shall attend to the prisoners at my earliest convenience. You have my word. If you would excuse me, sir, good night.' Smith strode towards the passageway where he descended to a cutter on the outer wall of the quay.

Saint-Joséph, trembling with exhaustion, attempted to take stock of the seventeen ships moored in the New Arsenal. Three groups of four ships and one group of five ships were moored in the four quadrants of the broadly square arsenal.

Two fireships entangled together, one secured, one loose, were on fire. The tide had drawn the loose fireship onto the secured fireship and now the corner of the basin which contained five monstrous seventy-four and eighty-gun ships-of-the-line was alight with blazing tar. The flames licked the flanks of three, then four, silent, huge timber monsters rocking on their lines, oblivious to their fate.

'What would you have us do, sir?' asked Jobert.

'You will note, gentlemen, we have one secured fireship alight and snagged with a loose fireship. The other unlit fireship is drawn south, away from our ships, by the out-going tide. The remaining fireship is swinging on its moorings away from our ships. The as-yet-unlit fireships are drifting into quadrants where the embers cannot reach them. They become much less of a threat as our luck with the tide holds.

'It is the wind that dogs us. You will note the onshore wind blowing the embers north across the basin. The greatest threat is the ember storm driving towards the opposite quadrant, where two frigates and two seventy-fours, the *Centaur* and the *Commerce de Bordeaux*, are moored. As the last action of the battle, we must man the pumps on the two seventy-fours and save them. Sadly, at the cost of the two twenty-four-gun frigates. What say you, gentlemen?'

Jobert looked at the washed-out men about him. 'Lads, how can horsemen stand idle while the *Centaur* burns? Sergeants, take all your men with Major Avriol and the Captain. Voreille, fetch Koschak and the sniper teams to me on board the *Bordeaux*. Move!'

At midnight, Jobert watched the British return.

On this occasion, the cutters were crammed full of men, hundreds of French sailors held prisoner in ships at anchor in the Inner Harbour. Attaching to the hospital's steps with boat hooks, the cutters disgorged their human cargo. Those at the head of the masses were surprised by wretched, torch bearing Spaniards guarding a backdrop of battleships ablaze, while cloying tar smoke roiled on the surface of the water and the docks.

'Young Moench!' called Koschak, 'do you have your fife with you?'

'Always, Sergeant Major.'

'Then shut this fucking rabble up.'

Drawing his fife from the inside of his waistcoat, young Moench piped a long, shrill shriek. The noise of hundreds of men subdued with a groan, then hissed for silence to those still surmounting the steps.

'Shut up and listen in,' yelled Koschak. 'Who is the senior officer present?'

'I am!' A man pressed through the murmuring crowd.

Saint-Joséph stepped forward. 'Is that so, sir? I am Captain Saint-Joséph of the French Mediterranean Fleet, representative of Admiral Brueys d'Aigalliers. How many men are with you, sir?'

'The British have taken half of us off, sir and are now returning for the other half. Perhaps there would be three hundred here, sir.'

Saint-Joséph summoned his final vocal reserves, waving to the blazing docks. 'Sailors of France, the Republic requires all hands to the pumps. Now!'

'It is midnight,' said Jobert. 'Regather our men at the guard-room, Sergeant Major. Leave all this to the navy.'

At the guardroom, the soot-begrimed chasseurs found Duque and four of their 2nd Company mates.

'Lieutenant Neilage now holds both gates of the city,' said Duque. 'Lieutenant Neilage has received messages back from General Masséna that the army, due to their exertions today, will be unable to enter the city before dawn tomorrow. I am posting this guard over you here, then I am returning to the Royal Gate. You need to sleep before dawn.'

Jobert peered into the warm guardroom reeking of unwashed bodies and resounding to the snores of the physically shattered.

Koschak pressed the remaining men into the room, to slump against the bodies of their comrades and melt into the stone floor. Then, Koschak put his back against the guardhouse wall and, with buckling knees, slid to the ground.

Jobert winced as he bent. 'If I get down, I will not get up again.'

'Perhaps you might feel better, sir,' said Duque, 'with a bath and a shave before supper?'

In his weakened state Jobert found Duque's impertinence unexpected, causing him to explode with laughter that convulsed his body. Half giggling, half attempting to regain his breath, Jobert wiped the tears from his eyes and looked for Koschak's reaction.

Koschak's chin had slumped against his chest. All he contributed to the conversation were ragged snores.

In the dull grey dawn of the 19th of December, although the ferocity of the flames was conquered, the embers within eleven timber hulls burnt down to the waterline glowed and fizzled. The acrid tar smoke squatted over the arsenals and the port, choking the few sailors moving around the wharves on fire piquet.

Through that wafting, sulphurous miasma shuffled 2nd Company, walking their smoke-agitated horses away from the Royal Gate, across the slippery cobblestones of the silent streets of the city, through the Italian Gate and onward for the two-hour ride to Revest.

2nd Company had left Captain Saint-Joséph, as he had directed them, snoring in the inner compound guardroom, swaddled in blankets from the general store, under a naval guard.

A few hours later, at nine o'clock, the infantry probed carefully into Toulon.

At nine-thirty, the generals and the People's Deputies entered triumphantly.

At ten o'clock, the executions began.

A week later, Koschak tucked his head into the freezing rain as he opened the door to allow Chabenac entry into the smoky heat of old Quandalle's cottage. 'You would have heard he has declined promotion, sir?'

'I had not, Sergeant Major.'

As Chabenac shook his wet cape and took a seat by the fire, he saw a small, broken cask under the table with gunpowder dust crushed into the timber interior. 'Shall I pop this on the fire?'

'No!' Jobert jerked from a sheaf of documents at the cottage table and thrust out his hands for the splintered, sulphur-smelling cask. 'That is mine.'

'Quite so.' Chabenac suppressed his surprise as he handed the filthy cask across the table. 'What was the final bill for your jaunt into the port the other evening?'

Jobert placed the lid on the ink pot and rifled through an inner pocket of his waistcoat withdrawing a small slip of parchment. 'There were seventy vessels in the Mediterranean Fleet in August. About sixty in port and ten at sea. Twenty were removed by the enemy during the four-month siege. Five were destroyed out in the roads during the evacuation. Of the thirty-six in port that night, eleven were burnt to varying degrees.

Due to the shallow arsenal basin, much will be salvaged. Twenty-five were returned to the Republic unscathed.'

'You saved twenty-five out of thirty-six. Impressive.' Chabenac stretched his muddy boots across the front of the blaze in the small hearth. '2nd Company did well.'

As Jobert poured two cups of rum, the single candle illuminated his scowl. 'Yes, we did. 2nd Company most certainly did very well.'

'What of this declined promotion?' asked Chabenac.

'With Saliceti promoting Avriol to brigadier-general within the Army of the Rhine, Saliceti also approved Avriol's request to take a major as his aide de camp. Avriol approached me with an offer of promotion. I declined.'

Over the rim of his cup, Chabenac raised an eyebrow in gentle enquiry.

The dribbles from the straw thatch puddled noisily outside the timber shutters. Jobert rolled his head to the noise of chasseurs working in the barn yard beyond the windows. 'I feel that I belong here with them.'

'Indeed, you do, brother. Aide de camp is a waste of your talents. You will be chief of squadron soon enough.'

Jobert nudged a large leather-bound volume across the cottage table. 'Avriol gave me this as a parting gift.'

Chabenac whistled softly as he opened the front cover of de Guibert's *Essai General de Tactique* and turned the first few pages. 'Are you aware that Avriol is not the only major Saliceti has promoted to brigadier-general? Bonaparte and Victor are promoted amongst others.'

'That is not surprising. For any of them.'

'Have you also heard the 24th Chasseurs is now reduced to a three-squadron regiment?'

'Hah! I knew that would happen.'

'We lose two squadrons as reinforcements to the Army of

the North. The 24th Chasseurs is assigned to the Army of Italy and placed under General Masséna's division.'

'Masséna's division?' asked Jobert.

'Yes, Saliceti promoted him to divisional commander. The regiment has orders to return to Avignon, due to lack of forage in the Alps over winter, then to report to Nice by the 1st of March next year.'

'Is that so? On return to Avignon, I will request a month's leave from Raive and return home. My grandfather is not well.'

'No, not Raive. Lieutenant Colonel Spiccard is now regimental second-in-command. Raive has been promoted to colonel and posted to General Masséna's staff, all thanks to Citizen Saliceti. We will see Raive in Nice next spring.'

Jobert cocked his head in calculation. 'With Avriol and Spiccard no longer chiefs of squadron ...?'

'Colonel Morin will say more at dinner this evening. You will not be surprised to learn that, based on captain's seniority, 1st Squadron's Fergnes and 3rd Squadron's Clemusat will be our new chiefs of squadron. Yes, you are the next senior captain in line for promotion.'

The cottage door swung open, revealing a caped Orlande with a tray of steaming cups and food. 'Excuse me, gentlemen, rum coffees and fresh raisin cakes with butter?'

'Yes, please, Orlande,' Inhaling the delicious aroma, Chabenac straightened. 'Butter, you say?'

Orlande set the tray on the table, as Jobert pushed aside his paperwork. 'Yes, sir. All thanks to madame.'

A curious smile creased Chabenac's cheek. 'Madame?'

'Madame Moo, sir,' said Orlande sweeping his red fringe back from his face and pressing his glasses back on his nose. 'Our cow from the dragoons.'

'Of course. Has 2nd Company named her remaining calf?'

'Easter, sir.'

'The company's joke,' said Jobert. 'He has to live up to his name.'

'Hah! I see.' Chabenac raised his laced coffee in toast. 'Then, as it is the season for it, I wish the little fellow a merry Christmas.'

Jobert's adventures, in 1794 and 1795, continue in
Duty on a Lesser Front

Visit **www.jobert.site**
to learn more of Jobert's adventures.

Author's Notes

Making up a story and then sharing it is marvellous fun. Especially when the characters that are created can sneak into a corner of history, taking upon themselves the colours and flavours of that period. How do I have any idea of those colours and flavours? I know because I took advantage of years and years and years of patient, painstaking research of dedicated, professional historians. Thus, I owe a significant debt of gratitude to those historians, whom I have listed in a bibliographical appendix, not only for assembling the facts, but explaining their analyses so clearly.

It remains a mystery why the planned destruction of the French fleet on the last evening of the siege of Toulon was so slight, especially the failure of the Spanish demolition parties to enter the port. Jobert's chasseurs provide a fictitious resolution to the historical oddity.

What is real and what is not? I have included a Chronology of Events as an appendix. After thirty years of crippling debt, France spiralled into anarchy. The chronology describes that descent, lists the historical events referred to within the story and gives some sense of the chaos impacting on the characters during 1793.

The 24th Chasseurs à Cheval, an actual regiment in the Revolutionary and Napoleonic armies, was raised in March 1793 from a regiment of patriotic volunteers, the *Chasseurs Volontaires*. During the Revolutionary period, the 24th Chasseurs à Cheval saw service across southern France in both the Army of the Western Pyrenees and the Army of Italy. With artistic license, I have borrowed this fine regiment to support the story of André Jobert.

Who is real and who is not? A list of characters, the Dramatis Personae, is also included as an appendix. Characters within the list with their names underlined actually existed, such as Colonel Morin, the 24th Chasseurs à Cheval's founding commanding officer. If the character's name is not underlined, such as André Jobert, then the character was invented.

There are two other appendices to assist the reader. For those unsure of metric measurements and their conversion, a very down-and-dirty guide is provided. For those unfamiliar with military organisations and ranks, again, a very simple guide is included.

I hope you enjoyed Jobert's first adventure as much as I had writing it. Jobert's adventures in 1794 and 1795 continue in **Duty on a Lesser Front**. I welcome your feedback on Jobert's website (**www.jobert.site**), or even a quick note just to say 'Hi!'.

Rob McLaren
Veresdale, Queensland
September 2020

Bibliography

Bourgeot, V., *Les Tresors de l'Emperi*, Paris, 2009

Bucquoy, E., *Les Uniformes Du Premier Empire, La Cavalerie Legere*, Paris, 1980

Bukhari, E., *Napoleon's Cavalry*, London, 1979

Calvert, M., Young, P., *A Dictionary of Battles, 1715-1815*, New York, 1979

Chandler, D.G., *Napoleon's Marshals*, London, 1987

Chandler, D.G., *The Campaigns of Napoleon*, New York, 1966

De Lee, N., *Nations in Arms 1800-1815 - French Lancers*, London, 1976

De Marbot, JB.A.M., *The Memoirs of General the Baron de Marbot*, London, 1892

Dodge, T.A., *Warfare in the Age of Napoleon, Vol. 1*, 2011

Doisy de Villargennes, Chuquet, A., *Soldiers of Napoleon, The Experiences of the Men of the First French Empire*, 2008

Duffy, C., *The Military Experience in the Age of Reason, 1715-1789*, New York, 1987

Elting, J.R., *Swords Around A Throne*, London, 1988

Erkmann, E., Chatrian, A., *The History of a Conscript of 1813*, London, 1946

Fuller, J.F.C., *The Decisive Battles of the Western World*, London, 1970

Forczyk, R., *Toulon 1793 - Napoleon's First Great Victory*, London, 2005

Glover, G., *The Forgotten War Against Napoleon - Conflict in the Mediterranean 1793-1815*, London, 2017

Haythornthwaite, P., *Napoleonic Light Cavalry Tactics*, London, 2013

Haythornwaite, P., *Uniforms of the French Revolutionary Wars 1789-1802*, Poole, 1981

Letrun, L., Mongin, J., *Chasseurs à Cheval, 1779-1815, Vol. 1-3*, Paris, 2013

Maughan, S.E., *Napoleon's Line Cavalry - Recreated in Colour Photographs*, London, 1997

Napier, C.J., *Lights and Shades of Military Life; The Memoirs of Captain Elzear Blaze*, London, 1850

Petard-Rigo, M., *La Cavalerie Legere du Premier Empire*, 1993

Smith, D., *Napoleon's Regiments, Battle Histories of the Regiments of the French Army*, 1792-1815, London, 2000

Walter, J., *The Diary of a Napoleonic Foot Soldier*, London, 1991

I also acknowledge the insights and detail provided by the Wikipedia, Google Maps and YouTube websites.

Chronology of Events

The following chronology list the historical events
that are referred to within the story:

1789

5 May   King Louis XVI convenes States General to find a
solution to the severe financial crisis facing France

17 Jun   A break away government, the
National Assembly, is formed

14 Jul   The creation of the National Guard
and the fall of the Bastille

Aug–Sep   The Declaration of the Rights of Man,
cessation of noble privilege and medieval guilds

1792

20 Apr   France declares war on Prussia, Austria and Sardinia

20 Sep   In northern France, the French defeat
Prussia at the Battle of Valmy

21 Sep   France is declared a Republic and the
National Convention established

6 Nov   In the Austrian province of Belgium, the French
defeat Austria at the Battle of Jemappes

1793

21 Jan   King Louis XVI of France executed

1 Feb   Britain and the United Provinces (the Netherlands) declare war on France

23 Feb   Declaration of levee-en-masse

1 Mar	Twelve chasseur à cheval regiments raised, including the 24th Chasseur à Cheval
3 Mar	In northern France, the French are defeated at the Battle of Aix-la-Chapelle
7 Mar	Spain declares war on France
10 Mar	The National Convention forms the Revolutionary Tribunal
18 Mar	French forces capture Mainz, on the Rhine and declare the Mainz Republic formed
18 Mar	In northern France, the French are defeated at the Battle of Neerwinden, near Liege
Mar	Uprisings in the Vendée
30 Mar	Austria and Prussia lay siege to Mainz
5 Apr	Successful and popular commander, General Dumouriez, defects to the Austrians
6 Apr	The National Convention forms the Committee of Public Safety, thus beginning the period known as 'the Terror'
Apr	The Deputies, or Representatives, of the People are established by the Committee of Public Safety
29 Apr	Marseilles revolts against the Republic
30 Apr	Naples, Portugal and the Papal States declare war on France
May	Concentration of military force for the retaking of Marseille under General Carteux at Valence
5–24 May	In western France, Republican forces face a series of defeats in the Vendée
23 May	In northern France, the French defeat at the Battle of Famars is followed by the siege of Valenciennes
29 May	Lyon revolts against the Republic

2 Jun	The National Convention enacts severe legislation against opposition
10 Jun	The Jacobins control the Committee of Public Safety as a 'revolutionary dictatorship'
24 Jun	The Constitution of the Republic of France is adopted
25 Jun	Avignon revolts against the Republic
6–8 Jul	Federalist forces from Marseille enter Avignon to support the uprising
20 Jul	General Carteux departs Valence. Bonaparte abandons a powder convoy and joins Carteux's staff
24–27 Jul	Republican forces recapture Avignon. Bonaparte writes a propaganda essay, Le Souper de Beaucaire, which attracts the attention of Robespierre
23 Jul	On the Rhine, Mainz recaptured by Austria and Prussia
27 Jul	Robespierre elected to the Committee of Public Safety
29 Jul	In the north, Valenciennes captured by Austria, Prussia and Britain
8 Aug	General Carteux departs Avignon for Marseille
14 Aug	Carnot joins the Committee of Public Safety as the Minister of War
17–23 Aug	Carnot declares another levee-en-masse
18 Aug	In northern France, the French are defeated at the Battle of Lincelles
24 Aug–8 Sep	In northern France, the British lay siege to Dunkerque
25 Aug	Republican forces recapture Marseille. Bonaparte re-joins the powder convoy

Siege of Toulon

27 Aug	Toulon revolts against the Republic and invites British and Spanish fleets to secure the port
30 Aug	Outside Toulon, General Carteux arrives at the head of the Ollioules defile
5 Sep	Promulgation of 'Make terror the order of the day'
6–15 Sep	In northern France, the French raise the British siege of Dunkerque with victory at the Battle of Hondschoote, defeat the Dutch at the Battle of Boxtel, but are defeated by the Austrians at the Battles of Menin and Courtrai
7 Sep	Toulon invested by Generals Carteux and Lapoype
9 Sep	The National Convention enacts laws that force farmers to surrender grain without payment
12 Sep	In northern France, the French are defeated by the Austrians at the Battle of Avesnes-le-Sec
16 Sep	At Toulon, Bonaparte re-joins General Carteux's headquarters
17 Sep	The National Convention enacts the Law of Suspects, whereby anyone can be imprisoned or executed without proof
20 Sep	Bonaparte initiates a bombardment of the British fleet
1 Oct	At Toulon, Lapoype attacks the fortresses on Mount Faron
9 Oct	Republican forces recapture Lyon, releasing reinforcements for Toulon
10 Oct	The kingdoms of Naples and Sardinia reinforce the defence of Toulon
15–16 Oct	French victory at the Battle of Wattignies relieves the siege of Mauberge and alleviates the threat to Paris

15–17 Oct	Vendéen forces are defeated by the Republic at Cholet and Le Mans
16 Oct	Queen Marie Antoinette is executed, upon which Russia declares war on France
18 Oct	At Toulon, Bonaparte is promoted to the rank of major having established eleven batteries focused on the allies' western defences
18 Oct	Austria and Prussia attack across the Rhine into Alsace
22–29 Oct	French lay siege to Nieuport held by the British
23 Oct	At Toulon, General Carteux is replaced by General Doppet
13–16 Nov	At Toulon, General Doppet is replaced by General Dugommier
25 Nov	General Dugommier holds a Council of War at which Bonaparte's plan for the attack on Toulon is adopted
27–30 Nov	In Alsace, French are defeated at the Battle of Kaiserlauten
30 Nov	At Toulon, an allied sortie from the western Fort Malbousquet results in a decisive counterattack by the French
8–22 Dec	Republican forces defeat the Vendéen uprising at the Battles of Angers and Sarenay
14 Dec	At Toulon, as General Masséna's brigade arrives, Bonaparte initiates the bombardment of the allies' western Fort Mulgrave
17 Dec	French forces simultaneously attack Fort Mulgrave to the west of the Inner Harbour under General Dugommier and the fortresses on Mount Faron under General Lapoype

18 Dec	After three failed attempts to capture Fort Faron, General Masséna succeeds in securing Fort D'Artigues
18 Dec	With Fort Mulgrave secure, Bonaparte bombards the port of Toulon across the Inner Harbour, forcing the allies to evacuate the city
18 Dec	British and Spanish demolition parties re-enter Toulon to undertake the destruction of French naval ships and stores remaining in the port. Only sixteen of forty-one vessels are burnt to varying degrees
19 Dec	Republican forces enter the evacuated city of Toulon
22 Dec	Masséna promoted to major-general. Bonaparte and Victor promoted to brigadier-general

Ready Reference –
Military Organisations

A very simple overview of military
organisations in this period:

Squad/File/Patrol – Cavalry soldiers were grouped together
in threes or fours to patrol, cook and sleep together as well
as ride together in larger formations.

Section – Twelve men, when at full-strength, or three
squads/files, commanded by a corporal.

Platoon – Two sections, twenty-four men at full-strength,
commanded by a sergeant.

Troop – Two platoons, fifty men at full-strength,
commanded by a second lieutenant.

Company – Two troops, one hundred men at full-strength,
commanded by a captain.

Squadron – Two companies of cavalry, commanded by
the senior captain of the two companies.

Battalion – Six to eight companies of infantry,
commanded by a chief of battalion (major).

Regiment – Three or more squadrons of cavalry or
battalions of infantry commanded by a colonel. A cavalry
regimental commander had two chiefs of squadron (major)
who could assist him by commanding one to three
squadrons on independent tasks.

Brigade – Two or more regiments of infantry or cavalry,
with supporting artillery, engineers and logistic support,

commanded by a brigadier (a rank of general).

Division – Two or more brigades, with associated support, commanded by a major general.

Corps – Two or more divisions, capable of significant independent operations, commanded by a lieutenant general.

Army, or Army Wing – Two or more corps, commanded by a general.

Ready Reference –
Measurement Conversion

A very approximate conversion of metric measurements:

One inch is approximately two-and-a-half centimetres.
Ten centimetres is approximately four inches.

One metre is approximately one yard, or three feet.

One thousand metres, or one kilometre, is approximately two-thirds of a mile (five-eighths). One mile is approximately one-and-a-half kilometres.

One kilogram is approximately two pounds.

One litre, or one kilogram of water, is approximately two pints.

Dramatis Personae

This story is a work of fiction within a historical setting. In the list below, those characters with their names underlined actually existed, otherwise the character is a creation of the author.

The 24th Regiment of Chasseurs à Cheval
(Napoleonic ranks in brackets)

<u>Morin</u>   Colonel, Commanding Officer
of the regiment

Raive   Lieutenant Colonel (major) and
second-in-command of the regiment

Avriol   Major (adjutant or chef d'escadron)

Fergnes   Captain, commander of 1st Company
and 1st Squadron (1st and 7th Company)
Regimental fencing master

André Jobert   Captain, commander of 2nd Company
and 2nd Squadron (2nd and 8th Company)

De Chabenac   Captain, commander of 8th Company,
junior company of 2nd Squadron.
Posted regimental aide de camp

2nd Company, 24th Chasseurs à Cheval

(Napoleonic ranks in brackets)

André Jobert Captain, commander of 2nd Company and 2nd Squadron (2nd and 8th Company)

Geourdai Lieutenant, company second-in-command. Promoted to captain, company commander of 8th Company

Koschak Company sergeant major (marechel des logis chef)

Moench Company trumpeter

Neilage Second lieutenant (sous lieutenant) and troop commander. Promoted to lieutenant, second-in-command of 2nd Company

Voreille Second lieutenant (sous lieutenant) and troop commander

Pultiere Sergeant (marechel des logis) and platoon commander

Bredxieux Sergeant (marechel des logis) and platoon commander

Huin Sergeant (marechel des logis) and platoon commander. Promoted to second lieutenant, troop commander in 2nd Company

Yinot   Sergeant (marechel des logis) and platoon commander

Duque   Corporal (brigadier) and Jobert's groom

Orlande   Jobert's valet and cook

Siege of Toulon

Saliceti   A Jacobin Deputy of the People assigned to report on the performance of the Army. A friend and sponsor of Napoleon Bonaparte

General Masséna   Brigade commander from the Army of Italy. Promoted based on his performance at Toulon. Future Marshal of France under Emperor Napoleon

Admiral Brueys d'Aigalliers   A senior naval officer of the French Mediterranean Fleet

Captain Saint-Joséph   Naval staff officer to Admiral Brueys

Captain Sir William Sydney Smith   British naval officer directed to destroy the vessels and the supplies within Toulon upon the evacuation of the British and Spanish forces

Major Victor   Commander of the 5th Battalion, Volontaires Bouches-du-Rhône at the siege of Toulon. Future Marshal of France under Emperor Napoleon

Captain Bonaparte   Artillery officer. Promoted Brigadier General as a result of his performance at Toulon. Future Napoleon I, Emperor of France

2nd Coy   100

Troop   Troop   2 x 50

Pl   Pl   Pl   Pl   4 x 24

SS   SS   SS   SS   8 x 12

Cpt Jobert

Lt, Ned Sgt M, Trum.   Groom
                                Valet

Troops   2nd Lt   Vore
          2nd Lt   Hu...

Pts   4 x Sgts   Pul Bred Yin

Sect   8 x Cpls

Printed in Great Britain
by Amazon

53318192R00211